BECOMING TERRAN

MARK ROTH-WHITWORTH

UNTREED READS PUBLISHING

CONTENTS

Becoming Terran

By Mark Roth-Whitworth

Ebook ISBN: 979-8-88860-182-2

Print ISBN: 979-8-88860-183-9

Published by Top of the World Publishing, a Texas limited liability company, inclusive of its affiliates, subsidiaries, imprints, successors and assigns, including eLectio Publishing and Untreed Reads Publishing, with offices at 1008 S. Main St., Georgetown, TX 78626 ("Publisher").

www.untreedreads.com.

Printed in the United States of America.

FRANCOISE

1

FOUNDLINGS

The sky was a hard, hot blue with nothing more than faint haze on the horizon, the air dry and dusty to match, and the grass around the hotel brown in patches, the water supply having been irregular for weeks. The young Fulani woman stood near the locked chain-link fence, looking across fields to the distant hills, and smelled the occasional stink of the oil pumpjacks from the fields. Her sister, five years younger, had been brought out with the other laundry workers, and the girl held onto her trying to be brave, only the occasional sniffle revealing her fear. Behind them the crowd, a few oilfield workers scattered among the rest of the hotel staff, stood closer to the building. They smelled of sweat and fear as well, the occasional burst of gunfire echoing in the air. Rebel troops had come in first thing in the morning, having taken the oil field and the services, as well as the hotel, herded them all together and out, locked them into the fenced area, then ignored them. They had been standing or sitting for hours and the north African sun was hot, even in the winter.

The shooting quieted down late in the morning. Another few hours, and she saw a white man being shown around by one of the rebel officers, and was flanked by another white man and an Asian, clearly with him, and a rebel trooper. His clean, dark hair was neatly cut over a thin face with a pencil mustache, a face that was neither kind nor gentle, with hardness in every line. They came close, and the rebel officer pointed at the people behind the fence. "What shall we do with them?"

She had seen men in the hotel who were hard, who had let greed lead them to accept offers they should not have, and took a chance. She stepped to the fence, leaving her sister behind. "Please, m'sieur, water? Toilet?"

The man looked at her dismissively, began to turn back to the rebel officer, then did a double take, and stared at her, a tall, slender African woman with a classical oval face and high cheek bones. Finally, in badly accented French, he said, "You can pee in the dirt."

He didn't move. Staring back, she realized that she had only once or twice seen someone dressed in clothes that fit so perfectly, and both of them were important people. With that, she bent and reached under her hotel uniform skirt, pulled down her panties and dropped them, stepping out carefully. Then, carefully, deliberately, she pulled up her skirt, exposing herself to him, and incidentally to the men around him, thrust her pelvis forward and pissed through the fence, forming a crude heart in the sandy ground, then let her skirt fall back to her knees. There was some murmuring behind her, but the man ignored the officer, the rest of the crowd, and kept staring through her performance. Finally, a minute or two later, he broke eye contact with a clear effort. "Get the hotel people back in, they'll be needed. Secure the oilfield workers," he told the officers. "Clean her up, and bring her to me in the hotel office."

Two hours later, dressed in a businesswoman's suit found in a suitcase from the checkroom, she was led into the office. It was not a large room, with only enough space for the desk and a couple of guest chairs. The walls were tan, with heavy beige curtains cutting the brightness of the sunlight flowing in the windows. "You can go," he said to the Asian man who had brought her in. The Asian stepped out, shutting the door behind him, cutting off the view of her sister sitting on the couch outside. He stared at her for a while, running a finger over his phone, as she stood in front of the desk, his look more than stripping her naked. Finally, he asked, "How old are you?"

"Twenty, m'sieur."

"And you're a maid at this hotel."

"They 'ave started me working in accounting...."

"You're eighteen, if that. Any other family here?"

"Only my sister. Our maman died in the virus that came through a few months ago, along with some of the oilfield guards and hotel staff."

"You and the brat didn't go home."

"The staffing company for the hotel told us we needed to work another year to make the money to go home."

He nodded. "You service anyone the hotel tells you to?"

Her features grew cold and immobile, and she looked far older than her age. "No, m'sieur. They only offered me twice, and I only serviced one, someone close to the owner of refinery."

His stare had become like a spotlight. "How does the hotel see you, other than this?"

She changed her whole body language. "Why, m'sieur, I am just a young woman from Niger, without much education, who can certainly be useful if the tasks assigned me are not too compli... complicated," she said, pretending to have trouble with the longer words.

He broke up laughing. "What's your name?" She told him, and he replied, "Too hard for me. You'll be Francoise. You'll address me in public, as M'sieur Tolliver, and in private as Phillipe." She looked at him, and he added, "Oh, yes, you're hired. I'll buy out your contract. We'll find something to do with your sister, school maybe. If she's anything like you, she could be useful in a few years. In the meantime, we'll get you a wardrobe, and you'll be introduced as an assistant. You will use that other personality, the simple girl from Niger, and will give me reports on what you overhear. Understood?"

"*Oui, m'sieur*. Of course, the first report I should give you is that your French accent is terrible, and French speakers probably laugh at you behind your back."

His mouth fell open. He closed it and rose, nodding, and came around the desk. "By damn, you just earned a raise. You'll give me lessons, then." She nodded, and then he slapped her face, hard. "You will never be insubordinate."

She stood, cheek red though the dark brown, showing no emotion. "*Oui, Phillipe.*"

Later, when now-Francoise and her sister, who was to be called Amelie, were alone in one of the hotel rooms near the office, the girl looked at her. "What you did today...."

"Years ago, I told you that you should not remember papa striking maman, only good times. You should not remember this, either. Just remember I am always on your side, and will do whatever I can for you."

Amelie looked at her for a few minutes, then asked, "But who is on your side?"

Francoise's face grew harder. "Every chain has an end. For this one, I must be there for me. I must stand up to the world, as hard a place as it is." She held out her arms, and her sister came close, and she leaned over and held her close, keeping her warm in the coolness of the hotel.

2

BEGINNING TRAINING

Over the next week, Francoise and Amelie were given immunization cocktails, the paperwork was arranged, although the two of them understood little of all this at first, and were asleep from the effects of the shots for most of that time. Within weeks, they were in Paris, where one of Tolliver's main corporate offices was located. Francoise waited with Amelie in their hotel room, sometimes coming into the offices, where she would sit and study what information she had been given. Along with clothes, she had been allowed to bring a few things from Africa, including a musk oil her mother had worn a few times. They had also given her a modern phone, and a quick lesson in how to use it. She spent a lot of time trying to understand who Tolliver was, and the world into which he had brought them. The days went by until he finally called her into his office. A man and a woman were sitting there.

The woman, a stern expression on her face, her hair a bland brown, looked at her. "We will be putting you and your sister into accelerated learning. We expect she will be ready for university level in three years. You will receive an intensive version, and will be at university level in about a year."

"May I ask why the accelerated learning?"

"So that you can understand better what you hear, so that you can tell what is important and what is not," Tolliver said, and Francoise nodded.

The woman reached up and handed her a media. "This has all the information you will need to begin. Read the introduction, and show up in the location it provides tomorrow at 0800."

"*Oui*."

The man, older, a little gray in his dark hair, wore a sports jacket and a shirt with an open collar. He rose from his seat and walked around her, looking her up and down, like a laboratory subject. After a couple of minutes, he turned to Tolliver. "I don't see any problems. We'll want to run several tests, but I think she can be done within two months."

She looked at Tolliver curiously, and he said, "Do it, then. Francoise, we're going to do some minor genetic modifications that will fit you better for the purpose for which I intend to use you. Your skin will be a bit lighter, your hair will be lightened, the curls looser, your bust larger, and your immune system will be jacked up, which will also give you immunity to several common drugs."

She said, in her emotionless manner, "As you wish, *m'sieur*. Will this just be for me, or for my sister as well?"

Tolliver looked at the man, who said, "*Non*. We will wait for puberty to begin before we make modifications to her genes."

Tolliver nodded. "By then, we'll see how well you deliver results." She nodded. He looked at the two and said, "That's all." They rose and left, shutting the door behind them. Turning back to her, he handed her another media, colored red. "You will begin studying this. Marsden is your first target. When you've finished, let me know what you see in this, and anything else you can speculate on." He paused and sniffed. "The perfume you have on, I like it."

"*Oui*, Phillipe." He nodded again, and turned to reach for a bulky AR headset. She started to leave the room, but he called to her. "You said your mother died at that hotel. What happened to her body?"

Puzzled, she looked at him. "They cremated all those who died, to prevent the disease from spreading. I have her ashes in a small urn."

"Did you want them sent home for burial?"

"*Oui*. I had intended to do so."

"Do it. Here's a charge number." He handed her a slip of paper. "That will be all." She left the room.

That night, back in their room after dinner, Francoise told Amelia about their mother's ashes, and then about the genengineering, and the advanced learning. "They're going to change what you look like? Forever?" her young sister asked, a worried look on her face.

"Just my hair will change, and my skin tone. My face and body are still my own." She smiled. "As is my mind. The person who could do what I did was part of what got Tolliver to pay attention to me in the first place, and saved us from whatever he was going to let the insurgents do."

Amelie thought this over for a while, then looked up. "What is advanced learning?"

"I have heard and read a little of this. For the intensive learning, they are going to implant electrodes or whatever in my head, just as the advanced countries do to their air force pilots and such. That is not a big deal, I hope." She looked at her sister. "Do not worry, this is something that has been done for thirty years around the world. It won't change who I am, or my love for you." She took a sip of juice. "You, on the other hand, will be expected to work hard to learn what they give you."

She did not tell her sister what she had already come to understand, about the look he had given her, that first day in the hotel office. It was not merely sexual, but considering how he could use her, her looks, her intelligence...or her organs, should he need them for something. She, like everyone around him, was a *thing* to be used or discarded.

At their next meeting, Francoise and Tolliver both had the bulky AR headsets on, looking at information on Krock, a trillionaire he intended as use as her first target. After a while, she said, "I noticed, and this was not in your notes that you sent me earlier, his avoidance of general biotech. That may be related to several relatives who jumped into genengineering early, and had themselves modified, to find that the modifications failed spectacularly."

"Interesting. I had not noticed that."

"I had to dig into his biography. The accelerated training is already helping me do research."

"Very good. Anything else?"

"He seems to have issues with families with older money from the East Coast of the US, and is cozy with several Russians, and oddly enough, several Ukrainians."

He nodded. "Very good. More background that I had not put together before." He reached out, in the real world, and took a sip from a mug in front of him. "I have my own issues with old East Coast money. Give me another report in two weeks. I want to see if you find anything else, and I want to see how the accelerated education is working."

"*Oui.*"

Later that week, she was taken to a hospital, where she spent five days, in bed or a recliner, some of the time listening to the sounds of the room, the pumps, and the smells of the disinfectants as her body dealt with side effects from the first round of gene editing. Most of the time, however, she spent in AR, either going through her course of education, or in discovering how to use AR most effectively for how she wanted to use it. She avoided the real world as much as possible, to avoid the aching in her bones, the itching over her entire skin, and the presence of the hospital. Other than the nurses and the doctor, her only visitor was Amelie, trying to assimilate how her sister now looked.

"They will do this to me, as well?"

"*Oui,* though they tell me in two years or so, when they do you, it should be faster, easier, and less painful."

Three weeks later, she spent another week in the hospital for the second round of genengineering, which included metal and biosilicon nodes in her head, similar to those used by the military. This round of changes left her with much more severe pain, and she went deep into AR, to the point where she found herself unsure what was

AR and what real world, in the effort to escape the pain that came through in spite of the drugs. Deep down, she found that there were paths to invoke physical effects in her body. More than once, she *knew* that she had just run a mile. Once she came up from an orgasm with someone she remembered from school, only to find the agony of her real body, and skipped away. The accelerated education was another escape, and she went through nearly three weeks of studies in days.

Finally, the pain was down to something manageable by drugs and a cranial headset that sent electrical signals to the brain to block it. She was back in the apartment that she and Amelie had been given, but the first evening, after Amelie was supposed to be in bed, she had gone through half a bottle of vodka with orange juice, that she heard was called a screwdriver, before the pain let her fall asleep. It did not help that she knew Amelie was sneaking looks from her bedroom, worried about her.

Slowly, as the days crept by, she managed to get to sleep with less and less alcohol, or perhaps the alcohol did not work as well for the pain as time went on.

Late that week, she was in AR, lying in bed in the apartment, almost ready to stop and sleep, when she felt Tolliver coming into her AR presence. Somehow, she wasn't sure what he did, but they were *there*, back on that first day, and he was watching as she pulled up her skirt, but she was wearing the finer clothes she had now, rather than the hotel uniform, and her skin and hair were the way they looked when she looked in the mirror earlier that day. She felt herself peeing, and then the other people faded away, and he was in front of her, and she fell to her knees, in the wet dirt, and he used her over and over. It went on and on, until from somewhere, she pulled the memory of the orgasm with the oilfield worker who had courted, then dumped her, fed that to him, and he finally climaxed, then let her go. She woke to the real world, the urine-soaked bed, and the sweat on her skin.

Free for the moment, she yanked off the headset and buried her face in the pillow. After a while, she got up and rinsed herself off, changed the sheets. Then she got the vodka she now kept in her things, and some orange juice from the refrigerator, having found that alcohol, unlike other drugs, also distorted the input from the AR, to where she could shut down.

Since before she was in double digits, she had edited her own memories far more than she had ever told her sister, first to assure herself that maman and papa loved her, then to assure her sister of the same. After they left Niger, she did it even more, remembering what had happened, and then deciding what she should have done, to be ready for the next time. Once she had done that, whenever the memory came up, so did the second version. The morning after the mental rape, she used the AR to put herself into the state where she was not merely separate from her body, but was someone else, watching, and coldly following what he had done. It took hours, but she finally found how he had come through her security. Then she started researching how to redirect intrusions, and over the study course hours of the next several days, she set up canned memories and paths such that he would be redirected to, and would take his suggestions and play it out however he wanted, all without her being present...if that had any meaning in AR, other than to know it was happening.

Then she packed up the memories of the mental rape and put it into the storage for the system, closed it off, inaccessible unless she called it up consciously, as she had been doing without the AR for so many other memories for the last years, and washed it all down with vodka and orange juice.

3

IN PLAY

In the months since Tolliver found her, Francoise had been busy. The body modifications complete, a woman assistant had taken her shopping for the kind of clothing that people in what was about to be her social circle would wear. Among the clothes they bought there was a white linen suit that Francoise desired. The woman argued against it, but finally admitted that perhaps it would work. They added a blue blouse, and allowed her to add the jewel-toned green one she desired, and a wide-brimmed, low-crowned black hat. Then there were extensive lessons in manners, and protocol, until she followed them automatically.

A month later, she had her first taste of accompanying Tolliver on a business trip. While he was in a meeting with several other trillionaires, she was out in a room where there was a light buffet and drinks. She was nibbling on a sweet cake when two men came over, picked up cakes, and turned to her.

"I 'ave not seen you bevore," said one, with dark hair, dark eyebrows, and a heavy Russian accent. "You are new?"

"*Oui.* I 'ave just joined M'sieur Tolliver's team, and this is all so *exciting!*" she burbled. "All zis travelling, and meeting important people...."

The men rolled their eyes. "Th' excitement'll wear off purty soon," said the other, a man of medium height and sandy hair, who spoke with a Midwestern American accent. "We all jus' wind up standin' 'round while they argue." He smiled at her, and held out a hand. "Kin Baker. Ah'm with Mr. Waters." She shook his hand.

"Yaroslav Ossov," said the Russian and shook her hand as well. "I am wis gospodin Kagalovsky. Ve might as vell relax. Someone vill tell us vhen meeting is over. Come, let us get drinks, and make comfortable ourselves." He nodded towards a couch. The three chatted for a while about the city, until all heard the announcement over their phones to be ready to leave.

Francoise stood and shook their hands. "It has been a pleasure, I hope we run into each other again!" Seeing Tolliver coming out with two aides, she followed behind. As they were coming out of the building, she put on her AR headset and spoke to him through it. "M'sieur Tolliver, I should probably be in a second car, at least until I can change my clothes, and someone can scan me for bugs."

He glanced back with a hard smile. "Very good, Francoise. We will speak later." Three cars pulled up, and they got in, with her in the last car.

Later in the evening, after dinner, he called her to his room to report. "I was not able to get much useful from zem, although Waters's man seemed to be curious about our interests in the Chicago area, and Kagalovsky's man seemed interested in North Africa." She paused, "Oh, and you may want someone to examine zis," she said, pulling out a brown-stained napkin from her bag. Opening it, there was a partly dissolved pill. "I saw M'sieur Baker drop it into ze drink he was bringing me, and I managed to spill ze drink and partly mop it up."

Tolliver leaned back with a thump against the back of his chair. "Well. Well." He nodded. "I was *not* expecting that." She looked at him, curiously. "It's not that uncommon to try to slip a new person something that will make them more talkative, but that you caught it is most certainly uncommon."

"I had heard other women in the hotel talk about someone slipping things in zheir drinks, and what zhey would do."

He took the napkin, and put it on the table by him. "You had better remember all of those conversations, because the next meeting, I will throw you to the wolves, and we will see how you do."

"*Oui,* Phillipe."

The next meeting was only three weeks later, and she found that he was not exaggerating about the wolves. This was a large meeting of over twenty-five of the trillionaires, and over the course of a day, she was approached by no less than five men and two women, all of whom were very friendly. One woman, especially, used an approach of commiserating about the meetings, and their employers. The second day, one of the men who had approached her the day before spoke with her quietly about making money on their own, and suggested that he could assist her in setting up a private account unknown to her employer, and they spoke for a while about this, and exchanged contact information.

The meeting ended with a large lunch the next day. It was the day after that when Tolliver got around to having her report. She gave him a long report on all of the conversations, as well as recordings she had made with the hardware implanted in her head. Finally, she got around to the last man. "Zis man seems to have been actually sent after me. He spoke with me for a while, ze first morning and afternoon, and zen sought me out for the private chat ze second day, to speak of private accounts, and how I might make money on my own."

He leaned forward, resting his chin on his palms. "Who does he work for?"

"M'sieur Krock."

A sharp smile came to his face. "Not Marshall, who controls Krock Industries, but Krock himself?" She nodded. "Very good. I think you should allow him to help you set up the account, and put whatever you get from him in it. You will, of course, report it all to me."

"*Oui,* and let you know whatever I can peel out of him."

"*Oui.* Now, tell me why you're telling me this. He's quite right, you could make money on your own."

Francoise snorted. "For a short time. After which, I would either be somewhere very unpleasant, or dead. You 'ave my sister, you 'ave had things implanted in me, and I presume your own bugs in me. On top of zat...why should I trust him? With you, at least, I know where I stand, you 'ave spoken of possible futures for my sister and myself." She paused. "And you made sure that I could 'ave our mother's ashes buried. Why would I trust anyone of zem to even care? No. I chose to sell myself, and will stay bought." She smiled a hard smile of her own. "Besides, it was Krock who owned ze 'otel."

"Very good. Go see Peterson in Finance, and have him set up an AI trust for you."

She looked at him, confused. "An AI trust?"

"Of course. The AI is set up, incorporates in a data haven, such as in the Caribbean, one of several US states, South Ossetia, or a few others - I don't care to use Taiwan, with Wu having as much control as he does there - then assigns you as the trustee. All the income goes to the AI, and you have its trust to borrow against, and use to pay back the loans...while you've used the money for whatever you want. No taxes."

Her look grew pointed, giving her an almost fox-like look. "So zat is how they are avoided in developed nations." He nodded.

After that, she went with him to a number of meetings over the next year and a half, where she would pretend to take notes, or was left outside the meeting, or wander around during breaks in the meetings with one of his people supposedly minding her, but who would find some reason to ignore what she was doing. Some of those notes she made were based on her now-enhanced hearing, which was something she could control, such that she was not knocked out by loud music or noise. Some were from approaches the aides of other trillionaires made, and some even from ploys little fish billionaires tried on her. Several times, she had taken a proposal, and offered AR sex using the program Tolliver's people had installed in her AR. When the other party was done, she would probe them through their AR without their realization.

One day, they were in his office, reviewing the status of three of his projects, when she turned to him. "*M'sieur* Phillipe, a few questions, if I may?"

"Certainly."

"There are proposals out for raising the seawalls around New York City. Why are we not bidding?"

"Garrick and Kelly are from old, East Coast money, and have connections with all the local politicians, so they have the whole mid-Atlantic tied up between them. As profitable as that would be, it's pointless." He paused. "Though perhaps they should be nudged.... Perhaps failures in their work might change that in the future. I shall think more on that."

"Convenient accidents, M'sieur Phillipe?"

"That would be impolite, although one does always need to pay attention to one's employees. A moment." He called someone, and she heard him tell the man to contact someone else. "Have it arranged that the cement used for the glass block windows in the seawall, when they get to them, are less resistant to salt water than fresh. Much less." He hung up, and turned back to her. "More?"

"*Oui.* I see Marshall, of Krock Industries, is almost out of the 400 wealthiest families, with the loss of the oil fields and refinery where you found me, plastic recycling, and nuclear fusion replacing fossil fuels for electricity. On top of that, your moves resulted in a serious loss of stock value. The news is saying that Krock and his wife have been trying to retake control. Still, I understand they were both associates of your father, and built the seawalls protecting your home town of Chicago and the steel mills along the lakefront near there in Indiana from the rising lake level."

"Why go after him? As my father's associate, they were nothing to me. But years after my father died from one of those new diseases, Marshall, with Krock's aid, drove my mother's pharmaceutical industry in Paris into near insolvency, which was why she killed herself. That made him a target."

"From my studies, I understand that the 400 control most of the world, and have for centuries. Playing games against each other to change status has always been normal, but the projects I work on for you are aimed not merely at weakening one or another, but destroying them, wiping them out of the 400. Will not others notice it, and attack us, especially since there are many more of them?"

His smile grew predatory. "Ah, but times have changed. From the time that the 400 arose, the world was always opening up, new parts of the world becoming available, new markets and products. That is no longer the case. We are in the end times, the end `game. The world, and the markets, are closing down. What was once valuable property is no longer, between the risen sea level, the climate-change caused storms, and whole regions which are no longer habitable, and cropland that is useless. The millions of refugees are no market, just problems for someone else to deal with. We are now in a dominance game, which all of us are playing, and those left standing will win, and the rest will be nothing. I intend to be standing when the cards are laid out."

He looked at her intently, a look she had seen other times, as he was clearly considering how to use her. "You are one of my cards in the game, and not the least valuable. I have others of which you are not aware, and it shall stay that way."

She stared back, her own smile beginning to mirror his, growing from a mindset she was gaining, of judging how someone could be used, offering as little of herself as possible. "An eight, perhaps?"

"More of a jack, because I know you are not one to play others' games against me."

His projects in petrochemical and construction industries were where he used her, and he had her begin to look at fusion plants. Thinking about what he had said later, she could see that his moves in pharmaceuticals and especially genengineering were what he kept her away from. She shrugged, deciding that she would find out why, eventually.

Not long after that conversation, Tolliver announced that her sister would be going to a boarding school outside London. "But why? She is doing well in her lessons, and I am the only relative with whom she has any contact."

"She needs to learn to interact with other people of her station, and a boarding school such as this will fit her for her future work. I hope to have her take up your current work, when she is older, and you advance to more important positions."

"You plan for me to advance?"

"*Oui.* You have, shall we say, a limited shelf life in this role. Another few years and your real role will be clear to our opposition. I find you quite useful, and so you will move onward, picking the fruit that I knock down."

That evening in their apartment, she and Amelie had a difficult conversation. "But I don't want to leave you! *Tu es tout ce que j'ai!*"

"*Ma cherie*, I know, I know. Nor do I want you to leave, you are all I have. But we have no choice in the matter. He has decided."

"Can't we just leave him?"

"*Non.* I know too much, so he does not dare allow me to leave. And..." she paused, looking at her almost fourteen year old sister. "We live in a world where choice is a valuable commodity, and we have little. You were still a child when we came with mama to the hotel, because there was no work in Niger, and you remember summers, hot almost beyond bearing? That is the climate change that you learn of in your classes, and whether it will abate or not, we do not know. "

She sighed, and looked at her sister, who was growing close to her own height. "I looked at what chances we had, that day the hotel was taken, and I made a choice for both of us. At least until you come of age, or he decides to use you as he has used me. Then, you may have a choice, before you know too much of his business." She chuffed a sad laugh. "Look at me, see how he has changed what I look like? And there is more that you can not see, nor will I tell you about, that I have had to do. I must live with the choice I made, and there is no turning back."

Almost all of Francoise's expressions and body language were self-edited, from her early life, and from the training she had been given by Tolliver. She worked to allow herself almost none. But she set her face to show what an unedited look would be like, for her sister to see. With one look, Amelie flung her arms around her sister, and buried her face in her sister's blouse.

"It will be bearable, *ma cherie*." Amelie looked up at her. "If nothing else, we can visit in AR," Francoise said, composing a happier smile, and added, "And I can show you things to do in AR that the people you meet may not know, so there will be secrets only you and I know." Her sister smiled wanly, then hugged Francoise again and held on, taking comfort in the softness of her elder's silk blouse, and the smell of the musk oil she wore.

4

MOVING UP

The next summer Amelie was allowed to spend the first and last months of summer break with Francoise, who seeing her as she arrived, realized she was becoming a young woman. She was accepting of the school, and told Francoise how different it was than the schools she had been in before. Between the drugs Tolliver's people had given her for advanced learning, the personal tutoring, and Francoise's help, she realized that they actually expected her to learn things she didn't know, and that they expected her to study. She mentioned that she was starting to feel more at ease, but complained there was still a lot of prejudice. "And then there are the crude boys who pinch or grab a feel."

That last had her older sister shaking her head, wondering about that after all these years. "While you visit, let me give you some of the protocol and manners lessons I was given. They may help you demonstrate the others' preconceptions of you were, ah, misplaced. " Also, perhaps you should consider a martial art. That may give them pause." Amelie smiled at that.

In between those two visits, Tolliver had the young woman's hair lightened and her curls loosened. She was only in the hospital two days, to Francoise's week, as the technology had improved considerably. Still, her older sister made it a point to visit her in the hospital. When she went back, after she went through people not recognizing her, she had an easier time in the school, the racism less overt as her skin was lighter, and the classism less as the others realized how much money her sponsor must have. Amelie discovered, too, some of her sister's lessons allowed her to push their buttons, rather than allow them to push hers.

Some months later, Amelie was speaking with her sister over AR, and began the call with a hard smile of her own.

"Very well, you have something amusing for us to hear," Francoise said, after one look.

"*Oui.* I have not spoken about the martial arts class I took before, I had chosen karate as the obvious, and was doing well, until perhaps three months after I started. We had a competition with several other schools of martial arts, and I was shocked to watch this older man, who was an aikido master, simply walk through four of our top black belts. They could not lay a hand on him, yet he had two of them on the floor as soon as they attacked. Afterwards, I spoke with my sensei, and explained that I might return, but that I wanted to learn aikido before I went any further. He understood, and even put in a good word for me to the aikido school."

"I am not familiar with this 'aikido'."

"It is a school with no offensive moves, but one uses one's attacker's energy against them. At any rate, I have been taking lessons for three months now, and earlier this week, one of the crude boys was walking up the hall as I was going the other way, and no one else was around. As he went to pass, he grabbed my breast. A moment later, he hit the floor face first." Francoise' smile grew. "He looked up, his nose bleeding, and said that he'd get me for that. I smiled down at him, and said, 'Really? You know Louise, your mate Riley's girl, the one who's one of the biggest gossips in the school? You come after me, and I'll tell her how I put you on the floor for grabbing me." He looked up, opened his mouth, then closed it, got up, and went off towards a bathroom to do something about the blood. He's been staying away from me since then, and I heard from the gossip that he's passed along who our patron is, and offers that as a reason for doing so."

Francoise laughed, and clapped. "Brava! You are learning two martial arts then, and only one is physical." Amelie smiled even wider.

THE YEAR AFTER THAT, having completed the majority of her education online, with heavy use of the implants, Francoise was made assistant to Corson Norris, the CEO of TCC, Tolliver's international construction firm.

Norris shook his head. "I see he wants me to have you as an assistant, but I got no use for a spy."

Francoise's expression hardened into one that she had perfected, based on one of Tolliver's expressions that he used with equals, one that gave nothing away, that said that she was in control of the interchange. "I am no longer to play that role, *m'sieur*. Our opponents have seen through that facade, and so *M'sieur* Tolliver desires that I become useful in other roles."

He stared at her. "Damn, he had me fooled. Okay, what do you have I can use?"

"I have a business degree, and a master's in project management, including a minor in finance, all done through intensive advance learning, aided by the lower version of military grade AR."

His mouth fell open, and he stared at her for several minutes. Finally, he came to himself and shut his mouth. "The man is always farther ahead of me than I expect. Let me see how well you perform - we need to arrange a deal with Gliance for a notable building she wants in West Oakland, across from San Fran, and then for the Wu's to provide the sand for concrete."

"I assume you mean the correct sand for concrete, not the low-quality rounded-edge sand?"

He nodded. "Okay, you are what you say you are. The Younger

Wu happens to also be in San Francisco, and so you can approach him after we have the deal with Gliance."

The next day, she was in San Francisco, and was ushered into Gliance's suite. As all the trillionaires Francoise had seen, the woman was extremely well-dressed, attractive, and hard enough to have been carved from stone, from her severely-cut brown hair to her elegant but moderate-heeled shoes. Cold blue eyes looked her up and down.

"Are you here to discuss my building, or spy on me?"

Francoise displayed the expression she had used with Norris, but an even harder one, that gave nothing away, that implied "I directly represent Tolliver, and so we are equals."

"M'sieur Tolliver no longer employs me in such duties, as must be obvious, given your question."

Gliance nodded. "Very well. Are you empowered to negotiate for the entire project, or just part of it?"

"The entire project, madam. I understand this includes acquisition of the property, code compliance with tsunami and earthquake-resistant construction, and providing utilities."

"That is correct. There will be some issues concerning the property, as it has an ethnic history, and some of the owners are refusing initial offers. I expect once we have explained it to them, they will find some other hovels."

"This is not a problem, madam. There are always safety inspection issues, especially with older properties, and some that were grandfathered in when the properties were purchased are no longer permitted." As Francoise said that, she felt an unpleasantness deep inside, but brushed it off as irrelevant. "Once the property is acquired, we expect to have a deep enough basement, waterproof, of course, and to raise the ground level by ten meters, with a drive leading up to that, and parking beneath. This will provide a better view of the bay and the sky than your original proposition."

"That seems quite acceptable. Let me say that I just had dinner with the Younger Wu the other evening, and he has expressed interest in their providing some of the construction materials, with a discount for recognition of their collaboration on the project."

Gliance nodded, and looked out the window for a moment. "A very pleasant dinner companion, and someone I intend to work with in the future."

Francoise filed that comment away for the future. To distract Gliance from her apparently unintentional slip she asked, "Do I understand correctly, that this is to be a private museum?"

Gliance was clearly pleased. "Quite. Many of us acquired great works of art, and find them less enjoyable unless we display our acquisitions. We are even proposing to open it to the public, for a nominal fee, once a year."

The discussion continued until the major details were agreed upon, and Francoise signed for Norris. The next day she met the Younger Wu at a well-regarded restaurant in San Francisco, where she was escorted to his table, in a quiet section of the restaurant suitable for private conversations. He stood, tall with a medium build, black hair fashionably cut, his suit western but with Chinese influence, and shook her hand. They sat, ordered drinks, then appreciated the view of the city and the ocean. Looking north, he commented, "The coast here is lovely, but further north, there are scenes that resemble old Chinese pen and inks, perhaps Shen Zhou."

"That is the artist who drew landscapes, but not the high islands?"

He nodded. "You have done your research. I must congratulate Tolliver on his staff."

"*Merci.*"

"Speaking of which, do I understand you have moved up in Tolliver's organization? If so, congratulations."

"I have, and *merci* again. I have just arranged for a contract with Gliance, for which I have been told we will be looking to you for some of the construction materials."

"Yes. She and I had dinner the other night, and spoke of it. A very pleasant woman to work with.... I understand we will have some recognition for our contributions, as I believe the project will be highly regarded by many of us."

"That is my understanding. Though I do wonder whether the upcoming elections here in the States will impact the project."

He laughed politely, and shook his head. "The proles pay for us to entertain them, while we choose who they will pay attention to and vote for. And those elected that are guided by us will always outnumber the few who are not." He took a sip of wine. "Besides, they are blind to the absolute submission they have given to us, and having done so, what could they do to *us*?"

She looked at him and nodded, but made a mental note of the thought.

A week later, she was back in Norris' office. This time she was sitting, sipping coffee, as he looked up from her report. "Good job, and even better than we hoped for. Are you ready to work on a major project?"

"*Oui, m'sieur* Norris."

"Very well, we're building a two towers in Abuja. You'll pick up from someone who's left, assisting the project manager. You can start working remotely this afternoon. I want you to become fully familiar with the project before we make an on-site visit, however."

She nodded. "Very good, *m'sieur.* Nigeria's capital is a very nice location. We shall visit there together?"

"Yes. You'll accompany me, and shadow me as I deal with things. After we return, you and I will review the office."

After several weeks of her remote work, they spent two weeks in Abuja, then returned. A week later, she was back in Norris' office. "I see from your written report that you followed what I did and how I did it. I am pleased that you saw that there is something going on there that is continually delaying the construction, and I expect you to resolve that. Do you have any other comments?"

"Other than that the managers there assumed I was your, or someone's, fancy lady and nothing more."

He nodded. "To be expected. Given your experience as a spy, that may work well to start, but you will have to establish your authority."

"*Oui.* Do you have any recommendations as to what I might wish to take with me?"

"Hire your own assistant. Anyone there might spy on you, and undercut whatever you do."

"I have full authority to do whatever is necessary?"

He looked at her as she sat in the guest chair, perfectly dressed in a white suit with a jewel-tone blue blouse, her face calm. "If it were someone else, I'd caution you. However, when Tolliver sends you to me, I have no qualms. That construction is already over budget and behind schedule. Do what you need."

"*Oui.* I shall be on my way then."

He nodded, and she rose and turned, making sure he appreciated the view as she left his office, as she had as Tolliver's spy, knowing herself as still his agent. In Abuja, she was given an office in the corporate headquarters that was less than her authority deserved, in a corner of the building that never seemed to be cool. Her assistant Alain, a young man she had brought with her from Paris, shared an office with two people, of whom one she assumed was a spy. Things seemed to go very slowly, and took forever, until a Wednesday, three weeks after she had arrived, she reached the decision that she was being stalled. She had expected to have concrete pouring a week and a half before, and with that not even begun, she reviewed what had been going on using her senior managerial level clearance. Thursday, she called Abiola, the assistant to the chair of the BPE, who the current manager had been working with to deal with the permits and licenses, as well as local labor. When the call was over, she took lunch, and then had Alain place a call for her to Okoturo, the chair of the BPE.

Picking up the call, she saw an older man with a full head of white hair and a modest beard that was gray and black. On his face was a polite, curious expression, and she decided to take advantage of that, "*Bonne après-midi*, M. Okpara, I am Francoise Trouve. I have been sent by Mssr Norris, CEO of TSSC, to look into the reasons that the new towers we are building has fallen so far behind schedule."

"*Bonne après-midi.* A pleasure to speak with someone who speaks one of our official languages."

"But of course, I was born in Niger."

"A neighbor. Delightful. But about the reason for the call, I have been wondering that myself."

"Really? I am being told there there have been issues with paperwork, and a shortage of labor."

"That seems odd. Your company has filed all the papers?"

"Supposedly the end of last month, along with the appropriate, ahh, fees, which seem a little higher than expected."

"That is fascinating, as I have not seen any reference to them."

She nodded. "In that case, I shall have to look into this more closely, and if it would not be considered rude, may I suggest to you that you might consider that as well?"

The man on her screen nodded. "I think we have an understanding, madame. Shall we reconsider this issue next week, perhaps, mmm, Monday afternoon?"

"That seems like adequate time for me to have pulled in some additional corporate resources. Let us agree on this, and have our people arrange a time?"

"Quite. A pleasure, madame. *Bonne après-midi* ."

"It has been. *Bonne après-midi.*"

Her next call was to the Paris office, and arranged for a computer security specialist and a forensic accountant working remotely to investigate the records. Monday afternoon she called the chairman and exchanged reports with him. Before they disconnected, they had coordinated plans for the next day.

Tuesday morning, the senior staff found they had been called to a meeting at two in the afternoon, and to cancel any other appointments following that for the day. The time came, and they found themselves waiting in the corporate meeting room, decorated in current fashion with a west African flavor even to the curtains, down the hall from the Directors' office. The minutes ticked by, and several managers asked Rochefort, the Director, what this was all about.

"I've no clue. But before you ask me how this woman has the authority to call a meeting like this, all I can tell you is she was sent by Mssr Norris, and I haven't been able to reach him all morning. Until I do, I have to accept that she can do this."

They continued to speculate, the room growing warm with worry, until at nearly quarter after the hour Francoise strode in, stark white linen suit, jewel-toned green blouse, and a Nigerian-print light scarf, trailed by a handful of security guards, and two federal Nigerian police. She looked around the room with *the look*, which said nothing, offered nothing, then deliberately putting on the expression she privately referred to as *the face,* one that she had learned from Tolliver when he dealt with people who had become a problem to him. From the reactions of the executives around the conference table, she decided it was a success. She could see they felt they were being judged as to whether they were of use, an opponent, or nothing, something to be disposed of, in whatever manner she chose. Few could meet her eyes. She turned to the Director, sitting at the head of the table, and stared at him until he moved, and she took that seat.

"You need not make yourself comfortable, M. Rochefort. I have spoken with Chairman Okpara, who I find to be quite a congenial and agreeable gentleman." Rochefort stared at her, his expression turning from worry to serious concern. "In addition, I called upon resources from Paris, and we have resolved all issues that have been delaying the construction of the new towers to our satisfaction, though I believe they may not be so to some here, For example, I believe Director Anenih of finance and Director Anouilh of Technology will find of concern that their private accounts at Neue Deutsche Bank have been frozen, pending a legal review of the sources of significant monies recently deposited."

The Accounting Director, a woman in her fifties, actually gasped out loud, and her eyes went wide. The Technology Director, a heavyset man in his late forties, his western-style suit perhaps half a size too small, said nothing, but his jaw could be seen clenched and his hands drew into fists.

"Both of you, by the way, are suspended without pay, effective immediately. Madame Anenih, these gentlemen," she said, as two of the federal police came to stand beside the woman. "are taking you into custody under suspicion of tax fraud. Francoise nodded, and the two men took the woman's arms as she rose, and escorted her out of the room, face pale under her hijab, shaking in shock between the officers.

Franscoise leaned back in the chair. "You should know, M. Anouilh, that your senior IT staffer has just been terminated, and is being escorted out of the building for following your instructions to hide a number of transfers of funds. One hopes that his bonus for such work will tide him over until he finds a new position. I would suggest that should you see him in the street, you avoid him, as he may not be especially friendly towards you now." She motioned to security. "Escort this soon-to-be former employee off the premises." Two security officers strode up on either side of the man, and with them standing there, he rose and preceded them out the door.

Rochefort stared as the door closed behind his head of Technology surrounded by security.

She looked at the man, sweat beading on his forehead as he tried to remain impassive. The expression on her face that of a cat that has just cornered a mouse. "Now, concerning the primary issue that I was sent to deal with, I will say that you, M'sieur, may find that the, ahh," she looked at her watch, "now former assistant Chair was deeply unhappy to find you had given him a 33-67 split on what we shall continue to refer to as the 'appropriate fees and baksheesh', oh, *pardon*, 'for consideration', and may decide to open his heart to M. Okpara to reduce his sentence."

Sweat was now dripping down his face, and his hands gripped the arms of his chair as Francoise's expression grew even harder.

"Why M'sieur Rochefort, you appear concerned. No need, we have not requested that you be arrested and extradited. You will find, however, that your account in the corporate bank are frozen, pending fuller investigation, and that your current month's salary, and last month's, have both been deducted, which should cover the baksheesh that was not paid to meet the schedule, but split between yourself, your Directors, and the former Assistant to the Chair of BPE. Should you return to France, there will be some legal issues concerning taxes, I believe. At any rate, your office and files will be cleaned out, sanitized, and the remainder returned to you.

You will find in here," she handed him an envelope, "the information about a storage unit we have rented to store these things, given that your multiple landlords might have an issue with your being unable to pay rents in a timely manner. You are now dismissed from TSSC, and there will be neither pension, nor severance, as this dismissal is for cause." She looked down at a mobile, then up at the man. "My assistant has just sent out a note offices-wide that if you are found on-premises after this, they are to call security, and you will be arrested. "Security, please escort M. Rochefort off the premises."

"You can't do this!" His voice rose to a rusty tenor. "You're just...."

"Just what? Just someone's fancy woman, put into a position for which she is not qualified? We can debate this, but that would be a waste of time. If you like, I can call M. Norris, who you could not reach, but if that is not sufficient, I can call M. Tolliver."

At that name, his face went white.

"Gentlemen?" She looked at the security men, waited as they escorted the man out, then looked around the room. "Madam Nnadi, you are appointed acting Director of Technology, and M'sieur Lavigne, you are Acting Director of Technology." She looked straight at Thomas, who had been Rochefort's assistant. "You will join me after we all take a break, in, say, thirty minutes, and we will call the Secretary and his new Undersecretary, and straighten out all the required paperwork, such that we can begin preparing to pour concrete for the towers tomorrow."

She rose and strode out of the room, Alain beside her, leaving behind a room full of shocked and shaking managers who had found themselves in a new world, far less safe than they had thought themselves.

The towers were completed before the end of the year, to the satisfaction of the authorities in Abuja, and Norris had her begin to administer construction of a data center in South Ossetia, long since a breakaway region from Georgia, only recognized by a few countries. The project seemed to go on forever, and was nerve-wracking, dealing with both the bureaucracy and the baksheesh that was necessary to get the site, provide for power and secure housing for the staff, and to connect to the international backbone for the lines.

When the data center opened, after almost a year and a half of dealing with the details, she brought her sister to Paris for a short holiday. Amelie could hardly stop talking about the new breakthrough in physics, and the United States, the EU working with Nigeria, Ukraine, and China all rushing to build the first faster then light probes, with India and Japan collaborating on the projects. As Amelie pointed to the screens on the wall, Francoise finished her drink and ordered a second screwdriver without her sister noticing. "Think of it, Francoise! Reaching other stars in weeks or months!"

The elder sister, now with a slight buzz on, smiled. "It is as I have heard of the space race to the Moon." Shaking her head, she added, "*M'sieu* Tolliver has a hand in that, with his aerospace company, but I am not involved. I work with technical construction here on Earth."

"Perhaps *M'sieu* Tolliver will find me a job there, once I have finished my degree."

"We shall see. You know how he does what he wishes, and changing his direction takes time, and even so often fails. Ah!" she exclaimed, looking up at the waiter. After ordering, she added, "Once I completed the education he has provided, he moved me into being an actual manager, and I assisted in several construction projects. *M'sieu* Norris oversaw all of what I have been doing, and has begun to trust smaller projects fully to me, especially if we have done something like that before, like the data center I just completed in South Ossetia." She took a sip of her drink, and added, "Which is what we are celebrating."

"Is not South Ossetia known as a data haven?"

"*Oui.* But then, construction of the data center includes an area owned by *M'sieur* Tolliver, which should not surprise you."

"*Non.* What is your next project?"

"I am the project manager on the construction of a seawall with locks protecting Odessa, in Ukraine. I trust you find this a positive thing?"

"*Oui,* Francoise. I am sorry, with the people I am in school with, it is hard not to pick up some enthusiasm for improving the world, and there are anti-trillionaire sentiments."

"I understand. It is not a bad thing, but remember where we are, and why." Her sister nodded with some unhappiness. "I find this project complicated, partly because I am overseeing a counterespionage program." At her sister's look, she added, "Remember when the UN and part of New York were flooded, and it turned out that part of the seawall there had been sabotaged during construction? I do not intend that to occur on my project." She did not mention to her sister that the sabotage was courtesy of their patron. With that, they turned to dessert.

The seawall was detailed work, but nothing that had not been done before, and she had it well in hand within four months, all the permits signed, and the pilings set in, the framing for the concrete walls well under way. She took a break to visit Amelie, then it was back to Odessa, to oversee the beginning of the pouring of the concrete, and continued work at that for another seven months until Tolliver, now using her as a troubleshooter, pulled her off that project to work on one in Africa.

The next two years passed quickly, with Francoise handling two more major construction projects, dealing with so much that it seemed as though she hardly had time to do anything other than work. She did, however, make it a point to talk to Amelie weekly. Then, coming up from all the work, it seemed no time at all until she was outside London to attend Amelie's graduation. Her sister had done very well in her schoolwork, and even made a few friends, mostly among the less hide-bound students, after the genengineering. Francoise, sitting in the audience, glowed to see her sister walk across the stage. After, she wanted to take her out for a meal together. "But Francoise, my friends are having a party!"

"Not to worry. Why don't you ask them how long the party will run? I expect it will last late into the night. If so, you and I can eat, and I will drop you where the party is afterwards." Her sister found this agreeable and they went off together, arm in arm.

At the restaurant, they sat and ordered drinks. Francoise took a sip of her screwdriver, called the waiter back, dressing him down, and demanded a fresh one, with Polish potato vodka. She realized after that Amelie was shocked but trying not to let it show. The drink appeared, and she took a sip, and put it down, thanking the man. As he left, she looked at Amelie. "I am sorry. I find myself taking after the people in the circles I work in." Amelie nodded, still clearly disturbed. Later, after the onion soup they both had, Amelie's quiche, Francoise's salmon en papillote, they were finishing Napoleons as Francoise sat back and looked at her sister seriously. "I fear the time has come, *ma cherie*, for you to make *the choice*. You have some vague ideas of what I had been doing, before I was moved into management. He did hope you would pick it up—that was why he did the body modifications to you—but our opposition has not underestimated my role for years now."

Amelie stared at her, sucking her lips, then said, "Sister, I have no interest in business and meetings," she said, then lowered her voice such that only Francoise could hear, "nor playing spy, especially for *him*." Raising her voice to normal, she went on, "Perhaps it was how mama died, but I have found biochemistry and genengineering of great interest. If we could make people more resistant to the new diseases with a simple change to the genes...."

"I understand, and envy you. He may find this acceptable, and sponsor your college for such subjects, though he will expect you to work for him after you graduate for a few years at least. I can certainly speak to him about it."

Amelie let out a big sigh. "Thank you so much, sister. I was hoping it was not so impossible a choice that he would find it unacceptable." She squeezed her sister's hand. "Well, I had one other choice, but I really didn't think they'd let me in on the starship project."

Francoise laughed. "You would do that?"

"*Oui,* in a heartbeat. Several of my friends are trying for it. They've already been taking prep courses for physics and engineering, and have been talking to people on the project." Her face was animated. "The first faster than light interstellar probes got back last year, and now they're building a human-rated ship to start research colonies. There's at least two of the nearby planets that are habitable and terraformable without taking thousands of years." She paused. "Had I thought *he* would give me the chance, I would have asked you about that course of study, since you told me *M'sieur* Tolliver has a company that's part of the consortium that's building the ship."

Afterwards, they hailed a ride, and Francoise let Amelie off at the house of the party and returned to her hotel. She was sitting in the room, a drink in her hand, considering the bottles of orange juice and vodka, when he called. She put on the AR headset, much sleeker than the bulky ones she had started using years before, and appeared in a virtual room.

When she told him what her sister had asked about, he sighed. "I was hoping, since she has the looks, but if does not attract her, it will not work. People will see through her. Very well, if she does well in the field of study in the university, I will let her work for me for a few years, and see how she does. Good genes run in your family." Then he looked at her, and she saw a look she hadn't seen in two years. Before she could do much, he had her, and once again she was back in the field. She tried to turn on her canned program, but this time he saw it and shut it down, and she had no recourse but to endure it, for her sister.

After he had let her go and left, she stood and thought first of wanting to leave bleeding trails from her nails in her arms, her breasts, then thought about how completely he owned her, and Amelie was a hostage. There were thoughts of incense, of old things from Niger. Instead, she went and stood in the shower, the water as hot as she could stand it, and washed herself over and over, until she felt as though the washcloth were sandpaper.

5

NETWORK 3 NEWS

"This is Jasmine Johnson, Network 3 news, the most trusted news source on the Net, with a brief rundown of the latest news. From New York, the northeaster hitting the mid-Atlantic region brought the highest tides yet to the region. Water from the East River has gone over the seawall again and flooded the ground floor of the UN, in spite of the wall of sandbags. The neighborhood nearby is also flooded and several buildings have also sandbagged their sidewalks. Some are running on their own electrical generators, including a major network provider."

"It also appears that at a number of spots along the river, sections of the seawalls that were raised not long ago have been breached again. The president of the city council held a press conference, in which he castigated the mayor for her choice of construction firms to enhance the seawalls. He has also called for an investigation into the failure of the existing seawalls."

"James Garrick, the trillionaire CEO of Atlantic Construction, the firm that originally built the seawalls along the East River, has issued a statement to the press that he stands behind his firm's work. He says not only will he work with the city to investigate the cause of the failures, but have his own company investigate as well. He assures us that if there were failures on the part of his company, that there would be consequences."

"More storm news: the rain brought by the storm has resulted in floods in Pennsylvania, Ohio, West Virginia, and Virginia. Reports are that much of the corn and other crops in those regions may have been lost." She paused, then went on. "In spite of the rain, the mass lobbying of Congress has had a large turnout in preparation for the demonstration on the Mall tomorrow. Jake Roberts was on the street, and spoke to some of the lobbyists. Jake?"

"This is Jake Roberts, and I'm speaking with Mr. Stone, who was here to see his Congressman. Sir?"

"A lot of us are fed up with paying taxes, while billionaire members of Congress pay less than ordinary middle class people. We want them to raise their own taxes, instead of tax cuts, before they raise ours, and to do something about the sea level rise."

"Thank you, Mr. Stone. Jasmine, back to you."

She looked to the other commentator at the table. "And now, for why owners of old systems are paying more for fuel, here's Jose Lopes with the international news of the Americas. Jose?"

"Hello, folks, I'm Jose Lopez, covering Central and South America for Network 3 News. The heat wave around the equator is still stressing South America after nearly a month. Refugees from the extreme heat have been fleeing Ecuador and northern Brazil, pushing mostly south, but some, using boats, north, towards Central America. This, in turn, is pushing refugees already in Central America north towards Mexico and the United States. Oil exports from Venezuela have been affected by the heat, which has resulted in partial shutdowns of several oil fields, as well as a refinery. Because of that, gas prices in the US, Mexico, and a number of South American states have risen, and there are already protests in a number of countries about not being able to afford fuel for very old gasoline or diesel-burning vehicles, and blackouts, preventing EVs from being charged, as well as shutting down air conditioning, a critical utility with this heat. Now, let me pass it over to Josepha Erikson, covering world news, who has a lot to tell you, especially about Africa."

"Thank you, Jose. Josepha Erikson here, covering the eastern hemisphere. In both central western and southeastern Africa, the highly infectious respiratory hantavirus is spreading, especially in the camps of refugees from the extreme equatorial heat. In what is being taken as a mixed blessing, that very heat appears to be preventing the illness' spread to northern Africa due to transport breakdowns and road collapses from the heat. You might remember that they had their own influenza epidemic with a fatality rate several times normal only a few years ago. Meanwhile, the heat is affecting southern Europe, though it seems to be resulting in increased crop yield in areas where drought is not an issue. Russia's grain production, in the newly opened cropland resulting from global warming, has been up, resulting in a drop of European and African prices. In Greenland, the government has announced that it has now covered seventy-five percent of what's left of the glaciers with aluminized plastic, and solar panels on top of that. They say this will provide fifteen percent of the Ireland, Great Britain, and Scotland's summer energy, as well as five percent of France's needs. Finally, China and Southeast Asia are working at recovering from the recent typhoon that flooded many coastal cities. In addition, China has been rounding up notable Mongol spokespeople, claiming that they are subversives, and that they are receiving money from Taiwan. Taipei is denying that claim, pointing out that they have no control over how wealthy individuals or corporations care to spend their money. There was an implication that Wu Jishu, the CEO is known as the elder Wu, and is reputed to have built his empire up from his tang ancestors. might be involved. However, a spokesman for the elder Wu, who is unusual in having businesses in both Chinas, denies that his companies have any complicity in such actions. And now, here's Charles Drummond on the stock market."

"Charles Drummond here, covering the economy for Network 3. With the flooding in the east, as well as in New York, the markets have started falling, expecting a large drop for the next few weeks or more. Some large players appear to be waiting in the wings to buy at discount prices. Because of that, we expect the market to return to normal before the month is out. Meanwhile, unemployment claims are expected to rise sharply due to jobs lost during the current flooding, as well as the flooding that is expected to afflict the Midwest. Now, back to Jasmine for some cultural news."

"Thank you, Charles. The new art museum and office building in West Oakland, California, was just completed. There was a lot of criticism as the former historically ethnic neighborhood it is in was bought or otherwise forced out to make way for this magnificent building., and Gliance, the trillionaire who was the driving force behind it, has promised that it will be open to the public once a year, after she and other trillionaires have enhanced it from their private art collections. However, many may find it inaccessible, as they're saying tickets for the show would be between five hundred and a thousand dollars. Now over to Ann Hail, the Network 3 meteorologist...."

ROSE

6

BUTTERFLY'S WING

Judy excused herself and went into the hotel bathroom. Walking into the end stall, she closed the door, pulled some toilet paper off, and finally gave in to the cough that she had managed to hold off. There was, of course, blood in the phlegm. She threw the paper in the toilet, then used it and flushed. Before she opened the door, however, she drank from small bottle. *If it'll only keep me from coughing for the next few hours* she thought as she left the stall, and rinsed her hands lightly, drying them the same way, hoping they wouldn't be sterile. Looking in the mirror, she touched up her short blond hair with a comb, and then calmly walked back to the lobby, and to meet Stephanie and that pig of a trillionaire Senator.

"GEEZ...JACEY, quick, look at the news feed on Network 3!"

"Got it, Rose. What...what the hell is going on?"

"They were reporting on that trillionaire Senator, Waller, who looks like he's dying from the cell collapse virus, and the cops went into a charity hospital and they're arresting this dying woman for having deliberately infected him."

"That her? In the bed with the IV on? And they're arrestin' her?"

"It looks like they just cuffed her to the bed, and are reading the woman her rights."

"Hey, newsfeed 7's got a statement that her automated pers'nal asst's playing, 'bout her sister dyin' 'cause the Senator killed the medical assistance for a whole class of diseases, and since she's dyin' anyway, she was takin' him with her." Jacey started laughing. "She wants her enemy buried at her feet."

"Going all Ancient World, huh?" Rose shook her head. "It says she was only 19, but she looks younger in the recorded video. Dunno what the rich will do if this goes on, maybe live by themselves, with nothing but robots around?"

"Hah! People'll hack the robots." Jaycey paused. "Got it—what you just said 'minds me of an old science fiction book by Asimov that my bro' gave me to read a few years ago. This planet of super-wealthy, livin' all alone, did everything in virtual, and only time they ever saw another real person was to have sex for reproduction. Book was so old, they didn't have in vitro fertilization."

"I can see the trillionaires doing that, though I don't know where. Didn't they try to buy New Zealand?" Rose asked, thoughtfully.

"Yeah. The Kiwis had the nerve to tell them no. That was right before the tourist industry slumped, and New Zealand's economy went down the tubes. They're still trying to get it back up."

"They're lucky nobody hit them with some new disease."

Jaycey looked at Rose. "You still in the camp that thinks some of them are genengineered?"

"Hell, yes. Never saw so many appear so fast as they have the last fifteen-twenty years."

"Speaking of diseases, how's the required course goin'?"

"We had to put on full anticontam gear and go into a ward for the long-termers. Couple of the therapists lost it. After we got out, they quit the course, which means they'll be looking for new jobs."

"They better be lookin' hard. With all the disease class exclusions from coverage, unless you're workin' full time.... Can't really blame 'em though, with people having body parts shriveling up and falling off...."

"Please! I'm trying to heat up dinner," Rose said, annoyed.

"Sorry I brought it up." The oven dinged, and Rose took both dinners out and brought them to the table that barely fit, with room for chairs, in the kitchen. Jacey sat down, looking over the table at Rose, pale from lack of sun, with her short curly retro blue hair, tired, bringing over some forks.. "Smells okay, though I'm so tired of fish, anyway. How's the commute?"

"Metro was crowded, and there were a lot of people, all rained on, from the demonstrations and lobbying Congress about corruption and taxing billionaire Congresscritters. Slow. The Anacostia did not look friendly."

"With the rain?"

"It's high, and big waves. The tops of some reached the top of the floodwalls along the river."

"Crap, that's *high.*"

"Well, what do you expect, with the ocean as high as it is, crops growing in Greenland, and bushes on the edge of the Antarctic?" Rose shook her head.

"They decide on a company to raise the floodwall tops?" Jaycey said, just as the door opened. The two women took one look and were shocked as their roommate staggered in, shut the door behind him, leaned against it, dropped his backpack, and slid down, crying.

Rose jumped up and ran over. "Isiah, what's wrong?"

He was a skinny dark-skinned man in his late twenties, rain beading on his waterproof jacket and the hood covering his head, pants damp from the rain, face contorted in pain. It took him a while to talk without breaking down again, but he finally said, "My folks called. A seawall in South Carolina just failed, and took most of my grandparents' town. The Guard came in to do what they could, but a lot of it was finding bodies. They're both dead." Tears dripped down his cheeks.

The two women got him up and over to the couch, and Rose

made some green tea. While she waited for the water to boil, she came back to sit next to him. "When's the funeral, or cremation?"

"Cremation. End of the week," he said, his head hanging down. "They got so many bodies, and the ground's so soaked. They seen a coffin or two from the graveyard in the church come up."

"I hate to have to bring this up," Rose said, "But first thing tomorrow, you'd better talk to HR, and start the paperwork for updated travel papers, and your immunization records, so you can travel three states away."

"Damn, woman, always thinkin' of more to do." He looked at her, then hugged her hard, then looked the other way, at Jacey, also dark-skinned, short hair in tight black curls, strongly built, and hugged her, too. "Don't know what I'd do without the two of you. We was really lucky to find each other for roomies."

"Hey, you were there for me when I got mugged, and he broke my arm getting my pack," Rose said. The three of them talked for a while, with Isiah talking about memories of times with his grandparents, and finally the women got him to bed, with something to help him sleep.

Afterward, the two of them sat on the couch with drinks. "You look pissed," said Jaycey.

"Just remembered that it was Waller that was blocking funds for floodwalls and seawalls for Maryland for years, and in return, they didn't get the money they needed to maintain and upgrade the ones in South Carolina and Mississippi."

"Hell, I'd forgotten that," Jaycey replied. "Now I got me some real sympathy for that woman that infected Waller. Lots don' like him, but he had his votes bought and paid for, nobody takin' it away from him, and he don' care what we think, we ain't rich."

Rose stared at her. "Y'know, it just struck me—I wonder if something's going on. I mean, this is like the second or third big money somebody who's been taken out. The supermarket heir, then the media guy...."

"You mean, like a war between the trillionaires? That'd be scary. You hear they're talking about genengineering for some diseases required just to get on a plane?" They both shook their heads, then Jaycey looked up. "Hell, gettin' late." I think I'll skip the online game tonight." She tossed down the rest of her drink, and got up, a little woozy. "Bedtime for me," putting her glass in the dishwasher, and heading towards the bathroom.

"'Bout right," replied Rose, who did the same, started the dishwasher, and went to get ready for bed herself.

A WEEK LATER, Rose was in the crowded office she shared with three other nurses, working on documentation from the day before when Christine, the head nurse for the division walked in, along with an older man with several people who were clearly with him. Rose looked up, and as Christine called the four of them, she realized who the older man was. "Morning, Representative McCauley." He looked at her, and she added, "I'm in your district."

"Well, hello. You are?"

"Rose Josephson." She could see Christine getting a sour look on her face, and so she stepped back, to let Christine take control of the visit, which turned out to be McCauley asking the nurses about what more Congress could do to help speed up the clinical studies. She let the others give the usual responses, including asking for more nurses, which got a flash of a smile from Christine. Then he turned back to Rose. She could see Christine's expression close up as she said, "We could use a lot more money for maintenance and construction, so we could open up more wards." She shook her head. "They can't even keep all the elevators running."

He frowned. "Is it really that bad?"

Christine began to talk around the issue when he interrupted her. "Let Ms. Josephson finish."

Rose could see trouble coming from Christine, but replied, "Yes. There's one elevator they've been waiting for parts for four months." Her face grew serious. "We're the best there is in the world, and we'd like more support to keep it up. As it is, we have too high a turnover because of that."

He glanced at one of his aides, who nodded, and Rose could see words appearing on her mobile as the woman subvocalized her notes. "Thank you for your honest answer." He turned to look at Christine. "I think we're done here. What's the next division?" Christine led him and his people out, and Rose noted a glance she wasn't sure she could interpret from the aide.

Later, Christine called Rose into her office. "What the hell were you thinking, Rose? That's not how you talk to a visiting Congressman."

"Christine, I once heard an interview on a news stream, where someone was asked why they voted for someone, and they said, 'because they called me up and asked me to'. How are we ever going to get anything if we don't at least ask." She could see the woman was angry, but she added, "Besides, he *is* my Rep." The expression on Christine's face looked like she'd run into a wall.

"Please don't do that again. The Director will tell us what we get to communicate." That ended the conversation, and Rose left, each woman annoyed with the other.

That evening, however, Rose was surprised when she answered her mobile. "Hello, this is Amie Glossner, Representative McCauley's aide. Do you have time to have a private talk, now?"

"Yes...this is a good time. What's this about?" She pulled her AR —augmented reality - glasses on, and set privacy on her mobile.

"The Representative has tasked me to speak to you a bit more, without your manager standing over you."

Rose laughed. "I'm surprised. That's more concern for my job than I expected."

"That's why I work for him. So, what he wanted to know is just how bad the situation in Building 10 really is."

Rose took a deep breath. "What I get from people that have been here a long time, is that we're in a fifteen- or twenty-year cycle, where we've got whole wings, on multiple floors, closed off, needing rehab, and either the money's not there, or they don't get through the bidding process because of personnel churn at the level just under the director. That, and there are things like elevators out all over campus, and they're out for years."

The line was quiet for a minute. "That's...appalling."

"Tell me about it. And some of those elevators—if they're out, you have to go the long way around to get from one wing to another."

"And personnel churn?"

"Every few years, there's someone new under our Director, and the contract rebids wind up going to other contractors. Usually, most people move from one to another, but we do lose people who'd stay if they were feds like me. But then, you know how they like to claim that it saves money to outsource."

"Of course," Amie replied, and Rose saw her rolling her eyes. "That's been true forever. Going back to the physical plant though, if the Congressman added riders in the funding bill to require that the contracts be given out and work started within a year, would that help?"

"Oh, hell, yes, and if he would add a separate line item for the physical plant. Right now, they have to beg the other Institutes and Centers for money. I've been at the NIH for seven years, and seen something take almost a year before they even sat down to write the contract. For that matter, there's like eight guys taking care of the HVAC for eight buildings."

Amie nodded. "Ok, I think that covers most of what we can try to do something about. Thank you very much for your time, Ms. Josephson."

"You're very welcome." They hung up, and Rose sat there thinking about this for a while.

FRANCOISE II

7

RAFE

"Father, you can *not* let this go through. People will be in the same position as in the States, where they have to choose between medicine, food, and rent."

"Son, if we do not pass this, Commons will ram it through, and it will be more stringent," his father said, looking up from his seat in his study at his son. Behind the young man were the shelves filled with books, some several hundred years old.

"Stringent is not what this is, it is not just austerity, it is deliberately cruel, cutting the dole when you are also cutting funding to the NHS. You have to know this, given that you have to pass through the crowds of demonstrators every time you enter Parliament."

"With the unrest in the world, including these constant disruptions of the global supply chain, we have to do something to help British corporations."

"Which, the ones owned by the Chinese, the Russian oligarchs, or the American multinationals?"

"Now you're being unreasonable. This is the way business has gone in the last seventy years and more."

"*I'm* being unreasonable? When are you going to penalize the corporations for moving jobs overseas?"

"That would make things worse, don't you see?"

"No, I don't." Rafe shook his head. "You're refusing any compromise." He snorted. "This is going nowhere. I'm going out now."

His father shook his head sadly. "As you get older, you'll see how this all works."

"I see it *now*," Rafe said, pulling the door to the study closed firmly behind him. Pulling out his mobile, he made a call. "Hullo, Amelie."

"Rafe, how are you? What's up?"

"Would you like to go down to the Old Java shop with me? They might still have some of those nice French pastries."

"*Oui.* Zat's too tempting. Where shall I meet you, at ze shop?"

"Quite." A while later, he got to the shop, and saw her standing outside, staring at the pastries in the window. "Hullo there."

"Rafe! Let us go in." They went in and were soon seated in a far corner, coffee in front of both of them, a scone for him and a chocolate mousse in a tart shell for her. She looked at him. "Zere is somezing wrong, *oui*?"

"My father. He and the rest of the Lords are going to pass the austerity bill."

"But zat is vile! Cannot he see ze effects?"

"He's blind to the fact that it was exactly this that resulted in the breakup of the United Kingdom, and before that, in the Irish Potato Famine."

A look that occasionally came over her face, not pleasant at all, but very, very hard. "Perhaps you might suggest an alternate title for the bill, such as 'let zem eat brioche'." Rafe looked at her. The hard look on her face had, for a moment, become deadly, then softened, as if on purpose.

"He might blow his top at that," Rafe said, mildly.

"He should remember what followed zat."

They ate more of their pastries, and sipped the coffee. "Amelie, I am more than familiar with father's Tory friends and associates, and their approval and disapproval, but there are times when you come across as someone who could terrify them."

A look of pain washed away her former expression, and her French accent grew heavier. "My life since Francoise and I left Niger, I do not like to zink about, much less speak of it. But I 'ave seen my sister deal with our patron, the trillionaire Tolliver, and I 'ave 'ad some dealings wis' him, and one learns from a master."

He stared at her. "You say 'master' in a way that implies more than one definition."

She took a bite of her pastry and chewed it, looking at him for a while. "Not many would see zat, but *oui*."

As she put the pastry down, he reached over and took her hand. "Let me make an offer - whenever you need someone to speak to, or just to be company, when things get very bad, call me."

Several looks flashed over her face, hopeful, distrustful, appreciative. "I will remember zat. Perhaps I may ask it of you someday."

"But?"

"When one lives in ze world I do, trust is ze most dangerous zing in ze world."

"Perhaps I'm just a young spoiled upper class British lad...but I give you my word that offer is real."

"How odd...'your word.' You say zat like someone from centuries ago, or from a novel."

"Perhaps it comes from reading the wrong literature growing up." They looked at each other, then both laughed. "My late mother liked historical romances, and, oddly enough, some early science fiction and fantasy. I admit when I read them, I noticed that many ended with a happy ending."

"Zat is something I 'ave seen in entertainment, but is not something of ze real world."

"No, it does not tend to happen, especially when serious money or power is involved."

8

GROWING IN IMPORTANCE

Francoise wasn't sure how three years had passed so quickly. She sat in the audience in what had become her trademark white linen suit and jewel green blouse, and saw her sister, in the traditional collegiate robes, walking across a stage again, to receive her bachelor's degree. Afterwards, Amelie came over with young man from her graduating class. "Francoise, I'd like to properly introduce you to Rafe Maxwell."

"*Bonsoir.*" She paused for a minute, then asked, "You are the son of the Tory Whip in the 'Ouse of Lords?"

"I am, madam."

"You are looking forward, no doubt, to taking his seat when ze time comes."

"Actually, no. I am somewhat declassé, going on the next level at uni in accounting and finance."

Francoise raised her eyebrows. "Really? Will your parents be 'orrified at you becoming a tradesman? What are you planning on?"

He smiled. "Working for a different party, and trying to keep the well-off from making life for the working classes nothing but misery. As the old saying goes, 'there, but for fortune....'"

"*Intéressant*, zough you may find zat you take anozer course as time goes by."

Nodding, he replied. "I am not so naive as to think that I can change everything, but perhaps I can keep things from getting worse."

Francoise nodded in return. "A more reasonable goal, and perhaps somezing achievable." Turning to Amelie, she asked, "Shall we be off? I 'ave a reservation for dinner."

"Of course. Rafe, I will be by Charles' later for the party."

"Please do. I'm looking forward to you joining us, if for no other reason than keeping several of the crowd from building cloud castles."

Amelie smiled, and kissed Rafe on both cheeks, and left with Francoise.

Shortly, they sat in a well-appointed North African restaurant, large prints of classic black and white photographs on the walls alternating with imported handwoven fabrics, and wooden screens, the aromas of African spices, and traditional music from several nations playing softly in the background. Amelie had finished her attiekke and was considering dessert while Francoise lingered over her ebbeh and looked at her younger sister. Between them, they spoke French. "There is something in you, a touch of hope or some such, perhaps. Is it your friend's fault?"

"There is, and it is. He seems to be genuinely working to earn something of me that I'm not familiar with, except between you and me—trust."

"That is very, very dangerous."

"As if I do not know. But he has spent much of his youth..." Her sister smiled as the young woman said that. "Reading, and finding roles, if not people, to admire. He seems to want to be one of them."

"I wish him luck, especially if he draws the attention of a trillionaire, or even a billionaire, and annoys them." She looked at Amelie intently. "Are you considering trying to steer him out of such straits?"

The younger woman looked thoughtful. "That is not something that I would do without long and careful consideration."

"*Bien*. Remember, even I can only do so much." Her sister nodded, and then they ordered dessert. Afterwards, they said good night, and Amelie went off to party with her friends, many of whom Francoise found leaned socialist, and honest with herself as always, she knew her presence made them uncomfortable. But then, she was a direct agent of one of the people who had made the old nobility into nothing more than a title and a curiosity over the last two centuries. Letting her hair down was not something she dared to allow herself.

Several months later, Francoise was put in charge of a major construction project, building a dam on the Milo River in Mali. The more she worked on the project, the more complicated it became. Whole villages needed to be relocated, which the government gave assurances would happen. This worried her, since she had been offered nothing that suggested where the people would go. Finally, sitting in her office, late at night, a screwdriver in a tall glass near her, she saw her reflection in a window, and realized that she had the same look that Tolliver and that other trillionaires had on her face, and shuddered, then pushed the thought off, and chose to decide that was the government's problem.

Eight months into the project, though, her geological team sent Pierre, their team lead to speak to her in France. A stocky man, clearly not using the obesity-control drugs, with thinning dark hair. He was clearly uneasy, from the situation, and from Francoise's presence. Though she was only in her late twenties, her association with Tolliver implied much. "Madame, my entire team is tremendously concerned," Pierre said.

"And your concerns are? Will not the dam handle the river?"

"Madame, the dam will be fine. What we worry about are the banks and the basin behind and beyond the dam."

"Was this not considered before?"

"It was, but only a few anomalies were observed, and since much was done by the government's people, they were discounted. As the emphasis on the project has moved to the construction, we took some time to look further, and what we found were caves, and old mine shafts in the cliffs that everyone said they knew nothing about. We sent robots into the shafts, and found played out tin mines. In addition, we found large parts of the banks above the dam site that are buried garbage piles."

"And you fear?"

"That in a flood, the river will carve its way around the dam."

She sat back and looked at him for a while, seeing him fidget under her stare. A few drops of sweat showed above his forehead. At last, she said, "I shall speak with the government's geologists, and will get back to you." He thanked her profusely, shook her hand, and left for his hotel.

Francoise spent much of the next week chasing down government officials and geologists. Finally, she called Pierre in, and told him that the government had assured her that they had looked at the issue, and were planning on doing some reinforcement of the banks, forwarding some of the government's documents to him. After he left to return to Mali though, she stared unhappily at nothing. Having worked with them for over a year, she knew how much credence to put on the assurances. At last that evening, with much to do next day, and catching up with what she had put aside to deal with this, she took a drink of her screwdriver, shook her head, and put the decision out of her mind.

ROSE II

9

ISOLATION

Christine called the senior nurse into her office. "Rose, we're getting a very special patient." Rose tilted her head, curious. "The patient is Mr. James Garrick, the trillionaire. He appears to have been infected with a virus similar to the ones they think were genengineered while he was overseas a month ago, one that, so far, looks like over a thirty per cent fatality rate." Rose's eyebrows rose. "Congressman McCauley requested that he be treated here, and that he wanted you on the case." Looking up at her, Christine said, "I told you not to make trouble, Rose." She shook her head. "All I can say is good luck. He'll be brought in tomorrow morning."

Rose had nothing to say, so she nodded and left. That evening after dinner, Isiah looked at her as he was loading the dishwasher. "What's wrong, Rose. You're really quiet this evening." When she told him what was happening, he was quiet as he got the dishwasher going, then got himself something to drink. "I know you work with a lot of dangerous diseases, but this is one of the new scary ones, right?"

"Yeah. I'll be working in a full anticontagion suit, or in VR."

"Full bunny suit?" She nodded. "So you gonna look like the ether bunny," he said, with an innocent look on his face.

She sprayed out the sip that had been in her mouth, laughing. "You bum! You couldn't have waited till I swallowed!"

He put his drink down and wiped up the area on the floor. Hanging up the wipe, he came over and hugged her. "You gone be ok, honey. Just don't skip any steps. We make sure we don't do that in the lab, you don't do that in the ward."

She nodded, glad to be held. "This is scary. It's one of those if you don't beat it, you're dead in a week or two."

"We're the NIH. We're the best there is, and I don't care what China or India says. We've all had the genengineering to enhance our immune system to get our jobs." She nodded, her head against his shoulder. That night, the three of them opened up the large futon in the living room, and slept together, with Rose in the middle, to keep her safe for the night in the face of the danger she was facing.

In the morning, it was all signatures and checklists as Garrick was brought in, moving his isolation cylinder, like a giant test tube on its side, the top third clear, the rest white, on a wheeled platform through the sterilization lock, with Rose and two other nurses, in full suits, on the other side to bring it into the sealed room. Every connection double checked, and checked off on the lists in their VD. Zana lowered the frame at the foot of the bed, and Rose and Cherise spread the carrier's legs and pushed it so that it straddled both sides of the bed. Then they opened the clear lid, and rotated the isolation cylinder, Garrick sliding down, off the pad inside, down the bare clear ceramic, and onto the bed. They pulled the cylinder up and moved it back off the bed. Finally, he was installed in the room, IVs and sensors, and Rose turned to him. She could see his eyes open, and apparently tracking. "Good morning, Mr. Garrick. Welcome to the NIH Clinical Center. How are you feeling?"

"Rotten, but then I wouldn't be here if I felt okay."

Rose smiled, surprised that someone like this, in this situation, would make light of it. "I promise you that we're going to do better than anyone else, anywhere, to get you through this."

He snorted, which turned into a long gagging cough. Finally it stopped, and he lay there breathing for a bit. "That's something I haven't heard in a long time. You sound like someone who believes in their job."

"I do. I could make more money somewhere else, if being here wasn't important."

He looked at her, a hard expression that, beyond the worry about infection, scared her. He nodded. "You'll do, you'll do." His breathing grew a little heavier, and she adjusted the oxygen, which appeared to help some. His eyes closed, and he seemed to drift off to sleep. She inhaled the cold, self-contained air of the suit as she checked all the readings, verifying what the other two nurses had done, and the three of them left, pushing the opened isolation cylinder through the airlock to be sterilized.

They sat in the second chamber, white ceramic and stainless steel around them, as the lights went through the cycle from UV and infrared back to normal. "Why do we get to sit here for fifteen minutes, if we are sterile?" asked Zana, who had only come on recently.

"We get to rest," Rose smiled. "Well, unless you really like second or third degree burns." He looked at her, surprised. "Didn't they tell you that the last ten minutes was the beams bringing the outside of our suits to 175C?"

"It was warm, but I, ah, must have forgotten that."

"Don't. Ever. We've practically been autoclaved. Just a few more minutes to cool down."

"I'm just glad that after this, we can do almost everything in AR."

"True." She turned. "You ok, Cherise?"

"Yeah, yeah, but you know how it is, dealing with level four isolation's scary."

"I surely do. Shoulda seen me last night." Then the all clear rang, and they went to unsuit.

~

LATE IN THE AFTERNOON, Rose sat down at a desk in the monitoring station near the isolation chambers, pulled on a full AR headset, and walked into a virtual hospital room. There, Garrick was sitting in comfortable clothes by the window, looking out at fall on the campus. "I see you're feeling a little better, Mr. Garrick." It concerned her that there was a faint reddish cast to his image, which suggested strain or pain.

He turned, and looked at her, the blue around her stronger than the light in the virtual room. "Enough to get into AR, though the bluish tint to the light in this room is annoying."

"Sorry. We have heavy UV lighting to help disinfect the isolation chamber, and it bleeds through to AR. There's also the body state shading that the AR adds, to help us be aware of the condition of your physical body."

He nodded. "It's still tremendously better for me to be able to do things in AR, rather than just lie in bed feeling rotten." He rubbed his chin with the side of his hand. "Actually, I do feel better. At least I'm breathing more easily. Are you using a new drug?"

"Yes. The medical staff who got you into the isolation capsule were using the standard scrips. We're authorized to use newer ones that have been proven out here, but haven't completed general release trials." She paused. "I admit that we get extremely nervous when an extreme case like yours comes here, and we have to deal with it...on the other hand, as I said, we're the best there is."

He turned, and really looked at her, that terrifyingly hard expression back on his face. She felt like a sample under a microscope. "So, if I make it through, you wouldn't be interested if I were to offer you a job at one of the medical centers that I make donations to, at twice the salary."

Rose felt her stomach drop. She could...but then thought who she'd have to work with. Swallowing, she looked at him, her image going slightly bluer. "I don't think so. They do refinement. We're the ones who do the original work that they follow up on, and that's not even beginning to talk about the majority of the people I work with, people I like, some whom I admire." The conversation dried up, and they looked at each other for a while, then he turned to look out at the campus. They could faintly hear Taps from the Walter Reed Military Medical Center across the way, and Rose realized how late it was. "I need to leave. If you need anything, or start having problems, just ring. Someone's here twenty-four/seven."

"Thank you, Ms. Josephson." She walked out of the virtual room and got ready to leave for home, thinking about the conversation.

That evening, over dinner, she talked to her roommates. "I'm not sure about this guy. One minute, he's the creep, no, a monster I expected, looking at me like a bug, and asking if he can buy me, and the next, listening to why I won't be bought, and thinking about the answers."

"Well, there's somethin' you should consider," said Jaycey. Rose looked at her. "He knows damn well that he could die in the next week or two." She smiled as she took a bite. "'Minds me of some English nobleman from, what, the 17th century, who wrote something like, 'it greatly settles one's mind, knowing you're going to be hung in the morning.'" Rose and Isiah chuckled.

When Rose got in the next morning, Zana was there. "He's had some periods of difficult respiration since I got on for graveyard shift, but seems to be better now. If it gets bad again, I think we need to clear his lungs."

Rose nodded. "Let me call the doctor now, before you leave." He nodded, and went back to monitoring, while she called the doctor on the case and got approval. Turning back to Zana, she said, "Not only can we do it, he said that was a good idea to do it now, and prune the crap on the aeolli as well." Pulling on the AR headset, she looked at what Zana was seeing, and said, "He looks to be awake. I'll talk to him, and warn him we're going to knock him out." Garrick complained, but not for long, and soon he was out. Rose commented as Zana was leaving, "Great. Vacuuming his lungs, and next I'll wash his windows, I mean eyes...."

Zana laughed. "Better you than me. I do not do windows," which left Rose chuckling.

It kept her smiling for a while as she worked on the tedious details of supervising the microbots swarming through Garrick's lungs. Finally, though, it was done, she flushed the 'bots to be incinerated, and had the system stop the anesthetic. It was the better part of an hour before he woke up. In the AR, she walked into his room, to see him start to sit up, then begin coughing, wet hacking that kept up for several minutes. In the real room, she had a setup to draw it out of his mouth, and when he stopped, her teleoperated robot gave him some water to wash his mouth out, then to drink. Then she used it to help him get the AR headset on, and they were in the virtual room.

He shook his head. "What did you do to me? I feel like I'm breathing freezing air, or like my lungs have been sandblasted."

His image was purple, suggesting that his body was stressed, but improving. "In a way, that's what we did. You were coughing a lot overnight, and we cleaned your lungs."

He looked at her. "Surgery?"

She shook her head, her image gaining a yellow cast. "Haven't needed to do surgery in a long time. Tubes not much thicker than a hair going down your throat, with hundreds of microbots at their ends, vacuuming up the thick liquid, and cutting off growths caused by the infection."

His mouth opened as she explained. "That...that's something out of science fiction."

"We've been doing it for years, and it's being used by high-end hospitals around the world. Within a few years, we're looking forward to the prices coming down, so it can be used in ordinary hospitals."

"Selling those would make some serious money," he said, looking hungry.

She stared at him, coldly. "That's why I'm not interested in whatever you offer. I became a nurse to heal people, not make money off them being sick, or dying if they can't pay." She turned. "Excuse me, I shouldn't have said that, but it's something I feel strongly about. Let me run checks on you." She dropped out of the room abruptly, and was back the monitoring station. She started the standard checks, and added some additional ones to keep herself occupied.

Several hours later, as she was finishing lunch, Garrick called. Chuffing, she put the headset back on, and was back in the room. "You needed something, Mr. Garrick?"

"I think I have to do something that is very hard for me, something I don't do. Ms. Josephson, I need to apologize." Rose looked at him, puzzled. "You understand that I live in a world where the only time someone apologizes, if ever, is when they're walking out the door, and if anyone ever asks, they deny having ever apologized."

She stared. "That's...bizarre. No, it's scary. The first thing that comes to my mind is that your stress levels, all of you, have to be through the roof."

He stared back. "That's your first thought?"

"Well, and how cold a world that has to be to live in. You're like a bunch of...of cavemen, and if you make a mistake, you'll be dead."

"That's how it is, Ms. Josephson. That's how it's always been."

"Not in the world most of the rest of us live in. We haven't lived that way in a long, long time. Friends and family help each other when we need it." She chuffed, softly. "The night before last, when we knew you were coming in, and how dangerous admission is, my roomies were all over me, giving me reassurance and comfort. I can't see how you would ever get any of that, if where you live is that... precarious." She paused. "It must be immensely lonely."

He considered her words. "Not really. I've got all my people, who deal with the details, so I can handle the big picture."

"But are they friends? If a competitor of yours offered them enough money, would they leave without an apology?"

He opened his mouth to answer, then closed it, and with a thoughtful look stared out the window of the virtual room at the campus. After a bit, he turned back to her. "People in my situation tend to use a lot of words like loyalty, and calling, but in general, I admit, we mostly consider people like that..."

"Suckers."

"I wasn't going to put it that way, but yes. And yet, here I find my very life depends on people, on a woman, who actually believes in her job, and because she thinks that way could well save my life. On top of which, she's not looking for a payout."

"Other than to beat the disease, to beat death another day." She saw his look. He clearly was unused to thinking along these lines. She lowered her head for a minute, then looked at him. "I'd better get back to monitoring, especially since you're not the only person I have to care for, Mr. Garrick. Oh, and you might want to rest for a while, not push yourself, right after the work on your lungs."

He nodded. "Thank you. Oh, and it's James."

She paused, and thought for a minute. "Rose," she said, then turned and walked out of the virtual room.

10

TRACKING THE VIRUS

Over the next couple of days, Rose got into a habit of going into AR and spending some break time talking to Garrick, until the third day. Early that afternoon Rose was catching up on reports, when Christine called her into her office. "Rose, please shut the door."

Rose did so, concerned. "What's up?"

Christine looked at her, and then shook her head. "Not for you to worry, Mr. Garrick seems pleased with you." Her look grew serious. "We just got the report back from the lab. It appears that it was a genengineered virus." She paused. "For now, that's under security, but we need you to talk to Mr. Garrick and see if you can piece together how it might have been introduced to him, and write it up for the epidemiologist and the police."

Rose exhaled, loudly. "Crap. But shouldn't the FBI be doing this?"

"They have no one available used to AR. They have asked to piggyback on your interview, and may suggest questions."

"Okay.... Can we do this now? He's been doing a lot better since they had me do the work on his lungs, and he's awake now and working in AR."

"Let me contact the man who called. I expect he wants this

ASAP." A short while later, Christine called to Rose that the man was on the link, and she should start.

Back at the monitoring station, she sat at the desk and put on the AR headset. Before she virtually walked int his room, she found she could speak with the agent, and set a passthrough, to allow him to hear, and then activated the security protocol. As she came in, Garrick, sitting in bed and working on a virtual screen, looked up. His eyes opened wider, as he saw the red warning of security. "Rose, what's happening?"

"Please activate the security protocol on your AR, James." He did so, and she told him what she'd just learned, and about Mr. Leon, the FBI agent listening in.

He leaned back with a heavy sigh. His look was abstracted for a minute, then he said, "About two, no, almost two and a half weeks ago, I was at a meeting with several other people of my class in San Francisco, and afterwards, two of us went out for drinks. My assistant had arranged for escorts for us, to show us around. I think it was a day or two later that I started feeling ill." Pausing, he worked on his screen. "A minute." It was more like five when he looked up, his AR self shifting to a darker blue.

"What's wrong?" she asked sharply, her AR self gaining a faint reddishness.

"Duong, the acquaintance I went out with. He's dead. He and the escort hit it off, and they found the two of them in a hotel room, blood all over, as though they'd coughed their lungs out. The robot maid reported them not moving, and housekeeping came in, then security, who called the police."

"The escort you were with?"

"Let me call the escort service." He called out with privacy set. When he got off, he looked up. "She's in a hospital. I've told them where I am, and asked them to put her in isolation five minutes ago, and get her started on treatment."

"Forward me the information, and we'll get in touch with them." She paused. "Mr. Leon asks that you include the escort agency contact."

"I will. Thank you," he said, clearly shaken.

She saw the data arrive in the AR, and nodding at Garrick, left the room.

Rose stayed a little late, until Christine called her in and got the answers they were waiting for. "So," Rose said, "this woman came to the ER about a week and a half ago. That would have been about the same time that Mr. Garrick was starting to feel ill enough that he went to his medical. I don't know about you, but that suggests to me that the other escort was the vector, given the other man and the escort were dead already."

"That's what the hospital is thinking, and the police in San Francisco depend on their advice. They've been backtracking the other woman. One thing they found is in her social sphere, in a semi-private section, she's apparently in the antioligarch fringe. As of yet, they don't think the woman who died deliberately exposed herself to the disease to start, but that after she found herself ill, went after Mr. Nguyen."

"May I tell Mr. Garrick this?"

"I suppose. He's got enough pull to find out anyway."

Rose opened Christine's door, and returning to the monitoring station, she went into AR to check Garrick. Seeing that he was awake and working, she walked into the virtual room. He looked up as she did, and nodded. He wound up what he was working on, and looked at her. "You've got more information?"

"We do." She told him what she'd just heard, and he sighed. "I'm glad Anika's being taken care of. She was very pleasant company, and I'm pleased that you don't think she was the vector."

"No, since she seemed to come down with it about the same time you did, while the other woman and Mr....Nguyen, were dead over a week ago."

"We had two escorts. Neither was assigned to Duong or me, so Lydia, I think her name was, went after Duong purposely."

"Any idea why?"

"Not really. I didn't get anything of her background other than the usual anonymous escort information." He paused. "Wait, she made an off-handed comment about people starving in the favelas outside the Bay Area, and I know that one of his industries is in agribusiness."

"Let me pass that along, if you don't mind. Then, if I don't get out of here, I'll miss the next train, and won't get home for an hour and a half." He nodded and she left, sending what she'd learned along to Christine.

Two mornings later, Rose walked into Garrick's AR to find him seated at a desk working his screen when he looked up. "Morning, James. They found the answer, and it wasn't that she was just crazy. The woman's mother had died in an accident with a robot harvester on one of his farms in the Central Valley, and her father in one of the food riots the next year, when a lot of corn was shipped to Africa for animal feed."

He sat there, looking at her, for a while. Finally, "What do you say to something like that? That there are a lot of people in the world, and accidents happen?"

"I don't know about her mother's accident, but if people weren't starving and homeless, there wouldn't be riots." She looked at him. "You are aware, I assume, that this isn't just a lone vector?"

"I am. I know several other people in my class, or billionaires, have died lately, and they turn out to have been infected purposely."

"A few months ago, one of my roommates lost his grandparents to a flood from a seawall failure. That was right after Senator Waller, who had been blocking appropriations for upgrading of the seawalls, died from an escort who'd infected him as she was dying, because he'd also blocked appropriations and coverage for a whole class of diseases. You understand my roommates had some sympathy for her."

He nodded. "We may have to do something..." he began.

She barked a laugh. "Offer thoughts and prayers, or more intrusive security measures?"

"What else could we do?"

She paused, then asked, "Tell me, will you be using escorts again?"

He looked at her for a time, then he smiled. "Do you realize how hard it is for two people like me to get married, or even meet someone? I'm not even talking about the hundreds of pages of prenup agreement."

Rose laughed. "More than a century and a half after the right to vote, and there's still a lot more men among the ultra-wealthy than women." He nodded. "Century...right, that's what's been lurking in my subconscious. A while back, one of my roommates told me about an old science fiction book, where these really, really wealthy people lived on the planet of another star. There were a strictly limited number of them, and they had millions of robots...and did everything in virtual. The only time they saw each other in person was to have sex to reproduce." She shook he head. "In-vitro and artificial wombs weren't in the story. Is that how all of you are going to wind up? That is, assuming that you don't have your AIs hacking each others' robots?"

He stood there, in the virtual room they were sharing, and stared at her for a while, his expression not quite the hard, dangerous one. "So what would you do?"

"Be the one to find a way to end homelessness and starvation. Give people places to live, at least, and utilities, and food, and water, and medical care, for a start. Then maybe make something that's not make-work for them to do?" She snorted a laugh. "Well, you asked, and I'm not a trillionaire, nor am I the kind of person to become one. I want to make life better for everyone. You want profit, and nothing else matters." They stood there a while longer, and then she said, deliberately offhandedly, "By the way, we think that we've gotten it licked. They've given me a specific antiviral that I've had in your IV, and it seems to have won. Unless things change overnight, we'll be moving you to a normal recovery room tomorrow." Seeing a smile on his face, she nodded and left.

~

He watched her leave, sitting in the virtual room for a while, then dropped out, aware of his real body, with its aches and pains, in a bed, in an isolation chamber that had lighting with bluish-purple overtones, and he put his AR headset on the table.

That evening, well after dinner, he put it back on, set security to max, and called some people he knew.

11

CHANGING TIMES

Almost a month later, Garrick was ushered into the office of the honorable Senator Cortes from the State of New York. "Senator Cortes, thank you for seeing me."

The Senator, black haired, well into her fifties, and attractive enough that the media loved videoing her, shook his hand and sat down, "As you know, Mr. Garrick, I make a point of not seeing wealthy petitioners, but as legitimately a resident of New York, and some things that your staffer said to set this up, I made an exception. What is this donation you are planning to make for the 'public good'?"

"I know that you've seen that I signed two letters over the years with several other trillionaires calling for our taxes to be raised. However, recent events have made me consider the situation more seriously."

She leaned back. "Are you referring to your recent, ahhh, near-death experience?"

He gave a soft laugh. "That's a good way of putting it. I will note that the FBI are calling it an assassination attempt, though I was not the primary target."

"I find it hard to believe that this has changed your way of thinking that seriously."

"Back in the late nineteen hundreds, there was a former governor of Alabama named George Wallace. He was a racist and pro-segregation most of his life. That was, until he survived an assassination attempt. Within several years, he renounced those positions, and apologized for them. While I was in the clinical center of the NIH, I had some long discussions with a nurse there who saved my life, and I've been thinking about those discussions."

Cortes stared at him thoughtfully for a while. "What, exactly, are you planning on doing?"

"For a start, I've started a committee to raise funds to support political campaigns for you, and others around the country. We will include advertising in the conservative press and broadcast media, countering their commentators. We would also like to fund both voter registration and turn-out-the-vote drives. I've put five billion dollars aside for these campaigns, and I'm expecting to add more. What I would like from you is your recommendations as to what organizations that do that should be funded, and your public endorsement of those organizations."

Cortes' mouth slipped open in surprise. "That...that is a lot more than signing a letter." She saw his expression grow intense.

"If you like, you may view it as a thought to my afterlife. No one lives forever, and perhaps I would like to be remembered after I'm gone as someone who had to look death in the face, and decided that perhaps 'We, the People', was more than just a bunch of words." He shook his head. "That's really what I had to present to you, and I don't want to take up more of your time." He stood, pushing the chair back.

Cortes rose as well. "Mr. Garrick, I believe that we can work together on this."

He started to turn, then looked at her. "One other thing?" She gave him a questioning look. "Perhaps you can do something about increasing the budget of the NIH?"

A smile spread across her face. "I'd be happy to work on that."

"*Bonjour, M'sieu Marshall.*"

"Hello, Tolliver. To what do I owe the 'pleasure' of this call?"

"There is an issue that's come up recently that appears to be turning into a genuine annoyance, with which you might be able to assist?"

"Which is?"

Tolliver leaned back in his chair, looking at Marshall on the phone and rubbed his chin. "Garrick."

"I see. In this case, I find we are in agreement. This is far beyond signing meaningless letters, and looks to become an annoyance not merely here, but he's dabbling in the UN as well, to the point it will affect most of us."

"Since his recent incident, 'e seems to have changed in difficult ways."

"I agree. Pity that he didn't join his late dinner partner."

"It is. And he's unlikely to follow him, at this point, having apparently become rather paranoid about disease."

"Is he, now? Wouldn't it be amusing if, say, some simple mechanical thing happened to him?"

"So it would, so it would. Gliance and several others were speaking and we were wondering what might change his mind."

"The Wu's, of course, are not especially troubled by internal American events, but most of us could be, and the Wu's and their clients would be as well, should the UN stick its nose in." Marshall's smile matched Tolliver's. "I wouldn't even see this as a favor, should I find something to discommode him. Thank you for the thought."

"Ciao."

"This is Jasmine Johnson, Network 3 news, the most trusted news source on the Net, in front of the headquarters of the Garrick Companies. The trillionaire CEO, James Garrick, has recently been aggressively spending serious money to change the dialog concerning taxation on the wealthy, including both income and wealth taxes. He is even pushing to raise taxes on his own corporations, which has brought attacks from conservative media inside and outside the United States. Inspired by some of it, there is a truck convoy driving around and around the block, as you can see, creating massive traffic headaches." She looks around, her camerawoman following her, as a large, clearly heavy car pulls to the curb. Both doors facing the curb open, and a man and a woman in black step out and survey the street, then another man in well-fitting blue business suit steps out.

"And here's Mr. Garrick now. Sir, a question?"

Garrick looked at the reporter, and looked at her ID badge. "Just one. There'll be time for more later, inside."

"Do you really think that you'll be able to change the conversation, given the overwhelming attacks on you since you began?"

"The voters will make the changes. The people who own the media will change only when they're dragged to it by their audience, and they've spent many years convincing their primary audience that they know everything, and everyone who doesn't agree is wrong. They *will* learn better," he finished, emphatically, and turned to go into the building.

In his truck, part of the protest, John heard, "Hey, lookit!" and glanced over at the video on the dash in front of him. Luckily, his truck's anti-crash system stopped him from running into Clarence's pickup, ahead of him. Looking up, he saw Clarence pointing towards a fancy car that had just let someone out in front of the office building they'd been driving for an hour, around blocking traffic. He looked at the man, surrounded by three people walking towards the door. There were reporters around the man, and John realized it was Garrick himself, the man they'd been after. On the video screen, one of its four windows showed Johnson interviewing him.

John heard that, and was infuriated. "We'll learn better, will we? We'll see who learns better!" he screamed, and jerked his steering wheel towards the curb, trying to miss the end of the car. Instead, he scraped the end, jumped the curb, and slammed into one of the planters in front of the building, missing Garrick by meters. He was trying to turn his wheel to head towards Garrick when his windshield was shattered by shots, one of which hit his hand on the wheel by chance, and another his forehead. He was slammed backwards against the headrest, then into the wheel, and the truck stopped.

FRANCOISE III

12

FRANCOISE AND AMELIE

Amelie turned out to be very good at genengineering, and did a work-study with one of Tolliver's concerns an hour from London by rail, letting her commute from her university. There she found herself growing away from her sister, into her studies and social circle. Meanwhile, Francoise was deep into her work, her proficiency such that it became clear to those she worked with, as well as to Tolliver, that she was ready to promotion to the next level.

Francoise handled two more datacenters, one in Japan, in a relatively geologically stable location, and the other in Iceland, just outside of Reykjavik. She was, however, considered a hard and exacting manager, who turned away personal relationships, and even offers of friendship as a coworker were refused, politely or otherwise. Amelie, on the other hand, turned out to have an almost preternatural understanding of complex relationships, both genetic, and interpersonal, making her very well liked among her peers.

A year went by, and Francoise called Amelie, to have dinner together on a Friday evening at their favorite North African restaurant in London. After they were seated, and ordered, and gotten their drinks, Amelie looked at her sister. She had been growing harder, but now.... "Francoise, what's happened?"

"I've gotten a letter a few days ago, from division administrator's staff in Niger. There was a raid from Mali by troops affiliated with a would-be breakaway region. They were chased into Niger, and circled back, living off the land, as they say."

"Our village..."

"Was mostly destroyed. Papa is dead, as are the few relations we have."

Amelie took a drink, and put it down a little harder than she had intended, with some splashing onto the tablecloth, and nodded. "That part of our life has long been gone for us."

"*Oui,* and now it is closed." They sat there for a while, looking at each other, both trying to be indifferent, thought each knew the pain, until their dinner came. As they ate, Amelie looked up. "I have found something you might find interesting."

"*Oui?*"

"Remember how I said I wasn't interested in meetings and business?" Francoise nodded. "Well, with the eternal meetings, between having to attend, and trying to get things to happen, I seem to have discovered a talent for manipulating them, to the point where my coworkers ask me to deal with them."

"And, no doubt, to the displeasure of your managers." Amelie smiled, and her sister quizzed her on some of how she did what she did, and made some suggestions to be still more effective.

Another year and a half passed, and the next thing Francoise knew, her little sister had a master's, had decided to hold off on a doctorate, choosing to work full time at Tollipharm, where she had interned.

In the meantime, Francoise's responsibilities had grown. Tolliver had finally driven Krock Industries' stock down far enough that he had become the controlling stockholder, and shouldered most of the Krock family aside, appointing Francoise as a vice president. He also made her vice president of several other of his companies, with a mandate to assure 'reliability' to Tolliver himself—effectively, a political officer. She also traveled with her own entourage, including a driver and personal assistant who doubled as security, depending on where she was traveling. For Krock, she took a trip to the oil field and refinery where Tolliver had found her. There were only two people she recognized, a maid service manager and a man from the laundry, neither of whom she'd had she ever been close. She spent the whole day there cold and formal, leaving everyone with the impression that she had as much in the way of feelings as any statue. The only break in that emotionless face was in the hotel, where she called in the head of housekeeping, in front of the manager, and asked about the maids, and made them sure that if she found that the maids had been expected to be more than just maids, she would personally come back and stake them out over an ant mound, and she left them believing her.

For Tolliver, on the other hand, life had grown more difficult. The years when he could travel with little or no security were past. Now, when he was not in secure locations, he was surrounded by four well-armed security guards, not counting his driver and personal assistant. One security guard was killed, and another wounded, both in what should have been safe Western cities, not 'unstable' countries. Francoise knew, however, that he made a point of paying death benefits without any argument, something that she remembered fit with his arrangement for her mother's ashes. Besides that security, Francoise knew that he had several organizations to which he would assign jobs to that were never discussed, nor were they paid from the normal payrolls or contracts. She knew what they did, but by now she was resigned to that. Even so, she was disturbed when she had a meeting where a manager from one of those companies mentioned obtaining something from Tollipharm as they were preparing for an inter-company meeting.

The 400 were down to the 250, some having lost huge sums and control to others, some from personal attacks, targeted disease, and insurrection. One of the older 400 had died in one of those, killed as he was visiting one of his emplacements guarding the Greek border when they were overrun. Tolliver held on by the skin of his teeth and the viciousness of his counterattacks, and his reputation was not one admired by many, but he was a force unto himself.

Several times, a few of the 400 called meetings to try to reduce, if not settle, the inter-family feuds. Tolliver made it a point to attend them. As one session end, he walked into the cafe, and ran into Bandar al Sultan, from a side branch of the Saudi royal family. Al Sultan, slightly stocky, dressed in westernized traditional robes and kaffiyeh, had the barista make them a pot of Saudi coffee, and bring it to their small table. They each took a sip, and al Sultan tossed some candied fruit into his mouth. "I am somewhat surprised to see you here. I had not thought of you as a man of peace."

Tolliver looked at him and smiled. There was no friendliness on either face, no give, nothing more than a mask as each felt the other out, revealing nothing of themselves. He took another sip from the small cup, and then replied, "I am as much amused to find you here. Or perhaps I should not be, as I assume you are here for the same reason, to find out what they think they're going to do, and how it will affect our plans."

"Ah, surely we can find peace between ourselves...or, at least, perhaps in North Africa."

"We do both have interests there..." Tolliver said, leaving it open.

"True. But your interests are in the north of Libya, with the petrochemical industry."

Tolliver nodded. "I will confess that I do have some interest in the rare earths needed for batteries and superconductors in the south of Libya that you control."

"What I believe annoys both of us are the Allied Militias of Tripolitania, who seem to be expanding, which could become a problem for both of us." Al Sultan leaned back and took another sip of coffee. "A plague on their house would solve the problem, but would reduce a labor force that is significantly less expensive than automation."

"Do I recall that the several other generals are more interested in consolidating their current control than in expansion?"

"That is what my people tell me is the case."

"Perhaps if it were possible that only he and his faction were to become ill with one of those *interesting* plagues, his opponents might strengthen their hands."

"My very thought. Were you aware that at this time, he holds a smaller town as his base."

Tolliver shrugged. "Small? What, ten thousand people?"

"More like thirty-five thousand."

"Pity that they find his presence congenial." The two smiled like barracudas. "What do you know, it seems to me that this conversation is in keeping with this meeting concerning mutual peace. Perhaps my people should speak to yours."

"That seems like a profitable discussion. But it seems a shame to speak of business over such an excellent coffee."

Tolliver glanced around, and smiled another perfect smile. "Have you met our Mr. Garrick?"

Al Sultan followed his look, then turned back to Tolliver, and both broke into quiet laughter.

Tolliver came back from that conference and chuckled about Garrick in his semi-monthly meeting with Francoise. "I met Garrick, and he's one of the people pushing this council, as though it will make things *nicer*. He seems to have had a change of heart while he was ill. Talked about his nurse telling him bedtime stories, about an old book where wealthy people lived on a planet of their own." He shook his head, and looked at her. "That, perhaps, isn't the bad idea he seems to think it is. But he has clearly lost his way, and become a fool who will not last that much longer."

Then, one evening, Francoise got a call from her sister, asking if she could come over the Channel, and have dinner together in London, or perhaps at an old pub she had been introduced to in Reading. She had been missing Amelie, and told her she would happily cancel a meeting to come over. As she got off, she shook her head, wondering why she had lied to her sister, when the only meeting she had that evening was with a bottle of vodka and some orange juice.

Once she had taken the Chunnel, and gotten through security, followed by one security person, she found Amelie waiting. "Your hair is short!" she exclaimed. "I remember when you graduated the boarding school, and the curls fell halfway down your back."

Amelie shrugged. "It's safer this way, in the hoods I frequently need to wear."

They walked out and talked, Francoise's security hanging back so as to not listen in, and her sister managed to convince her to try an actual centuries-old pub in Reading rather than an expensive restaurant in London.

On the train, she looked at her grown up sister and smiled. She knew what Amelie saw when she looked at her, a professional upper class businesswoman, complete with security, formality masking... something hard and dangerous, though not to her.

"About your enhancements, is there some way we can speak privately?"

Francoise raised an eyebrow. "That can be arranged. Something personal?" She saw her sister think about the answer for a second or two, before she nodded.

They walked from the train station to the pub, not overly far, the weather warm and pleasant. Amelie told her that she had been introduced to the pub by a co-worker. From the outside, it certainly looked ancient, though it was clearly popular. Inside, Amelie asked for quiet, private seats, and they were shortly at a small table, at the end of a long nook that might have been a small extension two hundred years before, the security person seated at the bar. Wainscotting ran throughout the pub, and the tables were certainly well older than their parents would have been. They ordered, and Amelie sat with a dark beer in front of her, and Francoise with two screwdrivers.

Her sister stared as she drank the first as though it were water, then start on the second. Francoise started an inconsequential conversation, which lasted through their being served. Finally, not long after they'd begun eating, and she had obtained a third drink, she looked at Amelie. "*Bon*, that second one was enough that I can turn it off. Now we've some privacy."

Her sister's eyes grew wide. "Your implants go that deep?"

"They do. Luckily, I found out how to shut it out, mostly, long ago while you were at boarding school." She took a long sip. "So, what is going on?"

Amelie sighed heavily, and replied in a low voice. "I've been shifted, a couple of months ago, into genengineering of viruses, that can be used to cure some of the infectious ones. The people I'm working with have no idea to whom I'm related, all they know is I have a very high security rating. About a month ago, a colleague asked for some help on a project he's been working on, trying to limit its lifetime. I got my manager's approval, and we resolved his problem before the end of the next day. Before I left though, I started looking at what the one we had been working on did, and got scared. The simulations told me the effects.... Have you followed the news for the States?"

"I have to pay attention to all the news I can. What, specifically?"

"The trillionaire Senator who died a while back? From what I've read, it was this virus, without the lifetime that we just engineered in that killed him and the woman who infected him who died of it."

"You're sure?"

"*Oui*. I managed to get hold of some of the work they did after the bodies were found, and in her bag they found a small vial that smelled chemical, and analyzing it, they guessed that it delayed some of the effects. I know the chemical, which was first developed along with the virus."

They stared at each other. Francoise suddenly had a thought. "There is a trillionaire named Garrick. He's recovered now, but he was ill from an unknown disease. He was infected, along with another trillionaire named Nguyen, and a couple of escorts. One escort and Nguyen died. Garrick they took to the US's NIH." Francoise saw denial in her sister's face. "Wait."

Amelie pulled out a AR headset, hard set a security level, and looked online. Francoise saw her sister's face grow pale. She pulled off the headset and stared. "It's the one I worked on."

"I need to look into this. Between you and me, I know that some hostile takeovers are arranged by various means, but this hostile takeover I would consider beyond the pale." The sisters stared at each other. Francoise's face grew hard as stone. "I hoped he would not get you, too. Not as he has me, thankfully, but...."

As the waiter came by, Amelie caught his attention. "A screwdriver, please." The rest of meal was not comfortable.

13

NEWSFEED 5

"This is Charles Witherspoon, with Newsfeed 5, Great Britain's preferred newsfeed. The number one news story is the suddenly rising price of staples, and the Labour Party demanding answers as to the reasons behind the rise. There are demonstration around the country, demanding controls on food prices. The Tories are pointing to the millions of climate refugees in northern and southern Africa demanding food, and Russian willingness to provide it as foreign aid, as opposed to shipping it to the EU and Great Britain. Meanwhile, the same is true of the States and Canada, who are feeding Mexico and southern South America. The Greens are arguing that if it had not been for the massive desalination plants, millions would have died of dehydration already."

"Italy, Greece, and Spain are all demanding that the EU help them prevent refugees from North Africa reaching their shores, given that the plague that they may be carrying has a seriously high death and disability rate. We will not show the videos of the bodies being moved by front loaders into pits to be burned, which many are finding extremely disturbing. The European Commission, however, is pointing out that there were no other workable answers. Rumors are running rampant that the plague was genengineered, and several

African leaders are claiming that the significant fall in birth rates is due to another genengineered plague, but both EU and British authorities are denying that this is the case. Regardless of the denials, public sentiment is strongly disbelieving of such denials, and hundreds of people demonstrated in front of the London headquarters of several trillionaires, including Tolliver Industries and Olikovsky's Development Corporation. In addition, there have been two serious cases of people acting on the rumors, with the murder of the CEOs of Exxon, Shell, and two major drilling and pipeline companies, who were vacationing with their families. The vacation estate was almost completely destroyed, and only three servants and the son of the Shell CEO were found alive. A group calling themselves 'the Voice of the Unheard' has issued a claim of responsibility, promising more in the future. In their statement, they allege that the CEOs paid for the genengineering. Also among the dead was the president of Tollipharm, the company which is supposed to have performed the genengineering. The companies have issued protests, and denials, as well as requesting aid from the EU anti-terrorist task force."

"Speaking of terrorism, no one has claimed responsibility yet for the attacks in the States, along the coast of North and South Carolina, where under cover of night lavish vacation homes have been attacked and destroyed by explosive rockets. Coincidentally, the rain covering the coasts down to include Miami, where most of the old Miami Beach is now either covered by the ocean, or the waves are washing over the famous resorts."

"Finally, closing this hour of the news is a disaster in Africa. As if the killing head of central Africa hasn't been enough, a once a century flood has come down from the mountains on the Milo River in Mali, and the banks and sides of the dam that was completed only several years ago have collapsed. The collapse has now half-drained the lake above the dam. Entire villages have been wiped out, scores of thousands below the dam and along the river are reported to have died. The flood pushed the Niger River, beyond where the Mali joins it, to flood stage. The authorities are sending in troops to restore order and provide aid. The construction company that built the dam is denying responsibility, claiming that the government of Mali had assured them that their engineers were reinforcing the banks and sides around the dam. Refugees from the flood are spreading over northern central Africa, and there are demonstrations in several capitals, including Abaja in Nigeria, where security troops turned water cannon and rubber bullets on the demonstrators."

14

CONSCIENCE

For days, Francoise tried to work but got little accomplished. She spent the evenings staring at the news from Africa, the tens of thousands of death, hundreds of thousands homeless, homes and villages gone. She would occasionally take a break to make screwdrivers, one after another, drinking herself to sleep. The third evening, she staggered into the bathroom to get ready for bed, then stood there and stared at herself in the mirror for a long time. At length she sank down on the toilet lid and dropped her head into her hands. "I let all of those people die. I did not care to consider them." A thought struck her. "The times that I was there as he called and made arrangements for other trillionaires work to fail, bad concrete, whatever, he wasn't showing me his power, he was making me *complicit* in the collateral damage. He was molding me." A sob escaped her. "This is not me. I was not going to go where Tolliver is, I was going to be the weapon against all the trillionaires, and finally to twist in the hand that wields me, to kill my master. Instead, I am becoming him." She lifted her head to see in the mirror that her nails like claws had left red trails on her face.

She finished her screwdriver.

In bed, sleep would not come, until a thought crystallized,

drawing on old things Tolliver had said, and things she had gathered from some of the other trillionaires with whom she had dealings. "They intend to leave the Earth. That old story Tolliver mentioned, where they will live without a world full of nobodies." She lay thinking about that. "Perhaps that would be a good thing, let them all be *gone.* A move into the aerospace company, giving him some of my conscience as an excuse, along with Amelie's other dream as well." With that, she fell asleep.

Over the next few weeks, she planned her approach, then had the chance to set up an appointment to speak with Tolliver, who had been on trips fighting fires in his businesses, and maneuvering for advantage. Late in the day after he returned, she walked into his office. He sat there, feet on his desk, a mug of Vietnamese coffee on his desk. Looking at her, he said, "So tell me what you want."

"I think I'm getting stale, and was thinking about shifting to a different sector."

He looked at her for a while. "There's something else. What is it...." She knew he saw her eyes, with too many days of drinking. "Don't tell me you're developing a conscience."

"I want to do my job right. That dam in Mali...the geologists warned me that the banks might fail. I spoke to the government, but didn't go there and spread some baksheesh. They assured me everything was fine, and I finally took them at their word." She thought for a minute, and added, "It will not be good for our reputation, and for right now, I would not be welcome in those countries, which reduces my utility for those contracts.

"A conscience. What were you thinking about?"

"Something completely different." She snorted a laugh. "My sister likes her work, but still speaks of the starships. Perhaps aerospace?"

He stared at her a while with *the look*. She matched him, *look* for *look*. After a while, he nodded. "If you really mean to do the job right, with no mistakes, I will give you a chance. You'll be moving first to Kwajalein, and work with the current management team. See if you can get things moving faster. Everything seems to take longer than it should, and you know perfectly well how to fix that."

"I do, indeed. As usual, you will find my work acceptable," she smiled, "and my sister will be thrilled."

He shook his head. "Perhaps, but you know family will always fail you, sooner or later. You two have kept close, but things change." They spoke for a while longer of who would pick up the projects she was on, and she left to return to the apartment where she lived in the residential section of the office tower.

That night, he came to her again in virtual, and it was as bad as she had expected. But with one drink in her, she had some small control, and lasted until it was over.

15

THE STARSHIP

Several massive storms broke a number of seawalls around the world. New York City, Baltimore, Brest, Da Nang, Busan, others. The cities were saved, but tens of thousands died.

During the recovery, it was found that several of the seawalls had been built defectively. There came huge protests in world capitals, and the speculation about the plagues being engineered returned, in force. The UN began meetings, to try to hammer out a response, and the Security Council was in frequent session.

Meanwhile, far above the world, the first expeditionary starship approached completion. It was half a kilometer long, big enough to visit several star systems, and set up research stations on a world of each, with production machinery to build whatever each station needed. It would need another year and a half to complete in orbit, ending with the installation of the engine.

Francoise had been transferred to be president of one of Tolliver's companies, and vice president of two more, all of them involved with the construction the starship. She found herself on their interlocking boards, and dealing on occasion with one or another of the twenty-five trillionaires involved with the construction, as well as a number of other, supposedly unrelated projects. At one conference, she ran into the Garrick that Tolliver had mentioned, working the attendees, trying to organize some sort of council to try to come up with a way to reduce and ameliorate disasters. From what she could see, about a third of the people he spoke to seemed interested, and some number more were merely polite, while the rest were clearly uninterested, with the same attitude as her patron.

To her surprise, two of the trillionaires involved with Tolliver and the starship were among those interested. They were speaking with Garrick at the bar, and she maneuvered so as to wind up next to them, and start a conversation. For the first time, she found herself talking to people like them who seemed less than deadly opponents, who seemed almost human. At first, they were cautious, knowing who she worked for, but when the conversation drifted towards the starship, she saw animation, and something she only vaguely remembered from her sister's eyes when Amelie had spoken of the ship: a true dream. Not wealth, but the stars for humanity. They talked about building a lot of ships, and getting people to other worlds, so that if the worst happened, everyone would not die, and to lower the population of the planet even if the worst did not happen.

In their voices, she heard something that shook her to her core: they meant it. She took that away with her, telling Tolliver what he wanted to hear, but keeping that core back.

Tolliver laughed. "They're going to watch it go. How would you like to go with it?"

Her mouth fell open. "*Que*?"

"I'm going to be on it. As will a lot of people that are in the consortium. Thanks to what you're telling me, those three won't be picking any."

"Pourquoi?"

"You've not paid attention to the meetings at the UN. They're getting serious about setting up an international agency to collect taxes from internationals, meaning me, and the other trillionaires. It's been tedious, if rewarding, moving my trusts and companies around the world avoiding their taxes, but now they think they're going to prevent it. So, it's time to leave them behind."

"My sister?"

"Perhaps if there's a second mission. Or perhaps you can see her if you come back. You, however, have become critical to me, and you will be coming."

"As you wish, Phillipe." She lowered her head, as though she were accepting, giving him the illusion of dominance. Inside, she had come to see his true dominance was an illusion, and wondered when she would throw it over.

Several weeks later, back in her role as president of the company installing the drive, her purchasing head came to her, a short, blond haired man. "We have run into a major bottleneck."

She looked at him. "Which is, m'sieu Hardison?"

"We are unable to purchase the high-temperature superconductors the engine requires. We have been trying for over a month, and have been unable to find a provider."

"Why not?"

"None is for sale. The next year's output is already committed, they tell me."

A thought struck her. "What companies?"

He told her the names of the three major ones. "No one else can provide anywhere near what we need."

She nodded to herself. Those three were owned by opponents of Tolliver. "Let me see what I can do, and I will get back with you."

That evening, she was watching the news before she went to bed, and they covered a demonstration in New York. They spoke to one of the organizers, who argued that the engine of the starship was also a horrific weapon. "We've seen one of the engines of the probes cut a canyon on the dark side of the Moon, when it was activated and focused. There has to be some sort of control over them."

For some reason, that stuck in her mind as she readied herself for bed. She had trouble going to sleep, then sat bolt upright. *"That man. With that as a weapon to leave a farewell present, as he would say,"* she thought. *"They were correct, there must be some way to shut it down."* A thought worked its way into her consciousness...perhaps something out of the cinema. Then she realized, if she had the nerve to use it, that she had the answer to her problems.

The next day, she called in her chief engineer, and asked him how much it would effort would be involved if he had to use low-temperature superconductors, which would mean installing the cryogenic systems to cool them.

He thought for a while, made several calls, and turned back to her. "Perhaps two months. Since we have not yet begun using the industrial printers inside the engine compartments, they could be programmed to add that. It is, of course, old and well-known technology."

She called the head of purchasing, and in a three-way call, got the details. Several days later, she spoke with Tolliver and told him, "We found a way to save some serious money, which would speed up the construction by ten months and get around a bottleneck that some of your opponents have arranged."

"Very good. But then, I trust you to deal with such issues expediently. Do whatever you need."

"Thank you, Phillipe."

Ten months and two weeks later, she flew to Kwajalein with a plane full of Tolliver's co-conspirators and staff. A week later, she found herself thrust into her seat as the rocket left Earth, looking out the portholes as the sky went from blue to darker blue, to black. As they approached the ship, she stared in wonder. It was a miracle, a dream, lines and curves, ugly and beautiful. They boarded, and almost everyone on board were chosen people. There were only a few of the original crew who had been on board for months, overwhelmed by the crowd that came on from the ship that had brought her and Tolliver up.

Over the next few weeks, the final work was completed. There was also a large supply ship, unexpected by the few regular crew, which carried a huge amount of supplies of all kinds, not things of use to research stations. Most, though, were large sealed containers, with only identifying marks.

Finally, as the ship-day was over, Tolliver called her. "Might as well say so long to your sister. We will be leaving in the next few days."

"But what about the original crew and researchers?"

He laughed. "They will be left in the space dock." She lowered her head in assent.

That night, well into the vodka, she called her sister. "Amelie, I need to say *adieu*. I don't know when, or if, I will see you again. It's probably a good time for you to publish that paper you've been working on for several years, you deserve the credit for all that work. I also have a present for you -- expect a data dump to your personal storage from an account with your birth name. I know you do not like business, but you will have to deal with my affairs."

"What do you mean, *adieu*? And why deal with your affairs?"

"I wasn't allowed to say anything sooner. I am sorry, but I seem to have been selected by *m'sieur* to fulfill your other dream. How this turns out, who knows?"

"My *other* dream? Francoise, what's happening?

"I assure you that you, along with everyone else, will know soon enough. Know that I have always loved you. Take care of yourself." She rang off. All night, she had a hard time sleeping, even with the vodka, with all the noise as the ship was prepared for leaving.

In the morning, the news was all over, that the UN had finally been notified of the unapproved people and supplies on the starship from the joint world space administration, and was demanding Tolliver and the others return earthside immediately and present themselves to the UN commission overseeing the starship.

Tolliver and two other trillionaires were on the bridge, listening to the news, and to the engineering reports from the crew that had come up from Earth with them to replace the original crew, who they considered unreliable. Finally, Tolliver told the captain, "Move the ship's orbit. I want us over New York in twenty-five minutes."

One of the other trillionaires looked at him and smiled. "How pleasant, all those heads of state at the meeting at the UN just now."

Tolliver smiled back, and Francoise knew that smile. She knew, as surely as if he had told her, what was coming. She was buckled into the second engineer's seat, that worthy having been ushered out to the space dock before they left. Not needing to hold on in zero G, she fell into her thoughts, circling around and around to three things. As clear as if it were before her, she remembered what she had done to catch Tolliver's attention that first day, that complete and infinitely degrading act of submission. The mental note that she had made when the younger Wu had spoken of everyone's blind submission, and his throwaway remark, 'What could they do to us?'. Then sitting in her room drinking, looking at the news of all the people dead and homeless when the dam collapsed. Finally, it all came down to her understanding that the latter was the direct result of the former. *They died, because I allowed him to make me into the tool he desired, and I didn't care until it happened. But I am awake now, and if I do nothing while he destroys New York using the starship's engine, I will be as much the monster that he is. When Amelie asked about the dam, I laid the blame on the government officials, and she knew how they are. If I do nothing this time,* she *will know I have become as him, and have to live in a world that reviles him, and me, and even her dreams of the starships will be worse than dead.*

While it all coursed through her mind, the ship had altered its orbit as using maneuvering thrusters, dropping slightly, to bring them further north and east in their orbit. When they reached position, she unbuckled from the seat, drifted over to the engineer's shoulder, and looked at the controls before him. She had worked with his managers, and her presence clearly left him nervous.

Tolliver called to communications. "Connect us to the UN."

AMELIE

16

THE WHISTLEBLOWER

Amelie walked into the local office of New Scotland Yard, working hard at not showing fear. The room had a stale, sweaty smell, overlaid with disinfectant as she walked up to the reception desk.

The older, stocky woman there looked at her. "May I help you, Ma'am?"

"*Oui.* I spoke to the National Crime Agency a bit ago, and they sent me here. I need to speak to someone concerning whistleblowing, and we are speaking disaster-level."

"Disaster level?"

"Genengeineered diseases, for a start."

The desk officer stared at her for a minute, and then picked up a headset and put it on. "Mr. Baker, this is officer Thomas at the front desk. I've got a young woman out here who's either mad, or she's whistleblowing on gen...geneered," she stumbled over the word, "diseases. And she says that's just a start." She listened, and then took off the headset. "If you'll have a seat there, ma'am, officer Baker will be out in a few moments."

Amelie had almost rolled her eyes at the woman stumbling over the word genengineered in 2095, but she was too focused on her report to pay that much attention.

A few minutes later she saw a man of average height, with thinning unruly brown hair, come out a door. He looked at the desk officer, who nodded to her, and he walked over. "How d'you do, I'm officer Baker. Before we begin, do you wish to remain anonymous?"

She shook her head sharply. "*Non!* I am Amelie Trouve. May we speak privately, somewhere?"

"Of course," he said, and led her into a witness interviewing room, outfitted with four dark-green government-issue chairs, a plain table with a keyboard on it, and a screen on the wall. Waving her to a seat, he asked, "What's this all about, then?"

"Before we begin, can we have a solicitor present? I am not familiar with procedure for such things."

"Of course. Let me call the duty solicitor." After some confusion, a harried-looking woman with a long British face. brown hair up in a bun with a lock that had come undone, walked into the room. There were lines of strain on her face, her office clothing rumpled. "I just finished advising someone, and you're lucky that you came between situations." She stuck her hand out. "I am Barbara Jefferson. May I ask what this concerns?"

Amelie shook the woman's hand, and repeated what she had said before, and the woman sat down heavily. "This is not my area of expertise, but I can guide you, at least to start. I would recommend engaging your own solicitor."

"Certainly, if you can recommend one. I have had no experience or need for one before."

Jefferson nodded. "I will have to check to see who would be good, and willing to accept a new client." She turned. "Mr. Baker, may she and I speak in privacy before we start?"

"Certainly," he answered, and left the room. As the door closed, Jefferson reached over to the keyboard and hit one of the function keys.

"Privacy, for lawyer-client discussions." She sat down again. "Can you give me the short version?"

Amelie, who now felt a little more comfortable, began. "I am a senior genengineering designer for Tollipharm, over on the west side of the Silicon Roundabout." She reached into her shirt pocket, and pulled out her ID badge to display. She went on, "Several times in the last four years, I have been called in on projects due to my high security clearance, and my experience in developing designer drugs and targeted viruses. I have evidence here," she said, pulling out a small media, "that four times, the tailored viruses my company was working on were made to kill, not heal, and that they have been used. You may, perhaps, remember the American Senator who died of an unknown disease? Or the trillionaire Garrick, who was saved, while another trillionaire, Nguyen, died, along with the woman who infected him?"

Jefferson's look grew horrified, her eyes wide. "You have proof?"

"On the media, in one folder, I have the design of that virus, as well as others. I also have several other designs for death-dealing viruses. Although I do not have the details of the all the plagues that are causing huge number of deaths that have spread in northern and southern Africa, and the one in Central America, I strongly suspect one or two of the designs on the media are involved."

"Are you alleging that Tollipharm knew?"

"They were designed at the orders of Tolliver himself."

"Why are you coming forward now?"

"I just received a lot of information overnight from a source I absolutely trust to verify my suspicions, and who suggested with the greatest urgency that I come forward without further delay."

"It was their urging that led you to come forward now, then?"

"That, along with the data dump of much more evidence."

Jefferson nodded. "You might have had issues, if you've been holding onto this for a while, but since you just got confirmation, that should be good. Let's call in Mr. Baker, and give him your statement and the evidence."

"Speaking of which, this is, of course, not the only copy, and I do have backup plans if this gets quashed."

The other woman shook her head. "Don't bring that up to start.

Were times different, you could be in danger personally, and so it would be a good idea, but given the news the last week, it may not be an issue." The woman turned off the security, and officer Baker came back in to take Amelie's statement, and accept copies of the evidence to be examined. Before she started, she said, "Ms. Jefferson mentioned something about the news. What is happening? I have been too busy to scan the newsfeeds."

"Just yesterday, there were major attacks on several important military bases in the United States by the absurd Free Citizen Alliance. They claimed to have the Central American plague virus, and are prepared to use it as a weapon. The US had started sending assistance to Central America, but had to recall most of them to fight the insurgency. This was on top of the hearings the last week at the UN concerning multinational pharmaceutical firms and their possible connections to the plagues of the last few years."

Amelie shook her head. "Say, rather, definite connections." With that, she went on to lay out her evidence.

Three hours later, Amelie, accompanied by officer Baker, was at the central offices of New Scotland Yard, in a conference room with four men and two women. They had just been served tea when a younger man walked in, and looked to the older man, who had been introduced as Captain Catto. "Sir, it's confirmed. The virus that the lady here had on her media, labeled 'senator' is the one that the US NIH and the police in San Francisco reported that killed the US Senator."

They all looked at her. She stared back and decided it was time to push. "I trust, by the way, that none of you thinks of me as foolish enough to think that the media I have presented is the only copy, or that I have not made multiple arrangements to release this to the press, ranging from the Guardian to the Hindustani."

"That would cause worldwide panic..." the woman introduced as Ms. Haxton began.

"As opposed to the ongoing one?" replied Amelie. She had settled down from when she had walked into the station that morning, and was managing a fair impression of the impenetrable, implacable *look* her sister used to face off a trillionaire.

"David, get us online with captain Watson", Catto gestured at the room's conference connection. Glancing at the time, "He's probably at the UN right now."

Amelie looked at Catto curiously, as David made the connection. "The UN?"

"Young lady, I assume you haven't been following the news. A number of heads of state, and foreign ministers, are at the UN, holding hearings accusing a number of trillionaires and their corporations of being the source of some of the recent wars, of causing economic collapse, and of rumors of complicity with some of the major plagues. This morning's news was that Tolliver and a number of other trillionaires, went up to the expedition starship unexpectedly over the last two weeks, most recently yesterday, with a large number of passengers and supplies. They were ordered down, and from what I heard, just before we came into this room, the ship was maneuvering to be above New York."

Horror grew on Amelie's face. She opened her mouth to speak, when the door burst open and a young man looked in. "Sirs, the news feed!" David turned that on, and they watched as there was coverage from the UN Security Council chamber.

"You will return here immediately," the French ambassador was saying.

They saw the response. "This is Phillipe Tolliver. You wanted us to report and answer to the UN. We will give you an answer now, one that will be heard down the years as we leave you rabble behind." Looking up, he said, "Aim the engines towards New York."

A minute passed. The room was silent, except for Amelie's strangled, "*Non....*"

And then, in the transmission from the starship, from the background of the bridge, a woman, tall, slender, with a coffee and cream complexion, dark hair in loose curls, wearing an impeccable white linen suit with a green blouse, asked in a clear voice that carried, "Have you chilled the engine coils?"

The engineer she was floating next to said loudly, "WHAT?"

In the conference room, Amelie was standing, crying, "*Non, non, NON!...*"

In the transmission from the bridge of the starship, everyone turned to look at the woman, who said, in an utterly incongruously innocent tone, "Why, I thought you knew that I saved all that money, and sped up the construction of the ship by using low temperature superconductors instead of high temperature ones." She turned her head to look Tolliver with *the face* on. "Phillipe? The complete submission that I made to you the day we met, all these years ago? *I revoke it!*" With that, she reached past the engineer, and touched the screen before him.

And they saw the transmission from the starship wink out, and the feed from New York showed the city suddenly lit by a burst of light, everywhere shadows and light, as the fireball of the explosion of the starship grew, three hundred and fifty kilometers above.

"*NON!*" Amelie screamed. "*NON!*" She beat the table over and over. Everyone around the table stared.

"Young lady, what..." began Catto.

With immense effort, Amelie stood up straight, tears streaming down her face, but somehow managed the utterly cold *look* of her sister's, which gave everyone a pause. "Captain Catto, as I said, I am Amelie Trouve. The woman who just blew up the starship, thus saving New York from being a hole filled with boiling water, is..." she coughed, "Was my sister, Francoise Trouve, one of the chief assistants of Phillipe Tolliver. You will excuse me for a moment. It is not every day that I see my only living relative, my sister, kill herself to save the world." She sat heavily, her elbows hitting the table, and her head falling into her hands, tears spilling from them onto the table.

They led her to a small office, where Baker and Haxton sat with her, as she slowly regained control of herself. They had a small hot lunch brought in, and by the time it was over, Catto came into the room. "Ms. Trouve, do you have a passport available?"

"*Oui*. I carry it with me."

"Excellent. If you'll give us the key to your apartment, and tell us what to get, we'll send someone to pack a bag for you. You'll be flying overnight to New York."

She smiled wanly at him. "A moment, please." Reaching into her bag, she pulled out her mesh headset, and sent a message. As she took it off, she explained, "Sorry, I had to notify my employer that I have been called away on unexpected circumstances, and expect to be out for a week."

Baker couldn't quite keep a straight face, but gave a choked laugh. "A most responsible employee, although I suspect Tollipharm has other issues to worry about just now."

Her face fell. "Still...I learned much from my sister."

That evening, sitting in the plane, she saw the last of the sun far ahead, dark covering Great Britain and Europe behind them, and hoped that was not a sign for the world. At last, they came into JFK and were brought to a hotel downtown. Once in her room, she collapsed after the stress of the day, knowing morning would come too soon.

While dressing in the morning, she turned to the newsfeeds.

17

NETWORK 3 NEWS

"This is Jasmine Johnson, Network 3 news, the most trusted news source on the Net, with a brief rundown of the latest news. From New York, protests have spontaneously developed all over Manhattan's west side in front of corporate headquarters whose CEOs are known to have been on the now-destroyed starship. The largest is on 7th Ave, in front of the Tollipharm building. I'm hearing police reports of attempts to break into the building. There are also reports coming in from London of similar protests, and in Paris, where the gendarmes escorted the entire night shift of the Tollipharm building out, as well as several others, in fear of attacks. More now from Josepha Erikson."

"This is Josepha Erikson in London. We're receiving reports from Abuja, in Nigeria, that there are mobs around several datacenters that was build by TCC, owned by Tolliver, Our local sources say that they're accusing Tollipharm and several other major pharmaceutical firms of creating some of the plagues, and the police are coming in prepared for riots, as there have already been cars up and down the streets set afire, and trash dumpsters pulled into the streets to make barricades. In Mumbai and New Delhi, off-duty police have been called in to deal with expected disruption in the morning, it being the middle of the night there. Back to you, Jasmine."

"Thanks, Josepha. One of our reporters at the UN has heard rumors of a surprise witness being flown in from London, allegedly a whistleblower who can confirm some of the accusations against the trillionaires. This morning, snap polls are showing majority opinion has gone strongly against all of the trillionaires, turning them from admired celebrities to villains in days. Overnight, around New York, protests at the local homes of trillionaires had turned into firefights, with demonstrators pulling out firearms and improvised weapons. Half a dozen mansions have been wrecked, two set afire, and several condo buildings damaged, with their power out."

"Meanwhile, at the UN, heads of state, including the US, Ukrainian, Russian, and Chinese Presidents, along with the Prime Ministers and Presidents from many nations in Europe, India, Southeast Asia, Africa, and South America, have already begun meetings early this morning, and the discussions are continuing. In their home countries, Indonesia has already declared a state of emergency, as has Nigeria. Reportedly, the mayor of New York City has been speaking with the governor about declaring martial law."

"And now for the weather...."

18

WITNESS

Still groggy, with strong tea not available, Amelie clutched a cup of coffee as she was driven to the UN. There, she saw the repaired massive seawall with the transparent aluminum block windows that let light through while they protected the city against the risen sea levels. Looking around, she saw large crowds, uncommonly quiet, watching as she and others were escorted inside. They led her into a large room, to a reserved section of seating, and she woke to the realization that this room was where the Security Council itself met. Seated near her were people she'd never seen before, and others...people that she had seen that had testified to the US Congress and the Parliament of the EU, including the trillionaire Garrick that Francoise had spoken of, and others. Around the table, she saw the PMs of England and India were there, along with the Presidents of France, the United States, Ukraine, the Russian Federation, and Nigeria, and Chairman of the Chinese Politburo, with a number of famous politicians beside them. In this position, given the people with whom she was about to deal, she thought that Francoise would not mind if she borrowed her *look*.

The meeting started, and she listened, though she found herself drifting off, half asleep, as it ran on for hours. They took a brief break for lunch, then it continued again. Early in the afternoon, she was finally called forward. Putting on the *look*, she sat facing them all, telling everything she knew, and what Francoise had sent her before.... There were parts they had her go over several times.

"You are certain that Tollipharm created the Senator-1, and the ASE-3 viruses?"

"*Oui.* I myself am a genengineer, and based on my annual reviews, am considered a good one. I was called away one day from a project I was on to unknowingly work on the latter. It was only afterwards, looking over the data when I returned to my ongoing work, that I realized what it was. In private, I shared that with my...late sister, and she looked into it further."

Finally, the interrogation was over, and they let her go back to her seat. The whole scene was repeated with other witnesses for days. Finally, early in the third afternoon, Garrick was brought up. Amelie remembered that her sister had met him and thought well of him, not something she usually said of that class of people.

He spoke for a while. Some of what he said was what Francoise had told her, that the wealthiest of the wealthy were in a war, seeing markets, and the world, shrink, and looked to see who would rule. After Garrick was done and his testimony was discussed, they asked the aides if there was more corroboration, and she found herself called to return to the front, and again put on *the look.*

"M. Trouve," said the US ambassador, "We understand that you have some additional corroborating testimony, placed in your trust by your sister." He paused. "We also are given to understand that it was your sister, Francoise Trouve, who destroyed the starship several days ago, and thus saved the lives of everyone here, and millions more around the city. The entire Security Council, the United Nations itself, as well as the Mayor and Council of the City of New York, owe her a debt of gratitude that can never be repaid. For now, please know that she died a hero, and we will not forget it."

Amelie nodded, ashamed to find tears streaming down her face, and struggled to keep her sister's imperturbable *look* on. It took a minute or two, but she finally was able to say, with some difficulty,

"Thank you, *m'sieur* ambassador. My sister saved my life when I was young, and now she has done it again," she smiled through her tears, "along with that of a few others, in a slightly more spectacular manner."

"About the documents she provided you, I understand that they corroborate much of what Mr. Garrick said?"

"*Oui*. She was not merely one of Tolliver's chief assistants, she was to some degree a confidant. You will find that she documented attacks by him and his allies on a number of other ultrawealthy, the people she referred to as 'the 400', and their attacks and counterattacks, economic and otherwise, on he and his allies in return."

"May I ask," said the Chinese ambassador, "Why your sister released all this?"

She had her full Francoise *face* on now, and felt hot and cold at the same time. "*Non*. I will not speak of that, now, or ever. Take it that she has proven her trustworthiness to humanity, rather than to the 400." She heard muttering, and that died down. "Allow me to present several additional media to your staff." A young woman ran over, and Amelie handed them to her. "As I told Scotland Yard when I came in, these are, of course, not the only copies."

"Let me assure you that we will have them analyzed as quickly as possible," said the French ambassador.

She thanked them and was led back to the witness seating to watch still more debate. Finally, late in the afternoon, she and the rest of the witnesses were thanked, and the Council announced that it would break for dinner, and then return to a closed-door session.

19

THE TERRAN CONFEDERATION

The next day, she was among many brought back to the UN. As she walked from the car, she saw a very heavy police presence, and demonstrators on either side, one group calling for the arrest of the trillionaires and massive taxes, while a very small group the other side with signs asserting how the trillionaires had made the country great, and denying much of the evidence to the contrary. There was pushing and shoving when suddenly a woman pushed through the police line pulling out a taser. She screamed, "Traitors!" and fired towards Amelie. It was only luck that a police officer moved his plastic shield up in time to block the probes, and others grabbed the woman and hustled her away.

This time they were escorted to a viewing area for the General Assembly, to hear the report of the Security Council to the body in person, something that had never been done.

Once the members had filed in, all looking utterly drained, the US Ambassador, who was the current president of the Council, stood. His face was almost gray, and the lines in it deep as he announced in a hoarse baritone, "M. Secretary General, the Security Council wishes to present a report of its deliberations over the last two weeks in person to the entire General Assembly."

"Ambassador Young, given the events of the last two weeks, we look forward to your conclusions."

Young took a sip of water, and began. "None of the members of the Security Council, nor most of the countries of the UN, can deal with the current situation. We have been given direct testimony that some of the wars and insurgencies currently being conducted through the agency of nation states are, in fact, directly controlled and instigated by ultrawealthy individuals and corporate entities. A prime example is, of course, the threat to all of us personally, the entire United Nations, and the City of New York, by the late Phillipe Tolliver and his allies. This must not be allowed to continue. Therefore, with the consultation and agreement of the chief executives of all the countries on the Security Council, we propose to form a unified military force for the world. The structure and command will rotate, similar to the structure of the former NATO." He paused, as the buzz of conversation rose to a roar.

After it quieted, he continued. "In addition, there must be more control over individual and corporate actors who ignore the laws of the nation-state of which they nominally are citizens. We therefore also propose that the International Criminal Court include criminal actions by individuals and multinational corporation conducting their own wars. Finally, we recommend the creation of an International Civil Court, to deal with the effects and aftermath of actions by individuals and multinational corporations."

He took another sip of water, waiting for the noise to die down. "Your Excellencies, this has become a matter of life or death for all humanity. The one thing that can prevent this proposed force, and courts, from effectively dealing with disasters, insurgencies, and deliberate economic catastrophe is that they require a civilian guiding body that can make decisions and give clear direction. The history of the General Assembly has shown no such ability, while given clear direction such a joint military can end all this madness, and courts to resolve them. It is, therefore, the unanimous recommendation of the Security Council that the United Nations General Council consider reforming itself as a more powerful body. As much as the nations of the Security Council dislike the idea, the only solution that we see that might be acceptable would be to reform the United Nations as a confederation, which would allow the joint military to deal with issues anywhere, always assuring that troops from any state that requires action will be among the troops dealing with the issue. It would, in addition, have taxing power directly over multinationals, with the taxes divided between the country of origin, the country of destination, and the Confederation."

There was no containing the roar of voices, shocked, arguing, and so the Secretary General called a recess. Around Amelie everyone was talking, or screaming. She saw a few fist fights start, both in the audience and on the floor itself. The people in her viewing areas, mostly witnesses and minders, were quickly escorted to a conference room where they could wait safely. After a while, an early buffet dinner was brought in, and everyone waited and chatted.

"M. Trouve?"

"*Oui*? You are...the nurse from the NIH?" Amelie had a glass of sparkling water in her hand, but offered the other hand to shake.

"I am. Rose Josephson." She shook Amelie's. "A pleasure."

Amelie shrugged, "Given the situation, I suppose. But thank you. Had you not posted the source of M. Garrick's illness, I would never have caught the relationship to what I had been working on."

Rose looked aside, and Amelie saw Garrick come up, a cup of coffee in his hand. She snorted a small, quiet laugh, realizing that Francoise's *face* was starting to become hers, at least for now. "What," Amelie said, "Even a man of your wealth will drink that alleged coffee?" she pointed with her chin.

He gave a surprised laugh, nearly spilling some. "You get used to it." He looked at her, closely.

"You wish something, *m'sieur*?"

He started, seeing *the look* on her face. "Is that what you think, that I'm about to ask you for something?"

She shrugged again. "Of course. I am quite familiar with that exact *look*, *m'sieur*, from others such as you." She paused, and decided that emulating her sister was not a bad thing at all. "I am well aware how different people of your class are."

Rose looked at her, shocked. Garrick hung his head. "I...well, I suppose you're right. It's something you learn growing up, and there's never been a reason before to break it, or even think of it."

Rose looked back and forth at them. Finally, she said, "Ok, I know when I'm out of my depth."

Amelie looked at her. "You are an American. You are not well-off, but well educated. With a path in life that is not a choice between brutish poverty, and most likely an early death, or selling yourself to the highest bidder, knowing that the sale is permanent, and includes one's body and soul."

Rose's mouth fell open. She turned to look at Garrick, and to her shock, he nodded. "In much of the world," he said, "I'm afraid that she's right, Rose, and it's gotten worse in the last half century."

"But...our conversations, when you were ill..."

"Rose, you believe in what you do. Our conversations were the first time in my life that I had met and spoken with someone who did not live in the world that Mme. Trouve and I have spent our lives in." Shaking his head, he added, "Don't think that being as wealthy as I am protects you from that. But our little talks led me to think in a way I'd never done before."

Amelie smiled, though it was still a hard smile. "It is true. My sister told me she met you once at a conference, and then spoke with a couple of other trillionaires...and that they were among the few who thought you were not foolish." Looking at Rose, she added, "From what you say, Tolliver, had he been in hospital, would have laughed in your face, and treated you as the help."

Rose's expression grew indignant. Amelie smiled, and put her free hand on Rose's arm. "Madam, you are why we are all here. There was a time, for a few hundred years, when it was as though hope were born, with the Enlightenment, and the revolutions in your country and France, and everyone had that hope, even if it mostly failed. Much of that has been gone for most of this century. It is not naivete, no, you, and people like you, carry the hope, carry the dream. Were there no one to carry the torch, what is there to hope for? People can change, even as you seem to have led *m'sieur* Garrick out of the wilderness that people such as he live in. I am here, knowing that I could well be killed easily enough by Tolliver's underlings, or other trillionaires, for my witnessing and evidence." She choked up for a moment, her eyes glistening with unshed tears, and then there was a burning intensity behind the tears. "But I can do no less than my sister, who paid Tolliver back for more than I will ever know, with all the interest he had earned over the years." She paused. "The starship, too, meant much to me, and my sister knew that, but there was no choice."

Garrick looked at Amelie. "If we reach the other side of all of this, and the new international military settles their hash, I'll still be wealthy, though perhaps not as I am now, I presume. I will put money into building a new starship, and it will need researchers, the best there is, to study those planets out there."

Amelie stared back. "Are you offering me a position, *m'sieur*?"

"I hope I am. It all depends on how things turn out...but I can live with a new regime, one that brings civilization back." He gave her *that look* again. "I assure you, M. Trouve, this is a job offer, I am not looking to buy you."

She looked back at him with the same *look* for a minute, and then answered, "If that is in fact the case, I will accept." She smiled. "I will have to give notice to my current employer, Tollipharm, but as an officer of Scotland Yard said to me, I expect they will have bigger issues with which to deal."

Rose looked from one to the other, and shook her head. "I do not understand either of you." She paused, looking thoughtful. "Actually, I'm not sure I want to, because if what little I do get is what I think it is, I'll run off screaming and hide under a table." She took a sip from a cup that a waiter had brought around. "I guess I should thank you both, though, for appreciating what I do, and what the people I work with do."

Amelie looked at her, and replied, "What you do is more than you understand, for more than your patients."

Eventually, they were taken back to their hotels, where all had well-guarded rooms. Amelie was sitting in hers, a screwdriver in front of her, when her phone rang. She picked it up, and actually truly smiled, for the first time in days. "Rafe! This is an unexpected pleasure."

"It's been too long since we last saw each other, and when I read what had happened, I decided that I needed to call, for you to hear from a friend, to offer condolences and sympathy, and especially one who had met your...late sister."

She could feel tears in her eyes. "No one else has thought to call. *Merci beaucoup*. When all this madness is over, we must have dinner."

"We must. For now, I can only would offer to put my arms around you virtually, for whatever comfort that might be."

Now the tears fell. "Everything you say is a great comfort." She wiped her face. "But it is very late for you...."

"It is. We can talk another time, but know that if you call, I will always answer if I can."

"As will I." They spoke for a few more minutes, then disconnected. She sat for a while, then was able to go to bed.

~

THE STREETLIGHTS WERE JUST GOING off as his small caravan of four cars pulled out of the driveway, only to find the streets suddenly blocked by a crowd that had apparently been there all night. He heard a lot of screaming and yelling, then sirens as the police arrive. Leaning forward, he opened the window as an officer approached.

"Can you clear us a path through this...crowd, officer?"

"Are you Mr. Notaheart, of MeritTech?"

"I am."

"Sir, we've been sent to escort you to a secure location."

"That's absurd. We just need to get out of the city...."

"Sir, this is for your own protection. You may not have heard the news, but the CEOs of OnAccount and BigPort, who had condos in the same building, called an airtaxi during the night, which came to the landing pad on the roof of the building. They and their families got in, but as the taxi took off, it was rammed by several drones, and fell thirty-five stories to the street. Everyone was killed."

Notaheart's mouth fell open in shock, and he heard his wife's sudden intake of breath, and her hand jerked his arm. "Very well, then, lead us."

The officer was almost back to his car when there was a cry "Here's your 'whatever it takes, Notaheart!'", and an officer cried, "MOLOTOV!" as two bottles with flaming wicks shattered in the street by Notaheart's car, and the strong smell of kerosene and flames burst next to them. The police moved quickly to make room for the car to move past the flames, and an officer from another car came out with a fire extinguisher as the column moved away from the crowd.

AMELIE SPENT much of the next two weeks in her hotel, speaking with some of the other witnesses, and watching the uproar on the news-feeds. There were many in the US Congress, and the media, screaming into their microphones until they could not be understood over the feedback, about treason...and others asking them how they would prefer to die, with an genengineered infection, or a bomb. The madness in New York continued, given that many of the 400 and other ultrawealthy had homes there of course, and outside those that had not been destroyed there were protests that frequently became riots. Around the US, there were attacks on wealthy members of the US Congress and Senate who were suspected of being in league with the trillionaires. One of the Congressmen from Texas was at a rally against the idea of a world confederation when a self-driving car rammed into the rally and exploded by the stage, killing him and his guests, as well as many of the attendees. There were attacks in Great Britain, the members of the EU, and other countries around the world.

All of this went on for two weeks, and then for two days the General Assembly met behind closed doors, after which announced they would make their final recommendations in open session. That morning saw huge mobs of people outside the building, to be present, to watch what everyone knew would be history with a capital 'H'. Amelie and the other witnesses were escorted into the building to a secure viewing area.

Once everyone had entered, and the chamber quieted, the Secretary General rose. "Excellencies, honorable guests, delegates, this is a momentous day. We have worked for months to deal with catastrophe, insurrection, and unexpectedly, a personal threat to ourselves and this city. The Security Council, too, worked many long days, until the final report that they gave two weeks ago, to which the General Assembly has worked to formulate a response. I say to you, and to the people of the world, that we have achieved that."

He looked around the chamber. "We have looked and looked, and have found no path before us out of this wilderness other than the one recommended by the Security Council. We have, therefore, with the explicit agreement of the heads of state of the countries that form the Security Council, we are declaring the formation of a world confederation, forming ourselves into an interim governing body. We have appointed a number of committees. The first will be charged with writing a charter, a constitution, if you will, for a confederation of which all the nations of the world may be, and hopefully will be, members. The second will consist of the members of the Security Council, to form a joint military command, including a space Navy, under the civilian control of the Council and the General Assembly. A third will deal with international policing. The fourth will deal with international banking and taxation, and they will look at a limit to wealth, given that those who are wealthiest appear to know no bounds. All have been tasked to complete these as soon as possible. When complete, we will vote on them; once accepted as written or amended, the heads of state will be asked to approve the measures for their countries, pending a national vote in each country, to be held as soon as possible, to accept or reject the confederation. Once that is done, we will begin to work on a unified body of laws, drawing heavily on the charters of the United Nations and that of the European Union."

He paused, again, and then added, "We did not wish any one country to feel as though any other were pushing their language or name, and so we have chosen as a working name, to replace the United Nations with the Terran Confederation."

In all the uproar, Amelie could not but remember her old college radical friends rising to sing the Internationale.

20

NETWORK 3 NEWS

"This is Jasmine Johnson, Network 3 news, the most trusted news source on the Net, with a brief rundown of the latest news. Reports are coming in almost too rapidly to keep up with - mayors of several US cities, especially New York, have declared civil emergencies, and there are curfews from sundown to sunup. Many sources, both in the US Congress and the media, are claiming that this is a betrayal of the country, and selling control to foreigners. Great Britain, and many of the nations of the EU have declared martial law, in spite of which there are protests and scattered violence. For more from the Middle East, here's Namdar Hakimi. Namdar?"

"Thank you, Jasmine. There are large riots in Tehran and other cities, with one side primarily being heavily religious groups, claiming that this is another effort by the West to take over the country, and the other being mostly secular groups supporting the government, who say that the others are supporting wealthy imams and their backers among the trillionaires. In India, the fights are between one group of heavily religious Hindus accusing wealthy Muslims of fomenting the riots, the second group are Muslims, accusing wealthy Hindus of using this to attack them, and the government troops are having trouble separating them. Meanwhile, in Egypt, groups are also trying to brand this a Western takeover. In Turkey, there was a failed coup by mid-level military officers, and the PM is claiming that it was orchestrated by several trillionaires. Saudi Arabia seems to have moved to full-scale civil war, but reports are too confused to make any sense of. Back to you, Jasmine."

"Thanks, Namdar. For more on Central and South America, here's Jose Lopes."

"Thank you, Jasmine. Honduras, Columbia, and Brazil have all declared martial law, and troops are fighting in a number of areas. One thing that has many worried are reports of very heavy military helicopters over the better parts of major cities, and there are rumors of military arrests of wealthy families. Jasmine?"

"Thanks, Jose. The military helicopters and national police have been reported in many places, and recent reports have hundreds of people being delivered to the ICC at Den Haag. News organizations are being allowed to place a pool of reporters there, as criminal trials begin. What has been announced is that the charges range from slavery to mass murder to simple corruption, and we're promised the evidence as the trials begin. Now for the weather...."

21

A DINNER

As the campaigns and trials began, Rose returned to Bethesda, while Garrick and Amelie stayed in New York under police protection. Later that week, Garrick invited Amelie to dinner, promising that he had someone to introduce her to. Amused to find a Michelin-rated French restaurant near the top floors of the Empire State building, she arrived, and nodded to her guard to join Garrick's at a nearby table. At Garrick's table was another man, younger than Garrick, who clearly one of the wealthy from his look and his clothes. After her extensive practice in the previous weeks, she was able to put on her sister's face, the formal, emotionless one, easily.

"M. Trouve, how good to see you. This is Jaroslav Konevsky."

"Bonsoir, madame," he said.

"Dobriy vyecher, pan Konevsky." She shook his offered hand.

"Jaroslav, s'il vous plait."

"Amelie".

They all sat, and Konevsky looked at her, and nodded. "I met your late sister once, at a conference. You look much like her. She and I, along with the late Sinh Nguyen, wound up speaking of the starship, which was then under construction."

She nodded. “Ah, you were the ones my sister mentioned.” She relaxed slightly, but did not drop her sister’s face. “M. Nguyen was the, ah, brother of the man infected when you were, Mr. Garrick?”

“He was. And James, please.”

“He died, as well?”

“He was on the starship when your late sister chose to not allow them to sail off,” replied Konevsky. Seeing her look, he added, “It appears I was not considered quite reliable enough for M. Tolliver’s project.”

She nodded. “He could be, how shall I say it, intensely interested in his projects, and anyone not in line with that intensity was not looked upon with great favor.”

“Speaking of projects, James is working to convince me to join him on pushing the Terran Confederation’s creation of a civilian Space Agency, beside the space Navy, and investing in the construction of a new expeditionary starship. I understand he has offered you a position on it, if it is built.”

“He has, and I am interested. When I was in my late teens, I had difficulty making up my mind between genengineering and starship engineering.” She gave a short snort of a laugh. “I found it easier to get into the former, not least because of my sex.” The men nodded. “You would think after all these years…but then, Tolliver preferred that I go into genetic work, and I had no option to gainsay him..”

“I gather that was an excellent choice, at any rate. From the evidence you gave, you were clearly in demand within the company that hired you.”

She tilted her head in acknowledgment. “*Oui*, there is that.”

“It may also be,” Garrick said, “That he did not want you under your sister.”

She thought about that for a minute. “That is possible. I understand that he partitioned his projects, such that none knew the business of the other, so that no one person could become too knowledgeable. Unfortunately for him, I was close with my…late sister.” A brief downturn of her face was all the men saw.

The waiter came by, and they ordered. Moments later, their wine arrived, and each found it quite excellent. The waiter bowed, and left the bottle on the table.

"About building a new starship, do you actually think there is much interest now, after the destruction of the first in those circumstances?" Konevsky asked.

"*Oui*. In fact, more than just interest. I have heard from old friends and classmates, asking whether I thought a new one might be built." A brief chuckle. "And if so, whether I had an 'in' to apply for positions on it." She looked at Garrick. "I am not like Rose, but she is not the only keeper of the flame."

Konevsky looked curious. "A conversation we had while waiting for the riot to die down after the Security Council report, with the nurse who took care of me when I had the virus," Garrick told him. Just then, the first course came, and the three turned to enjoy the meal.

Over the next weeks, Amelia was amused to note that the outcry in the informal media began to drop precipitously as the convicted went to jail, and the money paid by them for the people and software to generate the outcry dried up. In the meantime, the same informal media that had been against the trillionaires all along grew larger, as did opposition traditional media.

22

ROSALYN, GENENGINEERED

"Mommy, it hu'ts and it's co'd."

"I know, Ahosalyn, honey, but it's somefing we need to do. They'ah puttin' gene-enginee'ahd cells into you, that will fix things that ain't 'ight. Othehwise, when you' oldeah, you'll get sick." The woman reached out and held the little girl's hand that didn't have the IV needle in it. "Heah, let's see what's on TV." She turned on the network TV, but almost the stations were covering the creation of the Terran Confederation and the trials at the World Criminal Court of trillionaires and their staff.

After a bit, the little girl looked up. "Mommy, what's it aw mean?"

Rosalyn's mother sighed. "The whole wo'ld is changin'. They just combine' all the count'ahies, oah most of them, into one, and the t'il-lionai'es who had theah own waahs, and made diseases to make lots of people sick, and wouldn't pay theah faah shaahe of taxes are going to couaht, and they goin' to put them in jail."

"They hu't people, and wouldn't pay theah shaahe to he'p them? Like Jimmy an' Bobby an' Ka'en in school?"

Her mother smiled. "Like them, but woahse, a lot woahse."

"An' the goveahment's gonna make them play faah?"

"Yeah, it will, and then things will be betta', you'll see. When you g'ow up, you'll see."

23

EXECUTIVE

Nearly a month after the creation of the Terran Confederation Amelie received a notification from Francoise's lawyer. She knew, objectively, that her sister had several, but had never dealt with them. Unlocking the message, she sat down hard on the nearest flat surface, which happened to be the writing table in the hotel room. Rereading the message did not change the import, that she was her sister's sole heir, and now had half a dozen accounts in banks that specialized in what was referred to as 'wealth management', and was worth hundreds of millions of euros, and dollars, and English pounds, as well as stock options that, should she care to exercise them, would make her a billionaire many times over.

Included in that, thanks to prearranged buy orders by her sister that took place since the starship's destruction, she now owned a twenty percent share of Tollipharm, making her the controlling investor, as well as a fifteen percent share in Krock Industries, the lead builders of the starship's engine.

Amelie sat there for a while, then called the room service, and ordered a bottle of vodka and a bottle of orange juice.

The next day she flew back to Paris, and the day after that was spent signing documents and accepting congratulations. She hired a staff, and her own security from a firm recommended by the lawyer, who told her that they had provided personal security to Francoise when she had needed other than that provided by Tolliver. She went back to London, and they drove to the Tollipharm campus, where she called an all-hands meeting.

Sitting at the head of the table, with video to all the employees, she looked around. "For those of you who do not know, my sister was Francoise Trouve, assistant to Tolliver. She left me a controlling interest in this company. Feel free to check. While you are doing that, this is how it will be. First, if you worked on any of the black genengineering projects, and knew what you were working on, it will make things easier for you if you will contact my aide, here," she pointed, and contact information flashed online for everyone else not at the table. "I will be having investigators go through the records—please note I now have access to *all* of them—and if you have not contacted my aide within a few days, the information will be provided to the Terran Confederation-affiliated police. Great Britain is not part yet, but that may change, and I do not imagine that is the kind of information that will stay private forever." She looked around. "I also do not believe that this country will look kindly on such designers, and though it may come as a surprise to some, Tollipharm is no longer under the protection of Phillipe Tolliver." A range of expressions greeted that comment.

She took a sip of tea. "Everyone who has worked in any capacity on them, if they are not arrested or released, will be working full time on curing the diseases." She had her statue-cold Francoise *face* on as she added, "Consider yourselves lucky. Where I my sister, you would be volunteered to be infected, so that we could verify the cure." She could feel the shock roil through everyone.

"Are there any questions? *Non*? Good. That is the end of the all-hands, as I need to speak to my managers." Before she left that meeting, she said, "I fully expect at least one or two of you to have vanished in the morning. I promise you that I will provide that information to the authorities, many of whom are not in a mood to accept gratuities. I will also note that I am assured my security is excellent."

"But this is England," began the vice president in charge of the facility.

"And do you think they will deny extradition, given the ICC trials?"

May, the VP, lost it at that point. "England will stand on its own!"

"*Oui*. And I have French citizenship. If you like, I shall begin to sing *Le Marseillaise*, after I remind you that you could follow in the footsteps of Charles I." There was dead silence after that. "*Bon*. I have business to take care of." She rose, and left with her entourage of two aides and security.

She flew back across the Atlantic to New York, to make deals and await for the results of the worldwide voting, after she cast her absentee ballot for France.

Saturday she decided to celebrate and arranged to have dinner with Garrick. She was at a table when she saw him coming through the dining room. She nodded to the table next to her, where her two security people were seated, and his security went to join then.

"So, to what do I owe the pleasure of this dinner?"

She took a sip of wine, looked at him, and leaned back in her chair. Thinking about it for a minute, she dropped part of her Francoise face, and replied, "It appears that I will not be accepting that job offer after all. Instead, I am dealing with some serious changes in my world, and I am sure you will understand." His expression was a query in itself. "I am my sister's heir."

He slipped into *that* look again, then with an effort, let it go. "Congratulations, I suppose."

"Not to worry, I'm not up with you, just a little fish." She smiled. "I can, however, guarantee that if you are infected again, Tollipharm, or whatever I decide to rebrand it as, will not be responsible."

"It's like that?"

"*Oui*. Furthermore, I expect that I shall look for higher prices on certain products in other fields. For example, I think I shall take the extra time to build a new starship engine with high temperature superconductors only, with interlocks to prevent it from firing in line with a large body."

"You...Krock?"

"Fifteen percent outright."

Garrick picked up his glass of wine, and held it up to toast. His smile, a real smile, was matched by hers. "I look forward, Amelie, to a long and fruitful relationship." He took a sip of wine, and looked at her again. "You're not her."

"*Non*. But I never had to sell my soul as she did, and I have other things in my life. But I am not Rose, either. Say, rather, that I live in both worlds."

~

As the Secretary General had requested, the campaigns around the world were kept short, and everyone was allowed at least a provisional ballot, since this was a question for everyone, not just officially documented citizens. The results came in, and most of the industrialized world had voted to join the Confederation, save for one or two, such as Great Britain, where the results were in dispute, or the current government was fighting a delaying action, or a number of smaller countries with hardline rulers. In the end, two-thirds of the nations of the planet had seen the advantages, if only for an organized force that could handle disasters rather than create them.

Later, on the one year anniversary of the aborted attack by Tolliver on the UN, the Terran Confederation brought in Amelie and in a ceremony broadcast worldwide, the Secretary General gave into her keeping an award that was to be the highest honor of the Confederation, the first Medal of Honor, awarded posthumously to Francoise. She had Francoise's imperturbable *look* on, thanked them graciously, and walked off the latest stage in her life with the award. That night, feeling utterly alone in the condo she had bought, she cried into her vodka and orange juice.

24

PRIVATE DEBATES

The understated elegance of the virtual room ranged from the decor to the current virtual inhabitants. "Is everyone here?" Gliance asked. She could see herself in the shared AR, tall, slender, her hair currently short and white, a modern woman of the end of the 21st century. Disgustedly, she mentally added *hiding like a criminal, rather than one of the 400 who ruled the world, until that rabble, with the help of those turncoats like Tolliver's Trouves, and Garrick, killed, imprisoned, or just emptied and closed out accounts...not that they found them all.* Someone said something, and she turned her attention back to the meeting. "I see two people missing."

Jerrie looked up at her. He was perhaps twenty years younger than her, in his early forties, and had been very active in trying to coordinate the response of some of the other trillionaires to the creation of the Terran Confederation, and its attacks against them. "That's what I was just saying, Mo and her people were stopped and arrested as they were about to fly out of Shanghai." Jerrie shook his head. "It's possible one of the aircraft mechanics called them in."

"And Olikovsky?"

"I've no idea. Anyone?" Everyone shook their heads. Most of them liked the Russian, although he wasn't as wealthy as most of them, he used what he controlled with precision.

"Very well, then, let's begin." She looked around at the one hundred and fourteen people. "We're down to this small number, and we will keep losing people unless we do something. Therefore, the floor is open to suggestions." She looked around. "Elder Wu?"

The elder Wu was well-respected among trillionaires, often considered one of their leaders. He lived on Taiwan, but had managed to stay on the right side of the Party in mainland China while remaining one of the controlling powers in Taipei. In his nineties, but with modern medicine looked no more than his late sixties. He affected the old style of a mustache with the sides hanging down, his hair gray, but his clothing a modern Tang suit. "The meetings that we had over the last few decades concerning reducing our intra-class warfare were perhaps a good idea after all, but focused on the wrong goal. It would seem to me that the correct goal should have been, and now must be, on taking direct control of the world, dividing it up and setting up a system to adjudicate disagreements." He took a sip of tea. "I confess I did not foresee this...Terran Confederation being set up."

Gliance nodded. "We knew they were talking about some sort of action, but perhaps Tolliver's threatened destruction was significantly beyond anything they may have expected, and pushed them over the line."

"He was a fool," elder Wu replied. "He was not making demands, nor offering them a way to surrender, or even back down. It was pure revenge."

"Tolliver was mad," Marshall injected. Midwestern American, in an older style suit, gray in his blond hair, he always tried to dominate any conversation. "Perhaps he was like any of us, but so much more so. He was determined to win, however he defined 'winning'. He, and the people he made war against, made the whole planetary situation so much worse." He shook his head. "I admit, I fought back, but never expected the kind of attacks he came up with - they were far more widespread, with far more collateral damage, than I, or most of us, would ever countenance."

Gliance saw and recognized Jim Warton, whose family owned the largest retail chain in North America, and was heavily involved in shipping. Dark haired and polite, he said, "I agree, and think elder Wu's on the right path. Why should we have to spend resources to buy politicians and other rulers, who can then be changed by unforeseen circumstances, like an unexpected turnout of troublemakers, rather than just take direct control?"

"I was thinking," replied the elder Wu, "more of regional governors, appointed by us. Let them deal with the minutiae, and if they perhaps go too far in an infelicitous direction, they will be the ones the populace will make trouble about, so that when we replace them, we are praised."

"The elder Wu's thoughts on this are salubrious," said al Sultan, his tenor heavy with a Saudi accent. "These governors' remit should be larger than the existing nation-states, and they should be able to redivide their territories to reduce internal issues, such as of Arabs and Kurds in Iraq. One qualification I would add would be that none of them be more than billionaires. Perhaps someone with under forty percent of a trillion. That way, they are not in our class, and will not have the resources to fight removal."

Gliance saw Gauthier laughing. "Yes?"

The elegant man, dressed in a casual French style that was not out of place, smiled. "I am reminded of the Sun King. Perhaps the governors should be encouraged to invest heavily in fashion, as Louis the XIV forced his nobles to do, thus making them spend large sums on clothing and things related to it, making great art, and not having the money to build private armies."

Soft laughter filled the virtual room.

"So what kind of time frame are you thinking of for setting up these governors, elder Wu?" Gliance asked.

"The development of our forces should begin within the next five years, but that depends on the effectiveness of our rabble rousers, and how aggressive this Confederation becomes. It may take much longer, perhaps twenty years or more for the enthusiasm to die down, while our base is built up with a new generation. For one, our think-tanks will have to be more aggressive in their attacks on this Terran Confederation, especially focusing on accusations of lack of individual opportunity. Of course, our social sphere tools will need to implement a more intensive and long-term opinion-shifting program." He paused for a moment, then went on. "It strikes me that they should wait not more than a year before they can claim to be on the forefront of current opinion. At any rate, we should also encourage the religious extremists to begin softening up the current nation-states. For that, M. al Sultan, can you have your North African militaries absorb Tolliver's?"

"I can have them link up with mine in Yemen, Afghanistan, and Iraq."

"Very good. M. Warton, can you perhaps have your Old Believers and the other extremists find a way to either unify or work together?" She saw him nod. "And M. Singh?"

"My Hindu militias and supporters will be ready when we call," replied the dark-haired man, with a thin mustache, in a collarless suit, lounging backwards in his chair.

"Very good." She recognized Jerrie.

"I highly approve of the idea, but we should, perhaps, have a plan B. May I suggest one that will also require long term planning."

"We need to deal with right now, but I agree, we will need to consider the longer term," Gliance answered. "So, what are you contemplating?"

"Perhaps Tolliver was right, get off of this planet, and settle one that we have full control over."

There was some hubbub, and then the virtual conference room grew quiet. Masterson looked disgusted. "You want to be some sort of colonist, grubbing in what will become dirt?"

Jerrie laughed. "Perhaps you missed the fact that this is not the beginning of the 20th century? That's what robots are for...oh, but I forgot, none of your investments is in production, only financials. Apologies."

Masterson was clearly annoyed, but waved it away. "How do you know that would work?"

"Because I've got some test cases running in Africa and South America, as well as a demonstrator on Mars," Jerrie replied.

"He is correct," said al Sultan. "We have been using such in our nuclear power plants, the newer fusion plants, and the newest matter conversion facilities, and they work quite well. Fewer fools to make mistakes."

"Where are you suggesting we go," Gliance asked.

"I've several people in the office where they've begun recording the results of the interstellar probes. If I remain solvent and safe, I was planning on waiting some years, and when we get a report of a viable planet that's not too close, editing the reports so that it shows the planet unfeasible for terraforming. That, of course, would give us a choice, and time to prepare a colonization ship. We could even have it look legitimate, with false identification of everyone boarding, and a false course." Jerrie sat back, looking confident.

There was a pause that grew. Finally, exhaling a white smoke from a silver tube, Lopez sat up. "What about the near term strategy? How shall we go about setting up governors?"

Now Jerrie looked annoyed as Masterson responded. "Buying essential Confederation personnel, and using them, whenever possible, to cause disruption and distrust. Those that are most effective, and gain their own following, will suggest who we should choose in each region. In the meanwhile I've set up a black channel, using non-connected banks in several of the few countries not in the Confederation. Some of it exchanges with *those people*, which I'd rather not do, but extreme times call for extreme measures."

Gliance grimaced for an instant. *Those people were, of course, the Mob and their friends.* Her thoughts drifted back to Jerrie's plan. "The one weak spot are the people you have in place in the exploration office."

"True. Several deaths would attract attention, but I have people looking into ways around that." He saw questioning looks. "This new thing, the bot-mediated mesh, seems to offer some possibilities that haven't been investigated. If it works out as well as is being suggested to me, they can't tell what they can't remember doing," Jerrie answered.

"Really?" Gliance asked. "That would be extremely useful."

On a private channel, he told her to contact him after the meeting, and he would tell her more. She agreed, and went on with the meeting.

"Let us return to near-term strategy. The first question, of course, is could these banks and the associates handle the kind of sums we need to move around soonest."

"I doubt that," replied the elder Wu. "However, if we were to make connections between our banks and other security sinks and those disconnected banks, through dummy companies and money launderers in those countries, and through property in the rest of the world, the usual techniques...."

"That might be difficult enough for them to follow, especially with your associates who would be an additional layer of security."

"Which was my thought."

"Does anyone else have suggestions?"

Several people had similar plans. "Then I suggest that we let our legal and financial staff come up with several specific plans of action, and then choose several of them, and let us break into individual groups, each using them, so that one breach does not affect all of us," she said.

There was agreement on this plan, though as most winked out of the meeting, a half a dozen stayed online. Johnson, from Atlanta, looked around, and said, "I think we are interested in the long term plan. There are just too many of the rabble, and sooner or later they will track most of us down. Just because they are rabble doesn't mean that all of them are stupid."

Gliance nodded, as did Jerrie. "I don't let my biases blind me. In fact, I find it hard to see why too many do allow themselves to be blinded, given our greatly reduced circumstances," he said.

"I didn't mention it before," interjected Warton, "but there's another route to deal with finances. For example, American conservatives have for a century and more used the ultra-religious, especially the ones who call themselves the Old Believers. Yes, some of them were in the 'Free Citizens Alliance', but more weren't ready to go that far. Money can be funneled through them, and I have to say that a good number of them would probably be quite happy to destroy the Confederation, or to leave Earth," he said, with an emphasis on the last word, "and build colonies where they had no one to contradict them in their beliefs."

"That's an excellent point," Johnson said. "I take it you have connections?" Warton nodded and smiled.

Never one to lose focus, Gliance looked at Jerrie, "Have your people found any potential planets yet?"

"Not yet, but I'm hoping for some more than a few hundred light years away." The others looked at him. "I'm being reasonable. A hundred years from now, they'll be stretching out well beyond that, and we want to not be bothered."

"I think we do want to be close enough, or close enough to other colonies, in case of an emergency," Gliance replied.

Jerrie nodded. "Not unreasonable. Let me have my people work up some possibilities, and I'll send you some proposals." There was general agreement, and the others winked out. Finally, it was just the two of them.

"Now about this mesh thing..." she said.

"Yes. You know they've been engineering these tiny bots, and injecting them into people, to monitor their health, and communicate with the monitors. These last few years, there has been work on getting them through the blood-brain barrier. What they've recently found is that those can be used to make very light-weight connections between them, and closely linked computers. They're referring to it as the 'mesh'. My people have found that if you have a heavy-duty controller for the mesh, you can see and know what they're seeing, and you can apply an electrical charge to the person you're monitoring, and they reject whatever they were thinking about. I'm told it's not especially painful, but they're working on going from individual memories to patterns of memories, so that you simply cannot think about anything that matches that pattern."

"How fascinating. One could assure that the person no longer remembers one thing, but they are still of use to one for other purposes, with no disappearances to cause suspicion." Jerrie nodded, smiling. "Do keep me up to date on the development."

25

RAFE AND AMELIE

Three evenings after Amelie received the Confederation Medal of Honor, her mobile rang. "Rafe? *Cherie*, this is a pleasant surprise. It has been a while since we last spoke."

"It has, indeed, not like when we were in uni together, and you and I and our friends would get together for a long dinner every few weeks. It's more than three months, so I have some news for you. Would you care to join me for dinner tomorrow evening?"

"Dinner? *Ça me ferait plaisir*. You will be flying over?"

"No, I will be taking public transit," he said, smiling, waiting for her response.

"You are here?"

"And have been living here for a few months. I've been wanting to call you, but the time never seemed right. Then I saw you accepting the medal for your late sister, and realized that if I were to keep my word that I gave you years ago, I needed to call."

"*Merci beaucoup*. That does mean something to me. *Oui*, I would very much enjoy dinner with you." With that, they made arrangements to meet at a restaurant he had been directed to by co-workers, and rang off.

The next evening, with dusk falling, her car dropped her outside the restaurant, and she went to greet Rafe, kissing him on both cheeks, which he returned. Seeing the car, he asked, "Your security?"

"*Oui.*" She shrugged. "But let us go in. I know I am running a little late, but the traffic...."

"This is New York. Everyone has complained about that for centuries." He led her in, saying "They offer continental cuisine, from French to Hungarian, so I assume you will find something to appreciate."

She smiled. "Continental? *Oui.*"

The restaurant was impressive, with a subdued elegance, small chandeliers, linen tablecloths and napkins, and designed such that the hum of conversation was soft and muted. They were shortly led to a small corner table. As they were seated, he said, "I arranged this so that we could speak with relative privacy."

"*Merci.*" She looked around, and her eyebrows went up. "This is pleasant. We are not being stared at."

"Even after the award the other day, I was told that this is the type of establishment that would consider that crude."

"I am quite familiar with such." She shook her head. "I am remembering you taking me out for coffee and pastries, a few years ago."

He smiled. "I've moved up, as they say. But I'm glad you remember that. It was not a good time for either of us, and that we were there for each other helped, at least for me."

"As it was for *moi.*" She nodded to herself. "So, what is your surprise?"

"I'm working in the Treasury Secretariat of the Confederation, helping to track down the trillionaires."

A smile split her face. "*Félicitations*!...but I should perhaps ask, given where you are now working, is there any issue with having dinner with *moi*?"

"No. I am not a manager or administrator, and you are not within the province of my department. Thank you for thinking of that."

"It is the world that I, and now you, move in. Speaking of which, I assume that your father was not amused with your move."

He closed his eyes for a minute. "No. He was already unhappy with me when I was working for the Labour Party, though he would have been more unhappy if he had known I was tracking opposition funding. It grew quite unpleasant when I also joined the campaign to join the Confederation."

"Oh, my, *oui.* Of course, I am sure you told him it was only a campaign for a non-binding vote...." They both laughed, remembering the history of the 'non-binding' vote that allowed the Tories to pull what was then the United Kingdom out of the European Union, and then Scotland out of the United Kingdom. "What are its chances?"

"We have another year to run the campaign, and we think it's gaining support. The Republic of Scotland, of course, is vastly amused."

"How could they not? Ah, the waiter." They listened to the specials, and ordered.

"Not a *prix fixe* restaurant, but I...well, I didn't want to seem as though I was trying to impress you."

"You do not need to. You are my old, who has shown himself a friend for years." Impulsively, she reached over and touched his hand as it sat on the table. Neither of them pulled their hands away until the meal came. Later, after they had finished, and added dessert, they left the restaurant. "This has been lovely, Rafe." She took a deep breath. "Would you care to stop over for a drink, and a private conversation?"

His eyes widened for a moment. "I should like that very much."

Her car came around and picked the two up. Once at her building, they went through building security, and up to her floor. She owned half of the floor, he found, as they went in, and took off their jackets. She got them drinks, a Speyside single malt for him, a screwdriver for her, and they sat on the couch.

"How was it for you with your father?"

"Very bad. I invited him to meet me for dinner...."

Rafe had been seated for a while, and was beginning to wonder if his father would even show up, when he heard, "Good evening, Rafe."

"Good evening, father. I trust this restaurant is to your satisfaction?" he said, looking around at the linen tablecloths, the old wainscotting, and pictures of famous nobility of centuries gone.

"Quite so. But since we're in a corner, and having dinner here, rather than at my club, I assume there are things you have to discuss that will not be."

"Father, please. Let us have a pleasant dinner, before we discuss such things."

"Very well." He looked down at the menu that Rafe had already studied. The waiter came over, and they ordered. "How did you find an establishment like this?"

"A school chum told me about it, and I've been here several times, twice with them, and once...with Amelie."

"The African-French girl? She would like a place this conservative?"

"Yes. She and her sister had the trillionaire Tolliver as their patron for many years,"

His father's eyes widened for an instant, and he looked thoughtful. That looked continured through dinner. Finally, they ordered liquors, and his father's face turned hard. "Tolliver. And African-French. Her last name is Trouve. Her sister was the one who destroyed the starship."

Rafe bit his lip. "Yes."

"And Amelie was one of those at the UN last year, providing evidence against a number of trillionaires, including several of the patrons of the Tories." Rafe said nothing. "Very well, tell me what I shall find extremely objectionable. Have you joined the campaign for the non-binding referendum to join this absurd Confederation, that will certainly collapse in disaster in a few years?"

"I did that several months ago. No, you may like this less: I became aware of a position that would use all that I learned both in school and in working as an intern. It will require my relocating." His father stared at him, hard. "I've accepted a position in the Budget Division of the Treasury Secretariat of the Confederation."

Anger swept across his father's face. "How, how *could* you?! How *dare* you? This is an attack on everything our family has stood for, for centuries."

"Yes, and it's time we stood for something other than our own privilege."

By now, his father's face was bright red, and Rafe began to fear that his elder might have a heart attack right there. "Father, surely it doesn't mean all that. We have lived through other vast changes in the world, from the First World War, through the Second, and the end of the Empire, and then the departure of Scotland and Northern Ireland. We can surely live through this, and show people how what we stand for is for the good of all, and Great Britain."

"If this, this Confederation does not collapse in a world war, there will be no more Great Britain. And our family will be nothing but a footnote in history." The man stood. "When you regret this decision, you may call me again, but not until you do." Rafe sat, watching his father storm out.

~

"THAT MUST HAVE BEEN HAVE BEEN *trés mal*. Oh, Rafe, I am so sorry." She reached over to take hold of his hand.

He nodded, then looked at her, and at what she was drinking. "I see the screwdriver, and I'm remembering what you told me about Francoise. It has been very bad for you, as well."

"It has. I miss her terribly. She was all that I had for so long...."

"I'm sure that it adds to your discomfort that people are already starting to refer to the Medal of Honor as the Trouve."

Amelie's head fell, still holding his hand. "To celebrate my sister's death, rather than her life." He felt tears fall on his hand. "Rafe, Rafe..." She raised her head and looked at him. "You are the only person in the world who understands, who would think of that. Only you." She carefully put her drink down on the coffee table, and took his from him, and put that down as well, and then wrapped her arms around him.

They sat like that for a while, arms around each other. At last she looked up, and there was an expression he had never seen on her face before. Her voice grew husky. “Francoise and I spoke about trust at dinner that time, after I introduced you at graduation, and I agreed with her, that the most dangerous thing in the world is trust.” She bit her lips, then said, “I yield. I yield. I have never said this before, but *mon amor*, you have me at your mercy. Do what you will, I give you my trust.” Tears streamed down her cheeks.

He looked at her, and felt tears in his own eyes. “Amelie, *mon amor*, I take that trust as the most valuable gift I have ever been given, and hope I may return it with all the trust it deserves.” He laughed, tears pouring down his cheeks, as they were still pouring down hers. “I believe that there’s only one thing for me to do now, and that’s out of absurd old tales from our great grandparents’ time.” He pulled himself free of her arms, got off the couch, and went down on one knee before her. Amelie’s mouth fell open as he said, “I cannot imagine anyone who could understand me, other than you, nor I you. My beloved, will you...?”

Crying, laughing, she flung herself off the couch, knees on the floor by him and wrapped her arms around him. “*Oui. Oui. Oui.* And what I tell you three times is true.”

TWENTY-FIVE YEARS LATER

26

BLOODY STRAWBERRIES

Rhys associated strawberries with blood since he was little, which was not unreasonable. When he was five he was riding in a hovercar, still uncommon back then, with his parents. They were on a small country road, going to a cabin on one of the Finger Lakes in upstate New York for a week's vacation. He still remembered how he'd looked forward to picking wild strawberries, and how wonderful they tasted when the IED went off, and the explosion flipped the hover upside down. The memories of screaming, tasting blood in his mouth as he tried to get free, terror at seeing his mother and father bleeding. He saw his father just hanging there, unmoving, while his mother was trying to move, as was their secretary, who was turning to help his mother. It still seemed as though they were there forever before the security hover circled, having assured that there was no further attack, came close. He remembered the big hook they put on the side of his hover, and flipping it back upright. After a while that seemed forever a medical aircraft was there, and people were taking care of them.

When he was older, he found out that had they been driving a wheeled car, they'd have died.

So he had a little frisson of discomfort when offered a strawberry tart for dessert. "I would prefer the chocolate torte, thank you," he told the waiter, and turned back to Amelie, his mother, who'd ordered chocolate mousse. She was looking at him over the white tablecloth and the small flower arrangement in the center of the table, and he knew she saw him, tall, slender, dark brown hair much like his father's, but with a tendency to curl that was hers. Still, he wondered if she saw him as a man, not merely her son. Her elbow on the table, she rested her chin on her palm. After a pause, she stated, "Strawberries still bother you."

Shamefacedly, he nodded. "I suppose I'll get over it someday." Changing the subject, he asked, "How is father?"

"Quite well. He's working late, or he'd be here. He claimed it was just cleaning up some details, but something bothers me about his attitude that I can't quite put my finger on. How is your job working out?"

"Fabulous, mother. They were very happy with me when I interned, and now that I'm employed there, they're letting me work on stabilization of gravity-control systems. I'm hoping to move up to work on starship stabilization fairly soon."

She smiled. "You know I'm somewhat jealous of you?"

"Really?"

"When I graduated from school, I was interested in both genengineering and starship engineering, but *that man* would only approve of the former."

Rhys nodded, knowing she meant Tolliver. "But for a long time, you have helped build starships through Krock." She nodded, and he changed the subject back. "What is it that is bothering you about father?"

"He's hiding something from me." Before her son could make a comment, she waved it away and went on. "*Non*, it's not just keeping something from his wife, it's that he's keeping something serious inside. I'm afraid he's got hold of something, and thinks he's going to protect us from whatever it is." She rolled her eyes. "He's still got too much Englishman in him, silly man."

A disbelieving look stole over his face. "Protecting *you*?" He looked at his mother, who had made her way into history books, and shook his head in disbelief.

She smiled. They finished dessert and shrugged into their coats, her hat already on. She kissed him on each cheek, and they left the restaurant, walking into the thin, chill wind blowing through Central Park.

IN THE HOVER carrying her home she thought how much easier her son and husband's lives had been than hers. Her thoughts spun away, and circled back to Rafe, her husband, and she decided it was time to find out what was going on at his work.

She paid the hover and went into the house, looking around as she did. Thinking about Rhys and strawberries, she was reminded of the first years after the creation of the Confederation, when she, then they, traveled with heavily armed police or private security. The attack that had hit their hover was only one of a series initiated by the former trillionaires, and their supremacist allies, or rather tools, to be honest, but it had been years since they'd had or needed regular security. She hung up her coat and the wide-brimmed black hat which she had made her trademark. Then fixed herself a bourbon and ginger, put on her elegant AR headset, and settled down to wait while listening to music.

Over an hour and a half later, Rafe, looking drawn and tired, came into the living room. It was a warm room, with bright fabric hangings from North Africa alternating with pictures taken from space, landscapes of the Moon and other worlds and bookcases with centuries-old books. As he took off his coat, he smiled at her. "I remembered you were eating with Rhys, so I called for some takeout for myself a while ago, but a drink looks like a good idea." He kissed her, then went to hang up his coat, coming back a couple of minutes later with a glass of red wine, sat in the comfortable chair next to her, and sighed. "I was going to ask how dinner was, but from the look on your face, I might as well cut to the chase. What's on your mind?"

"You are going to tell me what is going on, all of it. As our son said, you're protecting *moi*?"

He looked at her for a while, sitting there, slender, tall, elegant, her dark brown hair in loose curls currently hanging to her shoulders, in her late fifties, still young these days of genengineering. Finally, he shook his head. "I suppose that is absurd. You'd better set security on." She raised her eyebrows, then a couple of small red lights were visible in the room, and she took off her headset, her attention on him. "You remember that forensic accounting I originally did when I started, years ago? My manager began discouraging me from looking into some data earlier this year, something I found slightly odd, given my work?" He took a sip of his wine. "A couple months ago, work was slow as we were waiting for the Confederation Assembly to approve this year's budget. Just to warm up, I did some on us, and found most of what we have, though I must admit to being surprised I didn't find all. Then I started on the division itself."

Her look grew deadly serious. "I do not like that you paused just there."

"You've good reason. I found a hole in the Secretariat's wealth tax tracking. A number of trails just end, and then there are trails, later, that just begin. The trails change, and are larger or smaller, but no connection, while the individuals and corporations continue to exist, though there is some churn, with companies being created by other companies, and then the original companies going out of business. Finally, I went out for a drink with a friend in IT, and he did some tracing for me that got around where I didn't have the security to go. About two weeks ago, he passed his results to me while we were at the bar, and adding what he found to my trails, I found I was inside the event horizon, as it were."

"I trust it was not an Eldritch Horror."

"Actually, you could say that it was." She stared intently at him. "There were well over a hundred entities that had hidden links, loans, profit transfers, and false front companies that are worth many billions, and then dissolved, crisscrossing the world to hide them.

And some of it seems to lead to allegedly charitable places, such as several Old Believer megachurches."

"And each is in the range of tens to hundreds of billions of creds," she stated.

"Yes. And some of those names are familiar."

Her face grew serious and cold as ice, her Francoise *face*. "Some of the old 400." He nodded. "A moment, *cherie*." She downed the rest of her drink and went into the kitchen. When she came back, she was carrying a vodka and orange juice. "And did you find any links to your manager?"

He swallowed. "I'm not sure. I don't think I can get that deep without setting off alarms." Amelie smiled at him, not a nice smile. "Dear, you have a screwdriver, and that makes me very nervous, especially when you put on your late sister's face."

She smiled more broadly. "Even with the universal wealth taxes, we are still multimillionaires, and I control a number of companies. I shall call one or two, and have them do some looking." She suddenly managed an innocent voice that he'd only heard a few times, one where she imitated her late sister's naif voice, which deeply scared him. "I mean, we are only supporting the government against people who might not be the good citizens we are."

He swallowed, then downed the rest of his wine. "My dear, when you do *that*, I need something stronger. If you're going to drink that rotgut, I need one as well." He got up and went to mix a drink.

When he came back, he saw she had her AR headset on. She glanced at his screwdriver. "Now we are ready to play for real, *cherie*. I've called for security, who will be sending two people over to stay, and warned two informatics companies that I will be giving them a maximum security project in the morning." She looked thoughtful. "I'll have them try to send me preliminary results in a month."

"Do we know the people security is sending?"

"*Oui*, it's John, who has been here before, and a woman named Marie." He nodded.

27

FLYING

Rhys was in his study, wearing his AR headset, and had been pacing for a while. Finally, he flung himself into his chair, and the sound woke up his Artificial Stupid. "Is there something I can do, Rhys?" asked George, the AS, that ran in parallel with his AR local system connection, a configuration that people were calling a mesh.

He shook himself, and said, "Make this secure, please. Security level strawberry."

"Done, Rhys." The AI having some knowledge of human interaction, it paused before asking, "Since you just had dinner with your mother, does this concern her?"

He laughed a hard laugh. "With that security level? What else could it be? I suspect, as she does, that father's found something in the Confederation taxes or whatever. I'm hoping, no, scratch that, our conversation over dinner may have crystallized her thinking, I'm sure she's called for security no later than when she got home."

"So you're trying to find something that you can do, should she need you."

"Of course."

"Have you considered a stability-enhanced flyer, with armor?"

"Right, I...say what?"

"Is that not what you've been working on, for the military to use in storm or earthquake situations?"

He opened his mouth, then shut it and thought for a while. Then went into the mesh himself, wanting George to comment on his internal debate. "No experience flying them."

"Ask tomorrow to take the training. Is it not likely that your manager will agree, since it would give you better insight into what you are trying to accomplish?"

He thought about that for a while. Then thought some more. "Maybe I should get some friends to help look into what father does..."

"That would be a bad idea, Rhys. I gravely doubt that any of them have the security clearance for those systems."

He sighed, heavily. "You're probably right."

"Perhaps, then, you should give your mother a call tomorrow, assuming you can start training, to let her know what you will have access to?"

He pictured hitting himself on his forehead. "Coordination. Thank you, I should know that by now." He shook his head, then got a drink before going to bed.

In the morning, Anthony, his manager stared at him. "I thought you did not want to fly, you had some incident as a child...." Anthony's British ex-pat accent reminded him of his father's, and he decided to explain.

Rhys shook his head. "Incident isn't exactly that how I'd describe an assassination attempt," he said, softly.

"A *what*? You've never mentioned that. Who were they trying to assassinate?" Anthony kept his voice low, to match Rhys'.

Rhys bit his lip. "Anthony, may I close the door?" His manager looked at him oddly and nodded. "This is only between us." Seeing Anthony nod, he went on. "My mother is Amelie Trouve." Seeing his manager's incomprehension, he added, "My late aunt was the woman who made the boom heard 'round the world."

Anthony's eyes shot wide. "Francoise Trouve?"

"Yes."

Anthony stared for a moment, then nodded. "That explains a good bit, including how high a security clearance you have. No wonder you did not want this to get around. At any rate, I'll certainly sign the approval for the flight training. I agree, it will help you on your project."

That night, he called Amelie and told her his news. "*Ma enfant*, this makes me glad. I understand that when someone who rides is thrown from their horse, they are pushed to get back on again. It has been a long time since the incident, and it is time for you to move past it." He saw her look down. "Some things will always stay with you, and are part of you, but you move on to deal with the world."

"I don't know if I want to know what's going on, but you have security, right?"

"*Oui*. Your father and I had our little discussion, and I arranged for that immediately. Give me a codeword that I can send you via AR, should I need you."

He looked at her in the AR. "Strawberry. And use the mesh, if you would, that's most likely to get through, since George will find me wherever I am."

"*Oui. Au revoir*."

Tuesday, he came into work, got some tea, then went to the training room for the initial AR training. After the first hour, he took a break, and nearly threw up in the bathroom. More tea, and back in. The end of the second hour was a repeat of the first, except that he did throw up. Still more tea, and back into the room. The third hour ended at noon. Slightly nauseous, it was mid-afternoon before he had a few bites of a sandwich.

Two days later, it was the same routine, except this time he threw up after the first hour, and was only moderately nauseous the rest of the time. By the end of the next week's two sessions, he was getting through them with only mild discomfort. On the third Tuesday, something happened midway through the morning. He'd been rolled in AR upside down, and instead of resetting, he kept the roll going and came upright, the first time he had done that...and realized it was fun. By that Thursday, he was starting to get high scores, and when he finished for the day, he was notified that the following Monday, he would be co-piloting a real aircraft.

Monday morning he walked out behind the corporate offices to the landing pad and stopped, staring at the grav-control aircraft sitting there waiting for him. He swallowed hard, and walked to it. A long slender flattened oval about six meters long with a clear ceramic windshield, the short stubby wings with small electric propellers vertical, hovering about a meter off the ground. He climbed up the stairs, which closed up behind him into the body as he stepped into the cabin. A woman was in the pilot's seat, and an empty seat next to her waited for him. There were two seats behind the pilot and copilot's.

The pilot was looking back at him and said, "Hi, I'm Janine Smith."

"Rhys Maxwell." He shook her hand, sat and strapped in to the other front seat. Then he looked at her.

"Ready?" she asked.

"I suppose."

She gave a snort. "Well, we'll see. Start the checklist." Both put on heads-up AR glasses, and he began the checklist. She watched him go through it all methodically, then he reached to push the throttle. "Forgetting a thing or two?"

He looked at her, then hung his head. "You're quite right. I'm the project lead on the software for the stability system." He activated the stability subsystem, then brought the gravity control up, and could feel his weight on the seat lessening. When the gauge showed them down to two-thirds original mass, he brought the props on, and the craft lifted slowly at first, then faster. As they rose to five hundred feet, well above the top of the office building, he changed the angle of the wings, and they began to move forward as well as up. They flew for a while, doing straight lines and circles. Before he realized it, the session was over, and he brought them down, carefully. He thanked Janine, and headed back to his desk.

The schedule for the real world flying was two hours a day, three days a week. He enjoyed the rest of the week, and was looking forward to the following Monday. Halfway through that next lesson though, Janine suddenly cut the stabilization system as he was doing a sharp curve, and they flipped upside down, and were headed downwards as well as forward. He froze, unable to recover. She recovered the ship, and he unfroze only after she turned the stabilization system back on.

She looked at him, and he said, his eyes straight ahead, "There was an incident when I was a child, involving a flipped early hover, all of us hanging there, injured.."

She nodded, and circled another time. "You need to be able to handle the craft if something fails."

"Could you let me take it, then tell me when you're going to cut the stabilization?" She agreed, and they tried it again. When she cut it, he corrected, then overcorrected, and they wound upside down again, with him unable to recover. They tried three more times, the last time resulting in him rolling the craft repeatedly. She finally brought them down, seeing the wildness in his eyes, and the sweat pouring off him.

"We'll try again Wednesday." He nodded, wiping the sweat off his face, and went back to the office.

Wednesday, coming into the cabin, he said, "On the advice of my AS, I've taken something to relax me a little. Is that a problem?"

She looked at him, then slapped her hand at him. He blocked it, and she nodded. "Not one that affects your reflexes, so not a problem." They took off, and worked at flying, then the rolls. The third time, he managed to get them right-side up and stable, though they rocked a little. They flew for a bit longer, then he was turning them to head back, and Janine cut the stabilizer without warning. Again they flipped, and suddenly he found himself angry, angrier than he had been in a long time, immensely angry at Janine. Then, as though struck by lightning, realized who he was truly angry at were the fools who had tried to kill them when he was a child. His face froze into an unfamiliar expression, and the anger suddenly changed to something utterly cold and controlled, and he brought them upright, with almost no rocking at all. They did that two more times, and his expression never changed.

She threw a few more things at him, downdrafts, virtual clouds, and then finally asked to take control, and he let her, curtly. She brought them down on the pad, then looked at him. "I've never seen anyone go from unable to deal to cold perfect like that. I'd like to see you try again Friday, but with no help." He nodded agreement. "By the way, and this is a personal comment, but I don't know if it was the drug, or what, but the look you've had since that first time you recovered from one without warning is more than a little disturbing." She shook her head. "Hell, it's downright scary."

His look became quizzical, until he glanced at his face in the windscreen, and realized he'd put on *the face* his mother could put on, what she had called his aunt's face. It had always been genuinely scary, but for the first time, he truly understood it—not just a look, but inside, utterly controlled emotions, anger and calculation colder than ice at whatever was trying to use him...and how it could be used, ruling even every thought, and the willingness to do whatever was necessary to not be the one used. The smile he gave Janine clearly did not reassure her, but he said, "My apologies. I can't promise it won't come back." She nodded, and he left to return to his desk.

Friday, he flew without chemical assistance, and handled the unexpected without pulling on his late aunt's face, save for an instant or two. That evening, he called Amelie. "Mother, it's been a while, and I need to speak with you. Can we do dinner this weekend, some time?" Her AS, Marat, replied that she might have time for lunch, at least.

They met for brunch Saturday, in a trendy restaurant in the East Village. She walked in, gray slacks, trench coat, and her trademark low-crowned wide-brimmed black hat. He stood to say hello, and as usual, she kissed him on both cheeks, and they sat and ordered. She put down her bag, opening it as she did so, so he could see that she had a local security device, to block recordings of their conversation. "So," she asked, "What has been happening?"

"I'm now flying, getting ready to solo." As she smiled, he added,

"And I seem to have found an inheritance." She gave him a questioning look. "The second day I was trying to fly, with the pilot cutting stability, we rolled over, and I got angry, not only at her, but realized how much anger I still had for those men who trapped us." Her expression grew colder, and he went on. "As I did, this happened." It took him a few seconds, but he put on *the face*.

Her eyes opened a bit more for a moment, her face set. "*Ma cherie*, on the one hand, I am sorry that you found it, or ever needed to. On the other...there are times when it is a very useful weapon to have." They stared at each other, and then, with a little effort, he let it go. She gave a pained smile. "It would probably be better for your father not to know." He nodded.

"How have things progressed, if I may ask?"

"I spoke with your father the night after our last dinner, and he told me all, and yes, it is worse than you want to know. I have some people, in several places, looking into the issue from other angles, and have approached several old acquaintances in several Secretariats concerning it...which reminds me that I expected to hear from them this past week. This is, of course, a very delicate matter."

Knowing what she could mean by delicate, he didn't ask further. "Shall I assume," he nodded at her bag, "that you have called other old associates?"

"*Oui*," she smiled. Her eyes flitted one way, than another, and rubbing his chin as an excuse to turn his head, saw a flash of *the face*. "Several old, shall we say, fellow travelers." He smiled, knowing she meant other formerly wealthy people. Their food came, and their conversation turned to other things.

28

SECURITY AND SECURITIES

Back from brunch Amelie settled into her study. Putting on the AR headset, she used the mesh, adding an extra level of security, to contact her two informatics companies as neither had reported yet. Then she worked for a while, reviewing her corporations' reports until late in the afternoon, when Marat asked for her attention. "Madame, I have received a contact from Confederation Informatics, with an encrypted datafile for you. They apologize for running a week beyond what you requested for preliminary results, but believe you'll be pleased with the report. Security note: you need to be aware that several attempts were made to intercept or interfere with my reception of this data. I, and my counterpart at CI, believe that they were defeated, but of course one cannot prove a negative."

"*Oui*. Very good, Marat. Put it into, ah, I see you have already loaded it into the secure system using a housebot and deleted it from the connected system. Excellent. Let me know when my husband reappears." Exchanging her normal AR headset for a heavier set, tuned to the air gapped secure system, she decrypted the data and began to review it.

After Rafe got home and had hung up his coat, Marat informed him that it had tried to let Amelie know he was home several times, and she had paid no attention. Surprised, he walked into her study to find her with *that face* on. "Amelie? *Cherie*?" he said, louder than his normal tone, staying well away from her.

She jumped out of her chair and spun, going into an aikido stance she had learned in school, and stayed with when she was being sought by assassins. Seeing it was him, she relaxed her stance, breathed deeply, and came over. Kissing him, she put her arms around and leaned against him. "*Merde*. It is worse than we thought. There are at least something like thirty-six or thirty-eight of the old 400 who are involved in this, with hundreds of collaborators and hangers-on who would join them. There may be more, but all the links fade out at the edges. The interconnection is as bad as anything from before the Confederation, but CI has found what appears to be close to an actionable trail."

"Were your company's systems secure?"

"One hopes they are as secure as they think they are."

"The other company?"

"I have not heard from them yet...."

"Madame, one of the security people informs me there is a messenger at the door."

She looked up, puzzled. "Thank you, Marat. Have security escort them...no, have them scanned first." They waited, as the system used sensors installed around the front door.

"The messenger appears to be a gentleman in his mid-twenties, light brown hair, with a briefcase, and a firearm."

"Security? Escort the man into the front room, and relieve him of his firearm."

They waited until security reported, adding that the man had willingly handed over the weapon, looking uncomfortable holding it. Then they walked down the stairs and into the large comfortable living room. "John, Marie, thank you," Amelie said to the security guards.

The man, with a light coat on, looked up. "Madame Trouve?"

She nodded. "*Oui*. You are?"

"Art Carden. Carl Phillips asked me to hand deliver this to you." The young man acted as though he had done this many times before, but the pencil mustache on his round face twitched, giving him away. He reached into his jacket for his shirt pocket slowly, very aware of the two security guards with weapons suddenly aimed at him, brought out a media, and handed it to her.

"Why the firearm? The briefcase?" Rafe asked.

"A book and some papers, they're nothing, sir. Mr. Phillips called it a distraction." Rafe and Amelie both nodded. "And he pulled the gun out of a drawer and handed it to me." Art shook his head. "I'd no idea he had one, and I've never held one, but he told me that I could always threaten with it. He told me this was more dangerous than anything I've ever dealt with, but I was the only one available at the moment."

"But why send you in person?" she asked.

"He said he had no confidence that our systems were invulnerable."

She looked at her husband. "As I said, worse than we thought."

Marat spoke to her in mesh. *"Madame, the newsfeeds are reporting that an aerial transport has crashed into the main offices of the building which houses Confederation Informatics. There appears to have been an explosion, and there is a fire in progress."*

For a second she stood stunned, then *the face* fell into place, and she said, "John, call your superiors, and tell them to put maximum security on this house five minutes ago." Turning, "Marat, security max, now.. no, wait, Art, leave the briefcase, Marat will give you another jacket, and once the bot brings one, leave immediately, and assume someone is following you. Do your best to lose them." The man looked startled, with a touch of fear. "You have some fear. Good. Ah, here, change coats. *Bon. Au revoir*, and good luck." John let Art out the back door, instructing him to walk down the alley to the street before calling for a public hover.

The house grew quiet as Marat called up maximum security.

Shutters closed over the all the windows of the house, and drones came out of an unremarkable hatch on the roof, to circle the building. Just then, there was a knock at the back door. "Marat?"

"It is the young man, and there is someone next to him."

Amelie looked around, and John said, "I'll answer, Marie. You cover me." He went down the hall to the back door, while Marie, carrying a long bag, followed him, but opened a closet door and stepped in, her stunner at the edge of the open door. John unlatched the deadbolt and turned the doorknob, only to have the door rammed into him, and he fell backwards a couple steps. Art fell through the open door and to the floor as the other man leapt over him and rammed a stun-rod into John's stomach. He doubled over and fell twitching, retching. As the man straightened up from John, Marie shot him with the stun gun, and he fell, muscles locking, jerking, and there was a smell of burnt meat. There was the sound of a loud motor in the alley coming close, then stopping. She put the stun gun into her holster, and reached into the bag. Two men, each with a pistol, appeared in the doorway, then froze as Marie's rifle thundered in the narrow hall, the bullet hitting the wall beside the door, the smell of the propellant wafting from it.

Down the hall came Amelie's voice. "Housebots coming." Two housebots came out of the kitchen, came down the hall, and pulled John and Art back to the kitchen. There was the sound of the door from the dining room to the kitchen opening, and feet. Another bot came down the hall from the living room, stopping three meters from the men in the doorway, leaving Marie a clear shot. Stabilizers sprang out, and two cylinders, one on each side of the bot, tilted out, and there were red dots on the men. "I should not move, were I you," Amelie said. "That is a police-grade disabler that we legally own, and you would both require a trip to the hospital before the police take you to jail."

"Put your weapons on safety, and lay them on the floor," Marie ordered. They did so, and as they stood, Rafe came into the hallway holding a military handgun, a housebot behind him. "Housebot, retrieve the guns." The low unit, round and on rollers, scooted over and grabbed the pistols with two manipulator arms, then returned to stop beside Rafe.

"Both of you, on the floor, face down," he said. They did, and putting down her rifle, Marie bound them with plastic ties, then did the same for the other man, who was still twitching, but starting to move.

A minute later, John came down the hall limping, a thunderous expression on his face. "I wasn't expecting a high-power stun stick. The armor stopped a lot of it, but that one must be set to kill." He picked it up from the floor, and moved back.

"Amelie has called the police, and a security team should be here shortly."

"I 'ave also called Confederation Security, who is sending a couple of hovers," Amelie added from the kitchen, one leg out of the door, holding a stunner. "Is there anything else in the alley?" John looked out, carefully, and shook his head. "Go, Art, and do not take your time at it." He gulped, nodded, and ran.

With the door shut, Amelie thought for a minute, and called Rhys. "*Ma cherie*, protect yourself. I have my reports, one of my companies' offices have been crashed into by an aerial transport, there is a fire, and we have been attacked here at home, and have three invaders bound. The police and Confederation Security is on its way." She paused, and heard George tell her he would let Rhys know shortly. "*Non*, now! Tell him strawberry!" and she hung up.

With that done, and nods to John and Marie, who had the housebots drag the three men into the living room, and were keeping them covered. Amelie and Rafe returned to her study, to look at the media Art had delivered. Skimming it, they found confirmation of everything CI had sent, and more, clear evidence of corruption in governments, carefully chosen people who could hide the machinations and the extent of the wealth involved.

Rafe looked at her. "With all multinationals falling under the Confederation's remit, it's past time for us to regulate the investment banks, the way that we, and most member nations, did with with private banking. Doing that will give us control over the use, and misuse, by what's left of the trillionaires, and better control of the multinational companies. The law that was passed holding the executives of a corporation criminally responsible for actions of the corporations was a real shock that began the change."

"*Oui.* They hate being exposed in that way, and more, it will impede their schemes greatly. The Confederation is already taxing current wealth, but perhaps that should be raised, and include the current value of stock options."

He grinned a hard grin. "Another way of avoiding taxes, quite. Perhaps it's also time to fix salaries and put on far more permanent, and far more widespread price, and certainly profit controls, worldwide."

"Is that workable?"

He snorted. "During the British Empire, the value of the pound was stable from from the sixteen hundreds to the mid-seventeen hundreds, then again from the early eighteen hundreds to World War I. In other words, for two periods covering hundreds of years, inflation was close to non-existent. Then, since the world is now almost completely a single market, there's the question of whether a constant growth of GDP is even possible, much less sustainable. Besides, it will remove most incentives for relocating most businesses, when they cannot pay someone a tenth of what they would pay where the business is now."

He said. "Let us see..." he began, as the sound of a loud engine grew in their hearing.

"Downstairs!" Amelie yelled, grabbing the copies she had made of the media that lay on the desk, and thrusting them into a pocket. With her bulky security AR in her hand, they scrambled down the stairs, and saw John and Marie prone on the floor, ready for an invasion. "Quickly, to the basement" She motioned, and they started to rise to follow when the whole house shook, and they all fell to the floor. She looked up the stairs, to see that part of the roof had crumpled into the top floor. As they rose, there was an explosion, and the shutters on the bay window slammed in, then fell to hang crazily out.

She cried, "The basement," again, then screamed, and dropped to the floor as two of the windows suddenly had circular fractures and grew crazed, and a third grew a hole. Looking down, she saw that the AR headset had a hole in it, and her arm was bleeding. "Assassins!" she yelled, but even as she did, John, prone on the floor, Marie now behind a chair, were firing out of the now-open armored bay windows towards rooftop targets.

"See the view from the drones, Marie? They're on that rooftop!" John called.

"Now that we've got them backed down for a minute, yep," Marie answered. "Two more not with a line of sight to this window. M. Trouve, M. Maxwell, get behind something." Then she started muttering, "Wait for them, wait for them...."

As Amelie and Rafe dove for a couch, a bullet hit the floor right where she had been. The crack of Marie's rifle sounded an instant later, followed by a second shot from John. "Got one!" Marie's voice was victorious, and a "Hey, that one was mine!" John had hit the assassin as they lurched up after being hit by Marie's shot.

"Just making sure," he answered.

Rafe was wrapping Amelie's arm with a handkerchief when they saw an armored flyer with Confederation insignia on it coming straight in for the bay windows. Spinning, it stopped by the windows, and its door opened, smashing open the now-shattered windows. Needing no further urging, all four rose and ran, leaping into the interior. They saw both front seats occupied, with Rhys in the pilot's seat, and from the side of Rhys' head, Amelie saw him wearing *the face*.

"Mother, father, take the seats. Guards, on the floor, legs around the seats and hold on. Janine, let the Joint Air know we're coming up." They did, and Janine's mouth fell open as Rhys pulled away from the house, flipped the aircraft, and rose, upside down to expose their armored top, only rolling back once they were clear of the houses and headed up towards the security aircraft and temporary safety.

Rhys glanced back. "Where to, mother, father?"

They looked at each other, and Rafe replied. "Secretariat of

Justice, I think." Amelie nodded, and Rhys spun the aircraft, asking Janine to let the flyers accompanying them know where they were headed. In half an hour, they were coming down on the Secretariat's landing pad, and they could see heavily armed guards around the pad, and an armored vehicle. "I hope they're on our side," Amelie said. Just then, they heard them calling. Janine answered, and gave Rhys the thumbs-up for landing, and he brought them down as smoothly as they could want. Opening the door, Amelie led them out, and she, Rafe, Rhys, and Janine all holding out Confederation ID, while their security showed their corporate IDs. As soon as they were checked, and vouched for their security people, they were hustled into the building.

Inside, a number of people were waiting. One caught Amelie's eye, and she said, "*Bonsoir*, Barbara."

"Good evening to you, Amelie." She shook her head. "I must say, you have a penchant for interesting entrances." Both women laughed.

"We need to speak to the Inspector General's office."

"I will call my manager. Now, let me call medical support for you," she said, seeing the bloody handkerchief and the other scrapes and bruises from the shrapnel.

"*Merci.* Oh, there are three bound men in our living room that began the assault. The police and security should have them shortly"

Soon, an older man, dark skinned, with gray in his curly hair, came up. "Barbara, I was just leaving. What's going on?" he asked, with a north African accent.

"Michael, this is Amelie Trouve, and her husband, Rafe Maxwell. Amelie, Rafe, Michael Ukiteyedi, from Justice's Inspector General's office."

A medic rushed into the room, as Amelie answered. "*Bonsoir,* a pleasure to meet you, *m'sieur* Ukiteyedi, although one could wish it had been under more pleasant circumstances."

"*Bonsoir*, Madame Trouve. What exactly, are the circumstances? I understand that your house was attacked, someone dropped an aerial transport on it?"

She looked down as the medic was cleaning and bandaging her

arm, as well as some small bloody holes in her side. "It began with an attempted invasion, but then there were assassins following the transport. Also the building where the headquarters of an informatics corporation I own that had done some work for us the last month was attacked, and the last we heard, the building is in flames. But let my husband tell you more. He is a senior accountant in the Treasury Secretariat."

Michael and Rafe shook hands. Rafe told him what he had been doing. "I spoke to Amelie about it, and she had her people look into the hole, and we had just gotten the initial reports from them today." His face grew grim. "Mostly involving former trillionaires hiding under false identities, or residing in countries not generally recognized, or just not part of the Confederation."

"Let me be blunt, Michael," interrupted Amelie. "We found dozens of the old 400 involved in monstrous tax evasion and fraud, abetting serious corruption. Given the attacks, there was clearly more that they feared we would find.."

"You have the evidence, I assume."

"*Oui,* of course. Let us go somewhere secure, with display headsets, and we will show you the reports." Once the medic had finished with her, they left for a private office, while Rhys and Janine, along with John and Marie, were shown to a break room to wait.

They got coffee and sat. As Janine sat, clearly still pumping adrenaline, she looked at Rhys. she burst out. "You...your mother is *that* Trouve?"

He had been staring into his coffee, but looked up at her. "*Oui*. I mean, yes. Sorry, mother never lost her accent, and it tends to be catching."

"That look you gave me, the first time we rolled...now I understand where you got it from."

He thought about it for a bit, and took another sip of coffee. "Yes, well, that is what she learned from her sister, how to face down trillionaires and their agents, when all the power was on their side."

Janine swallowed more coffee, then looked at him. "Frankly, she's terrifying. I'm glad she's on our side." She paused, "Yet with all the money your family has, you just work in software."

His grew intense. "About the money - we *believe* in the Confederation. My parents lived under what there was before, and I have heard personal stories from the inside, not just read histories. What I got from them, and those stories, is that what matters is what you can do that makes things better for everyone, not just yourself. Mother still has her French citizenship, and father his English, but we are *Terrans*." He paused, then went on, "Just software? No, I work in stabilization systems, and hope my next position is work on starship stabilization." He smiled, and there was a light in his eyes. "When my mother was ready for uni, um, college, she was torn between genengineering and starship engineering. She was told to go into the former, but over the years she spoke to me of starships, and I caught that from her, and no one told me no. In the Confederation, anyone can try for their dreams."

The fire in his face as he spoke about the Confederation and about starships, caught her by surprise, and she couldn't take her eyes off him. "Are you trying to tell me a girl from West Philly who pilots aircraft has a chance to wind up a starship pilot?"

A grin spread across his face, though the intensity of his gaze didn't change. "Why, do you know one who's interested?"

Upstairs, the mood was far more somber. "So you came directly to my office because there are links to the Justice Secretariat?" said Michael.

"They only seem to point to one cluster, a deputy attorney general and his team," Rafe clarified.

"If so, we can resolve that quietly and easily, just call them all for a meeting in the morning as they arrive, and pick them all up easily. Just a minor point, Rafe, why do you think your manager told you not to play with this?" Michael asked.

"I found a link to him, but no big money. I wonder if there are threats to his relatives. Just a minute." He dove back into the documents, calling on his AS to help search, and a few minutes later, pushed the AR headset up. "I passed this over before, but just recalled where I'd seen it mentioned. He is a close relative of one of the leaders of the Old Believers, and there is serious money going to them."

Michael shook his head. "Right now, the question is how to proceed. The Old Believers will be a special problem in their own right."

"*Oui,* but the first thing is to ask the local and Confederation authorities to query all air traffic control and see what other attacks have occurred," Amelie said. "The second thing is if there were more, then all regional private air transport needs to be grounded. Third would be to send marshals to arrest the top people for whom we have incriminating evidence, as well as those who sent the transports crashing into us. Certainly, we have two chains of such, from what my husband found, and from whoever instigated the attacks on CI and on our home."

"That would be an extreme set of actions...."

"It appears to me that this is evidence of serious subversion, both of the United States, and the Confederation. Can you disagree?" she asked, *the face* still on.

He stared back, then took a deep breath. "No, madame, I cannot." From his headset, he called Confederation Security.

Hours later, they went down to the break room where Rhys, Janine, John, and Marie were sitting around a table. Rafe and Amelie came over with cups of hot water, and Amelie pulled some teabags out of her bag. "Someday," she said, "There will be actual tea and coffee in break rooms, not merely tea or coffee beverages."

"Mother, father." He nodded. "I should introduce you. This is Janine Smith, the pilot I have been training with."

"A pleasure. Call me Amelie", she said, as she shook Janine's hand, seeing a slender woman with warm brown skin, shoulder-length thin braids, and a very mixed, nervous look in her eyes. "Rhys, do you mean to tell me that you didn't tell her I don't bite friends?"

"He did, but there's a difference between being told that, and knowing it," Janine responded.

"Rafe," he said, and shook her hand as well.

"How are things progressing?" Rhys asked.

"Michael called Security several hours ago," she answered. "There were several other attacks against some corporate support buildings, but we were the only ones individually attacked. It is as though one of the old wars I remember between trillionaires has risen its ugly head, but this time it is against us." Sighing, she added, "The order has just been given grounding all private aircraft in this region. The United States authorities and Confederation Security will sort this out over the next few days."

"The first teams of marshals, supported by the local police, have gone out," Rafe added.

Janine blew out a deep breath. "I have to say, this has been an interesting evening." She shook her head. "Rhys, you sure know how to show a girl an exciting evening out," she added.

His *face* gone, the two smiled at each other, and he replied, "It's a family trait." The chemistry was obvious, and Amelie and Rafe chuckled softly.

"My evenings are usually a lot quieter, involving online fantasy gaming with friends." She took a sip of the coffee. "I should introduce you to them. One's a handicapped woman who makes really lovely jewelry."

"Handicapped?"

"Yeah, she's got some learning process disorder in her brain, so she sometimes has trouble making herself understood. She plays a good game, though."

Across the table, Marie turned to John, "They warned me this job could get interesting."

"These folks don't call security when a paparazzi is bothering them. That's why we checked out the body armor, as well as the weapons," John replied.

"I'm sure glad we did. The company requiring us to get on the mesh never meant that much to me until this evening, but it would have been a lot harder to find the snipers without the link to the drones through the house AI."

A man walked into the break room, and came over to them. "Gentlepeople, as Mr. Ukiteyedi does not expect more excitement before morning, we have a meeting room with several couches, if you wish to catch some sleep." Seeing them all nod, even Amelie showing some tiredness in her face, he went on, "If you would care to follow me. "

29

END OF THE FIRST BATTLE

No one slept well. Without saying anything, John and Marie took shifts. In the morning, Michael and Barbara came into the conference room to meet with Amelie and Rafe, and Michael said there would be some food and drinks up shortly.

Amelie asked, "What is the situation?"

"I gather it's touch and go," Michael began, when there was a knock at the door. Barbara went to answer it, and returned, followed by a man in a Confederation Security uniform, wearing a heads-up AR link under his cap.

"Captain Ross, this is my manager, Michael Ukiteyedi, and these are Amelie Trouve and Rafe Maxwell, who brought all this to our attention," she said.

They shook hands and Barbara and Ross sat. "We hope that we've gotten it settled. A number of the targets have been arrested and brought in, but some were gone when our teams arrived, and some were resisted with violence. A number of people were injured, and several killed. Two people that we were after resisted arrested and tried to escape, but their vehicle was shot down with a rocket that was not ours, killing one target, and injuring the other three aboard. Also, we're starting to get reports of violence around the world, though."

"Who was the target of that attack?"

"Edward Krock and his wife. She is in the hospital." Amelie nodded, then thought for a minute. "Do you believe it will be safe for us to return home today?"

"Perhaps, although we'll arrange for police protection."

"*Merci,* that would be good, especially since M. Krock now has even more reason to dislike me, given that I control Krock Industries. We will have to arrange to have our roof repaired."

"Mother?"

"Oui?"

"I assume we'll have dinner together this evening. I trust you won't mind if Janine joins us?" Janine smiled at him.

"Non."

"Oh, and for dessert, I think I'll have a strawberry cheesecake."

30

AFTERMATH

Gliance ran her fingers through her hair as she looked around at the virtual meeting. It had been nearly twenty-five years since she was chair, and they had not been good ones. There were only ninety-seven of them left, the families that used to bestride the world as titans, disposing it as they would, leaving the rabble to think they had any control. Looking at the AR controls, she began, "I see that we are all here. Do the committees have reports? Action committee?"

"Trouve and Maxwell's intrusions triggered premature actions, including violence and attempted coups around the world, which resulted in a number of significant losses when they were crushed. However, the focus on them allowed us to make some moves that we had not expected to be available yet. They either are not aware of, or unable within their own parameters to deal with either the conservative religious groups or the nationalists, and things are moving along there well, although it looks like triggering Plan A will have to be pushed back several years." Jim Warton ended with a self-satisfied smile. "We're planning on setting up an invitation-only discount club in our stores, with events to sell firearms and ammunition at discount rates."

"Ve vould appreciate your assistance in arranging for such around Russia and its allies," said Rybinsk, who had risen after Olikovsky's disappearance long before.

"We're happy to assist."

"Finance?" Gliance asked.

Johnson looked up. "From the family reports, as Action has reported, they not only tracked some of our hidden resources, but the Confederation forced many of us to flee to Taiwan and elsewhere." She rolled her eyes. "However, the damned Confederation hasn't hit any of our major resources in several years. I think it's past time for us to ramp up our serious moves against the Confederation."

"Security?"

"My security people, along with the reports I have from our moles, tell me that we are secure for now. An attack on the Confederation would definitively get their attention back on us, but I agree, our only real security is their destruction."

"Very good. Masterson, political committee?"

"The fervor of the public over the Confederation is slowly settling down. Our supporters, especially the ones who believe that they share our worldview, along with the amusing groups of nationalists, are coalescing. Were money and other assistance provided directly to them, rather than through the Old Believers and such, might push them to make a move, and right now would be too soon. We should begin to fund them, but it should take several years."

"Has your committee settled on any actions that we might begin to undertake?"

"We have disagreements. One faction is looking at the possibility, with the aid of an interesting weapon we have developed, of beheading the Confederation. If we arrange for civil disruption in the States, Russia, Nigeria, India, and the EU, that might well result in the collapse of our enemies."

"And the other faction?"

"We will have a starship. It will not take long to load ourselves, some tens of thousands of our people, along with adequate supplies and robots, and leave. There are several possible planets that could be colonized, and we will no longer be bothered. Let me note that the interesting weapon can be used internally to assure us that our people won't change their minds, either."

"Interesting. Very interesting. Those that would like to discuss these two options, let us meet after we close this session. Should we come to any decisions on either or both, we will notify the rest of you." She looked around. "Is there anything else? Unless there is any new business, I think this wraps up this brief meeting."

All but a dozen winked out, and she looked at Jerrie. "The ship is coming well?"

He smiled. "There are actually two of them. We have arranged it so that first one is 'having construction issues', then the other one has issues. Either will be ready within four years."

"Excellent!" replied Gliance. "Perhaps we should think about arranging for at-will flights to the station under false names, via private launch, to ramp up around then."

"Already done," replied Masterson. "We can get twenty thousand people up on a dozen flights, our employees mostly in large cargo containers, inside of a few days from launch sites in the West or Taiwan, but some from the rest of the world. We can do more if we simply seize the launch area at Kwajalein." The others all nodded. "If there's less urgency, we can get all thirty thousand up within a week or week and a half."

Looking at Jerrie, "What's the word on planets?"

"There's a few possibilities, but I'd be happier if we could spare another year, since there are two or three that looked very good from automated surveys."

"As we're looking at a target of about four years, we can. I do tend to think that we shouldn't wait too long to identify something perfect, or we'll never leave." She thought for a minute. "Have you considered loading all the cargo that we don't have to worry about?"

Masterson nodded. "We have, and will. Even technology in production isn't going to change for some things in a year or so."

"I'll start moving on that in three years, when the hulls and bulkheads are done, and the cargo bays prepared," Jerrie replied. "And it we have that part of the cargo ready, and we only wind up with twenty thousand to move up, so much the better."

"Now about this other option...there's no reason we can't activate both, with the starship as a fallback."

"I like that," replied al Sultan. "It is always good to have a Plan B".

"Tell us about these interesting weapons, M. Cheng Chen-Tao?" Gliance asked.

"Modifications to meshbots. Wireless power, provided by a controller within twenty meters, which allows them to move, and swarm, outside the human body."

"You say 'swarm'," commented the elder Wu. "That implies many things."

"Intentionally. They can move across a floor, or other surfaces, and will target anyone with an active mesh, eat their way through the skin, and shut them down. We hope to have improved capabilities soon." Cheng smiled, and saw answering smiles from the others.

"So," elder Wu said. "A close range weapon."

"True," Cheng replied. "But there are many ways to arrange delivery."

31

ENGRELAY NEOWEB, INTERIM—TWO YEARS LATER

"Jacinda Macsen here, with Engrelay NeoWeb, *your* source of curated, verified news of the Terran Confederation and beyond! If something's going on, you'll hear it here! First off, it's two years since the violent attacks in the United States and elsewhere, and the US Attorney General has brought to charges against a sitting Senator, two Congresspersons, two CEOs, and the leaders of three megachurches, Large and unruly crowds of both religious and anti-Confederation supporters of the alleged ringleaders are outside the courthouse in Washington, DC, as well as New York and other cities."

"In international news, the Southern African nations conference at the Confederation building in New York of has announced progress towards a regional alliance to deal with immigrants from the equatorial nations that are still considered uninhabitable, due to the climate change over the last century. And now for a news-related PSA from the Confederation Health Agency."

"This is Dr. Alter, from the National Institute for Allergy and Infectious Diseases, part of the NIH. For anyone who has interaction with the protest crowds, and does not have the medical mesh, we strongly advise you to contact your doctor, as many in those crowds are advertising that they are against vaccinations and other medical protections. Remember, there is no cost to you for these consultations or treatments, should any be required."

The view returned to Macsen. "In other news, the Confederation Space Agency announced the return of the starship Grissom. First reports say they have identified four extrasolar worlds that appear suitable for terraforming, and have placed research stations on those worlds, as well as several others. Stay tuned for details after this break!"

FINAL CHAPTERS: ROSALYN

32

THE MESH

Sissy looked up from wiping the counter and drawled to the two working with her, "Ah, hell, here come that stupid boob who can't talk. Somebody else take her?"

"Nope. I did that las' time," said Jessie. "Had to make it over again." She shook her head. "Billy there ain't no good, he jus' stares at her boobs, like he used to stare at Jane when she was workin' here."

Billy, who'd been bending over reaching into a fridge, stood up with some milk and shook his head. "Did not!"

But it was too late, Rosalyn had walked into the coffee shop and up to the counter. In answer to Sissy's greeting, she said, "Dou'le capp'ccin', who'e mi'k, no whip c'eam, no sy'up."

Sissy said, "Double, no milk, syrup?" Rosalyn repeated again, until Sissy got it, then she made it up as Rosalyn credited for it. As Rosalyn walked out, she heard the young man say quietly, "Don' think she's stupid, she jus' can' talk right." She would have slammed the door, if it would slam. *Just what I needed to start the day, a stupid teen making excuses for me to a couple of girls who had probably been cutting me down the minute they saw me. I can see how the day's going to go.* Anger welled up so fast that she had to wipe away tears with her free hand.

Which was how it went. First there was the long group meeting with the art show director, who told her, in a patronizing tone, that the jury had rejected almost three-quarters of her pieces as "too avant-garde", or "too niche market". Then the transit was running late, to get home to find a message that her caster had a burned-out furnace core and it would be another couple of days before he could cast her pieces.

She finally sat by her system, AR glasses on and a gin and tonic on the table, thinking *I'm just glad I live now, and not half a century ago, so I don't have to worry about paying for a roof over my head or food on the table. Just wish I had more of a clue of what the damn show jury wants.*

A while later, gaming in AR, Jamie, one of her game partners, called her in a private side chat. "Having a bad day, Ros?"

"How could you tell?"

"A number of people are having more trouble than usual understanding you, or at least in time to find your comments useful."

Jamie listened to her rant about the day, and as Ros ran down, said, "Wish Janine was playing. She usually understands you better."

"Ah do, too. We'f known each o'er foah six-seven yeahs, sin' she bought a pie'e of mine at a cahaft faiah, an' we stahted talkin'." Rosalyn gave a sad smile. "But she's not on planet."

"Not...on planet? Where is she? What's she do?"

Rosalyn's sad smile became a much happier one. "She's a Confedahation stahship pilot."

"You kiddin' me?!"

"Nope. She's the 'eal t'ing." She sighed, wistfully. "I miss heah a lot."

"Hey, you need something to cheer you up, I just read an article and thought of you. There's this Institute at the NIH, the NIBIB, down in DC doing research on using the mesh to deal with learning disabilities."

"Tha's paht of mah p'oblem...send me a link to the ah'ticle, woul' you? I am jus' *so* tiah'd of all this."

~

"Hi, I'm Awslyn Ahidge. I've an appointmen' at two."

"M. Ridge?" replied the young person at the reception desk after a pause. "Yes, we've got your information. Would you please sign this health information form?"

Rosalyn came over, read over the usual privacy information, and signed with a stylus on the screen. She sat and pulled out a reader, and had only read for a few minutes when the nurse came out to escort her into the examination room. The woman stepped out and came back a minute or two later with the doctor, a woman a bit shorter than Rosalyn, gray frosting her hair, and the traditional lab coat over normal business wear.

"How do you do, M. Ridge," she said, holding out her hand. "I'm Doctor Friel."

Rosalyn shook the doctor's hand, and said, "Ah've been ahead'ng goo' t'ings about youh t'eatmen's."

"Well, you must understand this is more than just a treatment," the doctor said as they both sat.

"I've ha' some genengeneeahing," Rosalyn worked to say clearly. "Ha' some p'eadispositions foah sev'al diseases, stahtin' when I was a little gi'l. But these ahe bots, 'ight?"

"Well, no. If you've read about the meshbots that have been used for twenty years or so now, these are new, and different. They're not 'bots. Doing this will change who you are. These meshecytes are genengineered cells that we'll be putting into your bloodstream will stay in it and reproduce, new things, not just corrected errors in your natural DNA. And should you have children, they will carry them."

Rosalyn swallowed. "Doctoah, I've bee' 'eadin' abou' the mesh for a few yeahs now, and I'm comfoahtable with the ahegula-r" she said, emphasizing the end of the word, "but even in VAh, I still have the accen'. You unde'stan' the pahblem is the speech impaihmen' is cauahsed by the impaihed language pa'ocessin' ability in my hea'."

"I do understand, and I'm very interested to see just how far we can take this. If you don't mind, let me begin by making clear what the mesh is and does, as opposed to the media's usual misunderstanding."

Rosalyn nodded. "The first component are the meshecytes, which have several functions. They have short-range communication, so that they can talk to each other. Together, they make up a cloud cluster, to monitor your vital signs, and look for markers of diseases. You'll wear a small unit that will monitor them, and that runs an AI. Together, in the event of an emergency, they can broadcast an alert to you, or to anyone nearby. If they get no response, and it's a critical alert, they will go through the nearest 'Net connection to call emergency services."

"Can it oveahe-eact? I don' wan' it cawing if, say, Ah'm on me'ication, and in dee' sleep."

"We'll be doing what's known as precision medicine, and part of the process of installing the meshecytes is to tune it. Another thing that this cloud in your blood can do is a certain amount of emergency repair, so that, for example, if you cut yourself, they will cluster at the wound, and close the veins to stop the bleeding."

"Ah hadn' ahealized it coul' do that f'om my e-eading."

"Yes, well, the technology has moved rapidly. The meshecytes will probably replace the older meshbots, and as I said, your body will reproduce them by itself."

"You ah*eally* wahen't 'xage'ating 'bout changing who Ah am."

"No. With the meshbots, you were more resistant to illness and injury, while with these, it's more so. But let me go on," Rosalyn nodded. "The other thing they do is that as they pass through the larger vessels in your brain, they can pick up the signals that your brain generates in thinking, amplify them, and broadcast them, again short range. The headband picks up the signals and amplifies them, and, under your control, feed some into the local network."

"Does it feed eve'ything? I mean...."

"Not to worry. As I said, it's under your control. It's also not reading your mind, but rather pre-verbalized thoughts. Pictures also, because we can read the visual cortex. You'll have AR in your head, without needing the glasses, with the same ability to control whether you're deeply immersed, and not seeing your real world surrounding, or not."

"Ah'at's the pah' I've 'ead mostly abou'. Saw some peo'le talkin' abou' hackin' the mesh."

"Of course." The doctor shook her head. "There's always the issue of security with servers, but the meshecytes themselves can't be hacked, unless they have physical access to your personal headband - they're effectively read-only. That's a closed circuit, with the base AI on the headband or wherever you want to wear it, and there is security in the protocol. It's akin to a phone call, rather than the Web, and code in the chips in the headband that prevent such access. In fact, for any connection to another person in mesh, you have to explicitly accept each and every connection, nor will it accept a third party connecting without being accepted, and their ID is always visible to you, and cannot be falsified." Dr. Friel smiled. "There are some things that have improved over the decades. They've even got filters, which help you from getting overwhelmed by incoming information, doing things like not giving you duplicates. However, here's where it gets interesting. In the mesh, you can store whatever you want, meaning that you don't ever have to forget what you record, and it is retrievable on request. But you can also invoke the AI, really, expert systems on the local unit, and they can provide advice, additional information, and as you wish, control the meshecytes in your system to do such things as aid in moving your tongue, which of course is what you're interested in."

"Wi' the...mesh 'ecord evahythin'?"

"No, only what you tell it to, other than purely medical information. It certainly doesn't have nearly enough storage to record everything. They can also be quiesced on your mental command, though of course this is not recommended."

"An' youah thinkin' aht the AI can use the meshecytes to contahol my tong'."

"You've gotten ahead of me. That's exactly right."

"Wha' do we nee' to do? Ah'm 'eady to tah'y the mesh."

"Let us do a full physical with blood work, so that we can decide how to proceed."

Rosalyn nodded, and Friel began the physical.

A week later, Rosalyn took the train from Philadelphia's 30th St. Station down to Union Station in DC, then the Metro up to the NIH, and went into the campus, excited over the email saying that they'd take her case. She was smiling as Dr. Friel said, " You'll be happy to know, M. Ridge, that we've done the initial customization, so we're not expecting any issues. You should expect to have a slight fever for a day or so." Seeing Rosalyn's nod, she went on, "You haven't had anything to eat or drink since 2100 last night?" Rosalyn nodded again. "Excellent. Alvin, here," she said nodding at the nurse, "will be administering the first round of meshecytes. If everything goes well, we'll be supplying you with a specialized headband, and some software to run, to work on tuning the meshecytes over the next two weeks, when you'll come back in for the final infusion." Standing, she added, "Since you mentioned it last week, rest assured that the software and the firmware in the headband is absolutely current on security." Shaking Rosalyn's hand, she left the room.

Alvin, a thin, middle-aged black man, had her sit back in the chair, changing the configuration so that she was lying almost flat, and then used the small cup-shaped unit that automatically identified the vein and inserted the needle with little pain. Then he connected the bag of infusion with the meshecytes in it, and began the drip. "This will take about half an hour. We don't want to do it too quickly, just a slow and steady introduction. I'll sit here for a few minutes, but if anything goes wrong after I leave, push this button, and I'll be in here with help in a minute." She nodded and he sat, monitoring the progress. Soon, though, he stepped out, and she lay there, trying to see if she was feeling anything.

He came back in after a while, double-checked that the infusion was completed and removed the needle, then went out to come back in shortly trailing the doctor. "How are you feeling?" Dr. Friel asked.

Rosalyn started to open her mouth, closed it for a minute, then said, "So' of feel a kin' of hum."

"Interesting. We've had people mention something about a faint hum before. Here, try on the headband." She handed Rosalyn something that resembled a custom AR headband, with a silvery mesh that would cover the top of her head, and a small box on it, around the size of the mouse her grandparents used on their computers. Pulling her thick dark hair tight, she put it on. Alvin reached over, and guided her finger to a button that caused the headband to snug tight but comfortable. Then he moved her finger to the button next to it, and she heard the hum, much more clearly. "You should give it a name. as you would any house AS, and say 'hello' to it."

She thought for a minute, then said, *"Hi, Ahlan."* Slowly her vision grew a little dimmer, and then she saw a ghostly outline of a man's head. It seemed to acknowledge her, and then the humming grew louder. "It's getting louder."

"That part's normal," said Dr. Friel. "Give it some time. Among other things, it's tuning to your auditory cortex." The doctor and Alvin sat, monitoring her as over the next fifteen minutes, the humming peaked, then after a bit she realized it was getting quieter. Looking up, the doctor and nurse smiled encouragement, and within half an hour, she could barely hear it. "Has it quieted now?" the doctor asked, and at Rosalyn's nod, said, "Now, call the name, and ask it to tune your AR."

She did, and for a while watched the fireworks behind her eyelids as the meshecytes were tuned to her visual cortex. That settled down, and now she could see the figure of Alan Turing. Asking him to dim the AR, she looked up at Dr. Friel and Alvin and smiled. "Can see AAh, now."

"Excellent. We'd like you to stay here another hour for observation, but we'll release you to go home after that."

"Can I use it wit' 'eag'lah AAH on the 'Net?"

"Yes, but it is configured for maximum security, which may interfere with some of what you may want to do."

"Can we do more in a couple weeks?"

"Yes. At that point, the mesh will be fully active, and can provide an active defense in depth."

After the hour was gone, she thanked the two, Rosalyn headed home, down to the Metro, then the train back to Philadelphia, and finally the trolley home. That night, her gaming friends commented on her being a little slow that evening. She put them off, saying that she had a new interface for AR, and it was going to take time getting used to it.

Over the following two weeks, she found herself getting used to the mesh, and the feeling grew that the meshecytes and Alan were getting used to her. Occasionally, she'd feel a slight shiver, but that never lasted long, although gaming had definite issues. The second weekend, she was in a fast-moving game with friends, and froze during a fight. She sat there, annoyed, and finally called, *"Ahlan, turn down the security on the protocols my game is using."*

"Madame, I will do so if you require it, but I strongly recommend against it. There is a current attack, spreading over much of the continent. It is using denial of service to break security, then downloading and running malware which is targeted not only at 'Net service, but also at mesh users. I have blunted a number of attacks on us."

Oh, shit! she thought. *"Canceh pahevious ahequest. Can you give me a visuah monitoh of the attacks?"*

"Certainly, madame." A virtual pane appeared, with four gauges, one for the 'Net, one for bandwidth, one for attacks, and one for mesh attacks.

It took a while before she was back in the game. When they started complaining that they'd needed her, she explained what had happened, which put a real damper on the game. Several players did things out of game, and Jamie returned with "She's right, it's really bad this evening." They wound down, and spent a while socializing.

Monday, as she was getting ready for a quiet evening, she found a message in her queue from Janine. Opening it eagerly, she found that they expected to be back in-system in a few weeks, and was looking forward to getting together. *Not many people get interstellar messages, even if they're batched.* She felt warmed by that, from a friend who cared.

More than just ready for the second visit, she found herself excited and worried at the same time. Now that she had a taste of the mesh, she liked it, but found herself afraid of more power than she could handle. She couldn't stop thinking, all the way down to DC, and didn't show it going in, but Dr. Friel got her to admit it, after reviewing her sensor readings.

"Don't worry, M. Ridge. If it does start to feel like too much, you can always turn it down." She talked her through it, then bringing it back up to the level that Rosalyn had been using it at the last week.

Then Alvin inserted the needle, and started the second infusion. As the half hour passed, she found that, rather than like the last time, when there was a hum, this time she was vibrating. Finally complete, he took the needle out, and they let her lie for half an hour, again. They came in, to find her fidgeting, her breath coming a little rapidly, and licking her lips. "How are you feeling, M. Ridge?"

"Li'e I wan' to get up an' *do* some'ing...ow!"

"What was that?"

"I fel' a faint sho' in my mouf as I'm tal'in', my tong', my li's."

"Dial it down some." Rosalyn did that, and the whole feeling quieted. "Let us run through the analysis before you go home. Do what you did last time, take time before you turn it up, then little by little. Come back in next week, and we'll start your training." She nodded, and the doctor ran through the checks.

"Doctor, I heahd about attacks on the 'Net that ha' an effe't on th' mesh, las' weeken', Alan ha' me no' turn down secuahity, there was a bi' attack."

"I know about that as well, and it concerns me. If you come across anything more, please let me know." After a while, the doctor sent her home to Philly.

Back in Bethesda the following week, she sat in the exam room again with Dr. Friel monitoring the sensors. The doctor had given her a wired connection to the system, and told her she was downloading an experimental speech therapy program that the project had developed. "Okay, now I want you to dial it up to just where you can barely feel the shocks. Then I want you to say what you said before, about the faint shocks." She did that, and then the doctor asked, "Do they shock come all over, or just in parts of your mouth.

"Pahts of my mouf."

"Tell your AI to see if it can push, rather than shock. I think it's giving you a stimulus, but it's too strong."

Rosalyn did that, then said, "Pahrts of my moufth."

Dr. Friel smiled, and asked, "Did you hear what you said?"

"No. I awways hear myse'f saying it righ' in my head, bu' then I crahinge when I heah a recoahding."

The doctor played back her first statement, then after she'd told it to shift from shock to push. Rosalyn's face lit up in a smile, and Friel smiled back, "It's not going to work overnight, but it sounds as though it might begin to help. Let the AI give you speech practice from the the software I uploaded. If you have anything that disturbs you, about anything, please contact me."

Rosalyn was still smiling as she left. Over the next few weeks, she practiced for what became several hours every day, though she dialed it way back when she was online with her friends and gaming, wanting to surprise them.

She found herself turning the meshecytes up, slowly, as she grew more comfortable of her control. On the other hand, as she did, she found the AI selecting events going on in the world that were making everyone nervous, and made her glad she'd done almost no tweaking on the security. The attacks on the 'Net, and major backbone support were increasing, seemingly from nowhere traceable. It seemed as though something new was going on, not seen this bad in decades, since the old days before the Confederation was formed.

She commented as much to Dr. Friel, talking to her over AR, who was equally worried. "I'd heard of small attacks before we started you on the mesh. So far, we've seen nothing on the mesh proper, which is running in parallel with the 'Net, and probably will for years to come since so much is connected. You might come in, and we can update your AI. Then you'll be able to tell it to increase its active security measures." Smiling, she asked, "Have you let your friends know how well this is working?"

"Naht yet, but I will, soon. Lis-ten-in' to myse-l-f, I'm sta-r-t-ing to soun-d li-ike I do in mah head." Nodding, she added, "I know, it ta-k-es time."

"That's wonderful. Keep at it." With that, the doctor signed off.

Not long after, Rosalyn got a surprise call. "Janine! You'ahre back in-systehm!"

"Rhys and I are in orbit now, and will be down today. Maybe we can get together next week or so."

"Ah'd love that!"

Janine had a puzzled look on her dark face. "Rosalyn? Your...well, voice? It's much more towards standard! I'm not just talking to an AS, am I?"

A grin took over Rosalyn's face. "No Ahtificial Stupid involved. Ah've been savin' it as a surprahse for all my f-riends, so you've just become th' fahst to know. Ah'm on the mesh, through a r-eseahch prog-ram at the NIH, and it's been helpin' me lea-rn to speak co-rrect-ly."

"Oh, Ros, I'm so happy for you! Give us a couple days to settle in for the time being, and I'm sure Rhys and his folks would love to meet you, and hear all about it."

"His folks? They'd be interested?"

"His mother would probably be interested in providing additional funding for this project."

"But, she doan' know me. She have resources?"

Janine smiled broadly. "My mother-in-law is Amelie Trouve."

Rosalyn's mouth fell open. "The millionaire? The *woman whose sister was...?!*"

"None other. I'll ask her not to scare you when you come. She only bites nasty people."

They wound down and signed off. Rosalyn leaned back in chair shaking her head. *Talk about having completely unexpected connections! A woman comes to a craft fair, and buys one of my avant-garde pieces, we turn into friends, and....*

She spent the afternoon talking to her parents, with her sister joining the call. "Can you geh me inta this pahogaham, deah? It woul' be wonde'ful to speak moah cleahly," her mother asked.

"You wehre neve-r much for tech-ni-cal, mom, but we can set up an appoin-t-ment, and see wha' she says."

"Meh, too," said her sister.

"We'll see wha't we can do," Rosalyn said, thinking that maybe she should plead with Janine's mother-in-law.

Two days later Rosalyn was out, and decided to stop in for coffee. She could see the look on the faces of the three teenagers inside, and smiled. Walking up to the counter, she said, "Dou-ble cappuccino, who-le milk, no whipp-ed c-ream, no sy-rup." All three looked at her, and then one went to make the coffee. As she walked out, she tossed over her shoulder, "Ah, the mesh is won-der-ful.", and saw the jaws drop on the three behind the counter.

33

PLANS AND REPERCUSSIONS

"They have done *what?!*" Cheng Chen-Tao hissed.

"The Abkhazians who were programming our bots apparently were dealing with the leaders of their would-be country. After they became aware of how well they worked in the SADR, decided to use some them on Georgian government officials that they saw as a threat. They purchased identical bots from us, had the same programming applied, and used them." replied Cheng Duyi.

"Chen-Tao is correct in his concern," said the elder Wu. "It will point the damnable Confederation directly at us, or at least at our eastern European associates. Worse, our pieces are not all in place yet for Plan A." He thought for a minute. "Were they shipped from here?"

"Give me a moment," replied Cheng Duyi, pulling on his AR headset. He was silent for several minutes, then pulled it off and looked up. "No. First, they were shipped to western Morocco, the area under control of the SADR. From there, they appear to have been transshipped to Abkhazia."

"Both unrecognized countries, and so not eligible to join the Confederation, unless they agree to become territories." The elder Wu stroked his chin. "If it becomes clear that Taiwan is the source of the bots, we will of course have the President's office issue a statement condemning the attacks, and that there will be repercussions for those who knowingly sold our products for highly unauthorized uses." Everyone smiled at that. "Until then, we need not say anything."

"I believe, however, there should be repercussions for using the bots without our permission, possibly leading to the discovery of them before we plan to use them," Nhleko said.

The elder Wu looked at Nhleko. "What are you thinking?"

"That the Abkhazians need to be taught a lesson. Perhaps, if there were some way to activate them in storage…."

Cheng Chen-Tao gave a hard laugh. "Or perhaps the people who did the work should be taught the lesson, elder?" Seeing elder Wu nod, he added, "Maybe an update to the programming?"

The elder Wu looked around, and then nodded.

34

ARTIST AND AGENT

"Rosalyn, it's so good to see you in person," Janine said, hugging her once she was through the door, then led her down the hall into a living room with modern, self-adjusting chairs and two couches. The room had a high ceiling, and there was a fireplace on one wall. "Let me introduce you, you know my Rhys, and these are his folks, Amelie Trouve, and Rafe Maxwell. Amelie, Rafe, this is my dear friend Rosalyn Ridge."

"Rosalyn, *ma chère*, it is a pleasure. Janine has spoken very well of you," she said, reaching forward to clasp Rosalyn's hands.

The woman before Rosalyn was in her sixties, loose ringlets of salt and pepper hair hanging to her shoulders. Rosalyn, dressed to the hilt, her thick brown hair in a French braid curled on top of her head, was nervous, and licked her lips. "It's an hono-r to mee-t you, M. T-rouve," Rosalyn said, carefully enunciating, with the help of the mesh.

"*Non*, none of this nonsense. Amelie, *s'il vous plaît.* May I call you Rosalyn?"

"P-lease."

"And this is Rafe." Rafe greeted her with a very British accent, but her focus was on Amelie. "Now come, let us sit down. We have some excellent coffee, or tea, if you prefer?"

"Coffee, p-lease." Amelie leading, they all sat, and called someone in the other room.

"So, Janine tells me that you are in some program that is using the mesh to help you overcome a speech issue?"

"Yes." This was far more familiar ground, having had to explain it to her friends and business customers. "I have a lea-r-ning diso-rd-er due to some p-roblem wi' the language p-rocessin' a-rea of mah b-ahrain. Alan, my peahrsonal AI in the mesh, is still wo-rkin' to use the meshecytes in mah bloodst-ream to hel-p me move mah mouth the ahight," she pushed herself to repeat the word, "r-ight way."

"Zat's marvelous. Please send me a link to your doctor. I should like to speak with them about supporting this work. It is a wonderful use of the mesh far beyond what the 'Net can dream of, to make real changes in the real world."

A man came in, carrying drinks, and handed Rosalyn coffee. "Dr. F-riel is at the NIH in Bethesda." Rosalyn sipped the coffee, then looked down. "This is wonde-r-ful coffee."

"We get good beans, and grind them ourselves," said Rafe, who had been sitting back, his elbow on the arm of the chair. "None of 'this packet in our machine will be great' garbage. I even drink it some of the time," he smiled, adding. "Though I usually prefer good tea."

Rosalyn was at a loss, wondering what to say to someone this important. She looked up, to see Janine smiling. "Really, Ros, she won't bite. Have you been in any shows lately?"

Grateful for the lead, she could move into comfortable territory. "I'll be in a ju-ried show soon, but they only accep-ted about a quahrte-r of what I want-ed to pu' in. I can almos' unde-rstan-d 'too avan'-gahrde', but 'too niche mahrket'?"

Amelie, Rafe, and Rhys broke out in laughter. Putting down her coffee, Amelie managed to get her laughter under control. "Too avant-garde means that they may have seen one or two things like it in the last year, and aren't sure yet if it will become *en vogue*, or fade away, and don't want to look as though they had made the wrong choice before their peers. Let us ignore the fact that if they brought it in, they could make it *en vogue*." She shook her head. "They are second or third level people, unsure of themselves, and always looking to the big names to follow." She paused and took a sip of her coffee, then went on. "Too niche means they have no idea who'd buy it, or where it would go. It also means they really don't know the people who come to the show, since all they do is look at what the other big shows do."

"She's quite right," added Rafe. "I've had the misfortune of seeing some of what passes for high style since I was young, and far too much of it, sold in a smaller venue, would be kitsch."

"Would you permit me to see the full catalog of what you had offered to the show?" Amelie asked.

"Ce-rtainly. I can send my cat-alog...."

"Ros! Don't you have it in the mesh?" exclaimed Janine.

Rosalyn's mouth opened, closed. Then she shook her head. "I do. I did-n't even think of it. A-re you...?"

"Of course we are all on the mesh. Here, let me give you a virtual table," Amelie said.

Bringing up her AR via mesh, she saw a virtual table, and laid out from her mesh storage the entire 3-D catalog that she'd created in mesh before transferring it to display for the 'Net weeks ago. To her complete delight, the others wandered through it as though they were wandering through an opening in a gallery. Several times, she saw Amelie and Janine exclaiming over pieces. At last they were all virtually standing in front of the display.

"That small sculpture, the brass and copper tree, and that set of earrings and necklace that you have listed as item thirteen, are either of them going into the show, and if not, what are the prices?"

"No. The t-ree was 'too niche', and the other 'too avan'-gahrde'. Given how much time I spen' on them I was askin' twelve hun'red foah the t-ree, an-d fifteen hun'red foah the set."

Amelie shook her head. "I can see those were constructions, not cast. You are undervaluing your work and time. If you are having pieces accepted in juried shows, you should raise your prices by at least a quarter. I will give you sixteen hundred for the tree, and two thousand for the jewelry set."

Rosalyn's mouth fell open. It took her a moment to get out, in mesh, "No, that's too much…"

"*Non*, it is not. Janine, you and Rhys were planning on going to the art show, *oui?*"

"Yeah, we were."

"Would you care to wear ze jewelry set zat day?" Janine smiled broadly. "And you will go by ze show runners, and tell zem how much you enjoy ze show."

"Amelie, you are evil!" answered Janine, laughing.

Rosalyn looked from the older woman to the younger. "I feel like I'm takin-g a-dvantage of a f-riend."

Rhys looked at her, a serious look on his face. "You are not. My mother would not buy if she did not actually like them, and think them worth it. This is not a competition."

"And the circle of friends now includes you, Ros," Janine added. "Even beyond all that, why not help a friend, especially when she's dealing with the idiots of the world who are always with us, not to mention actual enemies?"

Rosalyn relaxed back in her chair, feeling it adjust itself to her new position, and looked at the others. In mesh, she said, "*We hear all the talk of the new world we're building. I, at least, don't run into many people who really believe in it. Certainly, it's not what you hear in some media, but if it was not for this new world, I would have trouble keeping a roof over my head, much less making jewelry. Thank you.*" She paused. "*What do you mean, actual enemies?*"

"The remaining members of the former 400 have hated me with a passion since I went to the UN and gave evidence against them. There have been a number of assassination attempts over the years," Amelie said, a hard smile on her face.

"We were attacked in this house several years ago, an assassination attempt, apparently related to our work ferreting out the ex-trillionaires. The house was damaged, even though it is armored. We paid for the repairs, since we can afford to have them privately done, and it frees up the public resources to repair the homes and apartments of neighbors who don't have such resources," Rafe said. He noticed the look on Rosalyn's face. "Yes?"

"Um, I, it's, ah, someone t-ried to assahssinate you? R-ight he-re?" Her mouth hung open for a minute, then she closed it. "So-rr-y, that just seems like something out of a video or a novel, not something that happens to someone you meet in r-eal life." Rosalyn paused, then added, "And you ah both he-re, so I can't ask 'how was the play?'" Rhys and Janine laughed, while Amelie and Rafe looked puzzled for a minute, then, having looked it up in mesh, smiled. Rosalyn took a sip of coffee. "About what you said afteah that though, I can just heah a f-riend of mine saying 'f-rom each acco-rding to theah abilities, to each acco-rding to theah need.'"

"Marx was a brilliant analyst. His prescriptions might have worked in his time, but not after...but now we have the means to make that possible," replied Amelie. "The world changes. When we can build machines that replace sweat shops, what should the people who worked them do, starve? Commit terrorism against people who have no control over resources, hoping to force them to do something that is beyond their control" She shook her head. "Once we broke the trillionaires and billionaires, who together owned eighty percent of everything, and turned those like myself into millionaires, the resources were there. Why should shelter, food, water, and utilities be owned by anyone other than those that use them? Why profit from others' suffering?" She shook her head. "Freed from that, we have no shortage of power, yet glaciers are coming back. Our starships have leapt ahead in their technology, and we are expanding into the universe, with all its wonders." Amelie's face grew more serious. "But do not be too quick to thank us. Some things have come to mind that I need to consider further that might affect you." Rosalyn looked at her, curious. "But not now. Come, lunch is almost ready."

~

After Rosalyn had left, Rhys turned to Amelie. "Very well, mother, spit it out. What unpleasantness are you thinking of for Ros?"

His mother's look was not pleasant. "I am still trying to find out where *la lie de l'humanité* were hiding their money and power. It has to be somewhere that kind of money is still meaningful."

"They have been using it, also," added Rafe. "The so-called conservative media has been doing its best in the years you were away, and there have been an increasing number of attacks and insurrections." A grim smile spread over his father's face. "I still assume it will be in one of the remaining wealth havens, unrecognized countries that are not part of the Confederation."

Rhys hmmed, then said. "That small thing in the ocean is a joke. Several of the others are frequently fighting, either for their existence, or to expand the territory they control." He looked at Janine. "Something funny, dearest?"

She shook her head. "I didn't grow up in a good neighborhood, and it just hit me as strange to listen to my husband and in-laws not merely talking serious geopolitics, but who are involved in it."

"*Ma cherie*, I was dragged, literally, into the world of the trillionaires as an ignorant child of twelve, and had to learn it just to survive. We 'ave succeeded, and now you're part of *us*. That last attack was not, could not have been a final throw, which means we are fighting for our very existence."

Janine smiled a grim smile back. "I won't ever forget flying in with Rhys to rescue you. I still get occasional nightmares. I surely don't want to do anything like that again." She leaned into Rhys' arm. They were all quiet for a bit.

"Have you seen any clues concerning their plans, Mother?"

Amelie's smile was hard and cold. "Zis is to be kept quiet of course, but Confederation Security contacted me not long ago. There have been several incidents lately. A large scale attack on the 'Net, with attempts to break into the mesh. Indications are that it came from several of the small countries that had a coup, or rigged elections, in the aftermath of when we were attacked, or since. There have also been some very odd attacks in several of the unrecognized countries. At first, it looked like power struggles, but then a minister was killed in Georgia, and being part of the Confederation, they asked for help. Security is still not sure what killed him. Most people there still have meshbots, not the new meshecytes, and his meshbots all reported normal, so they're looking into this, but it's taking time." She shook her head. "They have suspicions that these are tests of a new weapon, but nothing definite yet. They are thinking that something may be coming down the road."

Rhys nodded. "Who produced their meshbots? Could the factory have been hacked? If so, they might be able to tell from the programming."

"Something that sounds as sophisticated as that, of course, requires money and long-term planning," added Rafe. "But who set that up is the question."

"*Oui.* The bots were standard, and could have been produced in the West, or the East. They had the manufacturer's logos, but some had serial numbers didn't exist, and the manufacturers have been carefully investigated. The programming was another story, from what I hear," replied Amelie.

"Could someone have found a way to attack meshbots from a distance?" Janine asked.

"That's unlikely," answered Rhys. "They're designed to only respond to sources at a very specific distance, and many people don't have a full AI, but only a less expensive artificial stupid which is read only, unless it is physically connected. We are not sure how any of this interacts with meshecytes." She shook her head. "Then there's the point that some, not all, were strange."

"Strange? Wouldn't Taiwan be the most likely source? They're big in low-cost meshbots, as well as the related industries, and could easily produce custom meshbots." Janine ventured.

Rhys nodded. "That would seem reasonable, but it just looks too obvious."

"Perhaps manufactured in Taiwan, shipped to one of those other non-countries and someone there did the specific programming, then shipped from there?" she asked. The other three looked at each other, then at her, and Rhys tapped her on the nose with a finger.

Amelie and Rafe were nodding. "We have been beating our heads on the wall trying to guess, and here you point out the obvious, my dear." Rafe said.

"*Oui*. And the unrecognized nations are what I was thinking of, and I have contacts in several of them. They may be able to locate information locally, but getting it out is always an issue."

"And you're thinking Ros would be a useful mule," said Janine, harshly.

"I would not put it that way, rather, when necessity presses, one uses any tools at hand. However, we will not disguise it, rather we will offer her the choice. I suspect you may be surprised by her answer, *ma chérie.*"

Several days later, Amelie, Rafe, and Janine were sitting in the living room talking. Rhys took a sip of his coffee, "Mother, has Security contacted you about the possibility that Janine suggested, that the bots were produced in one place, and programmed in another?"

Amelie nodded, and her accent grew heavy. "Actually, zey 'ave, late yesterday. Right now, what zey have is zat se first attack was in Laayoune, in ze SADR, which is in ze western Sahara.. Zere was a closed-door meeting between ze minister of transportation, and ze man running ze major shipping agency. Ze guards outside heard yelling, zen nothing. By ze time zey got ze locked doors open, both were dead. Ze reports were odd, including no weapon marks. Zen one in Georgia, where ze finance minister and ze defense minister had a meeting, and ze guards outside here some odd noises. When zey opened ze doors, ze two were dead, though ze guards reported some blood on ze victims socks. Zat was ze one zat Confederation Security investigated." She took a drink, thought for a couple of minutes, then went on, her accent not as strong. "Zen, several weeks later, zere was a severe attack in Sukhumi, in Abhkazia. There was an office building near the central bazaar, and several dozen people were killed that we know of, and we don't know what happened, or why it stopped."

"Could the one in Abhkazia be a case where the bots were activated and released by accident?" Rhys asked, then he stopped, held up his hand, and thought for a minute. "Or two other possibilities - first, that they were working on a new batch, and there was an error in the programming. The last possibility is nastier, that they were given an update, and that attack was deliberate."

"Could the folks behind these attacks they be covering their tracks?" asked Janine. "Or telling the people who were doing the programming that they were not allowed to use them for their own purposes...at least yet. *Oui.* And if that is the case, then it suggests that someone elsewhere was running the whole thing. And now I agree, that level of organization could well be in Taiwan, with so many remnants of the trillionaire organizations."

Janine looked from one to the other of them, all with deadly serious faces. "What does this all mean?"

"That the Confederation may very well have to accede to China's demands that Taiwan be taken into the Confederation involuntarily." She looked at Janine. "Think it through, *ma cherie.*"

Janine was quiet for a bit, then said, "The bots were manufactured in Taipei, shipped dormant through Laayoune, and programmed in Sakhumi, then perhaps shipped back to Taipei. On the way, the people doing the planning wanted to test them, maybe that was the one in the SADR." Amelie nodded. "That seems reasonable. But now, who are they going to hit, and when?" She could feel Rhys nodding, and he tightened his arm around her.

"*Zat* is ze question, though the one in the SADR might have been done as a favor. Très *bien,*" Amelie said. "*Ma cherie*, you understand I am not being a difficult mother-in-law, but making sure that you are up to speed, as they say, not merely as part of this family, but to keep you alive since you are."

"I realized I'd be living in a world nothing like the one I grew up in when I said yes to Rhys. I suppose that first time, when we came for you, everything moved so fast that it felt like trouble in the neighborhood. Now that we're back for a few months from space, I realize how much more it is, especially as I read the news about the world since we left, and that it's time to watch out and pay attention. A smart person learns from someone who's been there how to avoid trouble, rather than finding new ways to land in trouble." She paused. "I've been studying other things, too," She paused again, calling on the mesh to help her pronunciation, licked her lips and said. "so *merci, belle-mére*." She could feel Rhys looking at her, but to her complete surprise, Amelie got up and came over with her arms wide. She rose and the two women held each other, and Amelie kissed her on both cheeks. Starting to let go, she was stunned to see tears in the older woman's eyes. "Amelie?"

"Other than *mon cher* Rafe, and *mon fils,* there have not been many times in my life when someone went out of their way to show that they cared about *moi,* not for who or what I was, *ma trés cherie.*" Amelie hugged her again, and Janine found tears in her own eyes, as well as a smile that seemed to have occupied her whole face.

"B*elle-mère*, first, you and your late sister were heroes of the world, not someone ordinary people meet. Then you were Rhys' mother, and a powerful millionaire. But I hear Rhys say things like 'we're Terrans,' not 'Americans' or 'British' or whatever, and meaning it, and that came from no one but you and Rafe, and where I grew up, that meant something. You could count on them...and things haven't been as bad as I hear about from before the Confederation, but there's still trouble. I married up, as they say...but now I know I'm part of this family, and family's big to me, that's what I learned from my family." Rafe had risen, a smile on his face, and she turned and hugged him, then they sat down together. "So, we think we know what happened. Now what?"

"It is time for me to look a little more deeply in those areas, and then speak with Security," answered Amelia.

"About sending Ros...," began Janine.

"Do not worry. I would not send her to all three, that would be blatantly obvious, but two...."

35

AN OPPORTUNITY, AND A MISSION

Rosalyn was gaming when she got a side call from Janine, who asked to talk to her via mesh. Switching gears, she connected. "*What's up?*"

"Amelie would like to get together with you. She's thinking of offering you a job that you might be interested in, though it might involve traveling to some unsafe locations.."

"Okay, now you've got me really interested. Let me guess, you can't tell me anymore, even over mesh."

"Got it in one. When would be good this week?"

Invoking her calendar, Rosalyn said "*Day after tomorrow.*"

"Would the evening work? Dinner, perhaps?"

"*Sounds good.*" She nodded. "*See you in a couple of days. I need to get back to the campaign.*"

Two evenings later, the cab left Rosalyn at the door in north New Jersey. Unsure of using the mesh to announce herself, she rang the doorbell, then Janine and Amelie were in mesh with her, and Janine opened the door. They hugged, and Janine hung Rosalyn's hat and jacket in a closet, and led her to the dining room, where they joined the others sitting around an eclectic array of appetizers, a scent of hot and sesame oils wafting from them.

After a Chinese steamed dumpling, Rosalyn leaned back and asked, "Amelie, I must ask - what's so impo-rtant that you didn't even want to talk on the mesh?"

Amelie put her wine glass down. "Everyone knows that I am a patron of the arts among other things. We," she said, waving an arm to include the rest of her family, "are on occasion also deniable assets." Rosalyn's eyes widened. "There are some artists of my acquaintance who I believe you would benefit from studying with for a bit. They are in different countries, but before you say anything, know that there is a distinct possibility of serious danger." She looked at Rosalyn, who had an odd expression. *"Oui?"*

Rosalyn ran a hand through her frizzy brown hair that she could never keep neat and stared at Amelie, slowly shaking her head. "You'ahre offe-ring me a chance that's r-ight out of a sto-ry oah game? Someone like me, who needed gen-enginee-ring to keep f-rom developing a disease that would have left me in pain my whole life, with this speech im-ped-iment?" She picked up a stuffed vine leaf, held it to her mouth like an old-time cigarette, and said, "The name is R-idge, R-osalyn R-idge." They stared at her, and then all four of them broke out laughing.

"My dear, understand that when she says there is a possibility of danger, she is not exaggerating," Rafe said.

"Of cou-rse I r-ealize that, or she woul' not have said it." Her face took on a harder smile. "I've r-ead about r-eal spies, so I can see why I'd be a good can-di-date. I mean who would give me a secon' thought, othe-r than foah a quickie?" she said, ending on a hard note. She ate a bite of the stuffed vine leaf. "Whe-re is the dang-er in this t-rip?"

Amelie nodded. "There have been several unusual deaths of important people in one of the countries I am interested in sending you to, and in the other, there are always issues."

Rosalyn's expression grew fierce. "I admit that's somethin' to be wo-rried of, but the Conf-ede-ration, and its laws, ahre what makes my life livable. With things seemingly getting wo-rse, and none of it due to the Confede-ration, but because of people against it, it's my turn to stand up. I'm in." She looked around the table, and saw expressions she wasn't used to—real warmth, and approval.

"*Bon. Très bon.* Very well. One artist that I would like you to visit is in the Western Sahara, in the SADR, which is where several apparent assassinations occurred. The artist's name is Zaim Alal. Art runs in his family, and he is named for a famous poet of over a century ago. Their art leans to the non-representational, but has an expansive flavor, something like the American West. I will warn you, though, that sexual roles are changing much more slowly than elsewhere."

"Of cou-arse. I assu-ah you that I have extens've expe-rience in being spoken down to, and know when to hol' my tongue," Rosalyn said, eliciting a wince from Amelie and Janine.

Amelie went on. "I will ask him to allow you to study with him for a few weeks. You will travel to and from there through Algiers, and then fly to Taipei. Aluaiy Pulidan is an artist I met at a show in New York some years ago. Her work is influenced both by traditional southern Taiwanese tribal traditions, and the abstractionism adopted in the north." She paused. "This is especially where it could become dangerous. Tensions are rising, since questions are being asked in the Confederation Assembly about large sums of money and resources appearing in unexpected places, and the source of some of that." She paused. "There is more, but I may not tell you that unless you choose to accept the mission."

Rosalyn licked her lips. "About the assassinations?"

"*Oui.* A government minister and a shipping executive."

"And you want me to see if the artist is involved? Is that the undehcove-r pa-rt of this t-rip?"

"*Non,* they are not involved in the murders. You will only visit these artists, study with them, and supervise the loading and shipping of the pieces they will give you. You will have assistance with this in Laayoune, but will probably work directly with M. Pulidan in Taipei. Each artist will supposedly be shipping to four different shows, two in New York, two in Paris. One show in each city will be canceled due to 'events', and other arrangements will be made to show them. About half of the pieces will have information and documents hidden inside the work. They must not be mixed up with the pieces going to the real shows." She took another sip of wine, and said, "You will, of course, have a chance to study with her for a few weeks as well."

Rosalyn swallowed, and slowly got out, "I've known of M. Pulidan, and admire he-r wo-rk." She shook her head. "I've neveah had the r-esou-rces to go off-continent. Yoah're going to send me ah-round the wo-rld, and study with well-known ah-tists on the t-rip. I have no way to r-epay you for this."

Amelie smiled. "Once you are safely back, with everything we are looking for, consider it work for hire. If you wish, make me a piece that is influenced by the artists with whom you will study." Rosalyn stood and reached out her hand, and Amelie shook it. "But now, let us not let dinner get cold."

~

TWO WEEKS LATER, Rosalyn returned to Amelie and Rafe's house. to be met by Rafe, who escorted her into the living room. She saw a man and two women, and she did a double take. "Dr. Friel! This is a su-rp-rise."

"For me as well. My director told me I was required to come."

"This is M. Hardy, and M. Whitmore. M. Hardy?" said Rafe.

"We have something for M. Ridge that you, her doctor, need to know about," Hardy said. He opened an envelope and pulled out some papers. "M. Ridge, doctor Friel, you are hereby served Confederation security papers, and are required to read and sign them."

Rosalyn and the doctor stared at him, then at each other. Then Rosalyn turned to Rafe. "This has to do with the t-rip?"

"Yes."

She looked at Friel and sighed deeply. "I'm so-rry, Doctor. This is my fault." Looking back at Hardy, she held out her hand for the paper. She read it through, using the mesh to help understand what she was committing herself to, and signed.

Watching Rosalyn, the doctor accepted the paper and signed. "Now can I know what this is about?"

"M. Whitmore?" said Hardy.

"M. Ridge has agreed to travel for us to several unsafe locations around the world. We have hardware, firmware, and software modifications to run on M. Ridge's AI and headband. In addition, we have some equipment that the Confederation is not officially providing to your division, but is a 'grant' from M. Trouve and M. Maxwell. It will allow you to work with the latest meshecytes that have been cleared for release."

"Oh, my! We've been hoping to get more funding for meshecyte work for several years." Her face grew serious. "The modifications...." said the doctor. "May we know what they do?"

"The hardware and firmware changes will circumvent any attempt to corrupt or invade her AI and mesh computer. We will also provide more secure encryption for her mesh computer and its storage. We ask that you monitor M. Ridge as we make these changes to assure that there are no issues."

Friel exhaled heavily. "I understand. Very well." Turning to Rosalyn, "Are you ready for this?"

"I said I wa-s when it was offe-red, so I su-ppose so." She looked at Rafe. "I do expect a theme song, like all the sec-ret agents in videos." Rafe looked puzzled, then laughed. Hardy and Whitmore just shook their heads.

Whitmore took Rosalyn's headband and worked on it for a few minutes. After testing, she ran the firmware update, and retested. Finally Whitmore ran the encryption package, and tested again. "M. Ridge, I've given your AI access to the encryption package, which includes how to encrypt and forget a memory until you release it. I expect that to take at least two or three days for you to learn how to use it. Feel free to contact me if you need assistance understanding it. Now please choose an emergency phrase. Invoking it will shut down the system immediately, and will not reboot unless you are wearing it, and your meshecytes report all normal, not under stress, that is, if you are not under threaten."

Rosalyn thought for a minute, and then said, "bug out".

They tested, and it crashed. It had begun to come up when Hardy pulled out a military handgun and aimed it at her right eye. She was utterly startled, and the system crashed again. He looked at Whitmore, who nodded, and he put the gun away, saying, "That needed to be tested."

Rafe, looked at Rosalyn. Seeing her stunned, asked, "A drink?" At her nod, he poured her some brandy.

"I…feel like I've wandered into a video," said the doctor.

Rosalyn nodded. "I'm r-ealizing now just how, how *r-eal* this is."

Whitmore packed up while Hardy said, "Our apologies for all this, but you may find you need this protection."

Rosalyn thought for a moment, then said, "Of cou-ahse. That was the point." The two agents said good-bye and left, and she looked at Friel, then said, "Rafe, could you possibly manage some coffee for the two of us, while we recover?"

"Certainly."

~

THREE WEEKS LATER, Rosalyn found herself aboard a planetary transport, coming down from two hundred kilometers to land at Houari Boumediene Skyport in Algiers. Passing customs, she brought up her mesh-mediated AR and followed directions to a well-dressed man and woman waiting for her. He introduced himself as Mahmoud Haddad, and the woman as his cousin, Clotilde Haddad. He was somewhat taller and apparently older than Rosalyn, while Clotilde was a little shorter, heavier, and younger. They led her to collect her luggage, then accompanied her by the rail link to the train station. Coming up there, they followed the AR signage to their track.

"We don't eveah go outside?" she asked.

He smiled. "You have never been here?"

"This is my first t-rip off No-rth Ame-rica."

"And here we think all Americans are well-supplied with resources." He shook his head. "I appreciate that you want to see my country, but we've barely begun to reverse any of the effects of climate change, and I didn't really think you would appreciate a walk in forty-five degree heat."

She looked at him, then shook her head. "Thahnk you, that was quite conside-rate. Ahre the two of you leaving me he-re, or....?"

"Oh, no. Given current local customs here and in the SADR, we are your security and guides for the trip, *in loco cognatus*, as it were." He looked around. "Our train doesn't leave for another hour. We can go to the lounge, or board now."

"I think I'd r-athe-r boahd now." As they led her to the boarding gate, she asked, "A-re customs still that st-rong, then?"

"They are fading, but change takes a long time in places where people have lived for thousands of years, though things are different in the SADR, and especially in Layoune," Clotilde said, a lilt in her voice that was unfamiliar to Rosalyn.

"Where are you from?"

"Burkina Faso. My cousin here found an opening with his firm, and I do a lot of this now."

Rosalyn wore a thoughtful look on her face as they walked down the platform following AR guides to their car. To her surprise, the two led her on to a small room that was still larger than the small compartments on American trains. "We have a r-oom to ouahselves?"

"Ah, you're not used to rail travel?"

"I've gone ac-ross the US by r-ail, but the r-oomettes are smalleah than this."

"Our tickets provided that we would not be sharing with up to four others." She nodded, and Clotilde sat next to her, as Mahmoud seated himself across from her. "Have you known M. Trouve long? Surely you are familiar with her choice of accommodations."

"On-ly a few months. We we-re int-roduced by her daughte-r-in-law, who is a f-riend and fellow game-r I've known foah yeahs."

He nodded. "I see. Not meaning to be rude, but I cannot place your accent."

Rosalyn gave a quirky smile. "It's not an ac-cent. I have a language p-rocessing diso-rde-r, that a new technique using the mesh is finally helping me oveahcome." She could see he was surprised, both by the disorder, and her mention of the mesh. He asked about it, and it was only when the train began to move that they realized how much time had passed.

"Clotilde, have you been an escohrt foar long?"

"No. I have only been doing this for six months or so, and I do not plan to make a career of it."

"What ahre you planning on, then?"

"When I save up enough money, I want to go to Europe, or America, to study. I want to be a nurse."

Rosalyn nodded, thinking how this is how it was before the Confederation, and things like free education, and a basic minimum income to live on.

In a bit, they went to the refreshment car and she asked the two to choose several local foods. With it, they got the strong, sweet local coffee, and returned to the compartment, to continue to talk and watch the scenery speeding by, into southwestern Algeria, with the low bare mountains and little vegetation, on into the Sahara as the sun set, then Mauritania, and finally into the SADR.

It was late the next morning that they arrived in Laayoune, in the SADR, having been in transit almost twenty hours. They could not take the shorter route through Morocco, which had disputed SADR's control of the western Sahara for many decades. They came out of the gate, and she saw that most of the travelers were wearing western-style clothing, but two, a man and woman were wearing versions of a short dashiki over pants, with the woman also wearing a headscarf. Roslyn realized that they were lit up in the mesh, and she and her guides went to meet them.

"*Bon jour!* I am Aderfi, and this is Markunda. You are M. Ridge?"

"*Oui.*" Rosalyn said, then added, "That's al-most all the F-rench I have." In mesh, she went on, "*These are my guides, Mahmoud and Clotilde.*"

"*Bon jour,*" Markunda said, and joined the conversation in mesh, "*We have dealt with M. Trouve for some years, and so we look forward to this visit.*"

"Usually students come for a longer visit."

Rosalyn, happy to continue in mesh, since her speech was perfect that way, said, "*She sent me to learn techniques and patterns from M. Alal, but I cannot afford much time away from home, as I am working on a number of pieces for upcoming shows at the end of the year.*"

Markunda's eyebrows went up for a moment. "*You are a working artist yourself?*"

"*I am. M. Trouve's daughter-in-law is a friend who introduced us, and M. Trouve was taken by two pieces in my catalog, and bought them. She says that she thinks what I might learn here would work with my own style.*" The other two nodded, and they left the station.

After they got to the artist's compound, and she had been settled in, Aderfi and Markunda escorted her to meet Zaim Alal. The conversation did not begin well. He did not have the mesh, and she could see that the still-extant speaking issues she had was leading him to think less of her. Glad she had brought some physical copies, she showed him her current catalog, which helped some. They agreed that he would see how things went working with his senior students for a week, although she suspected that he only offered that due to Amelie's influence.

The week began with resistance from the other students, who treated her as an interloper as well as dull-witted from her speech pattern. By Thursday though she had earned a grudging respect, having produced several pieces by combining both their techniques and her own. Friday she spent quietly, most all the rest of the household in prayers. Saturday, as the heat of the day subsided, she played tourist around Laayoune with Mahmoud and Clotilde, who had roomed with the household staff. They visited the newer city, on the other side of the dry river, and had a leisurely dinner of local food. As they ate, she spoke of how hard she was working, and he assured her that he and Clotilde would deal with the packing and shipping of the art so that she could stay focused on her work.

The next day she sat with three other senior students as Zaim Alal spoke about patterns and techniques used by traditional craftspeople, and how they were incorporated into his work. Finally, he assigned each of them a moderately complex project, to be completed by the upcoming Thursday, and bid them good day. To her surprise, hers was primarily a Western design, though with room for her own additions. She thought about it all evening, and began working on the final design the next day. which she finished by evening. Bright and early on Tuesday she was in the shop, laying out the metals for the project, marking the designs for cutting and other work. She worked late into the evening, only taking a few short breaks until one of the staff came in to tell her that dinner would be cleaned up if she were not there soon.

She worked Wednesday with the same intensity, and her piece was nearing completion by the time the others went to evening prayers. After dinner she went back to complete the polishing. In the morning, she and the other students sat with Zaim Alil. He examined each student's piece, commenting on them and giving critical approval, pointing out details to be improved upon on the next piece. Finally, he picked up hers. He held it, feeling the weight, and slowly turned it, examining it carefully inside and out. "You included enameling in the design."

"I did. You spoke of how t-raditional c-raftspeople inco-rpo-rated it in their designs, and how that was admi-red by t-radeahs f-rom elsewheahe."

"You also incorporated traditional designs into the makeup. That was not exactly what I had assigned. I was expecting Western design patterns, although I see you incorporated some into what I had specified should be exactly so."

"I am he-re studying with you, to leahn and unde-rstand how and why you-r patte-rns ahe as they ahe. I do Weste-rn style patte-rns all the time, but I'm heah, and so t-ried to follow youh lead in fusing designs from the West as well as other pa-rts of no-rthwest Af-rica." She smiled. "You have, of course, noted the deli-be-rate e-rro-r I made, to fo-llow in the footsteps of those who believe only Allah should c-reate pe-rfection."

He nodded, rocking a bit as he did so, his long graying beard moving with him. Finally, he allowed a small smile to show. "I see that Amelie's aesthetics remain excellent. Do contact me, as I would be interested in seeing where you take the designs you have learned here."

Warmth flowed from her heart to spread across her chest. "M. Alil, it has been an honah and p-rivilige to spend this sho-aht time with you, and I look foahwahd to a continued conve-rsation."

The next day, she made her farewells, and returned to the train station with her guides. "I t-rust that you we-re not bo-red du-ring my time he-re?"

"Not at all. I visited around—I have a friend or two here, and introduced Clotilde to them. Then the last day and a half I supervised the loading of the pieces that you will be shipping from Algiers for the shows." With that, he showed her the manifests and packing slips, and she saw that everything had been loaded correctly per her private instructions, stored as they were in her headband.

She sat quietly for a bit, suddenly reminded of the other part of this trip, its possible dangers, and resolved to keep it in her mind. She bid the two good-bye at the gate, asking them to keep in touch.

"Take care of yourself," he said. "I don't know if you've looked at the news, but tensions between Taiwan and the Confederation are very high, since they're not giving answers that the Confederation wants to hear."

"Thank you. I'll listen when we'ahe on the way. Take ca-re!"

36

TAIPEI

Listening to the news on the transport, she was distracted from the view of Terra from space. Mahmoud had not exaggerated—relations were very tense, both between the Confederation and Taiwan, but also internally in the US, the European Union, and China. Still, looking at Taipei as they came down, she saw how very different it was from Algiers. Dusk had fallen, and the city was a blaze of lights, like the cities of her childhood rather than the quieter lighting in modern metros. In the skyport, she got a mesh call which she followed to her guide. On the walk, she noticed a number of armed guards, something she hadn't seen in a long time. Passing through security, she met an formally dressed woman younger than her, perhaps in her twenties. They shook hands, but spoke in mesh. *"Welcome to Taipei, M. Ridge. I am Tsai Lìhuá. You have luggage?"*

"I do." Lìhuá led her to baggage claim, where Rosalyn had to show ID to reclaim it.

The uniformed man handed over two of the bags, but put the third on the counter. "There are tools in this bag. Why are you carrying them?"

Rosalyn was surprised for a moment, until her AI showed her

that Taiwanese security measures had been ratcheted up. "I am an ah-tist and c-raftspe-rson. I wo-rk in metal, and am he-re to study foah a sho-aht time with M. Pulidan, who is af-filiated with the National Taiwan Unive-ahrsity."

"Yet you carry your own tools?"

"Aahtists and c-raftspeople f-requently have tools they p-refeah, that are comfo-ahtable to them."

He stared at her for a minute, then handed over the bag. "This tag indicates the bag has been inspected. When you leave, it must be on the bag, and the contents will be verified."

"Thank you," she said, and took the bag. The women put the luggage on a cart, and took it to transportation, where a floater waited for them with a driver.

Lìhuá saw her surprise, and said, *"A driver cannot be taken over, unlike a self-driving vehicle, so there is less chance of an 'accident'"*

"Things are that unsettled?"

The woman held up a finger, and they loaded the luggage into the trunk and got into the floater. With the door shut Lìhuá continued. *"With the newsfeeds announcing the disclosure of serious amounts of money being moved into Confederation countries, events around what the Confederation is labeling 'disturbing', 'Net and mesh attacks in a number of countries, and something called a 'killbot' incident in a member nation', yes. Taipei's ambassador to the Confederation facing hostile questioning over them, the President has the nation at high alert."*

"Oh. Should I turn around now?"

"We believe you should be all right for the next week or so."

They drove on a road that ran along the coast, curved to parallel a river that emptied into the ocean, then across a bridge over the river. Soon they were in what was clearly a university district, and pulled up to a high-rise residence building, with the tall first floor designed in a traditional Taiwanese pattern of stone, with an entrance covering resembling a thatched roof. Getting out, Lìhuá took one bag, while Rosalyn carried the other and her tools. They went in, took an elevator to the fifth floor, and was brought into what looked like a hotel room. *"This is one of a few rooms we have for transients.*

Here's a key," she said, handing Rosalyn a wristband. *"Have you eaten?"*

"On the transport from Africa."

"Then let us join Professor Pulidan." She led Rosalyn up two levels to the top floor, and into a small lounge, with a wide doorway opening onto a balcony with a view across the river, and over Taipei. Seated there was a woman in her early fifties, not even middle aged these days, a cup of tea and a pastry on the table in front of her. Rosalyn had seen pictures of the professor, but in person, she was striking.

"Ah, M. Ridge. Welcome to Taipei, though one could wish the world situation was less fraught."

Shaking her hand, Rosalyn said, *"Thank you, and yes, certainly. Professor. I must say it's an honor to meet you. I've been admiring the work of you and your students since I was in college."*

The woman smiled. *"And that would seem to be a few years. Tea? A pastry, perhaps?"*

Rosalyn thought for a second, then said, "Actuahly, yes. I would like some tea, and a past-ry sounds about r-ight."

The other woman nodded, and looked at Lìhuá, who went over to a self-service counter. *"Amelie spoke with me about you, and mentioned your speech issue. Do you mind mesh conversations?"*

"Oh, no. I'm working hard with a specialist to use the mesh to train my muscles, and the brain paths, to speak more clearly, but a lifetime's patterns aren't changed in a few months."

"Very good. She also showed me your catalog, and you are no callow student. Call me Aluaiy, and I shall call you Rosalyn, if I may," she said, smiling at Rosalyn, who nodded, suddenly finding it difficult to look away from the older woman. Lìhuá came back with the tea and pastry, and they spoke for a while. Once they had finished their food, Aluaiy let the other woman leave, and led Rosalyn out onto the balcony. *"Lovely view, is it not?"*

"It is, though in mesh I notice what appears to be a screen above the ledge over the doorway."

The other woman turned around, and Rosalyn, taking a hint, did likewise. *"We do have reasonably good security. Mesh is far more secure than the Net, but even so, there are students, the government, and private actors. Where we are is about as secure as can be managed. You understand the situation is now worse than when your visit was planned?"*

"Yes. I saw armed guards at the skyport, and had my bag of tools searched."

"We shall spend what time we can, but be prepared to leave at a moment's notice. Is there anything in your luggage you would be unhappy to leave behind?"

"Some clothes, but they can be replaced. My computer was bought for me to be disposable. The only thing I would rather not lose are my tools."

"I understand. Given the circumstances, the first thing we will start on tomorrow is packing and palletizing the pieces for the shows," she said, emphasizing 'pieces'. She turned, again, leaning over the railing, and Rosalyn followed her lead, and their conversation turned to art.

The next day, they began the packing. Rosalyn's help was needed, as she was familiar with how Confederation and American shippers expected fragile art to be packed, as opposed to the less stringent Taiwanese methods. She found it interesting that at least one student kept placing artworks for one show with the other, and vice versa. After the second time, she didn't make any comments, but when he was not looking, corrected the misplacements. They were done by late afternoon, and seeing the pallets off to the cargo terminal at the skyport for shipping that evening, she and Aluaiy had a pleasant dinner. Their conversation began with Rosalyn mentioning the student.

"Ah, yes. I was sure that one of them is an agent, but had not determined who it was," Aluaiy said in mesh. *"Now we can keep an eye on them, and hopefully there will be no others. They are watching everyone who might have information."* Rosalyn gave a questioning look, and the other woman added, *"Some, but nothing definite."* The other woman took a sip of tea, and looked at Rosalyn. *"You have some hair coming out of that lovely barrette,"* giving Ros a picture.

She shook her head. *"My hair's thick, and has a mind of its own."*

As she reached up, Aluaiy leaned forward with a smile. *"Please, let me help,"* as she put the younger woman's hair back in place. With that, the conversation turned again to art, and the designs the older woman worked into her ceramics, which seemed to bring frequent smiles to both women's faces.

The discussions continued the next day, with several of Aluaiy's senior students joining in, describing the patterns they used, which made the mesh invaluable, being able to display them in AR. Still, every so often, several times they were interrupted, by one or two students coming to the wrong room, or a 'Net call, and Rosalyn found herself jumping when they occurred.

~

"WHAT DO YOU MEAN, security is after you?" Lìhuá said, softly but intensely at her younger sibling, who was standing there sweating profusely, in spite of the cool weather.

"It's some crazy thing. I was following Kuan-yu and his two mates, and we got into this warehouse that no one's been in for weeks. Chih-wei got the door open. I stayed by the door, but had my AI record everything it could enhance and see, figured I'd read it later. There were a dozen refrigerated containers powered on. Kuan-yu hit the button to open one, and alarms went off, and we were out of there. But we were chased. Kuan-yu meshed me that Chih-wei had been picked up, that I should hide, and he'd get in touch with me."

"Did the containers say anything on the outside?"

"Yeah, let me show you." They meshed her what the AI had recorded.

Lìhuá's jaw fell, then she put them on hold, and called Aluaiy to tell her what they'd found. She listened to Aluaiy, then signed off, and turned back to her sib. "Do you have a getaway bag packed?" They nodded, and she said, "Get it. We are going."

It was not long before they were at the University, and up in the lounge. Aluaiy led the two of them and Rosalyn onto the balcony. *"I'm trying to decide how to get this information out with you, Rosalyn."*

"I've already worked that out. First, Mei-ling, I need you to give me the memories from getting into the locked room, everything you recorded, until

you were running, now." She paused, and with their sister and Aluaiy nodding, Mei-ling gave her the recorded file, and she wrote it to her personal storage, then verified it. *"Now, erase everything. All of it."* She waited until they'd done that. *"Excuse us, this has to be private."* Blocking Aluaiy and Lìhuá, she asked, *"Have you had any training in locking memories?"* Mei-ling looked at her uncomprehendingly. *"Follow what I'm showing you. Mark that time period, then let me give your AI a key."* She had Alan generate a key and give it to Mei-ling's AI. "Now, *tell your AI to hide that entire marked memory so that you can't remember it without the key."* Nervously, they did as she said, and then their eyes flew wide open. "What did you do? What did I do? All I know is something happened, and I'm in deep trouble, but I don't know why."

"You were with f-riends who b-roke into a wa-rehouse. They ah-re p-robably in mo-ah t-rouble than you. You did the r-ight thin' to come to you-ah sistah." Mei-ling nodded, looking scared.

"Take the train, and go visit our aunt in the south." Lìhuá said in mesh. Mei-ling nodded, still looking scared, and left.

Aluaiy meshed, *"Rosalyn, you need to leave, now. They've just announced that all visas are being canceled shortly. I'm calling for a floater."* Rosalyn rose, then turned to Aluaiy and the two embraced, then she ran for her room and collected her bags, her tools in a backpack, and she was outside as the floater came up. As they drove along the street towards the bridge, lined with shops catering to the students, they started to see some with metal shutters over the windows. More and more were closed as they approached the bridge, which they saw it was blocked by half a dozen vehicles along and across it, a riot apparently in progress, bottles and stones going one way, and the police on the other side, with shields and helmets trying to cross.

"Is the-ah some way a-round?" she asked,

The driver, a young man who had mentioned he was a part time student replied, "Not a problem, this will be fun." He turned the vehicle the other way, and as they came along the road, turned onto a beach entrance. Then he gunned the engine, and they went skimming over the river. "Not to worry. Everybody does this one time or another. If you get caught, it is not an expensive fine." Shortly, they were on the other side, and up the beach, and back on the road to the skyport. She thanked him profusely as he let her off by departures. She went in with her ID and updated boarding pass ready. She checked her bags, and her tools seemed to clear, but when she went through security, two uniformed officers ordered her to come with them. They lead her to a room and told her to sit in a chair. The woman officer asked her the same questions about her tools that she had been asked coming in, and she gave the same answers.

Then the male officer asked her how she had changed her departure date and arrived so quickly, she told him honestly about the driver, and added, "I ha-ad to leave. I'm not wealthy, and cannot af-fo-rd to be stuck he-re fo-ah howev-ah long it is until the political issues ahe r-esolved."

"Yet that is a very interesting mesh headband."

"I'm in a special p-rog-ram, and my doctoah is using it to t-reat my language p-rocessing issue."

"So that is this accent you have?" She nodded, and started to say more when he came close. "Give me the headband."

"I can't just take it off that fa..." she began, as he reached for it. To Alan, her AI, she called *"Bug out!"*. As the man yanked it off, she jerked, fell backwards in the chair, and slumped down.

"What is this?!"

"I...I...can't just...do thah...." Her eyes rolled up, the lids fell, and she went limp, nearly sliding out of the chair. Grabbing her arm, he shook her, but she was unmoving.

The woman raised Rosalyn's eyelids, and shook her head. "She seems to be unconscious." She stepped out, and came back with another man, a stethoscope around his neck, who examined Rosalyn, then broke a small ampule under her nose. She jerked again, and began to stir. In a couple of minutes, she was sitting up again. The woman, looking at her, said, "You passed out."

"Yeah. I ha-ave...come to de-pen' on the mesh and headban' a lot..., an' mo-ah when I'm," she swallowed, "t-ahyin' to spea' clea-ahly."

The other man looked at her eyes again, and again felt her pulse. "She did seem to be in shock," he said to the other two.

The male officer took the headband,and put it on a scanning plate, and turned it on. After several minutes, he shook his head. "It tries to boot, then crashes."

"You may have corrupted the AI," said the doctor.

The male and female officers stepped outside for several minutes, then came back in. He handed her the headband, and said, "You may go."

She held the headband, staring at it with a distressed look on her face. "If it's boahkan, I can't affoad to 'eplace it." Rosalyn pulled herself together, heaved herself out of the chair, and with a "Tha-ank y-ou," left the room in the direction that the woman pointed her, arriving at her gate with twenty minutes to spare. On the transport, she leaned back in her seat resting until she felt the transport pull away from the gate and take off. As the sky out the portholes grew deep blue, and then darker, she first examined her headband, and pulled something small off that gave a small electrical spark as she did. Several other, almost unnoticeable spots lit up and turned dark on the inside. Wiping it all off with a rouge cloth she carried in her bag, she put it back on, Slowly, it came back up. After nearly ten minutes, Alan appeared. *"The headband was scanned, and several attacks were tried, but failed. The leeches that were installed are removed."*

She smiled. *"Thank you for the additional effects. Having me spasm and pass out worked well."*

"I gave those orders to your meshecytes before I shut down, madame."

"The data dump is secure?"

There was a brief pause. *"It appears to be, madame."*

"Please review it under security, and report."

A while later, the AI spoke in mesh again. *"Madame, the shipping orders are to Sukhumi, in Abkhazia via the SADR. From the little that is visible—the young person was by the container, not merely in the door, the labels inside appear to indicate they are functioning microbots, with military extensions, and ready for programming and activation. This suggests that they were made as weapons."*

"Use the contact we were given to have security meet us on landing in Philadelphia, and tell them I have had a more productive trip than I had expected." With that, knowing Alan was handling it, she closed her eyes, and let terror and exhaustion take her.

~

A WEEK LATER, Rosalyn was back in north Jersey, visiting Amelia and Rafe, Rhys and Janine having left to spend time with her family. They were sitting around with tea and coffee, and the two were looking at Rosalyn. "With ze danger you were in as you left Taipei, what you did was very brave, and I have been told to assure you zat ze United States and ze Confederation both deeply appreciate your actions," Amelie told her.

Rosalyn looked at her. She looked down at her coffee, then back up. "I'm just an ordina-ry pe-rson who makes jewel-ry, and lives in the woahld that you two, among otheahs, lite-rally made. F-rom what I've r-ead and heahd, I could have been living in a f-riend's basement, t-rying to find ways to pay them r-ent. Instead, I live in a place of my own, and can make a living doing what I love. You asked me to do something foah that wo-rld that I live in - how could I say 'no'? And you ahe the motheah-in-law of a deah f-riend, and welcomed me to youah wo-rld, giving me moah chances to do what I want, and to leahn f-rom masteahs. Again, how could I say 'no'?" She smiled. "Though I must admit, at that end in the ai-rospacepoaht in Taipei, I felt like I was in a game, and had the magic spell I needed to beat the bad guys." Shaking her head, she added, "Afterwards, when we were in the air, is when I got scared."

"*Cherie,* how you feel, and how you live, are a large part of why we did what we did, zose years ago, and what you are saying tells us that we made ze right choices."

Rosalyn's eyes began to tear. "How do I begin to thank you, when you tell me that?"

Rafe looked at Amelie, then at Rosalyn. "Nonsense, my dear. Amelie, shall we say that we have just acquired, oh, a niece?"

"By appointment? *Oui.*"

He looked at Rosalyn, and said, "Welcome to the family. It's not always a safe place, but we all care about what matters."

Rosalyn looked at the two of them, and to her embarrassment, started crying so hard she couldn't control it. Amelie rose and came to sit next to her on the couch, and put an arm around the younger woman.

37

FINAL PLANS

For this meeting, the virtual room had an elegant but understated Chinese flavor, with the elder Wu chairing the meeting. With Taiwan being the last major tax and data haven on the planet, the elder Wu had become recognized by the other former trillionaires as their leader, at least for now. The committee reports had been presented, and then Wu asked for new business.

"Elder," said Gliance. At Wu's look, she continued. "I had intended to report on the impact of what is known as the mesh, that its use has been growing exponentially, driven by both gaming and business. Its impact in surveys we have done that the groups who use the mesh heavily give negative results from normal propaganda, and advertising in general."

"You are saying that it has been found that the AI in the mesh-hosts they wear change their minds, and they do not buy what they are being told to buy, whether it is products or beliefs?"

"Yes. They fail to accept the dead cat on the table from our politicians. As time goes on, and with the meshecytes replacing mesh-bots, and so becoming inherited, this will probably grow. However, with the intelligence committee report, the situation is obviously critical. Last year, we attempted to control taxes by not planting ten percent of North American farmland, an attempt which I argued against. The predictable result was a strong response from the Confederation to the hundreds of thousands of famine deaths, and as we have just heard, is far worse than some of us anticipated. We have copies of the scenarios run by government policy AIs, and they appear to have chosen the most extreme, seizing complete control over all actual wealth, not merely money and stocks, but property as well, valued at over five hundred million dollars for individuals, and over fifty billion dollars for corporations. This is a declaration of war, that they intend to destroy us. I suggest that the time has come for an all-out attack the Confederation and see it fall, or that we should flee the planet. In addition, I urge sooner, rather than later, given that the report we heard concerning teaching the fools in Abkhazan a lesson has resulted in the Confederation paying attention, and probably seeing the patterns of disruption we have been building on for many years. She paused, then, at his nod, went on. "Given that Plans A and B have been in place for years now, we should, we *must* not delay any longer. The ship could be ready and loaded in a few months, while these bots, which we know work, can be prepared and positioned for use. For that matter, our instruments and their gullible adherents around the world are all champing at the bit to overthrow the 'New World Order'. I see reports from America, Afghanistan and Iraq, and India and Pakistan that our, ah, excessively religious leaders are going to move on their own, if we do not coordinate it. We already have people in Africa and South America in control, but they cannot hold on forever without the Confederation coming down on them."

The elder Wu stroked his thin gray beard. "Perhaps you are correct, and it is time to, as you say, 'pull the trigger'." He looked around, and saw that almost every face suddenly eager to be about it. "Very well, let the committees meet, and report on the sequence of steps," then added, "You have something to add, M. Gliance?"

She paused, looking thoughtful. "I would prefer an elegant and targeted method of delivery for the bots, one that does not announce its arrival until the bots attack. I believe the simplest method would work."

"How, M. Gliance," said Cheng Chen-Tao, "are you suggesting they be delivered? Shall we have our enemies come pick it up?"

All of the others in the room looked at him, and then the elder Wu, who had been staring at him, slowly smiled, as did the Younger Wu and Gliance, while Cheng Duyi and Radhakishan Ambani broke out laughing.

He looked around, and asked, "Why are you laughing?"

The elder Wu's smile grew broad. "M. Ambani, would you care to explain?"

"They will certainly accept them...when the small packages containing the mesh killers are shipped to them, with delivery guaranteed before 10:30 in the morning."

Cheng Chen-Tao stared at him, then he and the rest broke into laughter.

"And we can target them such that the entire top level of the Confederation is eliminated, and the rest falls apart as our agents attack on the ground," ended Ambani.

"What a pleasant a thought. We should have a party, to celebrate, as we watch them all fall apart," Lady Crossley-Spencer commented to Joan Krock, no longer a trillionaire, now reduced to a client.

"Perhaps we should plan the party after we succeed," commented Jim Waters.

Cepos Benjelloun nodded. "That seems to be to be a more reasonable sequence of events."

Krock's face grew harder. "Perhaps the Lady can plan the party, and if it would please her, I would be willing to represent her in the tedious business of planning the details of the overthrow of the rabble."

"I rather like that. Do so, if you would, Joan."

Later, in a small room in the huge estate belonging to the elder Wu, a dozen sat around a table, each with an aide or two. "We are agreed, then, on the order of events on the target day of Plan A?" asked Wu.

"I should like to make one suggestion concerning the 'bots," said Ambani.

"Which is?" Cheng Chen-Tao asked.

"As they are now, they are excellent weapons for assassination, being quiet and surreptitious. However, for our major push, we want fear and terror spreading among the targets. Is it possible to modify them so as to bring that about?"

Cheng Chen-Tao thought for a minute. "I believe it is. With the power available to them, compared to normal meshbots, they could broadcast mesh noise, distracting the people around from doing anything, and possibly interfering with mesh communication."

"That would be perfect," replied Ambani.

"Are there any other thoughts?" the elder Wu asked. His son, the younger Wu, motioned with his head towards Waters. He nodded.

"Since none of us is willing to accept the idea of being chased out of our home by the rabble, should things not end as planned, should we have a final weapon?"

"That is not a bad idea," replied the elder Wu. "What were you thinking of?"

Waters sucked his lips, then leaned back. "Modifying one or more major power generating stations. We could use that to show the rabble who's in charge."

"Is this doable?", questioned Benjelloun.

"I don't see why not." He saw Krock asking to speak, and nodded to her.

"Our construction firm built some of them. I can arrange for that to happen. However, it will take some time. Where were you thinking of?"

"New York, of course, perhaps Abuja, Berlin, and Tokai."

The younger Wu stared at him. "You are not a student of Sun Tzu,"

"No. And to be blunt, if it comes down to it, I want to take as many as I can with me."

There was silence for a few minutes, then the elder Wu said, "You are thinking very big. Tsunamis to strike Great Britain, France,

Spain on one side, and Japan, and the west coast of the United States."

"You saw that," Waters smiled. "Yes."

"That appears good to me, if it is feasible." He turned. "Mrs. Krock, please look into it." She nodded.

~

"CERTAINLY, Mrs. Krock, I'll get on it with my team right away." Joe watched as the woman and his manager left, and then sat down hard and slumped in his chair, going into mesh. A little while later Liz came in, and was about to say something, then stood there looking at him for a couple of minutes. He looked up, finally, and asked, "What's up?"

"I should ask what's up with you. You look really upset."

"We've just been handed a project by the boss, and I mean Joan Krock."

"Oh, crap. I've met Trouve, and she can be scary, but doesn't seem as though she's against us. Krock gives me the creeps. What's the job?"

"We're supposed to run simulations on matter-conversion generators, and find situation where they fail, especially if they fail catastrophically."

Liz started to say something, then stopped. After a minute, she said, "It's about lunch time. How 'bout we call George, and go out?"

"Sure."

A little while later, in their favorite restaurant, they were sitting with sushi and dumplings, and a few other things. As Liz was assembling the chopsticks she had pulled out of her bag, she said, quietly, "Let me guess, she's really interested in the cases where catastrophic means a very big boom."

"True."

"You know," said George, taking a sip of tea, "We covered some of that in school. The generators are designed to shut down gracefully, if possible, rather than fail. They're built to not go boom."

"Right. But there's no way to plan for all possibilities."

"Maybe we can find some that look like they should go boom, except there are deep safeguards," Liz said.

George smiled. "That sounds like fun. Like, something breaks, and the fuel tank bursts the valve system."

Mike looked at the other two. "So, what you're saying is that instead of a boom, the generator stutters, then shuts down?" George and Liz smiled at him.

~

"JAMIL, come here for a moment, would you?" Brian Chen called down the aisle.

"What's up, Brian?" Jamil Jones asked, coming into Brian's cramped office in the New York Metro Power Generation Engineering office.

"Take a look at this proposal." He handed up a few papers. "It comes from the company that built most of this station, and they want to significantly increase the output, without doubling the size of the plant. Something about it is catching in the back of my mind."

Jamil sat and looked it over. "Can I see the detail files?"

"I'll send you the location."

~

"MOHAMMAD?"

"Yes, sir?"

"I've heard from, ahh, an old friend. He tells me there's an urgent project proposal to double the output of our mass conversion generation for Abuja and the region around it. He suggests that we study it. Perhaps M. David might be assigned that task."

"But if you give it to him, it will be buried on his desk, and who knows how....oh." Smiling, he added, "I'll take it to him after lunch, sir."

SEEING friends in the gaming room, Bin called out in mesh. *"Hi, Arun."*

"Hey, Bin. How's your game coming?"

"Not bad. But let me put it on autoplay. Got something I wanted to talk to you and Tao-yi about."

They brought her in, and the three of them considered the modifications to the main Tokai generator Bin was looking at. *"These modifications to the generators? Tokai hasn't needed additional power in several years,"* Arun said.

"Why are they being called for?" Tao-yi asked.

"Orders from the top. Katsumi - he's my manager's manager, mentioned someone named Wu, wants it done soonest. But something about the design bothers me," Bin answered.

"I agree," responded Arun. *"Let's set up a cluster, the three of us, and run a simulation."* The others liked that idea, and soon enough they had it running. While that ran, they got back to their game. When they hit a break, the three of them went over to the cafeteria, got some desserts and drinks and sat around a table.

"Ah, the simulation's ended. What's it...huh?" exclaimed Bin.

"Right there," Tao-yi said, pointing in their shared virtual display. *"In a small generator, like the one outside Taipei that they have at elder Wu's estate, where I have to go to do maintenance occasionally, it would blow up. But in a large generator, with gigawatts of output or larger, the feed would become turbulent, the generator would stutter, then shut down in seconds."*

"That's ridiculous," said Arun. *"Why on earth would you want to do that to a grid-sized generator?"*

"But they want it on the Tokai generator...." Bin shook his head.

Tao-yi's mesh voice grew deadly serious. *"It's a threat. It's an ultimate threat."*

Arun shook his head. "But who would want to make such a threat?"

"You don't know who runs Taipei? You don't know who elder Wu is?" They shook their heads. *"The...the first time I was sent there, they ordered me around like a peasant. And the Younger Wu found me attractive,*

I guess, and he, he felt me all over. I didn't know what to do, and he reached inside my clothes. I managed to say that I was on a schedule, and he laughed, and said that we'd pick this up another time, and sent me on. Since then, I try to make sure there's a reason for someone else to be with me." She stopped, and they could feel her emotions leaking in the mesh, and could guess that more than once she hadn't been able to have someone with her. She took a few minutes to collect herself, took a sip of tea, then went on. *"After that first time, I looked them up. Elder Wu was one of the trillionaires who wasn't taken by the Confederation. Several visitors that I've seen there, them too, more trillionaires."*

"They're going to try again." said Bin. *"They'll do whatever, and this, and other grid generators around the world will be a threat."*

Tao-yi laughed, on the edge of hysteria. *"They think it will be. But they've made a mistake, a big one. Each of you run this again, and vary parameters, and I'll bet nothing changes. Whoever they had who designed this modification knew what would happen. We should help them."* An angry look flashed across her face. *"I think, however, that I could arrange for this modification to happen to the elder Wu's estate generator."* The others looked at her, horrified. *"What, you want them to win? Worse, what if they fail in whatever else they're planning? I've seen that American trillionaire Waters at elder Wu's. He'd do it just to get even with the Confederation. Do you want to join them in this?"*

The look on the others faces grew hard. *"That's not what we protested for while I was in uni,"* said Arun. *"Nor do any of us want to die. Can I help with your arrangements?"* he asked the woman.

She smiled a bitter smile. *"We will give him what the African woman gave Tolliver."*

38

VISITORS

Rosalyn stood outside security at Newark Aerospaceport, waiting for her visitors from Taiwan. A few years ago, this would have seemed like something from a video, but since she'd been friends with Janine and her family, life had been different. She was just looking around when she heard Aluaiy in mesh.

"Hello, again. Mei-ling and I are just about to exit security." A minute later, she saw Aluaiy, shoulder-length black hair, in dusty rose, the pants gathered at the ankles in the current fashion, and a young person, in the typical street dress of Taipei, the sibling of Aluaiy's senior student coming down the hallway. The older woman came up, and she and Rosalyn embraced "It's so good to see you in person, Rosalyn," said Aluaiy, and Rosalyn nodded, then turned to welcome Mei-ling.

"I hope this will be less, uh, exciting than the othah visit."

"I should hope so." She looked at Rosalyn. "Your speech is definitely better."

"It bettah be—I woahk at it all the time. Now I only slightly sound like I'm from Bahston." The two laughed.

Mei-ling looked at the two of them. "I don't remember that, is that an accent?" they asked, tentatively.

"Bahston is, that is, Boston." Rosalyn went on to explain, then glanced around, and said, "We can talk about this lateah. Let's get youah luggage and go back to wheah I live."

"It is not far?" Aluaiy asked.

"Well...a couple houahs, aftah we get out of heah. We'll grab the commutah rail, then anothah to Philly, a t-rolley and then it's a shoaht walk to my apahtment."

Later, as they settled in Rosalyn's living room with some drinks and snacks, Mei-ling looked at Rosalyn. "I...I thought you were a secret agent, like in the videos, when you were in Taipei."

Rosalyn snorted a soft laugh and shook her head. "I'm eveahything I said I was, an ahrtist and c-raftsman. I was r-ec-ruited by f-riends who I knew th-rough my aht to visit Aluaiy, and an ahtist in the SADR in West Af-rica, to collect infoahmation they already had and bring it back. I was not supposed to be in dangeah. I went into that thinking of all the books I've r-ead, and videos, and games, and thought I knew that it could be dangeahous, but I did it anyway, because it was a ve-ry se-rious mattah of Confedeahation secuahity, and like my f-riends, I believe in the Confedeahation, and that was woahth taking on some dangeah." She took a sip of her juice. "I'm just glad that ouh p-repahation woahked, and that I could handle myself when I needed to." Looking at the youngster, she could see that they were processing all this. "Before Aluaiy and I get into aht, let me tell you that this evening, I want to int-roduce you to some gaming friends seveahal of whom are gendeah fluid like you, and some t-rans, and see if you hit it off with any of them. I'm hoping you do, then we could ahrange foah you stay with them for a bit, while you find youah feet heah, and have someone like youahself to talk to about it in a society that's not actively hostile."

"Oh, that would be wonderful."

"Taiwan didn't used to be so hostile, but over the last twenty-five years, it has regressed a lot," Aluaiy said.

Rosalyn shook her head slowly, then, to Aluaiy. "So, have you been woahking on anything big since I was theah last yeah?" With that, the two women dove deep into a long conversation about the metalwork, ceramics, and jewelry that was both profession and passion to them.

The next day, Rosalyn took them around for some touristing, including the Philadelphia Art Museum, and several museums at the University of Pennsylvania, where Aluaiy was going to be presenting at an academic conference on the arts the following week. Mei-ling dragged along behind them, as bored as a teenager could be, although they perked up as Rosalyn spoke about how many ancient artifacts in some museums had been simply shipped out of the countries where they had been found. For dinner, she took them to a gaming hall. They went to the cafeteria, one of the new ones where food printers printed your order while you waited. After they'd gotten their food and drinks, they sat at a long table. As they ate, a number of people came over, and Rosalyn introduced them to gaming friends of hers who were there to play online, and party together in person at the same time. Mei-ling inhaled their dinner, and went off with Rosalyn's friends.

Watching them leaving, Aluaiy meshed, *"An interesting idea, this business."*

"It's not a business. It's a city recreation center. There are minor costs for cleaning and such, but otherwise it's for common use by city residents and their guests."

"Complete with the servers and networking?"

"Yep. I understand a century ago, companies fought in court to prevent localities from providing their own networking infrastructure. After the creation of the Confederation, a lot of those were either regulated down, or nationalized, and the costs are vastly less."

"How secure is mesh here?"

"Very. There were some attacks against the 'Net to mesh gateway last year, a few months before I first visited you, but the Confederation agency that runs it are very serious about security, and they've added additional protocols to prevent that." She looked at the older woman. *"What's up?"*

Aluaiy's mien grew serious. *"I need to warn you that I may have a tail."* Rosalyn looked at her sharply. *"The government suspects that I was involved in passing the information to the Confederation that I gave you.*

The opposition parties are pushing again to join the Confederation, and the ruling party, and those behind them, are cracking down on them, and punishing anyone they can to intimidate the rest."

"Crap! Give me a moment." Rosalyn thought for a minute, and sent a message to Janine. only to get a "On mission, will contact when I return" message. She took a deep breath, because it was still a big thing as far as she was concerned, and sent a message to Amelie.

A few minutes later, the woman linked in. *"Rosalyn, ma chère, bon jour. What is up?"*

"Aluaiy is here, and she has some security concerns." She brought Aluaiy in on the link and had her explain.

Amelie sighed, heavily. *"I pay attention to other things for a week, and the world goes to hell. Do you think you have been followed from Taiwan?"*

"I do not know."

"Let me contact some people I know, and we will get back to you," Amelie said, and closed the link.

"I hope her people can do something," meshed Aluaiy.

"I know that she has connections. In the meantime, I think we need to stay aware of what's going on around us anyway. That's what I got in a short course before they sent me on the trip, and that's what I certainly learned on leaving Taipei."

Just about then, Mei-ling cam over with a handful of teenagers and twentysomethings, along with several parents, and Rosalyn turned to greet them all. After a pleasant conversation, most drifted away, except for Mei-ling , the two parents and three teens. All seemed to get along, and it was arranged that Mei-ling would stay the next couple of nights with one family, then for two nights with the other, and then everyone would decide who they would stay with for the time being.

The next afternoon, Steve Zhou came over to Rosalyn's with Darcy, his teen that was fluid-tending-fem, who they'd seen the evening before. After visiting for a while, Mei-ling collected their overnight things and left with them.

A week later, Rosalyn, Aluaiy, and Mei-ling were driven to

Amelie's house one morning by a black floater that looked suspiciously like a government vehicle. Once inside, after Amelie had welcomed the three of them, they went into the dining room and she sat on the side to Rafe's right, at the head of the table. The two women and the teenager sat in the three empty chairs, across from seven men and women, all dressed formally. Amelie introduced the three, and then the people across from them: Jorgenson, Undersecretary with an aide from the Confederation Department of State, an Undersecretary from the Confederation Department of Foreign Affairs, a heavyset man named Presha from Confederation Security, and Taylor, Deputy Undersecretary of the State Department of the United States .

"Let me begin," said Jorgenson, the Undersecretary of State. "Professor Pulidan, we want to thank you for your work. Unfortunately, we have received information that Taipei is cracking down on opposition parties, and we believe that you may want to consider requesting temporary asylum."

"Is it really that bad? I only left a few days ago."

"Do you have a secure way to speak with anyone you trust back there?" Jorgenson asked.

"Yes...my senior graduate student assistant. Let me see, that's twelve hours away, so it's not too late. Excuse me." Aluaiy meshed Lìhuá, and was shocked at the young woman's response to her question.

"*Wait...*" Several minutes later, Lìhuá connected again. "*I'm up on our secure balcony. If you can stay there, do so! Your apartment was searched, and they left a mess, with the door open. We've cleaned it and packed what we can, but the worst is your art! Somehow they found out you were forwarding information in the art, and they've gone through everything that hasn't been shipped yet, and broke half of your back catalog, looking for media.*"

"*Lìhuá, protect yourself. If they come to interview you, tell them whatever you want, just not that you knew anything about what I was doing.*"

"*I've already had to do that. I'm so glad that Mei-ling is with you, because they know about them, and they've threatened me. I lied as well as*

I could, and claimed that our family was trying to decide to send them for 'therapy', and that I was as shocked as they were that my respected mentor would do such a thing as take them out of the country. If this keeps up, perhaps I should change majors to acting."

They spoke a little more, then signed off, and Aluaiy slumped back in her seat, clearly in shock. Given the formality and the company, Rosalyn felt a little uncomfortable, but put a hand on Aluaiy's arm, and the woman moved her arm, to hold the hand between it and her body.

"Aluaiy, my dear, would you like some tea?" Rafe asked.

"Y...yes, please. Green?" Rafe called Joseph, who came out shortly with with a mug with a tea spoon in it.

She sat there for a bit, quietly, trying to collect herself, as people quietly spoke around her. When the tea was ready, she sipped some.

Taking that as a signal that she was ready to continue, M. Taylor said, "Given the situation, we will offer temporary asylum, with a full Confederation visa."

Aluaiy looked at them. "This is all so unexpected that I will need time to consider."

"What abouht Mei-ling?" asked Rosalyn.

"We have spoken with M. Trouve, and she is willing to sponsor them for an American visa, although not a full Confederation one, as they are seventeen, and not considered an adult. Would that be acceptable?"

Aluaiy and Mei-ling both nodded.

M. Desai, the Deputy Undersecretary of Foreign Affairs, said, "M. Ridge, the information you helped bring back, and especially the information about the 'bots in that warehouse, which warns us that there may be a large attack planned were exceptionally above and beyond anything that was asked of you. The Confederation owes you a debt of gratitude. and in recognition of that, I have been authorized to inform you that you are being awarded a grant of art, to the tune of ten thousand credits." She paused, and added, "This is, of course, on top of the Basic Income and housing allowances all citizens receive."

Rosalyn's eyes grew wide, and her jaw dropped. Aluaiy turned and threw her arms around Rosalyn. Rafe smiled, and Amelie said "Congratulations. The work you used to do was good, but after the two visits I sent you on, it deserves this."

"I understand what this means, but if I may interrupt, there is something I need to ask you," said M. Presha. Rosalyn turned to him, seeing his dark eyes on her. "The information you brought back from Taipei was very good. However, we're wondering if there was anything more you can tell us. Anything at all. Taipei is claiming they had nothing to do with it, and that those were commercial warehouses."

The two women sat back, and Rosalyn thought for a while. "Theahe's only one thing I can suggest. The peahson who got that infoahmation is sitting heahe," she said, turning to Mei-ling. "But the only way they can give you any moahe is for me to unlock thei-r mesh memoahy of the event."

Mei-ling looked at Rosalyn, eyes wide. "What memory?"

"Do you remembeah, back in Taipei, when we and youah sisteah we-re standing togetheah, and you told us you were being chased?"

"Ye...es. But I don't remember what happened."

"That's because Alan, my AI, has the key to unlock the memoahy." Turning to Presha, "Will it make it any more dangerous for her to remembeah?"

"I don't think so," he said, shaking his round black face with close-cut hair slowly. "Given the situation with Taipei, this would be an important service that would reflect very well on your records when you turn eighteen."

Mei-ling licked their lips, then nodded. "What do I have to do?"

"Mesh with me, and tell youah AI to accept the memoahy key f-rom me."

"Ok..." *"Like this?"*

"Exactly. Alan?"

"Done."

Mei-ling sat there for several minutes, and then looked around in shock. "That was why they were chasing us? What I saw?"

"What they were afraid you'd seen," said Presha. "Do you remember any more, such as the warehouse signs or some such?"

"Yeah." They told Presha where the warehouse was, and he paused for a minute, accessing the mesh. Then he smiled. "That was exactly what I was looking for. Those are commercial warehouses... but they appear to have been leased to the government."

Everyone except Amelie, whose expression became hard, and the two Taiwanese looked shocked. "Excuse me, what does this mean?" Aluaiy asked.

"That it is suspected that the government of Taiwan, or the wealthy who live there and control the government were involved in the creation of the weaponized meshbots," replied Amelie, her face cold as stone, looking around. Rosalyn had heard Janine tell her about that look, and knew what it meant. "Has the Confederation retrieved and analyzed some of the samples from Georgia? Would the Confederation care to have my company Francopharm analyze some?"

"We do," replied Presha. "I must consult my superiors, but given your background, I suspect there are few laboratories anywhere that would be able to handle this as well."

That evening, back in Rosalyn's apartment, the day caught up with Aluaiy, and she slouched on the couch she was sitting on, almost going into shock. Rosalyn had been busy in the kitchen, but when saw it as she looked out to the living room, she came out and sat next to the older woman, reaching over to hold her hand.

Finally, Aluaiy sat up and looked at Rosalyn, holding her hand tightly. "That's years of work. I will be living on the pittance of a professor's salary, and the university will take much of the value." Tears fell onto her cheeks. "I am destroyed. I remember all my graduate work, my thesis, and the final defense for the doctorate. Then the appointment, the years of teaching and working, and each year, wondering if I would be reappointed for the next. The joy, celebrating with several of my students, including Lìhuá when they informed me that I was being moved to tenure track. The last five of of us at that party, on the balcony in the student union, looking out over the university at night, and the lights of Taipei surrounding the university, like a million stars. and so much seemed possible." She paused. "And now it is gone, crushed like a demonstration in the streets."

As she finished, Rosalyn said, "Aluaiy, you've lost that. You have not lost your aht, nor youah ability. I have seve-ral f-riends in local universities, let me see if they can find space for a guest lectu-rer. And it's only a week until the confe-rence at the Unive-rsity of Pennsylvania, but you can woahk in my studio, and perhaps do a piece or two."

"Rosalyn...." She looked at the younger woman, and said, "I don't know how to thank you." She paused, still working to pull herself together. Rosalyn rested her right hand on Aluaiy's shoulder, and the woman leaned her head on it, her eyes glistening with unshed tears.

The younger woman asked, "So, I know this is fast, but do you have some ideas for something you could make in a couple of days?"

"As I think of it, there were one or two that were in my personal collection that I might do in several days. Let me see what I can do."

"If theahe's any way I can help, let me know. Otheahwise, I need to think about what supplies and tools I'm going to buy with those r-esources they'ahe giving me."

The days were long, but went quickly, and by late Thursday, Aluaiy had completed both pieces she had hoped to get done, while Rosalyn was taking her time on a piece that incorporated a motif from the SADR that she had learned while there. Mei-ling had decided to stay with her new friends. The conference went off very well, and Aluaiy had even gotten to introduce Rosalyn, and let her speak for a short while concerning international folk motifs.

Monday, they began the week by sleeping in, winding down from the conference. Late in the afternoon, Aluaiy was notified of a number of boxes from Taiwan that had arrived, and had them delivered, then had Confederation Security in to open them. They turned out to be Aluaiy's clothing, and a number of other things that her students in Taipei, who had packed what they could, and separately shipped it, to try to avoid government security. The women looked at each other. "Rosalyn, these weeks have been terrible and wonderful, but your apartment really is too small for two of us, and with the studio being your other bedroom...."

"Ah ag-ree, Aluaiy. Actually, what came to mind was ah-rranging for an apahtment of youah own, and with my new resouahces, we could r-ent a r-eal studio, big enough for both of us."

"That's a very kind thought. How do we do that?"

"Mesh Taylor. See if he can ah-rrange it th-rough the US, maybe have it happen sooneah r-atheah than lateah, p-referably not fah from heahe, and I'll look for a studio."

That evening, Aluaiy had an apartment to look at, and Rosalyn had several studio spaces to look at. Aluaiy found a satisfactory apartment that was available for the summer.

"I'm surprised it was this easy to find places."

"This is Unive-rsity City. We'ahe ahround and west of the University, and other colleges. Students, and what they used to call bohemians, move in and out all the time. The stoahefront I found has not only enough r-oom foah both of us, but we could even do small shows theahe."

"Did you grow up here?"

"No, I g-rew up in the neaahby noahtheaste-rn subu-rbs. I lived in seve-ral a-reas afteah I left home, then I found this neighboahrhood, and it's been my home since." Rosalyn shook her head. "I g-rew up with a lot of unhappiness in school, especially in junioah high, but some continued in high school. Theah's none of that heah."

"What was the problem?"

"My language p-rocessing disoahdah. The populah kids thought it was fun to pick on me, and when they got going, 'stupid' was the kindest woahd they used.. Finally, I convinced my pa-rents to let me d-rop out, and take my last two yeahs of high school in community college. That was much, much betteah." She looked at Aluaiy and smiled. "The people theah we-re se-rious about getting theah degree, and too busy to give me g-rief. Then college... I took my fi-rst two yeahs at Moore, a small but good ahts college, r-ight on the Pahkway downtown, then managed to affoahd my last two at Temple. I did some shows at Temple, and was able to staht getting into ju-ried shows, and some lahgeah fai-rs."

"Whereas I stayed in academia." Rosalyn nodded.

With some help, they began to set up Aluaiy in her apartment, only two blocks from Rosalyn's. They took the next day off, to rest, and enjoy each other's company. Deliberately, they avoided the news-feeds. As evening fell on a pleasant afternoon, they walked down Baltimore Ave. for dinner, and chose an Ethiopian restaurant. "Have youah evah had Ethiopian, Aluaiy?"

"No. What is it like?"

"R-eminds me of otheah Af-rican cuisine, but one thing, don't be put off by the b-read."

"The bread?"

"The consistency is like a st-retch bandage."

Aluaiy looked at her and laughed as they walked into the restaurant, and the smell of sweet and hot spices surrounded them. They ordered, but when the order came, she looked up. "You weren't exaggerating. Good though, and I like the spices."

Afterwards, they walked along the street for a bit, then returned to Rosalyn's, since Aluaiy's apartment was not organized yet. They checked on Mei-ling, who was deep in gaming, and so presumably happy. It was a lazy, pleasant evening, winding down with wine, and each with an arm around the other on the couch.

The next day, they started working on the storefront, setting up a small showroom in front, and the back they cleaned so that they could start having tools, workbenches, and machinery delivered. Over the next several days, they organized it, and reached a point that it could be used. They put a few pieces in the front window, and Rosalyn arranged for a sign.

By Thursday, they decided it was ready, and had another pleasant evening, this time joined by Mei-ling, who took a break to be with them. When they asked them how things were progressing, they could hardly stop talking.

"It's...it's so *different* here. What I am, they call gender fluid, and it's not a big deal. The Zhous are wonderful people, and Darcy really *understands* me, although they find it hard to understand how different it is in Taipei, the way I was treated." They stared at the pizza in front of them, then seeing Rosalyn shake some oregano and crushed red pepper on several slices, then pick up one with her fingers and start eating, they followed suit.

"We went th-rough that a centu-ry ago," answered Rosalyn. "So ouah society has had a long time to undeahstand it. It's always hahdah when something is new, oah has been delibe-rately kept out foah political oah r-eligious r-easons."

Mei-ling nodded. "I guess…hey, this is good, but it's so different than the pizza I've had a few times before."

Rosalyn smiled. "Pizza, the all-Ame-rican food. This is East Coast style, the way I like it." Afterwards, they walked down the avenue, and showed Mei-ling their workshop. "Oh, wow," they said, looking at the few pieces in the window. "Those are…ok, maybe I'm starting to get a clue as to what the two of you do, and why it means so much. I hope I find something that talks to me that way." They walked them back to the Zhou's, and then went back to Rosalyn's for the night, as Aluaiy hadn't had a bed delivered yet.

Monday, Aluaiy got a message from the Fine Arts department at Penn, asking whether she would be interested in interviewing with them. She set up the interview for the next day with the dean of the department. When she got back to the shop, she came in and flung her arms around the younger woman as Rosalyn turned. "They not only want me as a guest lecturer this summer, they say that if things go well, they might hire me for the next year!"

"That's wonderful! We need to celebrate!" Rosalyn hugged her back, and they found themselves looking into each others' eyes. That evening they went downtown, to a small French restaurant that Rosalyn had been taken to once down on South Street, and was not prix fixe. Afterwards, they walked to the river, and enjoyed the lights. Turning to look at the city behind them, Aluaiy said, "It's like, and not like, Taipei."

"I should think not. Diffe-rent atmospheah, diffe-rent ahchitectu-ah." After, they walked up to City Hall, and took the trolley back.

Getting into Rosalyn's apartment, she went to her room, and Aluaiy to the spare room that had been Rosalyn's studio. Rosalyn was about ready to get into bed when Aluaiy came in and closed the door. "Rosalyn, I cannot tell you how much what you're doing has meant to me. I've lost my home, at least for a while, and everything, and you...."

"Aluaiy, what else could I do? You're a friend in trouble. Well, you're more than just a friend."

The older woman came over, and put her arms around Rosalyn, who returned that hug. They looked each other in the face, and then, there was a kiss that went on for a while. They finally pulled away, still holding each other. "I didn't know how you would take that," Aluaiy said.

"All that matteahs to me is whetheah I ca-re about someone, and whetheah they caahe about me." The two women held each other close, then Rosalyn pulled Aluaiy towards the bed.

Morning found the two of them sitting in the small kitchen, wearing bathrobes, chairs next to each other drinking tea, each with a large brioche that Rosalyn had ordered from a nearby bakery. Aluaiy looked at her, and said, "I suppose I should keep the apartment for the summer, since I signed the lease."

"And by that time, we'll know each other better, and you'll know whether you want to renew in the fall or not." She smiled at the older woman.

39

ENGRELAY NEOWEB

"Hello there, this is Jacinda Macsen, with Engrelay NeoWeb, *your* source of curated, verified news of the Terran Confederation and beyond! If it seems as though something's going on, don't worry, you'll hear it here! First off, news from the EU, where the newly elected conservative President of Poland has been making demands of the Confederation, and threatening to withdraw from both the EU and the Confederation. He is demanding the right to refuse to accept climate refugees, and has spoken of imposing work requirements on all citizens." [NeoWeb link]

"In Turkey, there was a coup attempted by religious conservatives, and fighting is still going on in the suburbs of Ankara. Local news is reporting that there have been air attacks on the Presidential Palace and the Parliament." [NeoWeb link]

"Jumping to the Middle East, troops loyal to the long-deposed House of Saud have staged attacks in Riyadh in an attempt to overthrow the secular government, and there are reports of heavy fighting around the airfield." [NeoWeb link]

"Meanwhile, in the United States, there have been demonstrations in a number of state capitals, with large ones planned for Washington and New York in a few weeks. The organizers are a coalition of political, economic, and religious conservatives, including the Old Believers' usual claim they are being discriminated against, and there are reports that supremacist organizations, such as the so-called Free Citizens' Alliance, are threatening violence."

"And now we switch to your local newsfeed, for more news and weather!"

40

AN UNPLEASANT HOMECOMING

"Hello, mother."

"Welcome home, *ma cherie*!" replied Amelie Trouve. "You and Janine are back?"

"We are. We just got back from the run to Alpha Centuri for our certifications. Janine's now qualified as a second mate, and I, as systems second."

"*Félicitations!* And so Janine has qualified as the starship pilot she dreamt of being! We will meet you at the gate."

Amelie and Rafe were outside the gate at the ancient air and shuttle port of JFK as Rhys and Janine came out, each with a small carry-on. She rushed over to her son and hugged him, then kissed him on both cheeks, then turned, and welcomed her daughter-in-law the same way, running her fingers through Janine's short, tightly curled black hair. "*Viens!* Come, get your luggage, and we have a hover waiting." They went down to pick up the luggage, and the hover came around to their mesh call. Loading themselves, they got in and headed home. A bot came out as they arrived, to carry the luggage in, and the four came into the living room, and settled down with drinks.

"Dinner will be ready in a little while," Rafe said. Seeing his son's look, he added, “No, we’re not printing dinner, and Joseph’s off on holiday. We splurged on a rather nice chef-bot that wasn’t outrageous.”

Rhys and Janine smiled. “We’re both *so* tired of printed food. It’s supposed to be the same, but it’s never quite right.”

“Let me say that *I* consider *this* food quite acceptable,” said Amelie.

“Then I’m quite looking forward to it, mother.” He took a sip of his drink, and then looked at her. “There is something I’d like your opinion on.” Amelie’s attention was on him. “We had lunch with an old friend, who works on Luna station and is the manager in the office that receives and registers the planetary survey reports from all incoming ships. Over the course of the meal, I mentioned, several times, about a couple of the planets we’d reported on when we came back from our first trip, and asked if he’d seen the three from the trip before the qualification run. He said he didn’t remember anything about any of them.”

She leaned back. “I’m sure they get a lot of reports....”

“There are plenty of probes, but not that many survey ships,” Janine said, “Nor are there that many terrestrial planets.”

Amelie ran her hand from her cheek to the back of her neck. She thought for a moment, then said, “Excuse *moi* a moment, then,” and pulled her slim and elegant AR headband on, and flipped down the glasses. The other three spoke of the trip, and of the continual changes to the New York metro, the capital of the Confederation. Finally, Amelie flipped up the glasses, and took off the headband. “You are right, *ma cherie*. The reports from your two trips show only one or two possibly habitable worlds, and all the others show as not viable, for one reason or another.”

“That’s...odd, mother. Two or three from each trip were certainly highly attractive.”

Amelie bit her lips, then said, “Now that you’ve filed the reports, so we cannot be charged with trying to get early reports, could you give us copies of your original reports?”

“Certainly. Actually, let me grab a headband...” he did so from the side table, and went into AR. His face slowly grew curious, and then clearly unhappy. This went on until Amelie called him for dinner. He came out, and they went to eat.

Afterwards, sitting around picking at what was left, Janine couldn't hold it anymore. "What did you find?"

"Our captain's logs are fine." He looked up, "As system third, I did look over the reports, while the captain usually discusses the report with Janine, she second mate and pilot." His parents nodded. "The ship logs are fine as well. The ship's voyage reports have been cleared, so there's nothing there. I used the ship's AI to check the transaction logs, and no changes were made before they were cleared. I've downloaded the reports to our usual report location, mother, so you can look at them."

"Do that in the morning, my dear," said Rafe. "This evening is a homecoming for our star voyagers."

She nodded. "Of course, *ma cherie*." Turning to Rhys and Janine, "So, have you heard of those twenty-somethings in Nigeria whose parents dug through trash shipped from the developed world, that are now millionaires, with the robots they invented are digging through landfills around the world for materials and minerals that are recycled. Have you read that they have endowed a chair at the University of Benin for, of all things, astrochemistry?" The others shook their heads. "I wonder if they're looking to get more Africans in general, and Nigerians in particular, on more starships,"

In the morning, Rafe, Rhys and Janine were finished their tea and coffee when Amelie walked in, her face looking as though she'd bitten something bitter. "What is it, dear?" Rafe asked.

"Everything that would show that the planets might be viable, all the signs on the numbers have been reversed, or flipped around the decimals, and the texts have been edited the same way." She looked at them, her face growing hard. "This is not an accident, this is deliberate."

"Mother, let me see which planets were altered." He grabbed a headband, and looked. "They're all ones further out, on the outbound portions of our trips, and in several directions, ones that I know we're less interested in." He looked at his mother, and his face hardened as well. "Someone's looking for somewhere to go." Rafe and Janine both put their mugs down as mother and son's faces hardened into *the face* and stared at each other.

"You think it's *them*," said Rafe, his voice suddenly hard.

Janine nodded. "Who else could be that sophisticated, and afford to do this?"

"They're tired of hiding like the rats that they are, and at least some of them are going to do what Tolliver intended," Amelie stated, factually.

"They've far fewer resources this time," said Rhys. "All ship captains are Confederation Navy reserve. Let me call the Navy." Amelie and Rafe nodded, and he made his call.

A day later, Amelie and Rhys were in the offices of Admiral Zelany, his adjutant standing by his desk. "If it were almost anyone else, I'd consider this a conspiracy theory. But you've long since earned your credentials, M. Trouve. M. Maxwell. Let me have my people look into this."

"Please, Admiral," interrupted Rhys. "We don't want to let *them* know, if it is them. Bring in several people you trust, and let my mother and me show you what we've found."

The admiral grimaced, but finally agreed. Hours later, he had his adjutant call for tea and coffee. "Very well, I'm convinced. Let me have the office closed and the staff brought in for questioning."

"If you do that, they'll know we're looking," said Amelie,

"Perhaps we could find a way for me to invite an old friend for lunch, or something." They looked at him, and Amelie started nodding. The admiral thought for a while, then nodded as well.

~

"DWAYNE, HOW ARE YOU?"

"Rhys, what's up?"

"How'd you feel about coming down from Luna Station to good old Terra? Janine and I are spending a few weeks at a house on the

Eastern shore in Maryland, and we're thinking of having a small party to celebrate our certifications mission, and being home again. You've got leave, don't you?"

"Well, yes...."

"Come on, old man, it will be fun."

It didn't take too much to convince him to come down, given that Dwayne knew that Rhys' folks had money, and it was likely to be a nicer time than he could afford. A week later, he was debarking at Dulles, having taken the shuttle to Terra Station, and then a shuttle down. A presence 'bot was waiting for him, and since he only had carry-on, it led him to a hover. It seemed a little staid and heavy, but he said nothing until he got in, to find a Naval officer waiting for him. As he sat, he suddenly found himself too heavy to move, and suddenly couldn't keep his eyes open.

He woke to find himself locked in a chair inside something he'd only seen in pictures, a full shielding cage. On the other side were two Naval officers, a Lieutenant and a Captain...and Rhys. "What the hell...?"

Rhys was standing, looking unhappy. "Dwayne, if this is all a mistake, I owe you an immense apology, and if you forgive me, I'll do my best to make it up to you. But first we have to find out if it is a mistake."

"What's this all about?"

"Let me question him, if you please, M. Maxwell," said the Lieutenant. "The reports from M. Maxwell's two missions—do you remember how many worlds of interest were in the two reports?"

"That's what this is about? I think there were... I think...I...I'm sorry, I don't remember."

"His last mission was not that long ago, and he's a friend of yours. You don't remember if there were any planets of interest?"

"I...I...," he twisted in his seat, unable to get out. "I just don't remember!" he said firmly, and then screamed. The captain did something, and Dwayne slumped, not unconscious, but breathing less heavily.

"Let me, gentlemen," said the captain. "Dwayne, can you tell us what you remember of the day that M. Maxwell's ship docked at Luna Station?"

Rhys watched as his friend showed an internal struggle on his face. "I…I knew that their ship was coming in, and a few hours later, Rhys called me to tell me he was in, and he said he'd filed the mission report, and invited me to join his wife, she's the second mate, and him for lunch. We did that, and they left, and I went back to work."

The captain leaned towards Dwayne. "Did you talk about his report, or the worlds that his ship surveyed?"

"Yes, no, not really."

The captain nodded, and stood. "Excuse us for a moment, and motioned Rhys and the Lieutenant to follow him out of the room.

After the door had shut behind them, Rhys looked at them. "Something's wrong. I don't think he's not telling the truth, I think he is actually unable to remember."

"I agree, M. Maxwell," replied the other captain. "The question is how to find out what he can't say."

Rhys face showed him looking inside his own head. "Captain, Lieutenant, I don't know how much you use mesh, but we use it very heavily on a starship. If you're willing, let me go into deep mesh with him, and you can ride in my train. as it's called." He looked at them, and the lieutenant started to shake his head when the captain rubbed his chin on the back of his hand. "That's new to me. What is this 'deep mesh'?"

"We connect in AR through the meshbots or meshecytes in our bloodstreams, going through the blood-brain barrier that way, and basically sharing what is almost the outermost level of conscious thought. Sometimes you get overtones of emotional reactions, as well." He shook his head. "The meshecytes, which I have, give clearer connections."

The captain and lieutenant looked at each other. "I can't see how it could hurt, sir."

"I agree," replied the captain. Looking at Rhys, he nodded. Rhys asked for a heavy-duty AR headband, and pulled out his own, designed with his mother's elegance, but all the power that could be packed into it with cutting edge technology. The three went back in, once the other headband had been brought in, and the lieutenant reached in to put it on Dwayne.

Rhys pulled a special cable that he had gotten from his mother, one legally only permitted to doctors licensed for it, and connected it to Dwayne's mesh-host. "Dwayne," Rhys began, "I've never done this before, but I'm asking you to trust me. I'll do everything I can to keep you from being hurt, but we're afraid something has been done to you, and we have to know."

Dwayne, almost rigid in spite of the relaxant, shivered, then nodded.

Rhys could feel the captain and lieutenant piggybacking on him, but he set up a filter, to try to protect his friend's, well, modesty. Slowly, he grew as close as he could to Dwayne's thoughts, then with this direct channel, connected to Dwayne's mesh-host, and almost felt as it they were thinking the same thoughts. Then asked, and thought, *what happened to the report?*

To his surprise, he saw Dwayne's mesh-host AI fork into two threads, one quiescing, and the other *twisted*, going around the receipt of the report, remembering needing the bathroom, looking at one of the other people in the office, sniffing, everything but what happened. He backed off a little, then came back into Dwayne's thoughts, aware again of the captain and the lieutenant.

Dwayne, my friend, I know this is almost like mind reading. Consider this, if you can read someone else's thoughts, you can read your own mind. Try to think around what's happening. What happens after the reports are edited? He knew his friend trying to understand, and then saw him activate the quiesced thread, trying to follow the twists of his own thought, until, suddenly, Rhys saw Dwayne see himself filing the edited report, and sending a copy of both to a recipient that sat under encryption to which he only knew the public key. Rhys made sure that the captain and the lieutenant saw that all, and recorded the key. Then Rhys saw something else. One thread of his mind in mesh had been monitoring his friend's health, and saw some of the meshbots moving towards parts of Dwayne's mind that controlled his heartbeat.

Using the additional power his headset gave, he sent the other meshbots to attack them, sending out chemical signals that started his friend's body's immune system to attack the rogue ones. Dwayne lost consciousness, and Rhys brought the three of them out.

"Call a medical code!" he said, and the lieutenant called. The staff was there in minutes, and had Dwayne on life support. Rhys yelled at them as they started to gurney Dwayne to medical. "Listen to me, you have to shut down his meshbots, immediately. Something just happened, and they're moving to attack his brain." They looked at him, and he added, "I was in deep mesh with him when it started, and I know what I'm talking about. Shut them down!" They assured him they would, and ran the gurney down the hall.

Rhys stared at the door shut, and the captain, behind him, asked, "What was all that about?"

Rhys turned, pain on his face. "The primary function of the meshbots is monitoring your health. A number of them released themselves from where they're supposed to be, in certain veins, at junctures, and had moved to take the bloodstream to carry them towards his head. There is nothing that should cause that."

"Could they have been hacked?" the lieutenant wondered.

He looked at the woman, and the pain left his face, and *the face* spread across his features. "No." he said coldly. "A hack would not have been so coordinated, nor respond that way when I led him to jump the fence, as it were. They were engineered that way, and put into him, and I have grave doubts that he knew about it."

"But who could..." began the lieutenant.

Rhys looked at the two. "The suspicions my mother and I had were correct. There's only one group that could afford the kind of money this sophisticated a procedure would require. The remnants of the trillionaires."

"That's hard to believe that there are any left with that kind of capability," said the woman.

"You don't understand what they had to start with. Even now, I would put down a cred if they didn't still each have tens of billions of creds, and some large companies all or partly under their control."

He added, "Did either of you note that before he went to shut down, there was a signaling attempt?"

"I'm not sure. Following you, we were in far deeper than I've ever been, and it was too much to all take in at once," said the captain.

"That's as deep as I've ever been, but when I'm in deep mesh with the bridge crew, especially when we're going in or dropping from FTL, I'm only a couple levels above that. I set a thread, using the AI to manage it, to look for signals, and it caught one, before the meshbots were using all their power to move."

"So it's a good thing we had him in a shielding cage," said the lieutenant.

Rhys nodded. "We need people on Luna Station to go clear the office, and tear apart his system, though I'm afraid that doing that might send a signal, or prevent a signal from being sent, to warn them." He thought for a minute. "We'll also need to make some guesses as to how long he's been under their control, and have people go through all the planetary survey reports, and compare them to the captains' logs."

"Unless they have people on some of the survey ships themselves," responded the captain.

Rhys looked at him for a moment. "Quite right. But I suspect that we'll find most of the missing planets' records in the official reports and logs, and that can be done fairly quickly, especially with the assistance of the mesh, to compare."

The captain nodded. "I'll contact my superior, and we'll have people there in hours."

Rhys' *face* smiled, and the lieutenant took a step back. "Hours? Then perhaps they should go in after hours, when the office is closed."

The captain started to open his mouth, then closed it, and a hard smile grew on his face. "An excellent thought, M. Maxwell," he said, and walked into the other room to make his calls.

41

SHOW TIME

"Good morning, M. Trouve, M. Maxwell."

"*Bonjoir*, Admiral Zelany. To what do my son and I owe this call?" The three of them, in AR, seemed to be sitting around a table.

"For one, we have to thank you, M. Maxwell, for assisting us in pulling in M. Kirschoff, and in his questioning using the mesh in a manner that my people are investigating very closely now."

"I am appreciative that you allowed me to assist. Had any other methods been used, my friend, if he still thinks of me that way, would be dead."

"The doctors asked me to give you their deepest thanks, as well, for telling them what was wrong. It would have taken much longer, and been fatal, without that.

"Ah, but Admiral, I hear a 'but' in all these thanks."

He nodded. "You are correct, M. Trouve. The team that went to the office that night found everything that he was unconsciously using, including the signaler. Unfortunately, they found something running that was expecting a signal at least once a week. He must have let them know he'd be on vacation, but presumably expected to signal on a regular schedule." He shook his head. "The link was followed, which of course went to a blind forwarder, which pointed to some code that generated a set of random mesh links, and even disassembling the code, were unable to decide which was the next one in the series, nor where they went. All were burner recipients, which seem to lead to several of the few nations that have not joined the Confederation."

"Mother," Rhys said. "Could any of them possibly be to old connections?"

"*Oui*, that is a thought. Admiral, can you give me a list of the numbers, if it is not too long, and I can check some very old records."

"We were hoping you might have some insight into that. I have them here," he said, and in AR, appeared to push a folder across the table, and Amelie pointed, and the folder disappeared into the table itself. "I will let you know as soon as possible."

"Thank you. M. Maxwell, I understand your friend wants to speak to you. You can reach him at this link, sometime after 1300 EDT."

He seemed to pour something into Rhys' hand, who closed his hand over it. "Thank you." The admiral cut the connection.

"I'll need to get off this link and go to my secure system, *ma cherie*."

"I assumed, mother. Love you," he replied, and cut the connection.

Several hours later, Amelie called the admiral. "Admiral Zelany, I have several hits. Three of them go to small corporations that handled communications for several of Tolliver's associates. As they are gone thirty years ago, I assume that they were taken on by those who were not on the starship that was destroyed by my sister", she said in a cold voice. "I did a little looking, and names that seem to pop up are an M. Gliance, M. Masterson, and M. Jerrie, and there are suggestions of an older man by the surname of Wu. I have heard mentioned of M. Jerrie in connection with a manufacturers of components used on starships, so I would suggest you follow those three up, and especially him, as soon as possible. I believe we know who Wu is."

"M. Trouve, you are everything I had heard of. Thank you very much, and my adjutant just disconnected to pass that information to our investigators, and to Justice."

"I am very glad to help, Admiral. We may be what is now considered a wealthy family, but I remember all too well before the Confederation, and you cannot know what that means to me. Now, I shall let you go, that you can apprehend these *racaille.*" They nodded at each other, and cut the link.

"MADAME."

Gliance looked up, an old useless habit when she was listening to her AS. "Yes, Jeeves?"

"There has been no signal from the office of the registry of planets on Luna Station this station morning,".

She looked sharply at her AR screen. "Really? Have one or two of our people, who don't know each other, sent to the office, perhaps an hour apart, and tell them to report as soon as possible."

"Very well, madam."

"And Jeeves, send out a message to Jerrie, Masterson, the elder Wu, and Warton. Tell them it may be game time."

Several hours later, Gliance was having coffee while talking to Jerrie in AR when Jeeves indicated that it had a message. She accepted it, and then looked at Jerrie. "The records from the ship that just came in a six months ago have been accessed by half a dozen people. Two of them were the ship's systems third...and the other I happen to know is his mother." In the real world, and the AR reflected that, her face grew angry and bitter. "Trouve. And since kidnapping isn't her style, I think we have to assume they've called in Naval intelligence. Are we agreed on a planet?"

"I think so. It may not be quite as desirable as several others, but one of our people was the civilian mission commander, and so all the reports filed will not differ from the filed reports. I'll have my agent file for the planet, and what, the dozen of us currently on this committee will cosign the contract?"

"That is what we agreed on. How close is the ship to ready?"

"It is ready. Only the reports show it as a month or two from being ready."

"Begin loading then, while we wait to see if plan A is successful," she said, and broke the connection. Looking around, she sighed. "I shall miss all this, but I would miss a lot more if they come after us. Jeeves! Start final packing."

"Yes, madame." There was a pause. "I have a message from M. Krock."

"Play it."

"M. Gliance, I understand the containers with the custom nanosystem are about to be shipped. Would it be possible to have four shipped to me? I have some special recipients for them, and will arrange to have them arrive as the others do."

"Message ends."

"Have the four shipped to her, as requested."

"DWAYNE?" Rhys could see him in a hospital bed, looking somewhat pale.

"Rhys...thank you for calling."

"Of course. Whether or not you still think of me as your friend, I have to apologize for the fraud, and for what happened, for what I did to you."

Dwayne shook his head. "I have no idea if I hate your guts, or have to thank you. What I do remember, now, is that they *mind-raped me*. I remember meeting a woman in a bar, the first day of a long weekend, who invited me to her place, and I remember waking up a few times, tied to the bed, and there were a couple of other people there, and screaming, and them putting something into my arm with a needle, and I fell asleep again every time. Finally, I woke up, and it was the end of the weekend. She was cold, saying I'd been rough, and telling me to leave. I remember staggering out, and getting a hover home. At work, when a ship came in, now I remember sort of zoning out and editing files, then refiling them with the correct timestamp, and then forgetting." Dwayne was breathing hard. "I understand you freed me, and I hear that your understanding of the mesh saved my life, but I need to think it all through."

Just then a nurse came in. "I'm sorry, you'll have to disconnect. We need to get your vitals down."

"We'll talk again, Dwayne, when you're better." Dwayne nodded, and disconnected.

42

PLAN A

"The mesh killers will be shipped to arrive tomorrow, first thing in the morning, Mrs. Krock."

"Ship these four immediately. Two are presents from the Younger Wu, and these two are from me, and I want them to arrive as late as possible this evening. With luck, they will deal with the traitor and her allies, and make sure she does not cause problems with the main attack."

"Yes, ma'am."

"Wu."

"Yes, Father?"

"I wish you to go to the starship. Should things go drastically wrong, and they are forced to flee, I want you to be my representative, and to provide some long-term planning for them. Additionally, if you are forced to flee, and from past interaction, I believe you may make a good alliance with Gliance, who seems competent and willing to adapt."

"Which is something that is difficult for many from younger

countries, and she and I have gotten along well in the past. Very well, father, I will load within a day."

~

THAT MORNING, Rosalyn and Aluaiy found themselves awake early, and decided to go to the shop. There they found, to their surprise, two packages already delivered. Looking at them, Aluaiy noticed that they'd been delivered after they had closed the shop. She picked them up, and meshed, *"That's odd, they are heavy, and lumpy."* Carrying both, she started to open the one addressed to her as she walked back into the workshop. Rosalyn had set up the tea kettle, and was setting up a pot of coffee when Aluaiy cried out. "Ow! Do you hear that noise in mesh?"

"I do. What on eahth...Aluaiy, I feel as though it's coming f-rom you." She looked at Aluaiy, then turned to Aluaiy's kiln, set it to high and opened the top. "D-rop them in!" Aluaiy stepped forward and dropped the packages, and Rosalyn closed the lid.

"Ahhh! My fingers! They're bleeding!" Aluaiy screamed.

Turning, Rosalyn grabbed a heavy pliers and reached out. An old rare earth magnet leapt to it, and she adjusted it to hold it in the jaws of the pliers, and turned, holding it to Aluaiy's fingers. The other woman was still screaming, and they saw small metallic things accumulating on the magnet. Rosalyn suddenly realized that the screaming in the mesh was failing. She took the chance to mesh Presha. *"Mr. Presha! Help!"*

"I'm about to go to a meeting. What's wrong?"

"We need a hazard team at our shop, now! We received two packages, one for each of us, and they contained what have to be the killer meshbots! Aluaiy's hands are being eaten, and bleeding!"

"Where are you?" She let him know. *"I'll have a team on its way asap."*

She paused and thought, then added Amelie to the mesh connection. *"Amelie! If you received a package, don't open it!"*

"Rosalyn, ma cherie, what's happened?"

She repeated what she had said, adding, *"Aluaiy and I can't be the only ones, and I thought of you."* She felt Amelie running.

"You were correct. I see two packages delivered. Wait...Rafe! Mon coeur! Have you received a package?" They could feel him respond he didn't know, and get up from his desk and walk out of his office, and his shock.

"Letitia! No!" Indirectly in mesh, they could hear a scream that died. *"Our receptionist just died in front of me! Her hands are bleeding, and there's blood coming out of her ears and mouth!"* They could hear him, though Amelia, call out, "Everyone stay away! James, get back, all you can do for her is die with her!"

Amelie added Presha to the connection. *"M. Presha, there are packages being delivered that contain the killer meshbots. M. Ridge just meshed me, and I have one, and my husband at the Finance Secretariat just had a receptionist die in front of him. This is a targeted attack. Contact the mail room and security for the Confederation Assembly!"*

They could feel his eyes widen. *"You're right. Excuse me, ladies, I'll have a team sent to you, M. Trouve, asap!"* He cut the connection.

Rosalyn got some disinfectant, but as she turned, Aluaiy fell bonelessly to the floor. Alan, her AI, told her that Aluaiy's AI reported her meshbots were fighting the invaders, which were trying to reprogram hers. She picked up the heavy-duty magnet with the pliers again, and ran it across Aluaiy's hands and arms. Finally, she heard the siren, and the EMTs were at the door. The team ran in, and Rosalyn meshed them to let them know what was going on. One pulled a device out of a pack and fired it at Aluaiy, whose whole body shivered, then lay still. "What did you do?"

"That just crashed all meshbots in her. We have this for cases where meshbots and other medical bots go off the rails, though I've never had to use it before. But now we need to filter them all out of her bloodstream, before they try to reboot. We can't do that here, they'll do it at Penn's isolation ward," replied the medic. Several of the team put Aluaiy on a stretcher and carried her swiftly out to the waiting ambulance. Hearing the police and the hazard vehicle arrive, people came in, and directed Rosalyn out of the workshop as two bunny-suited people ran in, and aimed devices around the workshop, and through the door she saw a small number of flaring motes in the air. Giving Rosalyn a quick debrief, when she told them about what was in the kiln, they thanked her, and told her that they would to take the whole unit. Turning it off, they loaded it onto a pallet that they sealed over and loaded into a compartment in their vehicle.

"Contact this office," the head of the hazard team told her, "and they'll arrange for resources to replace anything that we had to destroy or remove."

Seeing the ambulance about to leave, she called out, "Let me lock the shop, and r-ide with you!"

"They can't let you ride with them, with her in that condition, but you can ride with us, once we secure your shop," said the hazard team head.

"Thank you. Will I be able to be with heah?"

"They won't let you in the same room, but you can see her remotely."

"Can I wait theahe until she's conscious?"

He looked at her. "It may be a while."

"That doesn't matter." She locked the shop, and rode with them, terrified for Aluaiy. At the hospital, she was led to a room to watch over the older woman, who had been stripped, and was in a gown, lying in the bed unconscious, machines hooked to her, filtering her blood.

An hour later, a doctor came in, around her age, brown hair, wearing the universal uniform of scrubs. "Are you with her?"

"I am. How is she?"

"They sanitized her of the damn things in time, and we've got her clean. She'll have no connection to the mesh, though, since we've removed all the 'bots."

"Ahe you keeping he-r in isolation, or will you be moving heah to a less secu-re r-oom?"

"She'll go to the ICU. There was a lot of damage, and we've got some repair 'bots that we put into her at work."

"I'd like to sit with heah when she's moved."

He smiled. "We can do that."

"A question - would I have been as vulneahable? I have the new meshecytes."

He looked at her. "Interesting. No idea. May we take a sample of your blood? I'd like to have the isolation lab test that."

"Lead me to the phl-ebotomist."

~

After warning Presha, Amelie had Marat had bring up maximum security. Shutters once again closed and drones came out to circle the building. When Marat announced that the security team she had called for had arrived in a floater, she meshed them. "We'll be coming out in our floater from the garage. Give us coverage as we go to Confederation Security headquarters, *s'il te plaît.*"

The three of them, along with Joseph, Amelie and Rafe's dogsbody, left the living room and walked along the hallway, then down through the door into the garage. "Madam, shall I arm myself?"

"*Oui.*" He went over to what looked like a tool chest, opened it, then pulled a drawer out. Below it were several CA-9 2114 model military-grade coil pistols, and Joseph pulled out one.

"Are there more?" Jeanine asked. "I'm qualified."

Seeing Amelie nod, he handed her one, pulled a battery out of the charger unit, and handed pistol and battery to Jeanine, and took one for himself. The two of them checked the batteries then each shoved the battery home under the barrel. Next, he pulled out clips for both of them, shoving his into the handgrip. They then turned and got into the floater, closing the vehicle's doors and roof, and with Joseph driving, Amelie meshed Marat to open the door, and they floated out, the garage door shutting behind them.

"Janine, driving in this situation is among Joseph's duties for which he has special training." She looked at Rhys. "We are not out in the wilds. I do not expect what happened when you were young, *mon cherie.*"

"I think I could handle it now, Mother."

"Amelie," Joseph interrupted. "There's a report of a serious accident, and they're giving us a detour. Shall I take an alternate route to the detour?"

Her eyes were on the road. "*Oui.* But take a well-traveled one, even if it is not as short as either the detour or the alternate."

"Got it."

Fifteen minutes later, they were approaching the Confederation Security headquarters when Joseph spoke. "John? You heard that traffic report?" He paused, "That's what I think. Amelie, there was what they're calling another accident on the detour route. Marie thinks it was a vehicle with several people in it that is the same model and color as ours."

Amelie just nodded, her *face* coming on.

Joseph brought them down on Security's landing pad, John and Marie landed next to them. As they had arrived, they saw at the front of the building what appeared to be a full platoon of guards, all armed and armored, and two armored vehicles, each with a heavy automatic weapon and drone launcher. They all got out, holding up Confederation ID, while John and Marie held up their corporate IDs. They were hustled into the building, to find Presha waiting for them, with a small entourage. "M. Presha, we have the sealed package here for you," Amelie nodded to Joseph, who opened the small portable fire safe he was carrying.

"Excellent. We have a number of others, but this will let us compare them. Let M. Moussa here secure it." A white woman with very pale skin, piercing hazel eyes and tight, wavy black hair took the package, sealed it into a metal case with a handle, and walked off with her assistant. Turning to the lieutenant standing there, he said, "Please have M. Trouve's security escorted to the break room."

"Sir, they're armed."

"I see. Given what we're expecting, just hand me your pad and I'll authorize them to carry." He looked up at Joseph. "What are you loaded with?"

"Legal collapsing plastic baton rounds."

He nodded, signed the lieutenant's pad, then looked up. "We're not sure what form it's going to arrive in, but I would expect you to join us in a defense if the building is attacked."

Amelia, with *the face* on, smiled. It wasn't a nice smile.

He nodded. "If the three of you will follow me...." He led them, followed by an assistant, to the small conference room in his offices. and waved them to seats. "We've been able to burn out the 'bots with heavy-duty radar guns. In addition, a technical team has modified a number of units used by physicians to shut down meshbots that have gone rogue to work with a lot more power, to be used as an area weapon."

"I am glad to hear that, although it would be traumatic to people using the mesh."

Williams, Presha's assistant, shrugged. "True, but better that then dead." An hour and a half later, they went down to the break room where Joseph, John, and Marie were sitting around a table. They came over with cups of hot water, and Amelie, without a comment, pulled some teabags out of her bag.

"Is there something to eat, M. Presha?"

"We can have something sent up from the cafeteria."

She rolled her eyes. "Would it be acceptable for me to call out for delivery?"

"Certainly. Building security will bring it up."

She put on her AR headset, and put out an order. "Done." Getting offline, she looked around, then rose and walked over to talk to Rhys and Jeanine.

They spoke for a while, and then there was another knock, and a woman stuck her head in, the door opening away from Amelie and Rhys, so that only Jeanine was visible from the woman's viewpoint. "You called for food?"

"*Oui*. Please bring it in." Amelie saw a woman's hand on the outer doorknob as it opened, then three men rushed in, dropped the bags that had concealed their handguns and began firing. Presha, facing towards Amelie, was hit in the shoulder, and a second shot grazed his back, ripping through his jacket. John was slammed backwards as he was hit in the chest and shoulder, but like Marie, he had not removed his body armor, and returned fire with his coilgun, knocking down the man who had shot him, then fired at the second man. One of the other men fired at Marie, but missed as she dropped to her knees. He shot again, but it ricocheted off her shoulder, flying off into the wall, and she shot him with coilgun, and he collapsed backwards into the doorway from the two stun gun hits. A second later Williams's Beretta M11 thundered in the room, and the acrid smell of the ammunition The third assassin spun around, blood spattering the wall, and fell.

The woman, who had followed the men in, saw Janine and shot her, as the pilot was diving towards the table for cover. There was suddenly a splatter of blood on the pilot's leg as she landed, while a second shot missed.

As the woman stepped forward shooting, Rhys grabbed the chair behind him and swung it over around, hitting the woman's hand and knocking the gun to the floor and slamming the door open. Seeing her chance, Amelie grabbed the still-outstreched hand and pulled, spinning around to slam the woman headfirst into the wall. The room stank of gunsmoke, ozone from the coil guns, and blood. Her ears still rang as she looked around to take stock.

Williams called for backup as he, John, and Marie ran to kneel over the three fallen men. One of the men was moaning, the other shrieked, arched, and fell flat. Amelie fell to a crouch by the woman on the floor. The woman reached up to grab her, but Amelie sank a knee into the woman's stomach, who doubled over on the floor, moaning. "Is there a zip tie available?" Amelie asked.

"A moment," called Marie.

With the woman down, Rhys rushed over to Jeanine, helped her into a chair, and pulled out a handkerchief to put over the wound.

Williams had collected the guns and looked at them. "Ceramic, to get through detectors."

"A good thing," said Marie, massaging her arm. "They can't penetrate armor."

Looking at Presha, who was holding his side but aware, Williams said, "I've called medical emergency. We want to talk to them."

Marie stood and came over to hand ties to Amelie, who used them on the woman. "You've got this one at least."

Shortly, they heard footsteps in the hall, and Williams looked around the corner of the door with his handset. "Identify yourselves!" he called. They stopped, and held up ID, and gave their names. "Are you Confederation?"

The one in the lead replied, "Huh? Of course?" He turned, and the others all looked puzzled, but answered positively.

"Charlie...is that you?" Presha called from the room.

"Yes, sir, Williams called for medical and backup, said you had trouble." Ross, leading the backup, came in and motioned for the medical team to follow. Three were on the floor in a minute, working on the three men, while the other ran to Presha.

"Janine, how are you?" Amelie called.

"Hurts like hell, but I'm not bleeding out - my meshecytes are dealing with it. I can wait for the medic to take care of M. Presha."

Moments later, they heard heavy footsteps down the hall, and John, Marie, and Williams covered the door. Williams again called out, "Identify yourselves!"

"Secretariat security. There are insurrectionists in the building."

"Yes, we have four of them here, down. Show your identification," he called, and again put his handset around the corner, as they showed their IDs.

"M. Presha, are you all right?"

The EMT had stopped the bleeding, and shot him up with a painkiller. "I'm not well. Is that...Harry Smothers?" Presha replied.

"Yes, sir."

"Let them...come in."

The three men and a woman from security came into the room, and looked at the medical team and the men on the floor. "Sorry, sir," Smothers said to Presha. "There were some people who brought a food order, and as our people went to accept the food, they fired. We've got one person dead, and three more badly wounded."

Amelie looked at them. "I think that's all on my hands. I foolishly used one of my normal cards, which has my name on it, to order the food."

Smothers looked at her. "Ma'am, I don't think it's your fault. This isn't something that you think of happening."

She shook her head. "*I* should. I grew up under a trillionaire. Life has become settled, and I have not lived in that world for many years, for which I am grateful." she said, and sat heavily in a chair. "But it nearly killed us. I would not have thought they'd penetrate this far."

Charlie looked up from the one that had screamed. "Sorry, sir, this one's gone, and I don't think we can save him." He looked at the man working on the other two, and the woman who had gotten Presha's jacket off and shirtsleeve rolled up and was stabilizing him. "The bullet went through the muscle, and the other bounced off a rib. We need to get him to a hospital, but he'll hold for now. Let me get to the woman," nodding at Janine.

Smothers grimaced. "We'll take them. What happened?"

The medic cut Jeanine's pants leg open. Seeing no exit hole, she gave Jeanine a shot of painkiller, probed, and pulled out the bullet, then sealed and bandaged the wound. "Thank you," she said, then looked up at Amelie.

"Maman, don' let that bitch get away! She owes me for a pair of pants!" Rhys looked with a concerned look on his face.

"*Mon fils*, could you collect our lunch?" Amelie said, pointing to the bags on the floor. "I think we could all use some food." He nodded and went to collect the bags, then set them out on the table.

People grabbed what food they could as Williams stationed two of the security team outside the door, and the two others by the window. John and Marie split, with Marie covering the door, and John, complaining about the bruise he was going to have, the window. Amelie walked over to stand above the bound woman.

The woman had recovered by now and looked up. Clearly not used to being the recipient of *the look,* the woman shook herself, gave a shaky version of *the look* back, and spat. "Trouve the turncoat."

"And you are, madame?"

"An *American*. Mrs. Joan Krock to you, traitor."

"Ah, the widow of the former trillionaire. Interesting that you came after me yourself."

"We are all in this now, and you will be one of our triumphs, when we remove this, this dictatorship!"

Amelie, as strong as she was, never actually had the unbreakable control Francoise had found. At Krock's words, her early life poured through her mind like molten metal, her sister's utter self-humiliation as she sold their lives to Tolliver, their very names and looks ripped away at the trillionaire's pleasure. The little she knew of what Francoise had to do with the rest of her life, that she was willing to expunge by self-immolation as she destroyed herself and the first starship. The course of Amelie's younger life, and now the woman who had tried to kill her, her family, dare accuse *her*. It all coalesced and she lost control, rage flaming out like an open blast furnace, and *the face* blazed into a look that would melt steel. "Dictatorship? Turncoat? That would imply that such a thing as loyalty flowed any direction except up. Traitor? You dare call me traitor? You trillionaires, your kind were *never* loyal to any country other than the country of money and power. American? Do not make me laugh. You and your people worked long and spent much to buy the government, as you did other governments. I am from Niger, I am French, but most of all, *I* am of the Terran Confederation. *You* are the traitor. My sister spoke for us all, when she *revoked* our submission to your kind."

She took a deep breath, and regained control. *The face* returned, and looking down, deliberately, she kicked the woman in the side, hard. As Krock curled in pain, Amelie added, her voice cold again. "I could kill you, and not be charged, because I have witnesses to your treason. But I will let the courts take vengeance on you." She turned and began to walk away, then looked back. "And you have *failed*." With that, she returned to the table, Krock behind her crying, and poured some tea as everyone stared at her. She took a sip and stared at the cup. "Merde, dealing with her, the tea is getting cold." Then she looked over at Presha, lying on a collapsible gurney the medics had brought. "M'sieur, with this attack, I would presume more are coming to follow up on the confusion and disorganization from the killer meshbots. Should we assume that is why the troops are out front, and why they have not removed you to a hospital?"

"You have it...all correct. M. Trouve. I have...contacted my superiors, and...they have contacted the President, Confederation Navy, and the Security Council." He nodded ponderously. "We...are in better shape than they expect, thanks to...your early warnings this morning. The 'bots got to fewer higher-level people, and everyone...is expecting more trouble." Amelie smiled in response.

They turned on the newsfeeds, to see, twenty minutes later....

"...MACSEN, with Engrelay NeoWeb, *your* source of curated, verified news of the Terran Confederation and beyond! I'm here in the main lobby at the Confederation Assembly building, in New York, where the Security Council is meeting behind closed doors to consider the widespread attacks by package delivery of what are being called killer meshbots on the Confederation and the governments of a number of member nation-states. I'm hearing there may have been warnings earlier this morning, and there are Confederation troops inside the building, with New York City riot police outside...."

She stopped speaking as a thunderingly loud announcement came from the lobby's speakers. "AN ATTACK IS IMMINANT. TAKE COVER! UNDER DESKS, BEHIND CHAIRS, MOVE INTO OTHER ROOMS IF POSSIBLE. SHIELD YOURSELVES FROM THE WINDOWS!" Shock showing on her face, Macsen threw herself under a bench, her camerawoman right behind.

Moments later, there were several blasts. and after a pause several more, and several rows of windows were blown in from the front of the building. Leaning out, she looked that way, and began, "This is Macsen. I'll keep reporting as long as I can. Right now, I can see a number of yachts through where the transparent block windows in the seawall used to be. They seem to have cannons or rocket launchers mounted, and must have fired at us minutes ago, blowing out the windows in the seawall, then hitting the Confederation building. There's...." She ducked back, and another round of explosions could be heard as more windows were blown in, shatteringly loud. Looking out again, "I can see people injured, and now there are... wait, I can see large heavy vehicles, cars, trucks and floaters pulling up in front of the building. Some are flying the flag of the Free Citizens Alliance, and others have the logo on them of private security companies. They've come to a halt with screeches I can hear, and many armed and armored people are charging towards the building, shooting as they come, and private security seems to be with the FSA people...."

~

As THEY WATCHED the newsfeed from the Confederation Assembly, Amelie and the others heard loud noises coming through the window, and a security man at the windows yelled, "Everyone on the floor!" As everyone followed his order, he added, "There are three compact tanks out there, and a lot of individual vehicles following them."

"They're flying the Free Citizens Alliance flag," John added from under a table. Just then, there was the roar of cannon, and the whole building shook several times. They huddled there, then they heard sound of loud buzzing, and a few seconds later there was a sound of one heavy explosion, then another.

"What is zat?" Amelie shouted.

John stuck his mobile up into the window for a minute, as did one of Presha's security. "That was our guys," the security woman said. "Flew jet drones into the cannon mouth of two of those tanks. The tank crew didn't realize it, and tried to fire. They're out of action." She paused. "Crap! The vehicles are pulling up, and dozens of armed traitors are unloading and running towards the building. Several trucks rammed the fences to make openings, and they're getting through, though they're taking casualties." She smiled viciously. "They don't like our defense drones, and I'll bet they weren't expecting troops.

"I don't feel like sitting here waiting for them," Marie snarled, crawling to a window. She pulled the protective hood from her armored jacket over her head. It was a modern building, where architecture had returned to having windows that could open, She shoved the window up, then rolled to a kneeling position, and started picking targets. All the rest of the other security people followed her lead at other windows, except for the one guarding Krock. The sound of their guns was deafening, and the smell of ionization from the coilguns mixed with the acrid smell of the firearms filled the air. Shots came back, and Marie spun around backwards. "Damn it, got the same damn shoulder." She rubbed it, and cursed. "Someone got a bandage? It shoved my armor into the shoulder. A medic came over and helped her pull the hood down and the armor off the shoulder. Just then, there was a loud stuttering, and one of the security people spun, cried out and fell back, blood spilling from his head. The woman medic crawled over to him, looked at him, and turned to Presha, shaking her head. Amelie, looking around, could see cuts from shrapnel on the one of the security agents face.

LENNY SCHWEIR, on board to try to resolve some recent computer server issues, was in the break room on the command deck of the Terran Confederation Navy cruiser Glenn, watching the newsfeeds on screen and in mesh when he felt an explosion with a burst of air coming in the door. With that, the main lights went out, emergencies coming on. In mesh, he checked the command servers, the reason he was on board, and found them down. He leapt out of his seat and ran down the corridor towards the bridge. As he came in, smoke was clearing, and people were moving around, clearing things. Careful to stay out of everyone's way, he opened the cover to the server cabinets and sat on the floor, the cover behind him between him and the door. He moved a long coiled 220v cable that was used for charging bots, and opened the breaker box. Half of them were tripped. which concerned him. He considered it for a minute, then flipped the one least likely to cause trouble, the one for the support power like the bot chargers, and it stayed on. He had leaned in, and was staring at a number of blown-apart cables when he heard a loud voice behind him.

"Freeze!"

He started to put his hands up when he realized he couldn't be seen. Turning his head and leaning a bit, he saw a man with a commander's insignia holding a gun aimed at the captain.

"What's the meaning of this, XO?" the captain demanded.

"Don't play stupid. You're not attacking the patriots down there. O'Brien!" Another man in the uniform of a lieutenant came up beside the XO. "Take the weapons seat, and target the nearest airbases before they can get fighters into the air."

"Roger." O'Brian started towards the weapons console as the captain and the lieutenant at the weapons station began to argue.

Lenny thought as fast as he ever could, then quietly reached over and grabbed the coiled cable. Pulling out the wire cutter from the tools on his belt, he cut the female socket off and stripped the ends of the wire for a few centimeters, zip tied a big screwdriver from his belt to it. Holding the screwdriver, he plugged the other end into an outlet. Taking a deep breath, he leaned forward and yelled, "COMMANDER! CATCH!" and flung the screwdriver and cable at the man.

The commodore spun and fired at Lenny, who was slammed back against the edge of the cabinet. At the same time, the man had tried to catch the cable, and touched the bare wires. There was a spark, and the man jerked and fell backwards over a chair. The captain and two others leapt at the XO, who was shaking on the deck, while the weapons lieutenant attacked O'Brien. With what strength he had left, Lenny yanked the cable from the outlet.

In two minutes, it was all over, with the XO and O'Brien bound, and the captain ordering the weapons to target the attackers two hundred kilometers below. Then he turned and saw Lenny.

"Medic! Bridge emergency! Ihnat, you've got medic training."

"On it, sir" the young man said, as he ran to Lenny, and worked to stop the blood, who sat there trying to breath, feeling liquid in his lungs, and hoping his meshbots would keep him alive. He felt the slight shudder as they began firing the kinetic projectiles, and smiled.

"Why the hell did you do that?" the captain asked, standing near him, looking down.

Through the pain, Lenny smiled. "I...was in downtown... Manhattan the...day Trouve took out the...starship. She saved...my life...with her death. Could I do any less?" He bent in pain, and just then the medics came up to take over.

~

WILLIAMS SHOUTED, "They've got at least one automatic weapon," then paused. then he roared, "EVERYONE DOWN! Incoming!" A couple of seconds later, there was a massive sound, a shock wave that could be felt through the building, and the sound of some armored windows shattering, hot air slamming through.

~

"THE RIOT POLICE and the troops are fighting a pitched battle with the invaders," Macsen said, softly. Her camerawoman was angling to get the side of her head against the front of the building. "But they're falling back. There are too few of them, and the invaders are heavily armed..." She paused to use her mesh to enhance her vision. "I see them armed with shotguns and assault rifles, and many with body armor. Some of the police have fallen, or are still shooting, even though they are wounded and are being forced back." Macsen jerked back as the floor next to her grew some pockmarks, the shrapnel hitting her face and arm. The camerawoman had dropped the lens of her camera down, protecting it, but she felt herself hit as well.

"TAKE COVER, NOW!" burst from the speakers.

As Macsen and her camerawoman pushed back under the table, there were two immense blasts of thunder, and the whole building shook, and tremendously hot air, with the smell of hot metal, blew in for a minute.

~

NO ONE COULD HEAR for several minutes. Slowly as their hearing recovered, they heard the sound of heavy fliers, and some firing, but not like before. In through the broken windows drifted gunsmoke, ozone, and dust, along with the smell of crushed greenery.

"What just happened?" meshed Amelie.

Janine had risen to half standing, leaning on the table to support her wounded leg, looking out the window with her mouth open. She closed it and turned. "Something I hoped I'd never see in real life, a kinetic projectile from orbit. I saw training videos in the Air Force before I transferred to Confederation civilian air." She shivered, then waved out the window, which had a crack in the clear, hard ceramic, though the shattered rings where bullets had struck home. "The tanks are trashed, and most of the vehicles and people that were anywhere near are dead or flattened from the shock wave."

Within the hour, more medical help had arrived to stitch up Presha, and he took a call, then looked at the medic. "Give me a shot of upper. I...have to take this call." Unhappily, the medic injected him with it, and he spoke via mesh for a while. Finally, he said, "I'm leaving you in Williams's capable hands. That call was from the Executive Offices, and was for the Confederation President. She will be making a statement to the media soon. Medics, you can take me to the...hospital now."

~

PEERING OUT, Macsen's jaw dropped. "A good number of windows have been sucked out, towards the invaders. Many of them are down, though I can't see if they're moving. I have no idea what caused those blasts," she said, continuing her reporting.

Through the windows, the two newswomen saw a flight of heavily armed and armored flyers in US and Confederation insignia came along the East River, firing their weapons as they came. Several launched rockets, and the largest yachts were struck and left burning, with two of them breaking up. Following them, heavily armored floaters came down on the plaza in front of the Assembly, some landing on the heavy vehicles and crushing them, killing anyone still inside. The bays opened, and troops, some in US combat array, the rest in Confederation armor, came charging out. There was little resistance as troops rushed into the Assembly building, taking the invaders who had entered from behind before those that could still move were able to rise.

With all the noise, Macsen used the mesh to report. "I can see some of the invaders still outside are either firing from the ground, or trying to stand, but they are outnumbered by US and Confederation troops, who are rounding up the invaders, and forming an armed cordon around the Assembly. I'll...go out on a limb here, and guess that the Security Council was expecting an attack, and asked for support to be on standby. I'll see if...ah, they're giving us the all clear, and medical personnel are going through the lobby, giving aid to anyone who's been...." She paused, and muttered to herself, though her microphone was still on, "Why am I out of breath?" Her camerawoman caught it on camera as Macsen fell to the floor, with blood on her legs, a hip, and one arm.

Looking down, the camerawoman realized that her legs were cut up as well, but Macsen had caught most of the flying shards of glass. Holding the camera in one hand, she called for help, let herself be bandaged, then shook her head at the medics and picked up Macsen's microphone. "This is Breona Burke, normally camera for Jacinda Macsen, filling in for her. She was seriously injured by shrapnel from the invaders' weapons and glass shards from the windows, and has been taken off by medical personnel. Many other bystanders were injured or killed during the attack, but the murderous, ah, insurgent attack on the Assembly has been crushed by troops from the United States National Guard and Confederation Security, with support from the Confederation Navy, who broke the attack here in New York, and around the world in, um, Moscow, Paris, Beijing, New Delhi, Abuja, and other cities. From reports I'm hearing, the Confederation Navy used kinetic projectiles, solid shells fired from orbit that come down at hypersonic speeds with what I can personally assure you is a shattering effect. I'm told there were heavy casualties among the insurgents. The mopping up has begun, and I'm told that if anyone has been injured and help is not there, to contact the location that Engrelay NeoWeb has on the bottom of the screen. I'll need to move now, because we're being called in to hear a statement by the President of the Confederation."

Shortly after, the view from the newsfeeds moved to the press room of the Executive Offices, and President Sundberg walked in, flanked by military, police, and civilian officials. Stepping up to the podium, she began, "Citizens and Members of the Confederation, this morning an insurrection began against the Confederation with the delivery of over a thousand packages of targeted killer meshbots. This was followed a few hours later, by armed assaults here in New York, as well as in the capitals of a number of our major member countries, with many casualties, including one of my senior security officers in the Justice Secretariat. Fortunately, we received notification of these deadly weapons at the beginning of the attack, before most of the packages had been received, and were able to prepare a suitable response. I am happy to say that the attacks have been put down, although there are local holdouts. We expect them to be resolved shortly." She went on to take questions.

~

LATE IN THE EVENING, well into the second shift, Aluaiy opened her eyes. She looked around the hospital room, and then saw Rosalyn, eyes closed, slumped in a chair near the bed. Her voice came out breathy and weak, "Rosalyn?"

Rosalyn's eyes flew open, and she leaned forward, to grasp Aluaiy's hand that did not have IVs. "Aluaiy," she said, her eyes wet with tears starting. "They say you'll be okay."

"What...what happened? Why can't I mesh you?"

"The packages had the killeah meshbots that Amelie talked about. The EMTs disabled eve-rything in you, and heah in the hospital, they filte-red youah blood to r-emove eve-rything. You'ahe going to have to be r-ejoined to the mesh, though I think youah AI is still r-unning." She gestured at the monitor on the wall. "It's been an interesting day." On the screen, they saw a woman in a hospital bed, bandaged, with an IV hanging, just as Aluaiy was.

~

"HELLO, this is Jacinda Macsen, with Engrelay NeoWeb, *your* source of curated, verified news of the Terran Confederation and beyond! Please excuse my condition, but I was among the many seriously injured in the attack today on the Confederation Assembly building in New York. After it was put down, the President of the Confederation held a press conference, and reported that perhaps a thousand or more packages were delivered today to locations covering all major offices of the Confederation here in New York, and other major capitals. Each package contained mesh killers, meshbots that, on being activated by the package being opened, attacked anyone nearby with the intent to kill. This was followed a few hours later by armed insurrectionists, with aid from yachts identified as belonging to some of the former trillionaires. It is being considered as an attempted decapitation strike on the Confederation, and many of the Representatives are speaking of it as an act of war. There have been no claims of responsibility yet for the mesh killers, but Confederation Security is working with the American FBI, Interpol, and other agencies to track the source of the packages."

"A spokesperson for Confederation Security told us that dozens of people were killed or wounded, but that it could have been worse, had not someone whose package was delivered early in the day recognized what was happening, and contacted Security."

~

ALUAIY'S EYES GREW WIDE. "WHO...?"

"I think that would have been you and me who got the packages ea-rly, and I think we can guess who sent them.... I've heaahd things on b-roadcast, and no one's pointing fingeahs yet, but with what you and I know...."

Aluaiy nodded. "You saved my life."

"I wasn't going to let the woman I've discovered I love die in front of me." She squeezed Aluaiy's arm.

The woman in the bed bent her head to touch Rosalyn's arm, and nodded, but then her eyelids dipped. "So tired...."

"Sleep. You need it. If you wake up and need anything, I'll be heah and call the nu-rse." The two exchange a look that spoke volumes to each other, then Aluaiy lay back, and in moments was asleep again. Rosalyn stared at her for a while, unutterably glad. Finally, she sighed, and made a mesh link. *"Amelie, can you talk?"*

"Oui, ma cherie. How are you doing?"

"We're in the hospital. Aluaiy was hurt by the killer bots, and they had to crash and filter all her meshbots out. The damage is being repaired, but it will take days before she heals enough afterwards that she can leave. Since Aluaiy no longer has meshbots, I'd like to see her get meshecytes. Who should I contact?"

"M. Jorgeson. You have his contact information. Also, when she gets out of the hospital, let us assess the situation. The two of you may want to come up here until things settle down, since we do have our own security."

"Our shop...."

"I'll arrange to have an agency keep an eye on it."

~

ROSALYN GROGGILY OPENED her eyes as the morning shift came in, one of the cleaners singing softly to himself as he emptied the trash. As they finished, she saw the doctor she had spoken with the day before, and caught him as he walked by. "Yes, we ran the tests, and no, you were not as vulnerable, since your meshecytes aren't programmable, the way the meshbots are."

"Aluaiy needs rejoining to the mesh. Can you see that she gets meshecytes?"

"I don't know, they are fairly new...."

Smiling, she said, "I've made ah-rrangements. You should be contacted today conce-rning them. She's heah from Taiwan under asylum f-rom the Confede-ration, and they may have something to say." His eyes widened at that, and nodded. Going back into the room, she saw the other Aluaiy sleepily awake, and squeezed her forearm.

"What can we do about my mesh?"

"Al-ready taken caahe of. Ah've meshed Amelie, then Jo-rgenson, and you'll get the fi-rst infusion of meshecytes as soon as your doctoah says it's okay. The doctor heah tells me they wouldn't be affected the same way, since they can't be reprogrammed."

Aluaiy looked at her. "Dear lady, you need to get some sleep."

"You'ahe telling me? I'm going home, but I'll be back lateah." With that she kissed her and left.

Early in the evening, Rosalyn woke, took a shower and walked down to Baltimore Ave, and checked out their shop. Everything looked okay, so she stopped in a restaurant and ate, then took the trolley to the hospital. When she got in, Aluaiy was awake. They sat and watched the newsfeeds in horror. Dozens had been killed by the 'bot attack, including Representatives from several African and South American countries, as well as the one from Kazakhstan. Scores more had been injured, frequently when others were trying to help the injured before a sanitization team arrived from Security. Thousands had been wounded or killed around the world in the insurrection that followed, but most had already been put down. There had even been fighting on three of the five Confederation Navy cruisers before their kinetic projectiles broke the back of the insurrection.

43

A LAST SHOT

Rosalyn was sitting with Aluaiy in the ICU, surrounded by the usual smell of disinfectant, four days after the packages appeared and the insurrection that followed, talking about the older woman's first infusion of meshecytes that she had just gotten when her phone rang. She picked it up to hear a frantic Ju Zhou. "What's wr-ong?"

"Mei-ling! They've been kidnapped!"

Rosalyn froze for a moment, then said, slowly, "Take a deep breath, Ju, and slow down. What happened?"

Ju did as she'd asked, then said, "We, Darcy, Mei-ling, and I were coming back from picking up a pizza, and were waiting for a taxi, when this man came up from behind us, wearing wrap-around dark glasses, and pulled out a stun gun and pointed it at us, and told Mei-ling to come with him...."

Rosalyn sucked in her lips, then said, "Wait, this is impoahtant. What did he say, exactly?"

"He said, said, 'Come here, you slanty dicklette'." Rosalyn could see tears starting on Ju's face.

"Then what happened?"

"Mei-ling stepped towards him, then turned to run, but before they got two steps, a floater pulled up, its front on the sidewalk, and the man grabbed them, and shoved them in the back as the door opened."

"Could you see the driveah?"

"Yes, he had dark glasses on as well, but he looked Chinese. Then they drove off."

"Call the police, now. Give them my numbeah—they'll want more infoahmation about Mei-ling." Ju thanked her, and hung up to call. Rosalyn looked at Aluaiy and told her what had happened, then meshed for Amelie.

To her surprise, she answered immediately. *"Bonsoir, Rosalyn. Ah! What's wrong? I can feel you distressed."*

Rosalyn began to tell her, when Aluaiy answered her phone, next to the bed, and looked at it for a moment, then at Rosalyn.

"It must be the kidnapper. They say to come to a location, and 'bring my friend the spy' with me, or they'll send pieces of Mei-ling to us. They say not to tell anyone."

Through the mesh Rosalyn heard Amelie laugh, and looked at Aluaiy.

"They want to play this game, do they? Grabbing the young one off the street does not say much for their operational security, meaning they are playing far out of their league. It might make them more dangerous to the young one, but certainly shows them as fools. 'You give up, or we will shoot you', then they intend to take you away and shoot you. Tell me where and when they tell you to appear, and they will find themselves, ahh, as you Americans say, 'up the creek without a paddle'." Aluaiy repeated the information.

"I think I need to go, Amelie."

"Merci, ma chère. I will make arrangements," and signed off the link.

"The b-rief t-raining I had was to p-rotect myself, not woahry about othe-rs. But...I don't know about you, but I'm not suah what was more teahrifying." Aluaiy looked at Rosalyn, questioning. "The demand...or Amelie's laugh." She could see the lack of understanding in the older woman's face as they sat there for a moment. Rosalyn got up and got something to drink from a machine, and came back to the room where Aluaiy had gotten some tea from the hospital kitchen.

"Ah'll go," said Rosalyn. "It's not like you can. Ah'll tell them you'ahe in the hospital. They want me, anyway."

Aluaiy looked at her. "To quote a phrase I heard recently, I don't want to see the woman I love killed."

"I doan' think so. Amelie is making plans." They were each drinking when Amelie meshed back.

"We have fun and games prepared. Rosalyn, ma chère, there will be a package delivered momentarily. There will be a small stun gun, which you should put in a pocket for them to find, and a pendant. Put the latter on, making sure it is outside of any clothes. If you are under life-or-death threat, or hear a message via mesh to use it, align it towards them and close your eyes as you use this code." She gave her the code, and ended, *"Good hunting!"* she said, signing off.

Rosalyn swallowed, then looked at Aluaiy. "I suppose..." she began, as a woman with a package walked into the room, who said, in mesh,

"M. Ridge, you were informed about this package."

She nodded, took the package from the woman and signed for it, then the woman left. Sitting, she opened the package to find the small stun gun and the pendant, and put the the latter on. Turning, she said to Aluaiy, "Ah guess it's about time to leave." she said, putting on her light jacket, then pocketing the stun gun. Giving the older woman a kiss careful of the medical devices still attached to her, and a promise to come back, she left the hospital and called a cab.

Reaching the park, she paid and got out, walking around the corner and down Lindon Ave to the small park, then south onto Delaware Ave. It was getting dark, and the river was pleasant. On the other side of the street was a parking lot, and there were signs for a boat ramp. As she passed a tree, the door of a hover that was parked there opened, and a man stepped out, white, dark hair, wearing a dark jacket and dark glasses in spite of the lateness of the hour.

"You, in!" he said, pointing at the open back door. To her shock, he was pointing a handgun at her, not a stun gun. "Where's the other bitch?"

"She was badly hurt by one of the packages of killahbots. She's in the hospital."

A snarl crossed his face, and he waved the gun. "Move it!" Rosalyn went to get in, and from behind, he grabbed her arms and pulled them behind her, tying them with what she could feel was a zip tie, and shoved her in and slammed the door. He got in the passenger door and turned around, telling her to sit there and be quiet, while the other man, who looked Asian to Rosalyn, drove them out onto the street.

Rosalyn meshed *"The game's afoot..."* to Amelia when the man reached back and hit her across the face with the pistol, leaving her forehead and nose hurting and dripping blood. She looked at him, guessing he was local muscle with knowledge of the city.

"None o' that mesh crap. We've got a detector that tells us when you're using it."

He turned his head to see them take a turn, and Rosalyn told Alan to track them. The man turned and stared back at her. She saw them make several more turns, then drive onto the old Interstate, heading north. After a while they got off, heading to the near Northeast, then back towards the Delaware. She looked down, and saw the blood on her blouse, and suddenly realized that they didn't care if she saw where they were going, and what that probably meant. She felt paralyzed for a few minutes, and took several deep breaths, trying to give herself confidence that she wasn't feeling.

The man, watching her, gave a nasty smile, then, reached down in front of him and pulled out a small bottle of bourbon. Saying "Hate to waste it, but..." he opened it and splashed some on her. "You really shouldn't drink so much you fall down, bitch."

"Wheah's Mei-ling?"

"Where you'll be, soon enough. Shut up."

She hunched back into the seat. Finally, they pulled around a corner, and a rollup door opened in a building, and they drove in, the door coming down behind them. They came to a stop in front of a loading dock, next to a large truck with a shipping container on its flatbed. The men in front got out, the local pulling Rosalyn out. Standing on the dock above them were two more men, clearly Chinese. The building smelled of lubricants, cold metal, and dust.

"Here she is," said the driver, who hadn't spoken before.

"Where's the other?"

"She said she's in the hospital from the mesh killers."

"Did you search her?" the one on the dock with a dressy jacket asked.

"Why, look at 'er. What she gonna have?" asked the local.

The man above nodded, and the driver swiftly and efficiently searched Rosalyn, almost immediately finding the small stun gun. The man above shook his head, and the local muttered, "Well, shit...."

Rosalyn asked, "Wheah's Mei-ling?" when they heard a noise, and the teen came charging around the open door of the shipping container and jumped down from the dock. They fell to their knees as they landed, awkward with their hands tied behind, but got up and ran to Rosalyn, head against her chest. Glancing around, Rosalyn saw a door beside the rollup. She nerved herself up and said, "Guys..." They all turned to look at her, and she pulled her shoulders back to make sure the pendent was clear and aimed forward, and meshed the code. It flashed, blindingly, and darkened, then, as the men began yelling, flashed again. Rosalyn said, "The door," looking at the door. Mei-ling was still partly blinded by the reflection of the flash, but moved towards the door, with Rosalyn trying to push them faster. They were almost at the door when they heard, "Freeze, bitches," and a shot.

Rosalyn felt a tiny, powerful fist slam into the back of her right thigh, then a burning pain, and fell face first to the floor, trying to turn her head as she hit, slamming into her jaw and nose, then her ear and the side of her head, leaving her stunned. As though in response, the door burst open, and armored agents charged in to spread out past them, protecting them, and a loud voice said, "FREEZE! FBI! YOU ARE UNDER ARREST!"

Dazed, she looked back to see the two men on the dock drop to a crouch and tried to back away, but she felt a Sound, the backlash from weapon one of the agents carried as it echoed through the loading dock, and the two men fell backwards. The man who had been their driver raised his hands, and the local hand looked around, and said, "Shit, I didn't sign up for this," slowly put his gun on the ground and stood, hands raised.

As the agents collected the men, a man and woman rushed in through the door to Rosalyn and the teenager. They cut their bonds, and then the man, seeing the blood on Rosalyn's face and thigh, dropped to his knees and pulled out first aid gear. He gave her a calmative first, and as it hit, she called on her mesh to start closing the wounds. "M...mesh" she stammered, and he nodded, and put back one package and pulled out another. It wasn't long before he'd cleaned her up and put a leg brace on her.

"Even with the mesh, you shouldn't be putting weight on that for a week. You're lucky he only had legal baton rounds, rather than bullets," he said, then turned as the woman who had come in with him came up.

"Everything taken care of, medic?"

"Yes, ma'am. Minor wounds. Her face will be okay tomorrow, since she's got mesh."

"Ah, yes," She smiled. In mesh, she said to Rosalyn, *"The pendant you're wearing isn't just a flasher, it's also a passive mesh repeater, which let us follow you. When you used the flash, that was our signal to arrive."* She watched as Rosalyn stood with the EMT's help. *"I must compliment you. For someone without much experience or training, you've handled yourself quite respectably."*

"Thank you, though I'd really don't think I intend to have this as a new profession," Rosalyn meshed, with the edge of hysteria in her tone, then gave a shaky smile as the woman laughed with her.

Mei-ling, shaking like a leaf and clearly wanting to hold onto Rosalyn, gave something between a laugh and a cry. "For once, I am so happy to see the police.."

"Knowing where you're from, I understand. Ah!" the woman in

charge said, turning to look at one of her people on the loading dock. "We have their documents. We'll be letting the Taiwanese Embassy know, after we've debriefed them all."

"Ah think," Rosalyn said, "that you might get something useful out of the man who had the gun. He's obviously local, and seemed as if he didn't know who'd hiahed him, otheah than foah a kidnapping."

"Excellent point about the man."

With help from Mei-ling, Rosalyn stood. Thinking for a minute, then said, "I game a lot, and that gets me thinking - does this whole wahehouse setup seem a bit much for a simple kidnapping?"

The agent in charge looked at her. "I've been focused on getting you safe and arresting the kidnappers, too focused, perhaps. Agents, check out that cargo container, carefully." Turning back to Rosalyn and Mei-ling, she said, "We're going to bring you all into our offices, take your statements, and then?"

"Stay with you, please?" said Mei-ling, finally throwing her arms around Rosalyn. In mesh, she said, *"You saved me again. You are a hero, like from an old anime."*

She looked at Mei-ling, shaking her head. Remembering what Amelie had said, during her first visit, she replied, *"I'm a citizen of the Confederation, and tried to do what a good citizen should."* Looking at the officer, she said, "Ah think afteahwards, if you could transpoaht us back to my apahtment, Ah think we need a comfoahtable night."

Suddenly, there was the sound of shots from the container. One of the agents, and one of the Chinese men fell, and there was screaming. One armored agent staggered out of the container, tearing at their armor, screaming that it was eating him. "Back, everyone. Out the door! Do we have a sanitizer?" the woman by Rosalyn called loudly.

"I have one to use on one person at a time," said the medic.

"Get it, five minutes ago!" the agent yelled at him. Everyone was coming towards the door, except for the two armored agents and one of the men who had been on the dock, who had fallen, and lay there screaming and tearing at their arms. She pushed Rosalyn, Mei-ling and the medics out of the door, and pulled the American, now in handcuffs, after them. "YOU! What were all of you doing with the contents of this container?"

He looked at her, sullen, clearly nervous. "We were supposed to mail 'em all from a bunch o' offices, but the guys there wanted them two first," nodding at Rosalyn and Mei-ling.

"Did you know what these were?"

He shrugged. "Not my business to know. Why should I care, as long as I get paid?"

"Take a look in there, those men are being attacked by killer meshbots. What do you think now?"

He stood there for a minute, his face growing red. "They were gonna off me instead of paying." He was quiet for a minute. "Gimme a break, and I'll tell you everything I know."

The agent's smile was hard. "That seems like a reasonable deal."

~

"THIS IS THOMAS MASTERSON, for Philadelphia's Inky Net News, in Port Richmond. I can't show you the scene, since there are a number of bodies on the ground, including FBI agents, with blood around them. The police aren't clear on what's happened, but they've established a cordon around the warehouse, after several people ran to people they knew who had staggered out of the doors and fallen, and collapsed themselves. Wait, something's happening...the police are ordering everyone back another twenty meters, and they've just announced they're expecting assistance shortly." Masterson, paused, surrounded by the noise of the crowd, then he looked up. "I'm going to see if I can get close enough to the agent in charge from the FBI to ask for a statement...."

The video feed showed Masterson working to push his way through the crowd, when mesh and loudspeakers came on. "Please move back, do not crowd the line. The FBI has informed us that they believe that there has been a release of the killer meshbots, and are expecting heavy support shortly to sanitize the area."

With that, most of the crowd backed away, torn between being terror of the killer meshbots, and morbid curiosity. Masterson was finally able to get close to the agent-in-charge, standing next to a woman who was obviously wounded, a teenager, and a man in handcuffs. She could only reply that Masterson knew what she did, and to wait. The news feed broke for other local news, only to return fifteen minutes later.

"This is Thomas Masterson, still at the scene in Port Richmond. We're hearing heavy thrums in the air...wait, there are two heavy vehicles, both from Confederation Security. One is a transport, and I don't know what the other is, though it's floating down over the area...several weapons of some kind have appeared, and are pointing down, wait, there are what looks like small clouds of lights, like bright fireflies flashing and going out. There are more of them closer to the open warehouse door...the floater is circling the area, and now I'm not seeing any more of the flashes. They...they seem to have deliberately missed the bodies on the ground with their weapon, but now they're floating over each, and using something that doesn't seem to show anything, but as they do, the bodies are jerking, then stop."

Masterson watched as the floater dealt with all the bodies, then it rose as the transport landed. Out of what was an airlock door came a number of people in full armored contagion suits, running to the people on the ground.

"The people in the bunny suits are running towards three of the bodies on the ground, two further from the door, and one closer. Now three isolation tubes are being brought out of the transport, and the three are being hooked up to equipment, which may mean these people are still alive. They've moved them closer to the transport... wait, I hear sirens, here come three ambulance floaters, they're down, and they've loaded those three. Other people in suits are going over to the other bodies, and they're putting them in isolation tubes, but those seem to be just for isolation, not for life support." A short time later, the video feed finally panned to cover the scene. "All the bodies have been removed, and the armed floater has offloaded several people, all carrying what I assume are weapons. They're headed towards the door to the warehouse, and they're entering." He stood there for a while, trying to find words as he waited, then there was motion. "They're bringing several isolation tubes into the warehouse, doing something, and here they come. Enhancing my vision, I can see they have some boxes inside the isolation tubes, not a body. Now they're just spraying the area around the door, and inside the warehouse with the beam weapons that seem to disable the killer meshbots. Wait...I hear the agent-in-charge is saying there will be a press conference shortly downtown. This is Thomas Masterson, signing off."

44

CLOSING THE HOLE

Three days later, the doctor declared Aluaiy fit for release from the hospital, but advised that she not get the rest of the meshecytes for a few days yet.. Rosalyn had told Aluaiy of Amelie's invitation, and had come to the hospital that day with an overnight bag, so on Aluaiy's release, they called a cab and went to Aluaiy's apartment and had it wait while she packed an overnight bag, then they went to 30th St. Station to take the high speed train to New York City's New Jersey suburbs, where Joseph was waiting for them in the hover.

Amelie was there when they came in from the garage. "Ma cherie," she said, hugging Rosalyn. "Aluaiy, how good you could be here. I only wish it was under happier circumstances."

"M. Trouve, Amelie, if only. Thank you for inviting us up. We were afraid of further attacks...."

Amelie laughed. "If there are more, they will certainly include us here." She smiled. "Let Joseph, here, put your bags in your rooms...." She saw the look Rosalyn and Aluaiy exchanged, and went on. "Oh, how lovely, je suis heureuse pour vous deux, after being forced from your home and work. Joseph, put their bags in the large room, s'il te plaît. Come, we have some appetizers, and dinner will be ready soon enough." She led them into the sitting room, where Rafe was sitting in a comfortable chair.

He stood, and shook Rosalyn's hand, then turned to Aluaiy, and stopped, looking at her hands.

"I'm glad they got you in time."

"I will not be able to work for another week or two."

"Plan. Design," Rafe responded, and Aluaiy nodded.

"Ah wish Ah'd been able to stop them before they got you," said Rosalyn to Aluaiy.

Aluaiy looked at her. "Mei-ling is calling you a hero. Dear lady, she is not wrong."

"Rosalyn, ma cherie, you personally kept it from being much worse." Rosalyn looked at Amelie. "If you hadn't had the presence of mind to realize what was happening, and meshed M. Presha, and *moi*, they would have gone through the mailroom of the Confederation bureaus, or directly to offices, and to the Assembly itself. Had it done that, the Confederation would have been utterly disorganized when the insurrectionists attacked. Then you went into what we thought was just a kidnap situation to save Mei-ling, and from what I 'ave heard, a second attack of the killer meshbots would have been launched if you hadn't, then warned the agent in charge."

Rosalyn face grew red, and she shook her head. "As someone I know said, I'm just a citizen of the Confederation, trying to do what a good citizen should." Then her mouth compressed to a thin line. "Ah've been guessing who it might have been."

"You are most probably correct. There is much talk, but no one is pointing fingers yet. I hear that Confederation Security is working with the FBI at tracking where the cargo containers were shipped from."

"That would be ve-ry inte-resting."

"But Aluaiy, how are you feeling?"

"Still very out of it, aching in my arms and hands especially, and somewhat lost with only the first infusion of the meshecytes so recently. They seem...odd, though they're starting to talk to my AI."

"Ah'm cu-rious as to how that's going to wo-rk out. Ah didn't have an AI when they gave them to me, and had to build it."

Amelia led them into the dining room, where, to Rosalyn's pleasure, not only Rafe, but Rhys and Janine were sitting around the table. The two women greeted each other warmly, and then Janine said, "We get back from a trip to several worlds, go around to see family, and this is what greets us. *Belle-mére*, Ros, can't the two of you keep this world less interesting while we're gone?"

"Ah'm so so-rry, Ah've been busy," Rosalyn smiled. "This is Aluaiy Pulidan, who I met on my r-ound the wo-rld t-rip that Amelie sent me on. She was a p-rofessoah in Taipei, and now, once she r-ecovers, will be lectu-ring at Penn. Plus, she and Ah now have a wo-rkshop and studio near theah."

"It's a pleasure." Privately, Janine meshed to Rosalyn, *"Do I detect more there?"*

Rosalyn smiled. *"Very much so. But we shouldn't mesh—her meshbots are gone, and she's only had one infusion of meshectyes. and that was just the other day."* Looking at Aluaiy, she reached out and held her shoulder for a moment, then let go, adding, "Taipei is very different culturally. Aluaiy came with the sibling of her assistant."

Seeing Janine's look, Aluaiy said, "A 'gender fluid' teenager, which would get them institutionalized in Taipei." Janine shook her head, while Rhys pursed his lips.

"But Joseph is just bringing out dinner," Amelie said. "We should not let it get cold."

~

THE NEXT WEEK and a half passed pleasantly in Amelie and Rafe's company, with Aluaiy slowly getting used to using the meshecytes. Then a doctor and nurse from Confederation medical came in, and gave her the second infusion of 'cytes, and the doctor led her through tuning them. After they left, she hugged Rosalyn, who had been there during the process. *"It is so good to have this again, and you were right, there is more here than I had before. There's...an emotional overtone that adds a lot.*" They stood there holding each other for a while.

"It's nice to have you back, all of you."

~

AMELIE HAD JUST HAD hors d'oeuvres brought out in the late afternoon when the newsfeed reported that the incident the week before had indeed been caused by the same killer meshbots as the original attack, and seven people had been killed by them. Three others had survived, one apparently because they had not been attacked by a large number, and so their own meshbots had overwhelmed the killers, and two had the new meshecytes, were immune to the mesh part of the attacks, and were able to stop their attack. Although all three were in serious condition, they were expected to survive. The police chief then introduced the FBI special agent-in-charge on the case, who announced that this had been a second shipment of the packaged attacks.

"What we found interesting," the woman said, "is that the people who had been hired to ship the packages, and knew nothing about the contents, were over-eager to get paid. They had moved the small containers of packages that were already separated into mailing targets, and opened the larger container that was supposed to contain their payment. Instead, it contained active 'bots. Apparently, the intent was to have the packages shipped, and then kill the people who had done the shipping, to prevent any information concerning the source of the packages to become available to us. As my people went to investigate the shipping container, after we had rescued the two people who had been kidnapped, the original reason we had come, shots were fired, and a number of the packages burst open. Two of those who were hired are still alive, one in a hospital, and one who was far enough away that, seeing what was happening to the others, was brought out in time. We also have the container itself, which was scheduled to be removed in another day or two. We look forward to releasing further information as we obtain it."

Amelie and Rafe laughed. The others looked at them. "The shipping container will be tracked. All of them have IDs, even if they're only for one shipment. They will find where they came from, even if they were transshipped via a second ship."

At dinner, Aluaiy looked up at Amelie and Rafe. "Rosalyn and I have enjoyed your hospitality, but both of us want to get back to our shop, and I need to get to Penn, to begin giving the guest lectures they have offered me."

"I certainly understand," replied Rafe. "We were glad to invite you, but we understand that you're artists, and need to do art as well."

"Quite. Will you allow me to continue to provide additional security for the time being?"

"That would be app-reciated," answered Rosalyn. "Given what's happened r-ecently, until things settle out."

"I think you'll find they settle out very soon," Amelie said. They looked at her, but she said no more.

The next week was both slow and fast. Back in their apartments, and shop, they were busy working to turn designs they had been working on while at Amelie and Rafe's into physical form, and there were not enough hours in the day for all the work. On the other hand, tension in the world cranked up as high as it would go over the insurrection and the killer meshbots. The Confederation Assembly took testimony and deliberated behind closed doors for two days. Finally, Rosalyn and Aluaiy were sitting over dinner in Rosalyn's apartment, when they looked at each other as their AIs, monitoring the news, told them that the Confederation was about to make an announcement.

They both brought their mesh up to AR, and watched. The President walked up to the podium, with the entire Security Council behind her. "People of the Confederation, you all know of the attacks with the killer meshbots and the insurrection. The 'bots found in the shipping container several days later were the same, also designed to kill."

She paused, then went on. "The Assembly finds that these shipments constitute an Act of War against the Confederation and its member states. Confederation Security, with the assistance of the American FBI, EU's Interpol, Ukrainian intelligence, and those of the Peoples' Republic of China, have tracked the shipment back through two transhipments to the original point of origin, the port of Taipei in Republic of Taiwan. We therefore declare war on the country of Taiwan, and demand immediate surrender, and extradition of all members of the ruling party in the government, as well as all individuals involved in the act of war, to the Confederation Court in Den Haag. We offer Taipei seventy-two hours to respond. Should they fail to surrender, the Confederation will take whatever actions are necessary."

With that, she left the stage, flanked by the Security Council. Rosalyn and Aluaiy stared at each other, until Rosalyn, with a crooked smile, asked, "How does it feel to be the Ahchduke, except you su-rvived?"

A look crossed Aluaiy's face. "I think, perhaps, rather more like Poland." They stared at each other, then both laughed, with pain on their faces.

"I'm so so-rry foah what's about to happen to Taipei. I just hope theah aah not too many deaths."

"As do I. But this had to come, sooner or later. The former trillionaires that are left have become more and more coarse and violent in ruling my country." She hung her head, sadness in the lines of her face.

"You'ah not going back to youah apahtment tonight," Rosalyn said, firmly. Aluaiy got up from the table and walked around, and put her arms around Rosalyn.

~

MONDAY MORNING AMELIE, Rafe, Rhys, and Janine were sitting in the dining room, finishing brunch. Amelie was angry, having seen the news earlier. "So they got away."

"Apparently, mother. There was a colony ship that was scheduled to leave, and another that allegedly was still waiting for a number of final repairs to parts incorrectly built, and then the first ship had issues, and canceled the launch, and the second suddenly produced documents showing it was ready, and was supposedly going on a test flight before loading, and then it was gone. Afterwards, they found that it had been loading for about two weeks, since about the day after Security got to Dwayne."

"They were preparing," added Janine. "We don't know where they went, either because they never showed up at their test flight destination."

"Say, rather, that they were preparing Plan B, should their insurrection fail," responded Amelie. The others agreed.

"I wonder if they had people on one or more survey ships, editing reports before they were filed, in addition to Dwayne's office," mused Rafe.

"I understand both the Navy and Justice are looking into people who had positions such as mission commanders who've left, and they've found several who they can't seem to contact," added Rhys. "But unless we redo a mission, we'll never find such altered reports. It's unlikely that we'd rerun a mission, unless the unmanned probes showed something that looked very good."

Suddenly they all turned to the newsfeed.

~

THE CURRENT PRESIDENT of the Security Council was saying, "As we have received no word of surrender. Taipei shall suffer the consequences."

At that point, the newsfeeds all split the screen, to show from Taipei, the elder Wu. "Rather, the consequences you speak of will descend upon you. You have one hour to surrender, or New York, Berlin, Abuja, and Tokai will be destroyed. A further consequence, of course, will be the tsunami from New York that strikes Great Britain and Europe. Please feel free to prepare your surrender. Once you have, we shall appoint regional governors, who will oversee your countries and lead them towards more prosperity, and reasonable relations."

Amelie and the others sat, shocked, trying to come up with something they could do, when finally the newsfeed came up again.

"Hello, this is Jacinda Macsen, mostly healed thanks to modern medicine after the attack on the Confederation Assembly, with Engrelay NeoWeb, *your* source of curated, verified news of the Terran Confederation and beyond! We take you live to Terran Confederation headquarters, where M. Fedorov, the current Chair of the Confederation Security Council, is about to speak."

A big-boned man with a closely cut black beard stood up. In a strong baritone with a Ukrainian accent, he began. "I presume everyone has heard the threat the remaining trillionaires made an hour ago. We have have done everything we could to identify the weapons we have been threatened with, and none have been found, and so we believe that the threat does not exist. We will..."

~

THE ROOM WENT DARK. There was the sound of someone breathing heavily, and then "*Non! Non! FRANCOISE!*"

"*NON, mon amor, non.* It is not her come again, and we seem to all still be here," Rafe's voice came, calmly, even with his absurd British-accented French, and Amelie felt his arms around her. Then the emergency lights in the house came on, and Rafe added, "Well, it seems to have gotten dark earlier than usual. Perhaps we should suggest to Joseph to see about a cold dinner." The heavy breathing broke into laughter, and it took Amelie several minutes to catch her breath.

"May I inquire...?" asked Joseph, from the doorway.

"I'm afraid that was the final attack, old man, and this is all Narnia, or the afterlife, whatever."

"Stop it, Rafe!" Amelie said, her cheeks damp from tears. Just then, the lights and the newsfeed came on.

"Hello, this is Jacinda Macsen, back with Engrelay NeoWeb, *your* source of curated, verified news of the Terran Confederation and beyond!" Unusually, she paused, then went on. "We lost out link, and have no idea what's happened, and although there have been no explosions, New York was blacked out. as were, according to reports coming in, Berlin, and Tokai, but all seem to have come back online. There are no, wait, I'm getting a report of a huge explosion outside of Taipei, but we have no confirmation. Excuse me, New York is back online. We now return to the Security Council."

The scene in the Security Council was chaotic, with everyone talking into their phones, or clearly in mesh. Slowly, the scene calmed down, and the Chairman of the Council stood up again. "It appears we were partly correct in what we were saying before we lost contact. New York fell off the grid for a few moments, but power is being channeled from New Jersey, Pennsylvania, and New England, and the people in charge at the New York generation plant are promising to have it back online shortly. We are hearing the same thing is true of Berlin and Tokai, that Abuja never went down, but that Taipei seems to be on partial power, but there are indications they may be working on a restart. There are unconfirmed reports of a major explosion in the outskirts of Taipei, but we do not know where or what caused it. However, given this action, Confederation Security and the Navy will move with all considered speed. We will let you know as soon as we have confirmed data. Thank you, citizens of the Confederation."

He sat down heavily, and the news service cut to commentators.

~

AMELIE LOOKED AT RAFE, then at Rhys and Janine. "Well, that was interesting, and I admit not quite what I was expecting." Rafe hugged her tightly.

"Do you have any idea what happened?" Janine asked.

"I think I do," said Rhys. The others turned to him. "They tried to blow up the grid generators, and instead the control systems shut them down. You noticed the power flickering on and off, then it went off and stayed off. I've seen that in simulations in the starships." He turned. "Joseph, would you bring us all our usual drinks? I think we need them, and feel free to have one yourself."

It was evening, however, before there were more reports. Rhys' explanation was the correct one for the grid generators.

"The reports from Confederation Security are that the large explosion on the outskirts of Taipei was centered on an estate belonging to a man known as the elder Wu, who was reportedly a former trillionaire. We have no other information, though there are rumors it was unexpected, and that there are many casualties, although not as many as might be expected, given its location. We hope to have more information soon."

ROSALYN AND ALUAIY had the newsfeed on while they had their morning tea, listening, worried, to the news about Taiwan.

"THIS IS DONALD HYDE, with Engrelay NeoWeb, your source of curated, verified news of the Terran Confederation and beyond! At dawn local time, the Confederation Navy, supported by the Confederation Armed Forces, attacked Taipei. Official statements from the Confederation say that most of the air defenses were put out of action by kinetic projectiles from orbit early morning local time. Shortly after this, heavy Naval transports landed troops from the United States, France, Ukraine, Nigeria, and Vietnam. All government agencies were secured, and their security forces have been neutralized for the most part. Known residences of the government executive and the legislature, and of the former trillionaires were expected to be secured in the next several days." He looked sideways. "Let me pass you over to Kwan-yuet Ho, who can give us more details about Taiwan. Kwan-yuet?

"Thank you, Don. The legislature of Taiwan, the Legislative Yuan, has been called into session by General Hadley, who is in overall command of the Confederation Security forces. He has Security forces gathering the legislators and escorting them to the hall, to consider surrender and extradition. Casualties have been light on the Confederation side, and given surprise, the time of the attack, and the overwhelming force, they have been very light among the civilian population, although we hear that there have been attacks on the police and some of the Taiwanese military by students and dissidents, which has been an uneasy relationship for years. There are also reports of fighting around the country between pro- and anti-Confederation supporters. So far as we know, however, most casualties have been among the Taiwanese national or private security forces. Now let me hand you back to Don Hyde."

"Thank you, Kwan-yuet, for that view of the country. We understand that additional forces are landing as I speak, to secure warehouses and facilities capable of mass production of the mesh killers whose use provoked this war. The Confederation spokesperson says that they feel that the mission has been successful, and that this will signal the end of hostilities."

~

ROSALYN LOOKED AT ALUAIY. *"How correct do you think he is, about the end of hostilities?"*

"That remains to be seen, but with the military and security forces headless, organized resistance will take time...and there will be local resistance to that. I trust you remember the riots when you visited?"

"I do, indeed. The students will, I think, be for this change."

"A lot of the people outside of Taipei may agree with them. The students did not get their attitudes from nowhere."

Two days later, Aluaiy was drinking some green tea as Rosalyn finished up the ring she was working on. *"It has been a terrifying few weeks. I'm feeling addicted to the newsfeeds."*

"Hasn't it, though. I...wait, Alan's telling me there's news that we need to hear." Both of them connected to the news via mesh.

"Hello, this is Jacinda Macsen, with Engrelay NeoWeb, *your* source of curated, verified news of the Terran Confederation and beyond!" She went on, after a pause. "I have some disturbing news from Taipei. In the process of consolidating control over Taiwan, Confederation forces have, for one, found a large estate, where dozens of former trillionaires and their families appear to have held a party, ending with the entire domed mansion having oxygen pumped out, and replaced with nitrogen. Everyone, the family members, the party caterers, the regular staff, everyone is dead." She paused, with pictures of the estate, with vehicles removing the bodies.

"This is not the only disturbing incident. Confederation Security forces were contacted by several people who claimed to work with matter-conversion generators of all sizes, offering information about the power outage, as well as the explosion at the estate of the elder Wu. Confederation Security is looking into this report."

"They killed themselves, because they weren't going to be less than in command." Rosalyn meshed, horrified.

"The new emperors. I'm surprised they didn't arrange for the whole thing to fall into the ground and be covered, their own tomb."

"Those poor people working for them, with no idea, and no say." Aluaiy came over as Rosalyn put down the polished ring and put her arms around her. They stood like that for a while. *"We should have a pleasant dinner out this evening, after all this. Besides, I have something I want to discuss with you, that you might want to think about."*

"Something else?"

"I realize that it's very soon, but perhaps we should see if we can trade our separate apartments for one larger one. As I said, very different culture than Taipei."

Aluaiy's face lit up with a smile. *"Let me think about that..."* she said, as the two held each other close.

Printed in the USA
CPSIA information can be obtained
at www.ICGtesting.com
LVHW050738080324
773860LV00003B/389

9 798888 601839